CUT LIN

A NOVEL

BY

PETER L MASTERS

Copyright: Peter L Masters 2012

This work of fiction is dedicated to B.A. my old 'partner in grime' and to Chris Chisnall my old mate and legendary punk drummer.

Love and thanks to my wife and kids for their tolerance while this was being completed- remember kids, this is a work of fiction.

ONE

Chris Taylor gazed sleepily across the pristine tropical beach, saw intricate colourful shells lying by the warm waters edge, scattered and gleaming in the sunlight like so much forgotten treasure.

Despite the kind of life he'd led Chris thought he was looking good still, looking fit and tanned and although he didn't abuse the fact, he knew he still had that 'don't fuck with me' look, because generally, people still didn't fuck with him. He liked that.

"This really *is* paradise," he said to himself as the blazing sun turned his skin yet a darker shade of brown. He turned on the sun bed, smiling, relaxed and happy.

'Mad dogs and Englishmen' he thought squinting up at the sun and he picked up his glass from the powdery white sand, rattled the melting ice and noisily drained the last of his orange juice through the plastic straw. He looked across the beach and saw his family in the shade of a huge colourful parasol.

Clara, his young Filipino wife, was busy rubbing more sun block onto his two kids as they waved at him frantic and playful, big smiles amongst the frenzy of beach toys and family accessories. Clara as always looking tanned and sultry and young.

Chris smiled back and waved. He cherished their easy days on the beach, the powder white sand and crystal waters, the colourful darting fish, the rain forest backdrop with its chattering monkeys and big hovering fruit bats. The beach was a far cry from the chilly gray seaside towns of his misspent youth. After more than a decade in Asia, Chris rarely thought of England, hardly ever missed it at all, heard that things weren't too good there now anyway. The Philippines was his home now, finally he was settled down and had a family he adored. Settling down was something Chris thought would never happen to him; he was still amazed that it actually had. Life was good, simple… but good.

He looked up and saw Clara with the two nannies and the kids; off for another swim, arms full of snorkels, goggles and flippers, laughter with every small step. He smiled and waved again as he watched them.

Just another perfect day thought Chris as he lay back down and considered calling one of the boys to fetch him another orange juice. He decided to do it later and closed his eyes.

Clara walked over and stood close to his sun bed. She smiled, shaded her eyes from the sun and stood looking at him as the rest of the family ran noisily towards the sea.

Chris was nearly asleep; he didn't know she was standing there.

She stared at him for a while smiling, but then her eyes turned dark and serious and she slowly lost her smile.

Chris looked up and stretched and yawned and smiled. He was pleased and surprised to see her standing there, but wasn't too sure what she was going to say. She was looking kind of serious, ready to say something.

"By the way and I don't care *what* you say, ok? It doesn't matter... this is *my* decision. I don't want *that* Panky here and that's all there is to it!" Her English was excellent, just a hint of accent. She stood staring with her hands on her hips: a defiant pose.

Chris was surprised, almost shocked, all this coming totally out of the blue. "What?" he said, vaguely remembering a previous conversation, it seemed like weeks ago but was probably only a couple of days... a *very* casual mention about his old mate Panky *possibly* coming to visit... *possibly* he'd said. After ten long years Panky had finally called, said he *might* need to get away, far away and quick. No explanation why. Chris had said no problem, thought nothing of it.

"But he's my oldest friend," Chris said, smiling and relaxed still, not wanting to spoil the perfect day.

Clara just glared at him, thinking: Why now Chris, what's he running away from?

Chris tried his best to stay cool, "I said *possibly* visiting; remember... *he* said possibly!" Chris smiled and chuckled a little thinking it might help, but it didn't so he continued, "And anyway we grew up together, we were kids... you know, punks... we went through a lot of shit together... we were the boys from the brown stuff, you remember..."

Not impressed with the smile or the chuckle and remembering the occasional stories from Amsterdam very clearly, Clara stood firm and looked him in the eye. She said, "I know exactly what you two were like Chris, that's the problem... I don't want you going back to your 'old ways'... you promised me, remember?"

"Yeah, but me and Panky were close..." Chris said trying to stay calm, trying to explain things like it wasn't a big deal, casually wiping the sweat from his brow, "Like brothers, 'partners in grime', besides I'm a reformed character, you know that." He paused choosing the words carefully, "I don't even do all that mad stuff any more do I?" he said as he focused on the gold crucifix hanging just above her breasts, saw her turn in the sunlight, ready to leave him.

Chris didn't want her to leave like this and he wanted the chance to defend his old friend. He was tempted to say, "Ok, so some people might think he's a degenerate, troublesome, drug dealing, coke dependant, alcoholic, but that doesn't make him a bad person." He decided against it.

Clara stood defiant, looking back at him, glaring, "*You* might be a reformed character Chris, but I doubt if *he* is! I doubt that very much!"

TWO

The early morning streets were dark and deserted as the large black Mercedes cruised quietly past Amsterdam's central station; it slowed down, took a left turn, crossed the canal and entered the red light district.

Welcome to sin city.

The four Russians inside the Mercedes were big like TV wrestlers but real and serious.

Boris was sitting up front looking mean and ponderous; he glanced over to his driver and spoke in a curious whisper.

"So you're sure he's going to be there, huh?"

Vladimir, the driver, kept his eyes on the road, "Yes, I'm certain," he said. But he didn't sound it and Boris wasn't convinced. Vlad's eyes were focused on the road just a little too much; his big hands gripped the steering wheel just a little too hard.

Boris saw Vladimir's face twitch slightly, caught his furtive glance, caught him peeking across the car.

"Are you...err... absolutely certain?" asked Boris casually, his whisper a little louder now, his voice still husky and deep.

"Yes boss," said Vladimir, "Absolutely..."

As the journey continued, Boris laboured breathing was the only sound in the car.

The few remaining lights in coffee shops, bars and strip clubs were being switched off; murky canal waters lapped against empty pleasure boats and glimmering neon reflections rippled gently on the tide.

The car cruised quietly past a row of small red-lit windows. A solitary prostitute posed in her lingerie, her face caked in make up; she was old and fat and alone.

Another left turn and they entered the warm street, the Warmoesstraat. The tall ancient houses shrouded the street in angles and shadows and Boris sat gazing out the window, still in awe after nearly a decade, Amsterdam, a city so different to Moscow. No shortage of anything here, however bizarre your taste.

Boris liked that.

When he first arrived someone told him that Amsterdam is the 'Sex, Drugs and Rock and Roll' capital of the world. Boris thought it was probably true, but it was a shame they didn't play much rock and roll any more. After 40 years his favorite band was still Herman's Hermits.

The Mercedes cruised almost silently towards a coffee shop called 'The Other Twilight Zone'—the place where all the shit had gone down recently, where everything got fucked up and out of control.

It drove past slowly. No one even glanced.

The windows on the coffee shop were smashed, boarded up still. Tiny shards of glass caught the streetlight, shone like gems among the bloodstains on the pavement; yellow crime scene tape all around still, fluttering and flapping in the breeze like festive garlands.

No one said a word.

The Mercedes continued slowly along the dark street.

Vlad broke the silence, made a crack about 'the grave yard shift' but no one laughed. After eighteen months Vladimir Brodsky was still the new boy, the rookie, and everyone knew it, especially Vlad.

The car crossed another bridge and turned right, drove past a row of gaudy sex shops, lights flicking off as they closed for the night and then past the small Catholic Church—empty as always.

In the distance a dilapidated houseboat sat on the canal, a dim light trying hard to shine through a small dirty window.

Boris said, "Windows," and the Russians opened their electric windows in ritualistic unison.

The car filled with a warm Mercedes purr and a fresh early morning breeze. Boris liked to hear the places they approached on these early morning visits; he liked to hear what lay ahead. He liked to be ready for anything.

With the windows open, despite the chill, red light aromas filled the car; the red light air smelled of lust and fornication, smelled like centuries of it.

Boris lifted his eyebrows, smiled slightly and nodded.

Vladimir followed orders, cut the engine, turned out the lights. The car drifted, crept silently along the street towards the houseboat.

The Mercedes stopped and the Russians got out quietly. One of the thugs from the back of the car was carrying a baseball bat; the other holding a large petrol can.

Boris and Vlad stood in the dappled darkness, casually attaching silencers to their handguns. This wasn't an early morning social visit. This was strictly a business thing.

Boris nodded and they walked towards the houseboat. The car doors were left open—they weren't staying long.

As they stepped quietly down the gangplank, old timbers creaked and groaned in the dark. Heavy guys for sure.

A weathered sign said 'Home sweet home' and Boris smiled, sneered a little.

Another nod from Boris and solid practiced muscle pushed hard against the door. It opened almost silently and they entered without a word. The room filled instantly with shadows and shoulders.

The houseboat was a wreck, it looked trashed and deserted: chairs and a table lay scattered like victims; a sea of books, DVD's, and magazines carpeted the dirty wooden floor; bottles, cans and old party debris filled the gaps. Every draw and cupboard had been opened, rifled through, sleeves and socks hanging out like tongues whispering secrets.

The smell of stale tobacco and cheap perfume was their only welcome. This was not what they expected, not what they expected at all.

Boris scowled, shook his head slowly, said, "This is not a good situation." He looked over at Vlad thinking: Stupid vykovskyi!

Vlad just stared at his shoes.

Boris turned, sighed with frustration and lifted an eyebrow.

The guy with the baseball bat followed orders, walked through the houseboat, looked around and returned shaking his head. Nothing.

Silence in the room, all eyes on Vlad now as cold dark waters lapped against the side of the houseboat.

Vlad looked up; his defiant eyes returned the stares as he put away his handgun, his breathing quickened and then it quickened some more. Suddenly he spun and karate kicked a heavy punch bag hanging from the ceiling: a neck breaking roundhouse kick and accurate.

The guys stared silently, unimpressed, looking bored. Ok, he could kick, but he'd still fucked up again hadn't he?

The bag swung violently animating their shadows; sawdust trickled silently from lacerated leather.

"So, who told you Panky would be here?" asked Boris with just the hint of a sneer. Boris liked sneering.

Vladimir looked sheepish, "It doesn't matter, is a mistake ok?"

"It matters to me rookie… and I'm sure it will matter to Zoltan."

Panic in Vlad's blue eyes now. Vlad thinking: Bad idea to upset Zoltan. Vlad looked at Boris, "Okay, okay… it was Leary Katz…"

The two big guys from the back of the car sniggered, chuckled when they heard the name.

"Leary Katz the American?" asked Boris with a smirk and a little snort of air.

"Yes, Leary Katz the American," Vlad said quietly looking down at his shoes again.

"The American chemist?" said Boris, his voice riddled with disbelief.

"Yes… him… the chemist."

One of the guys snorted and the other cackled quietly.

Boris sounded amazed at Vlad's stupidity, "This… this chemist… he has brains like pelmeni, like pasta… and yet you believed him?"

Vlad stared at his shoes as he mumbled, he wasn't sounding very confident, and his voice was strained, breaking up a little.

"But he… he was there when it happened Boris… really, he was there that night, I promise you… he knows about everything."

"Then how come he's not dead… like everyone else?"

"He… he was in the cellar… hiding."

"Ok, leave this with me," said Boris, "Maybe later we can find this crazy chemist, this Leary Katz? But later…"

Boris stared at the punch bag and the others looked on silently watching him think; the bag still swinging, still animating their shadows; sawdust still trickling from its wounds.

As the dust settled Boris stooped forward, picked up a large shining kitchen knife from the floor and held it up, stared again at Vladimir. Boris's expression said: So what happened here? Who butchered the boxing bag and why? And where the fuck's the guy we're looking for?

Another small nod from Boris and the guy with the can started splashing diesel around, soaking the garbage-strewn floor, the cheap scattered furniture. Heavy diesel fumes filled the air.

Vlad gazed around aimlessly, sulking; among the cluttered debris of the coffee table he spotted a small broken mirror and two thick lines of white powder. He licked his finger and tasted the powder. It was cocaine and it was good. Very good!

Boris just stood there watching.

Vlad's quick glance said: Look at this, *maybe* someone is here after all… no one goes out and leaves quality coke just laying around, not even in Amsterdam…

As soon as Boris smiled his twisted little smile Vlad picked up the mirror and quickly snorted the coke in two big hits. The mirror was suddenly clean. Vlad stood erect, swallowing and sniffing, wide shiny eyed he grinned: redeemed and rewarded.

Across the room, splashed diesel continued to soak the houseboat, dry old timbers glistening and pungent; the disheveled bed more soiled and sodden than ever before.

Boris ripped a photograph from the wall, stuffed it into his coat pocket, thinking: This we can use. He then pulled a Zippo from his trousers pocket, opened it with a sharp metallic click.

Heavy fumes filled the air.

All eyes on Boris now.

The three huge Russians stepped back in unison towards the door, away from the Zippo; they knew from experience that Boris liked fire, in fact he loved it and nothing he ever did would surprise them. Boris was a scary guy—very scary.

"Is anyone ho… oome?" said Boris, his voice almost sweet now like a friendly Russian neighbour. His eyes shone bright and hopeful, almost certain that someone *was* around.

"If no one's home," he said smiling, looking back at the guys in the shadows, "We'll just torch the place, leave our friend Panky a little message."

A muffled cough and some small movement came from under the bed.

Four Russian smiles appeared: cheap teeth and cavities.

Boris, happy and having a little fun now, continued with his neighborly tone, he stepped slowly towards the bed. "Ok, how about... is anyone under the bed?"

The Russian smiles got bigger. Vlad sniggered, almost laughed.

A scantily dressed young girl crawled awkwardly from under the bed. She was New Age, from New York and she knew nothing. Clearly terrified and drenched with diesel she wiped her gaunt white face smearing heavy black mascara and blood red lipstick. She looked up nervously at her intruders, eyes glazed with fear and apprehension, her startled expression was Picasso ugly, thin and whimpering.

Boris looked down at the pierced and wired girl; saw traces of white powder on her nostrils, saw a street chic wannabe, black Jap tats on her lily-white skin, tangled peroxide hair wild with diesel, the flimsy sodden material of her thin blouse clinging to her small pink nipples.

Boris deep voice lost its friendly, neighbourly tone. "So where's the tough guy... little girl? Our comrade Panky?"

The girl sat up against the side of the houseboat sobbing, coughing, and dripping. Her eyes focused on the Zippo; she was shaking and scared; the smell of diesel filled her nostrils, the taste of it thick in her throat. She was thinking: And who the fuck are *these* guys? *What* the fuck is going on? She looked at Boris' beady eyes, thinking: Comrade Panky? She stuttered, gasped, and almost giggled through her tears. She remembered Panky's final words before he had finally stormed out of the houseboat that morning: He said, 'Look Soozie and listen carefully, the Russians are definitely after me… ok? If they come here… and there's every chance they will, you can be sure someone'll get hurt… so do yourself a big favour Soozie… got it?'

When Boris spoke he startled the girl from her reverie, "So, where… is… the tough guy?" He clicked the lighter shut, put it back into his pocket.

The boats dry old timbers creaked as the three huge curious Russians moved as one through the shadows. Heavy guys still. They got closer to the bed, looked lecherous at the trembling girl. Boris smiled.

Soozie tried to return his smile, quickly gave up as he pointed his gun at her head.

"Where…?"

"I… I don't know," she said between sobs, her small eyes darting nervously from left to right behind her fingers.

Boris lowered his gun, looked around at the guys, shrugged and sighed. He believed her. "If… and I said *if*, you see him again," said Boris pausing for effect, "Tell him Zoltan would like to have a little talk to him."

Soozie nodded and sobbed, thin pale hands covering her face.

Smiling with job satisfaction, Boris unscrewed his silencer, put away his gun.

The four Russians turned and headed for the door. They climbed the stairs almost silently and emerged as one from the houseboat: four guys just doing their job; four guys certain their message would be understood.

As he followed his colleagues the guy with the can was humming some quaint Old Russian folk song, casually leaving an acrid trail of diesel glistering in his wake. Just before he got back into the Mercedes with the others he threw the can; it landed noisily on the deck of the houseboat. Its inflammable trail finished close to the car, close to Boris' door.

Three doors slammed, but Boris sat with his open and stared at the houseboat and considered the morning's work.

Vlad was back in the driver's seat looking serious, sounding a little concerned, "You know Boris, I think she's far too young to be his girlfriend," he said.

Boris took a spliff from the dashboard, lit it with his Zippo. "This is true Vladimir," he said with some authority, through a thick cloud of smoke, his eyes fixed firmly on Vlad's, "But she's not his girlfriend."

"She's not?"

Boris lowered his Zippo to the ground.

Whoosh!

The trail of diesel caught instantly and quickly burned its way towards the old houseboat.

Booooom!!

In seconds the houseboat was a huge ball of fire; dry old timbers flickered and flared, sparks and thick clouds of smoke billowed into the early morning sky.

"Noooooo," said Boris stretching the little word about as far as it would go, "No, no, no… Vladimir… she is definitely not his girlfriend," he said staring at Vlad's blank expression.

Vlad thinking: Oh shit, Zoltan's going to be real mad about *this* little *'moment of weakness'*. They hadn't even searched for the money.

There were small explosions and hissing in the air as flaming fragments flew into the murky canal. The guys in the back of the car had their noses up against the window, warm fetid breath on cold glass, eyes wide with pyrotechnic wonder.

Vlad was stretched awkwardly across the front seat now, anxious to see the action.

Boris relaxed and smoked his joint as he watched the dancing flames, as he savoured the moment and took in the show. Sweat glistened on his angular face, the bright fire reflected in his dull gray eyes. "See Vladimir?" he said, with just a touch of Karloff eloquence, "She's just an old flame," and then he turned, stared at Vlad and he smiled just a little and said it again, but more slowly this time, "She's just… an… old… flame."

Soozie was up on the deck now, flailing her burning arms in agony; her thin scorched body was totally engulfed, her hair ablaze and smoking, her flesh bubbling and peeling in the heat. It was far too hot to scream and it was far too late. Thick black smoke spiraled into the early morning sky and the heat shimmered images like some macabre mirage.

Boris got out his mobile phone, slammed the car door and with a screech of tires the Mercedes pulled away.

THREE

As the huge guy breathed more deeply his smooth broad chest continued to expand and his pink face flushed with pectoral pride; again he flexed his rippling muscles and the big pulsing purple veins on his neck stood to attention.

He stared into the mirror; pleased with his pumped reflection, pleased with the way his huge body had developed over recent years, very pleased. His eyes then moved across the room, focused on a life-sized poster of his hero: Arnold Schwarzenegger. He smiled; smiled because some people actually called *him* 'The Terminator'—this he knew, but unless they were crazy or suicidal they rarely said it to his face. He wasn't called it just because of his uncanny resemblance to Arnie. (The Arnie in 'Predator' *not* the Arnie in 'Twins'.) And not because he and Arnie shared the same birthday either, nor was it because of his obvious and ardent fanaticism. It was simply because he didn't mind terminating people. That's the kind of guy he was: a terminator.

A few years back he was in South London with his brother, relaxing, having a few quiet beers, having a little fun after completing a deal. They'd just exchanged some semi automatic weapons for ten kilos of quality heroin, met up with some old Pakistani business associates; it was a good deal, nothing special but good. That was the night the Pakistani's said they'd never do business with the Russians again. Not ever. That was also the night some drunken guy in the pub laughed and said "Last Action Hero" was the worst movie ever made.

Big mistake.

Zoltan wasn't in a particularly good mood as it was. The drunken guy *must've* seen Zoltan's obvious resemblance, should have realised that he was not the kind of guy to wind up, but like most drunks he was full of bravado, wanted to have a laugh, wanted to give the big stranger some shit.

Zoltan didn't say a word, just slashed the drunk repeatedly with a jagged broken pint glass, gave him a hundred and twelve stitches in his face and his neck, another twenty seven defensive wounds on his forearms and a ten-day stay in the ICU. That's just the kind of guy Zoltan was—and that was when he was relaxing, having a little fun.

Zoltan looked across the room at his poster of Arnie again and smiled, he loved his morning regime, his 'figure forming physical' as he liked to call it. His English was getting pretty good now, easier to understand; his plan was to eventually have a vocabulary as extensive as Arnolds.

He stared at his reflection some more and smiled again.

A couple of years ago he'd had his cellar totally refurbished, got all the equipment for a very good price, new stuff too, top quality and mostly in red, his favorite colour. Regular cardiovascular exercise was essential at his age he'd been told and he believed it, it was good for the heart *and* the blood vessels the doctor had said. He was sure the exercise kept him looking young; fifty was the new forty he'd heard and he agreed, he was fit for a fifty five year old, very fit, still feeling strong and powerful. The steroids were a lot of hassle—all those injections, a literal pain in the arse—but they really seemed to help, the unquenchable thirst for violence was the only noticeable side effect; he didn't mind that, he considered it a bonus.

The cellar was still a little dank, dark too, but that didn't worry him; he liked his daily routine by candlelight, it seemed appropriate, it relaxed him, helped clear his mind of all the problems he had.

Zoltan's face was hard up against the wall, not particularly comfortable; at that angle it *was* hard to see his reflection full in the mirror, but he figured that training was like life itself, no pain no gain. The musty smell of old bricks and mortar filled his nostrils; his close-cropped gray hair was darker now with his sweat, his eyes were bright, clear with anticipation. Then his mobile phone rang. Was nothing sacred?

A female hand with long slender fingers and red polished nails held the phone close to his ear and he calmly listened to the anxious voice on the other end. Finally he said, "So keep looking," his voice was unaffected, matter of fact. He listened some more.

"Did you talk to this Leary Katz?" he paused, "Yes... Leary the chemist."

The anxious voice continued.

"Yes, yes... the American," Zoltan said, thinking: How many Leary Katz's could there be?

The flustered voice went on some more, explaining, apologizing, sounding a little scared.

Still calm, he continued, "Well I suggest you look for *him* too, ok? My sources tell me he was actually *in* the coffee shop when it all happened… yes… that's right, he was there, hiding in the cellar, that's why he's still alive."

The voice said it understood, said it would put things right, no problem.

Zoltan said: "And Boris… I want no more *moments of weakness*, ok… just find him."

The hand with the red polished nails took the phone and switched it off.

Zoltan sighed and flexed his solid muscles again, his face still hard against the wall, his nostrils still full of bricks and mortar, old and damp. His powerful arms were still stretched out; the iron manacles that encircled his thick wrists still held him off the ground; his muscular legs were chained, spread-eagled as before, his firm buttocks were smooth glistening with his sweat and the multitude of red weal's across his back were still fresh and swollen.

Taut red leather and silver zippers flickered in the tremulous candlelight as the tall, muscular dominatrix cracked the bullwhip and a sharp, vicious sound echoed around the old damp cellar.

"You want more Zoltan?" she said quietly and knowingly.

Zoltan Morozov nodded his head enthusiastically. "Yes… yes please mistress!" he said laughing, "I've been such a naughty boy again!" He sounded just like Arnold.

FOUR

The coffeeshop was closing for the night. A sleepy hippy swept the wooden floor and the few remaining customers sat quietly at the far end of the room in the shadows, in a haze of smoke.

Zoltan sat with a nervous Boris and Vlad either side of him. Zoltan looked massive and Boris and Vlad looked a little scared. Turning his head slowly in the silence, staring at each of the guys in turn, he looked way beyond menacing. His piercing gray eyes searched for some truth as he calmly smoked a joint, his back was aching like a bitch, but he loved that. Eventually Zoltan exhaled a billowing cloud of smoke and said, "That's very good Boris, but we still don't know where he is do we?"

Silence again.

"The thing about organized crime Boris… is that you have to be organized, ok? You cannot do things just because you want to or because you have a certain feelings, you understand?"

Boris nodded.

"Feelings are for social workers and priests, you understand?" Zoltan paused for effect smoke spiraling from his nostrils. "And tell me please," he said to Boris, "Do you really think that barbequing his girlfriend is some kind of compensation to me, hmmm… is that what you think… is it?" Once again Zoltan exhaled smoke high into the air, his eyes fixed firmly on Boris.

Boris looked down at the floor, not daring to speak, not really knowing what to say.

"And how do you know that what we're looking for wasn't on the houseboat, burnt to a cinders now? Huh?" Zoltan's voice was becoming a little louder, his square face more intense, getting closer to Boris'.

Vlad just knew this was going to happen, he knew the fire thing was a stupid idea, but he stayed quiet. He was still the new boy; still the rookie and he knew his place.

"But I told you," said Boris, nervous, anxious for the right words, avoiding eye contact, "We searched the place and anyway he… he wouldn't leave it there, he's not stupid Zoltan, this much we know… and besides, in my professional opinion, that *little* girl… she knew nothing. Not a thing!"

"And in *my* professional opinion *little* brother, you… are a *little* psychotic!" said Zoltan, breaking into an almost gentle smile, once again pulling deeply on the joint, exhaling high into the air with dragon nostrils. "But as we all know, sometimes in this business psychotic can be good," he said with a gentle knowing nod of his head, smiling at Boris and Vlad in turn.

"Just remember Boris, these *'moments of weakness'* can come back to haunt you… just find this Panky, ok?" As Zoltan stood up his voice got louder, more emotional, "I want to know where he is and I want to know it soon, *very* soon!" he said. He smiled like a wolf at an orphan's picnic, thinking: Ha! I've been dying to say that for years.

FIVE

Panky Wellard sat alone, snoring by the window of the 747, destined for Manila, The Philippines.

The humming engines and in-flight alcohol had induced a deep sleep; he was oblivious to the passenger chitchat, the rattling carts offering tax free trash and taste free food.

Hunched into his seat with his head slumped awkwardly to one side he continued to sleep; with his weekend stubble, his rumpled clothes and his bad hair, he looked a mess.

His snoring and the grinding of his teeth went unnoticed by the other passengers as they squeezed through the aisles searching in vain for an empty toilet. The constant hustle and bustle didn't worry Panky at all; he was miles away. Fast asleep. The last few days had been so tiring, such a nightmare, so unexpected.

He suddenly woke up, panting and confused, looking around, where the hell was he?

Panky sat hunched in Economy Class, his neck twisted and aching. He was suddenly very awake; looking frightened, haunted almost, wondering what the hell he was doing on an airplane. He shook his head, trying to lose the lingering memories of Amsterdam, those stupid kids, the retro punks. He held his head in his hands and breathed deeply, slow deep breathes with his eyes tightly closed. Eventually he remembered why he was on the plane and where he was going, remembered why he had to get away so quickly and all the problems he'd left behind: all the violence, all the destruction.

It broke his heart to leave Amsterdam, but he had to. He had no choice. Everything got so out of control. Still shaking slightly he reached for a Chivas Regal miniature on the left of the tray in front of him. He opened it without looking, drained it in one gulp, put the empty bottle with the other five empty ones and tried hard not to think about cigarettes. God he needed a cigarette! Still panting slightly, wondering if he needed more alcohol, he looked up over the seat in front of him, eyes searching desperate for a flight attendant, a stewardess, but no luck. He saw that the in-flight movie had finished; a luminous map of the world had taken its place.

He screwed up his eyes and stared: Jesus, the Philippines *really* are a long way from Amsterdam. Still a little anxious and in need of distraction, he flicked through the in-flight magazine, slowly flicked past the glamorous cigarette adverts. He threw it onto the floor in disgust, thinking: Hypocrites or what? His head was spinning; he desperately needed some kind of distraction and considered calling Chris. His mobile phone was in his pocket, it would be easy, but he decided to do it later, didn't want to appear a burden before he'd even arrived. With a sudden burst of inspiration he ripped open a small plastic bag and scrambled to put on his in-flight headphones, he plugged them in, quickly *flicked* through the music channels wanting to take his mind to a different place, anywhere, just somewhere different.

He *flicked* through the channels; short sharp sound bytes filled his ears. *Flicked* passed classical, *flicked* passed jazz and country, hard rock, r'n'b and then... and then he couldn't believe it!

Now was this totally weird or what? He was back in time, listening to Johnny Lydon, listening to "Holidays in the sun?" a classic by the Sex Pistols. What are the chances? he thought, such an old favourite and such an appropriate one. He didn't want a holiday in the sun either, he really didn't, but he had no choice, everything had gone so *completely* wrong. Running away was the only option, it was that or death. Running away is never easy, but death is so permanent.

Panky sat alone, looking more of a mess than ever with his headphones mixed in with his hair; his small reading light was shining down on him making him look tired and pale, he was fidgeting, trying hard to get comfortable, trying hard not to think about cigarettes, wondering what had happened to his world and also wondering where all the good times had gone.

Things were quiet now and on the entire flight deck Panky's was the only reading light still switched on and all the seats apart from the two next to him were full of peaceful sleeping passengers.

SIX

"This is not a good situation," said Boris as they strolled casually through the red light district.

"It could be worse," said Vlad.

"Worse, Vladimir, you say worse? What could be worse, what could be worse than this?"

Vlad grinned knowingly, "We could be running."

"Right now, I'm mad... ok? If we're running... watch out!" Boris hated running.

Although it was early still Boris and Vlad were both tired and their feet ached. They'd been walking around the red light district for hours and getting nowhere. They had checked every strip joint, sex shop, peep show, bar, coffee shop and restaurant they could think of; fortunately for them they knew all the places Panky used to hang out, the places he used to pedal his powders, it seemed logical to try those first, so they did. But nothing, nada, zilch, not a sniff. They even toured the windows where the girls worked, just in case he was hiding out there.

Boris and Vlad padded through the narrow alleys with acrid smelling puddles, sweat and testosterone wafting thick in the air. They peered and peeped into endless rows of 'windows'—they were actually doors to tiny rooms; the infamous little 'windows' with quaint red lights where men with eager smiles sneaked quietly in and curtains closed behind them. But Panky wasn't there and more to the point no one had seen him, which was unusual.

Although the big Russians were tired, the red light district was still entertaining.

'Suck or fuck?' the girl's said, with lipstick smiles, getting straight to the point as always, standing with their tits pushed forward, weary nipples peeking out, high mileage asses hanging heavy in red and black lace. No time for romantic chitchat here, it was all strictly business.

So Boris and Vlad kept walking, pounding the pavements, showing the same old photograph, asking the same old questions, but with no results. No one had seen either of the guys in the picture or if they had they weren't telling.

Vlad yawned and peered sleepily into the window of yet another sex shop. Dildos big enough to scare a cow stood proudly on display, along with inflatable rubber women guaranteeing cheap hassle free humping and cheap plastic costumes with zips, clips and strategic holes for easy access. The place was very popular. It had everything you could possibly need.

Boris was inside, patiently waiting for the owner to get off the phone. The owner stood in the corner chatting on the phone, smiling happily because someone on the other end was ordering a hundred 'grade A' rubber women. A good order from Japan again. Boris stood waiting, gazing casually at a solid wall of hard core porn: obliging goats and super hung horses in semi erotic poses, skinny dogs humping zoned out junkies. Boris thinking: Is a sad world, these dogs have no pride. It was nothing Boris hadn't seen before, nothing out of the ordinary, just the usual stuff.

Still smiling the guy taking the order wrote down an address and a credit card number, he guaranteed satisfaction, said goodbye, have fun, and hung up the phone.

Boris didn't mind waiting a few minutes, business is business, besides, he knew the owner well, so did Zoltan; the guy was from Yugoslavia originally, they were practically friends. Boris collected protection money from him on a weekly basis.

As soon as the phone went down Boris smiled his twisted little smile and thrust the crumpled photograph into the guy's face. It was the photograph he'd taken from the houseboat, the one of Panky smiling, standing shoulder to shoulder with his old friend Leary Katz. The owner shook his head. No, he hadn't seen either of them. Boris knew it was true, knew the guy was telling the truth. Why wouldn't he?

So Boris and Vlad continued walking, continued showing the photograph, but with no result. They agreed that they needed a beer, it was nearly lunchtime.

They sat outside a coffeeshop close to one of the canals, ordered a couple of cold beers and rolled a couple of joints. They felt they deserved a break, hoped Zoltan would understand. The air was fresh and crisp here, the late morning sun warm and bright. Pleasure boats brimming with middle class middle-aged tourists passed by; tourists excited by the city sites, cameras busy snapping at distant skin and promises of fornication; forbidden pictures destined for secret albums; tourists happy and safe at a distance with hopeful zooming lenses.

Boris and Vlad sat amused watching the action; the vibrant city never dull, easy money on every corner; so different to Moscow.

When the waiter arrived with the beer Boris pulled the photograph from his coat pocket, paid him, tipped him well and asked if he'd seen either of the guys in the picture. Why not, it was worth a shot, you never know?

The waiter picked up his tip, smiled, nodded and casually pointed to a table about fifteen feet away. There was Leary Katz!

Boris and Vlad couldn't believe it. They just sat and stared at him, realisation taking a while to actually sink in.

Leary Katz looked sad and ponderous; his Lennon shades down on the end of his nose, his Grateful Dead t-shirt—the yellow one today—was faded and crumpled, his frizzy 70's hairstyle flickering in the breeze like ginger candy floss.

To the Russians it didn't matter how he looked or what he was thinking about. All that really mattered was that Leary Katz was there, just a few feet away; sitting alone smoking a spliff over a coffee, looking stoned and preoccupied, switching off and putting down his mobile phone.

Leary suddenly looked up, saw the Muscovites staring at him and quickly realised that the waiter was pointing at him. He vaguely recognized Boris and Vlad; he'd heard about these Russian dudes from Panky, he'd heard about the things they did to people; heard that they enjoyed it! He picked up his phone. He was up and out of there! And fast! His coffee cup shattered on the ground, chairs toppled over as he struggled past them. He was off, not even looking behind, running madly, dodging tourists and locals alike he headed towards the crowded street market. As he ran he looked down at the phone held tightly in his hand, not pausing for even a second he sent a text, a long distance message. He didn't have to write the message, it was already prepared—he'd been expecting something like this to happen.

Boris and Vlad rose slowly, amazed at the situation, amazed at their luck. What else could they do? They ran after him.

Leary looked back, saw the big, cumbersome Russians heading towards him; he was panting, gasping, running for his life, no real idea where he was running to or why. He just kept running as fast as he could.

Boris and Vlad continued after him, gaining a little ground as Leary stumbled and fell; two big serious looking guys running through the busy streets, pushing through the market crowds, heaving chests anxious for air, faces flushed and sweating. They continued running, the pressure and the chase was on, then Vlad saw Leary turn off into a narrow alleyway, he smiled, "Keep going," he said to Boris as he stopped and doubled back, "Keep going." Vlad knew these streets; he knew them well.

Leary looked back again, saw Boris, red faced and tired, but determined, slower now, but still pushing his bulk along the street. Where was the other guy? Leary kept running dodging shoppers, avoiding people on bikes, thinking: Just keep going… just keep running. Then he fell. *Wham!*

His face landed hard on the cobblestones, his tongue almost tasting the street, his body twisted on the curb, blood in his mouth now, still breathless and wheezing. He looked up, saw Boris getting closer, the look of determination still there, still plodding along, still trying to catch up.

Leary Katz got to his feet, dizzy. No time, must keep running, he thought, Must get away.   He was off again, quickly gaining some distance from Boris. He was going make it, he was going to get away, the certainty propelled him faster, he was running faster, much faster than before, running with a renewed strength, he was getting away. He was going to make it. He swerved left into a quiet dark alley, his arm grazing the wall, hurting, there was blood but he ignored the pain, dizzy again, but certain now that he was free from the Russians.

Bosh! Leary bumped into someone big, the smell of sweat and his face in someone's chest, someone sturdy and unyielding.

Gasping for air Leary Katz looked up. Shit! It was Vladimir! Vladimir with a big smile.

Leary's trembling body spun easily, he felt himself being lifted off the ground, held by strong arms in a headlock, felt Vlad's breath close and menacing in his ear. He looked ahead as Boris turned the corner, Boris gasping still, fighting for air, looking seriously pissed off.

Leary felt hot breath as Vlad whispered into his ear, "You lied to me."

Leary was gasping, gasping and scared!

More hot whispers in the ear. "So where is he?"

Boris propped himself against a wall, held his heart, straining for oxygen and wiped the sweat from his face.

Leary's tired legs were struggling slightly as Vlad held him off the ground. "Where is *who* man? Who the fuck *are* you guys?" said Leary acting innocent, but not sure if he'd pulled it off, still panting and sweating, fear still obvious in his voice.

Boris moved closer.

Leary Katz could see Boris's eyes now and he didn't like what he saw. Leary wanted to live; he didn't want to die in some dark piss filled alley, not like this.

"You see my friend there?" whispered Vlad, quietly now so that Boris couldn't hear, still holding Leary firmly in the air, still breathing into his ear.

Boris was close now, smiling sadistically.

Leary could see him clearly and he nodded.

Vlad said, "As you American's say... he's got some issues..."

Boris raised his hands and cracked his knuckles, an ominous sound like breaking puppy bones echoed through the alley.

"So... where is our comrade Panky?" asked Vlad.

"Ok, ok I'll tell you where he's going dude," said Leary, "I'll tell you where he's going!"

SEVEN

The 747 engines continued humming as Panky sat in his seat by the window gazing ahead at nothing in particular, trying hard not to think about cigarettes, feeling like he'd been sitting there for days rather than the mere nine hours or so the journey had taken so far.

With stiff and aching limbs he stood up. Stumbling only slightly and mildly optimistic he went in search of a vacant toilet. Eventually he found one, entered, sat himself down on the cold silver bowl and removed one of his boots.

Smiling with anticipation he opened his hand and carefully shook the boot above it. Out fell three small white envelopes. Cocaine. Nice.

Leaning over the small counter near the hand basin, he carefully opened one of the envelopes. He pulled a hundred dollar note out of his shirt pocket and carefully rolled it into a perfect tube. Something he'd done maybe a million times.

Placing the tube up his nose, he lowered his head above the envelope and snorted the coke in two almighty hits: one huge sniff into the right nostril, another huge sniff into the left. Then a gasp, a wheezy kind of cough, a quick wipe of any residue onto his gums and he was done. Wicked!

He looked up and stared into the mirror. God he looked rough! A small drop of blood dripped from his nose, landed like a tiny splash onto the empty white envelope. "Much better!" he said to himself, casually wiping the blood from his nose. "God… I'm gonna miss Amsterdam!" Sniffing slightly he looked down at the bloodied envelope, then up again at his reflection in the mirror. Shocked, he let out a terrified gasp! He couldn't believe it!

Behind him in the reflection, he saw D.K. and Sid, the crazy punks, the kids from Amsterdam—the dead ones. They stood behind him, mocking and bloodied, guns in their hands, taunting grins on their faces. Panky thinking: Jesus Christ what's going on? He gasped again covering his face with his hands, hiding his eyes, scared of the reflection, shaking in an instant cold sweat, desperate for air!

Seconds ticked by slowly and his fingers spread cautiously, slowly revealing the mirror and his lone haggard image. Anxious and panting he stared into it, checking things out, making sure, his breathing getting slower now, kind of normal. Leaning closer, almost touching the cold surface of the mirror with his nose, he laughed madly into his own reflected face, wild eyes staring, lids kind of flickering slightly, sweating.

"Fuckin' mental or what?" he said and with small shallow breaths and a manic smile, he picked up the small envelope, licked it thoroughly and flushed it down the toilet. He unrolled the hundred-dollar bill, licked that too, put it back into his pocket and wished he could smoke a cigarette. He checked his pocket; his mobile phone was still there, good, he was going to need it. It seemed that things were taking a turn for the worse!

Panky thinking: Bad lingering memories are one thing, but coke induced hallucinations are entirely another! He had every right to feel nervous, not only had he never been to the Philippines before but he had no idea where he was going and no idea what to expect either. No bloody idea at all.

EIGHT

Chris finished his fifth orange juice and smiled across the beach at his wife Clara but she ignored him. They hadn't spoken for a while.

He looked over at Boy, his driver/bodyguard, gave him the thumbs up and a 'Jeez it's hot' kind of gesture.

Boy was standing in the shade of some coconut trees smoking a cigarette, looking relaxed and casually tough, flexing his muscles a little. As far as Boy was concerned guarding Chris' new Range Rover was easy work and despite the heat he liked it; it was probably the best job he'd ever had, but he secretly yearned for a little action, yearned for the chance to prove his abilities.

Boy adjusted his chauffeur's cap, grinned a response to Chris as he turned towards the sunlight.

It was then that Chris saw the large black handgun sitting in Boy's shoulder holster, a cold stark contrast against the white shirt of his uniform, a reminder of how things were here in the Philippines—or at least how they could be. Chris liked having Boy around.

As Chris picked up a towel and wiped the sweat from his face his mobile phone rang. He searched for it frantically among his belongings, not noticing that Clara had started walking over towards him.

He answered the phone. "Hey Panky, how the devil are you?" he said surprised and delighted, "Yeah, no problem, just call me... of course you're dying to check out the girlie bars... you're a man, what can you do?"

Clara was getting closer. Chris was oblivious, chatting, excited.

He said, "I know, yeah, hey, a night on the town would be... it does sound fun, yeah of course, sure, uh-huh... I know!"

Clara was close now and listening.

"I wish, ha! Of course!" Chris looked up slightly as he continued, saw Clara. "Can't can I? I've got family obligations, haven't I?" he said.

Clara stood frowning with her arms folded, grinning sarcastically, nodding to herself... family obligations... yeah right!

"Easy," said Chris, "just get a taxi from the airport... don't pay more than 500 pesos whatever you do, head straight for P.Burgos Street... that's where all the girls are, yeah! Chris was smiling at Clara as he spoke, raising his eyebrows saying: It's not my fault. "Yeah... no, just be careful, wear a condom... Ha! ...No call me when you're done, I'll send Boy my driver... of course I've got a driver. No problema, I can't wait to see you either mate! Excellent, yeah of course... and she's looking forward to meeting you too! Of course she is!" Chris switched off the phone, looking sheepish and hopeful.

Clara looked seriously pissed off! As she turned and stormed away her eyes were full of daggers, sharp and pointed daggers.

NINE

The 747 engines continued humming.

A weary looking couple and their screaming twin babies sat a few seats in front of Panky.

Panky watched as the flight attendant served them a dubious processed 'cordon bleu' meal. The joys of parenthood, thought Panky as he slowly took a packet of cigarettes out of his pocket. He stared at the box almost lovingly as he opened it, he smiled as he sniffed the contents, inhaled the bittersweet aroma.

The flight attendant served more food, smiled and ignored the screaming twins with occupational ease; it was only then she caught a glimpse of Panky sniffing the open cigarette packet. She looked over at the No Smoking sign, tilted her head slightly and grinned at Panky. It was a subtle, professional, high altitude hint; a flash of pearly white teeth between pouting pink lips, a smile full of disdain and authority, that hard stare. The flight attendant watched him, eagle eyed as she worked.

With small groans of satisfaction he continued to sniff the packet.

Dishing out more warm processed meals like a Las Vegas card sharp, the attendant thought: He might look a bit like Colin Farrell, but he's a druggie for sure. As soon as she saw Panky she expected trouble; she'd seen his type before and many times. She was quite prepared to file a passenger report, get him banned from the airline. The flight deck was her responsibility and she wasn't without powers.

Panky smiled at her suggestively, sniffed the cigarette box again, licked his lips. He liked women in uniform, they excited him—he'd had amazing sex with a traffic warden once, a meter maid, in the back of his car, an experience he'd never forget.

The flight attendant rattled her trolley forward, did her best to smile at Panky, beady blue eyes on his cigarette packet. As she reached him he looked up at her and smiled, waving the packet gently he said, "Nicotine dependant."

"Oh really sir?" she said, wondering why he sounded so proud, "And how many do you smoke a day?" She wanted to say sniff but thought it might sound sarcastic, wouldn't read too well in the report.

Panky held up his empty glass, offered it to her, "Oh as many as I can."

"This is your captain speaking," said a slick DJ voice from the speakers, "Please fasten your seat belts as we may encounter a little turbulence in the next few minutes." The voice paused and then continued, "As expected this flight will arrive in Manila in approximately four hours, that's 2.30 p.m. local time. Thank you for flying Philippine airlines, please remember this is a no smoking flight."

Panky looked at the flight attendant, wondered if she had said anything, wondered if the "this is a no smoking flight" comment was directed at him in particular. He sniggered audibly at his paranoia, closed his eyes and lay back in his seat.

Passengers gasped and children screamed as the plane shook and suddenly dropped.

Turbulence for sure, thought Panky, as glasses and bottles rattled.

The shaking continued; a few toddlers began to blubber and cry. After ten years in Amsterdam Panky could handle a bit of turbulence, he had practically thrived on it so he wasn't too worried. He lay back again and closed his eyes.

The turbulence continued, but not as heavy as before, Panky opened his eyes and sat forward a little. He glanced over at the two empty seats beside him. Oh God! He couldn't believe it! It was the punks!

A gory and bloodied Sid and D.K. were sitting next to him! The kids from his nightmare, they were back again and they looked so real! They were smoking, blowing thick clouds at him, sneering, offering the joints and laughing! Their hands were dripping with blood. Their faces mad and distorted!

Panky gasped, slumped back into his seat and held his head in his hands.

The plane started to shake more violently.

I can't fuckin' believe it, he thought... Those dead kids, I keep seeing them... keep seeing them...

A minute or two passed and the turbulence stopped.

Panky opened his fingers and peeked through. Phew! Once again he was all alone. He was shaking still but only slightly, thinking: I don't know if it's the coke or just the booze. I don't know what it is? He sniffed loudly, tasted a little cocaine burn in his throat and then gulped at his wine, thinking: Maybe it's some misplaced guilt thing? A mental problem?

The flight attendant approached, hips swaying with precision, wearing her best phony smile. She put a large glass of red wine in front of Panky, gave a small polite sneer. "Anything else sir?" she said, her contempt barely hidden in the syrupy warmth of her voice.

"Yeah, why not... some cold beer'd be nice sweetheart."

The flight attendant sashayed off sighing, trying hard to maintain her smile.

Panky thinking: Long as I can keep it together 'til I get to Chris' I'll be ok, things will be fine. He sipped his wine thinking: Looking on the bright side, if Chris is still the party animal he used to be, it'll probably be a riot—at one time Chris made Panky look like an angel, like Bambi; Chris was *the* party animal, a legend almost in Amsterdam—Panky now thinking: *If* Chris is still the party animal he used to be, I'm bound to have a good time... I just hope his wife likes me!

TEN

"I hate him!" said Clara

Chris smiled, "C'mon babe, how can you hate someone you haven't even met?"

"Easy!" Chris lost his smile.

Clara said, "You just want to show off don't you? Show your old mate how *successful* you've been!

Chris stared blankly. Sweating a little.

"I don't like the idea of someone like *that* sleeping under the same roof as *my* children, ok? Simple enough for you?"

Chris was going to say *our* children, decided against it. They were sitting in the back of the Range Rover with the kids and the ya-ya's. Boy was driving, trying hard not to listen; he hooted the horn as they approached their large house, trees and colourful plants all around.

Two uniformed guards with guns and salutes opened the tall gates and they drove up towards the garage.

"Relax honey," Chris said, "I've changed, he's probably changed too… ten years is a long time, all that mad stuff's in the past sweetheart… ancient history, right?"

Clara sneered sick of all the servility, sick of all the 'babes' and the 'sweethearts'. He'd be calling her *honey* again soon. She *really* hated that.

Chris said, "Hey *honey* don't worry you'll like him… really you will… he's Catholic.

ELEVEN

Zoltan sat behind the desk in his darkened warehouse smoking a joint and holding a nine-millimeter Beretta. It was one of his favourite guns, not just because Beretta's the oldest gun making company in the world, but he liked the grip too. It felt good. The gun looked small, strangely impotent in Zoltan's large hand, but it wasn't.

Boris and Vlad sat on the opposite side of the desk looking nervous.

The tall concrete walls and the pillars rising high above them made every small sound echo like solitary footsteps in an empty church. Like a good many churches the atmosphere here was far from relaxed. The warehouse stood alone by the docks, an unobtrusive bastion of the black economy.

Cars recently stolen from Germany, mainly BMW's and Mercedes, were undergoing cosmetic surgery, a change of identity, ready for the Middle East and Africa; shrink wrapped packages of porno fresh from Scandinavia stood waiting for distribution; wooden crates marked 'live ammunition' were stacked high on shelves and a selection of guns stood proudly on display. The marijuana, hashish and chemicals were at the far end in the shadows, samples set out ready for coffeeshop owners and street dealers alike; state of the art testing equipment sat on long wooden benches like a mad scientist's lab ready to prove the quality of the pills and powders. The place looked organized, ready for business. Apart from a couple of spotlights two long rows of pinball machines lit up the warehouse, dazzling chrome legs and highly polished fixtures shone; modern and psychedelic art work gleamed and sparkled almost bursting with brightness and colour.

The place was quiet now.

Boris and Vlad sat waiting for the inevitable. Boris thinking: This is not a good situation.

Zoltan finished his joint, put down his Beretta and slammed his hands flat on the desk and stood up. "What do you mean Manila?" he shouted, "Manila is like 10 thousand miles away!"

Boris said nothing as Zoltan's voice echoed, Zoltan looking real mad and Boris thinking: Oh shit, maybe he's missed his cardiovascular or something?

"What the hell's he doing in Manila?"

Vlad sat still not wanting to say a word. Zoltan had been known to shoot people in moments like this, shoot them dead without warning.

Zoltan picked up the Beretta, held it in his large hand, stared at it blankly, thinking.

Boris and Vlad stirred in their seats a little.

Zoltan said, "Manila the Philippines right?"

Boris and Vlad nodded in unison.

Zoltan said, "Ok, it appears we have no choice… Boris go get your shots this afternoon, you're going on a trip!"

Vlad almost smiled, the blame was clearly on Boris' broad shoulders and rightly so.

"And take Vladimir with you," said Zoltan.

Vlad lost his smile.

Boris glanced at Vlad but said nothing.

"And use you're Canadian passports ok?" said Zoltan, "We don't want the Philippine authorities to know that 'The Russians' are coming into town do we? We seem to have such a bad reputation just lately," he smiled, "Me... I cannot think why? Smiling at his own good humor Zoltan pointed the Beretta at his brother Boris. "Are you sure we can't find out *why* he's going there?"

Boris stood up in the dim light revealing his bloodstained hands, the blood splattered across his big white shirt. Boris nodded the affirmative, confirmed he was sure.

"Ok, what else can we do? I don't care what it takes, let's find this son of a bitch, this crazy vykovskyi, ok?"

Boris and Vlad nodded their heads in unison, happy that Zoltan was calming down a little, pleased he was no longer pointing his favourite gun at them.

Zoltan looked over to the side of the warehouse.

Leary Katz was sitting in the shadows stripped to his Grateful Dead boxers, tied to a chair with wire, he was barely conscious; he'd been tortured and by the looks of him Boris had done quite a job.

Again Zoltan looked at Boris and Vlad: "And get this trash out of here before it starts to smell," he said looking over at Leary Katz. Leary's hair was matted, thick with blood, dark clumps stuck to his bruised, swollen face, most of his front teeth were broken or missing; the missing ones lying on the floor near some rusty pliers in a pool of spit and blood.

Leary looked up slowly at Zoltan and peering through his puffy hideous eyes he made a strained guttural gurgling noise as urine soaked his trousers, trickled onto the concrete floor, pungent steam rising in the half-light. Leary looked into Zoltan's eyes; with snot and blood bubbling from his nose, he did his best to laugh, let out a few barely audible words. "Hasta la vista baby," he mumbled, and then he laughed again, tried his hardest to smile. He knew what was about to happen. It was obvious.

Zoltan lifted the nine-millimeter Beretta, aimed and pulled the trigger.

A shot rang out, loud and reverberating.

Boris and Vlad jumped. The sound echoed, a harsh ringing filled their ears, they were shocked, startled by the sudden intensity.

Leary's head jerked backwards, a black olive hole appeared between his eyes and his brains left a thick sticky impression on the wall behind him, a small Jackson Pollock in red, pink and gray.

Boris lifted an eyebrow, casually looked over to Vlad. Nice shot.

TWELVE

Panky stood in the airport sweating and looking at the crowds: people everywhere, rushing around shouting, looking lost and confused, struggling with massive amounts off luggage.

So this is the Philippines, thought Panky, Ninoy Aquino airport, chaos or what? Everyone looking so desperate and anxious like they'd never been to an airport before, like they had no real idea what to do or where to go. Maybe they didn't?

Panky took out what was left of his breath freshening aerosol and squirted it into his mouth. Nice. He shook the canister and aimed a squirt on his chest, another under his left armpit, finally one under his right armpit. He smiled as he realized he'd inadvertently crossed himself. Maybe it was a subconscious thing? He had just landed in a Catholic country hadn't he?

Panky was pleased he smelled a bit better, but was pretty sure he still looked like shit. With his small bag in his hand he plodded wearily through immigration looking at his landing card. At the bottom it said: Warning: Death to drug traffickers. Fucking super, he thought and felt the small envelopes of cocaine in his boot. They suddenly seemed bigger than before; they seemed to be crying out for attention. He tried hard not to think about them. His heart started beating faster; it was a long time ago, when he was still a kid, but he'd seen 'Midnight Express' a couple of times. He remembered it well.

He joined the endless noisy queue and eventually got his visitors stamp. The guy looked him up and down suspiciously but didn't say a thing. So far so good. He sauntered casually towards the middle-aged lady in customs and stood in front of her desk. She had a nice smile. Panky smiled back, sighed and felt relaxed.

She said, "Your first trip to the Philippines sir?"

"Yes it is," said Panky.

"Business or pleasure sir?"

"Pleasure… I hope!" Panky with a big smile now, trying to be amusing and friendly.

The woman's smile suddenly changed, it made Panky think of Piranha and he sighed quietly. "Would you like us to check your luggage sir?"

A bead of sweat trickled slowly down Panky's forehead and landed on the woman's desk. He couldn't believe it! Sweat on the fucking desk for God's sake! It seemed like the biggest bead of sweat he'd ever produced, it seemed to bounce in slow motion, positively cascade into the air. Un-fuckin'-believable! He was practically giving himself away! Panky thinking: I might as well have Drug Smuggler written on my forehead!

"I've only got this," he said holding up his small battered leather bag, smiling again. His heart was beating faster now, he was convinced Mrs. Piranha Smile could he hear it. Giving him away, his own heart!

"And you flew direct from Amsterdam sir?"

"Correct." Oh no… this was it, Amsterdam… the very mention of the place spelled trouble!

"A very sinful place sir, or so I'm told," said Mrs. Piranha Smile.

"Oh, not really," said Panky thinking: Oh not *really*! What does that mean? Why 'Oh not really,' for God's sake! What does *that* imply? He grinned.

"Would you like to make a donation sir?" said Mrs. Piranha Smile looking over at her colleague, a smiling friendly looking guy, who was casually putting on thin rubber surgical gloves.

Panky nearly smiled at him. Then he thought: Surgical gloves! Oh no! My body cavities! Rough internal probing, then at least fifty years in prison eating rice and getting shagged up the arse by mad people with aids! Or slightly worse… death! Sentenced without a trial, abused and beaten on a daily basis, finally hung by the neck or fried in the chair! "A donation?" he said.

"For our Christmas fund, for the orphans."

"But it's March?"

Mrs. Piranha Smile and her colleague stared at Panky for what seemed an eternity, smiles fixed; the sounds of the airport seemed to disappear.

Panky thinking: March? Christmas? A donation?

It was tense. Very tense.

Panky put a fifty-dollar note into his passport, handed it to the officious woman.

She glanced at the surgical glove guy and he smiled, she put the fifty-dollar note casually into her purse and handed Panky back his passport.

"Thank you sir," she said, "Welcome to the Philippines! Mabuhay!"

Panky left arrivals soaked in sweat, his head was throbbing, he wanted to turn around and go straight back to Amsterdam. He wanted to curl up into a ball for about nine months and make noises like a fetus. If only that was an option!

Outside he lit a much needed cigarette, savoring every puff, tasting the sweet smoke, floating and dizzy in nicotine nirvana, then the heat hit him again, more intense than ever and then the noise hit him, the noise was unbelievable.

Up ahead a massive crowd, all waiting for their friends and families to arrive, was literally squashed against a barricade of iron railings; arms and legs poking through; brave, hopeful faces up close to the sharp spikes, everyone shouting and hollering. It was crazy. Everyone seemed so excited!

Beyond the crowd the traffic was deafening. It seemed like every car was either hooting or revving or swerving madly; drivers hanging out their windows yelling, waving their hands like mad Italians. Exhaust fumes pumping into the air. Chaos! Mabuhay, thought Panky as he wandered past the incredibly young, but heavily armed guards, over to the moneychanger to get some pesos. Glad the guy spoke English but unaware that he'd just been ripped off Panky walked towards a long line of taxicabs, his pesos in his sweaty hand. The noise here wasn't so bad; the taxi's looked new and had aircon, but all except one had people getting in or loading huge amounts of luggage.

As Panky walked towards the taxi, two people bumped into him, two people just not looking where they were going, what's the story? He checked his pockets, stopped and smiled at the taxi driver.

"How much to P.Burgos Street in Makati?" Panky asked.

"For you boss, in this traffic... only two thousand. Plus tip!" The guy was smiling, real friendly.

Panky said, "How about 500 and a tip?"

The guy just laughed.

Another taxi was passing by, slowing down and Panky waved. The cab stopped and the guy smiled, real friendly, seemed like a nice guy.

Panky said, "How much to P.Burgos in Makati?"

The cab driver said, "You looking for a nice girl, no problem my friend, I take you, get in."

Panky was losing his patience; he scowled and said, "You deaf? I asked how much to Burgos?"

The cab driver said, "In this traffic, only two thousand five hundred, plus tip."

Panky sneered and waved him away, wiped the sweat from his face and lit another cigarette.

A small dark middle-aged guy, scruffy but with a big smile approached him as he puffed on his cigarette. "You need a taxi boss?" the guy asked.

"Yeah I do, to Burgos, Makati... how much ten thousand plus tip?"

The guy laughed as if it was the best joke he'd ever heard. "For you my good fren only five hundred, plus tip!" he said smiling proudly showing the remains of his long yellow teeth.

"A done deal!" said Panky feeling that things were starting to get better.

"My name's Ding-Dong," the little guy said, "You wait for a while ok? I'll be back," and he rushed off to fetch his taxicab.

Panky leaned against the wall, finished his cigarette and wondered if it was late enough for a few cold beers. He decided it was and looked up when he heard a loud echoing screech of tires and saw a bright yellow, hand painted, dilapidated 1974 Datsun Cherry come hammering around the corner.

On the side in scrawling hand painted red letters it said Ding-Dong and sure enough as the taxi pulled up alongside him there was Ding-Dong leaning out of the window smiling, happy as a leper in an all night pharmacy.

THIRTEEN

"How are you boss?" said Ding-Dong looking at his passenger in the rear view mirror.

"Ok I guess." Panky sat sweating in the back of Ding-Dong's Datsun Cherry, gazing through the cracked front windscreen at heavily grid locked traffic. He'd never seen a Jeepney before.

"You see the jeepneys?" asked Ding-Dong reading his mind, "Remnant of World War Two, gift from America."

Panky looked again; saw a sixty-year-old public transport system, noisy and colourful and pumping pollution. God bless America! The heat shimmering roads like the streets were bustling and busy, smoke and noise filling the hot air, people milling around in the haze, some frantic, most totally indifferent, weaving in and out of traffic, jumping from the backs of moving jeepneys, some hanging precariously to the outside seemingly happy, oblivious to the apparent dangers. Pedestrians shuffled along at a snail's pace holding umbrellas, bags and newspapers over their faces, protecting themselves from the relentless sun; not wanting to look tanned and poor like farmers even though they were.

Panky could actually taste the pollution, the sound of a million hooting horns and tired old revving engines filled his ears and slowly filtered through to his brain. But it wasn't just the intense heat and the constant noise

affecting him; the car's suspension was just a distant
memory; every pothole and bump – and there were lots
of them –jarred Panky's bones, gradually breaking his
resilience, slowly eating away at his core. The few
remaining springs in the seat were digging into his arse.

Ding-Dong must have sensed his discomfort; he
turned around and smiled at him, noticing the sweat on
his face, the look of anguish in his tired eyes.

Panky smiled back, but wasn't sure why.

"You like aircon boss?" said Ding-Dong, eyes back
on the road now as they struggled over a couple of
major potholes.

"Sure," Panky replied wondering if it wasn't the
silliest question he'd ever heard in his life.

"No problem my fren," said Ding-Dong passing a
small plastic hand held fan over to his passenger, the
small fan buzzing away, it's power coming from a thin
frayed wire running twisted and knotted from the
cigarette lighter.

High tech or what? thought Panky. Holding the
small fan close to his bemused face he said, "Is your
name *really* Ding-Dong?"

Ding-Dong smiled proudly, "Yes sir!"

Panky was amazed. Ding-Dong's parents obviously
didn't care, clearly hadn't considered all the jokes about
his name ringing a bell.

"Americano right?" said Ding-Dong swerving to
miss a couple of scabby dogs running wild through the
traffic, squabbling over a dirty diaper they'd found for
lunch.

"No British."

"British!" said Ding-Dong—it sounded like
Breeteesh—"Oh, I like British!" Ding-Dong started to

sing. "Rule Britannia, Britannia rules the waves," he sang happily, bobbing his head, humming the words he wasn't sure of. "You must like Beatles huh? She lub you, right?" Ding-Dong sang a little Lennon and McCartney, he was clearly an accomplished singer. "All Filipinos like Beatles... we like Tom Jones too."

Panky grinned hoping he wouldn't have to listen to a Ding-Dong rendition of 'The green, green grass of home.'

"Your first trip to Philippines boss?" asked Ding-Dong as the car coughed and ambled along.

"Yeah." Panky wasn't really into the chitchat; he was too busy feeling shocked. He stared out the window at a row of squatter's shanties; homes built from odd pieces of timber, old rusting sheets of corrugated metal, torn tarpaulins, pieces of cardboard, sad old tires slung on the roof to hold it all down when the monsoons came. He couldn't believe it. As the car crawled along he saw hungry faces at unglazed makeshift windows; saw a God fearing congregation sitting, waiting for something good to happen. Those that couldn't wait sat gambling in huddled groups on street corners, smoking cheap cigarettes, flashing jailhouse tattoos, drinking cheap gin. Countless dogs and thin dirty-faced children played happily among the dirt, open sewers trickled quietly into the garbage ridden river, discarded plastic floated on the surface like a crust. Panky thinking: Jesus Heavenly Christ... Third World or what? Where's Greenpeace when you need them? as the old Datsun trundled on through the heat, the haze and the traffic.

Ding-Dong was at the wheel humming a medley of Lennon and McCartney tunes, looking happy.

Panky sat in the back sweating profusely with the small hand held fan buzzing in his face and a thirty-year-old Japanese spring stuck up his arse.

The journey continued, with shanties and destitution still on his mind he spotted a large sign informing them they were now in Makati City, asking them to please keep it clean and green. The difference was immediate, breathtaking: a sudden *other* world. Huge shining skyscrapers reached high up into the distant heavens, smoked glass dazzled and gleamed, stretched upwards in a thousand different shades, highly polished marble facades stood proud, reflecting well-dressed business people and chic passers by; bistros and cordon bleu restaurants offered fine dining in a cosmopolitan multitude of languages. Cartier, Boss, Versace and Armani displayed the latest designer styles, so elegant and essential. BMW's and Mercedes sat in traffic with purring Jaguars. Wow! A confusion of images swimming and swirling in Panky's head now.

"Shangri-La boss, New World maybe?" asked Ding-Dong.

"Uh?" he said, a little dazed by all he'd seen so far, an hour or so of South East Asian reality?

"Your hotel my fren? Shangri-La? New World?"

"Err… no… no, don't worry I'll find somewhere," said Panky, "somewhere near the bars, more convenient… Burgos Street will do nicely… thanks."

Ding-Dong looked at Panky in the rear view and smiled a big one, "Oh… you look for nice girl huh?"

"I just need a few drinks…!"

"You must be very rich come all this way huh?"

"Ha! Now that's a good one Ding-Dong, really, if only you knew! I'm far from rich"

"But you from England, you must be rich right? British pound very strong."

"So I hear." He had no idea really, not a clue.

"You British, so don't worry, you find nice girl here no problem! You pogi guy huh? Bery handsome?" said Ding-Dong.

The car stopped again at some traffic lights on Buendia, their destination not too far away now.

Panky heard a small knock on the side window: someone was tapping. He looked and saw a small girl about six years old holding a naked crying baby over her shoulder. The baby was caked in dirt, flies buzzed about. The little girl continued tapping, looking sadly into Panky's eyes, made a small gesture with her hand to her mouth making it clear she was hungry.

Panky was moved to tears—a lump like a Scotsman's fist filled his throat. The girl held out her dirty little hand, the naked baby continued to cry. The girl's eyes were beautiful and sad. Panky opened the window, handed the girl some money, a handful of coins; he didn't even know how much.

Suddenly a dozen dirty little hands poked through the window, begging eyes and grubby fingers desperately seeking donations; small tragic voices through the window, tired sad little faces pushed against the glass. Panky was handing out money, trying to fill every little hand with at least something.

Ding-Dong looked round at the commotion. "Hey boss! What you doing? Police catch you, big trouble!"

"It's against the law to help starving kids?" asked Panky, handing out the last of his pesos.

"They're professional boss… big, big syndicate."

The car pulled away from the scrambling kids with as much power as it could muster; Panky's sad eyes met Ding-Dong's in the rearview mirror.

"You got children boss?"

Panky said, "I'm not sure... probably." Thinking: Fuck the law... they're starving kids, right?

"Probably, I like that! You funny guy boss!" said Ding-Dong laughing trying to lighten things up a little. "Me, I got eight children so far," he said happily, "They keep me poor, but I love them all." Ding-Dong's smile said he really did love them all and his car proved they kept him poor.

Panky smiled again, for some reason he liked this little guy Ding-Dong, he was ok.

"My name's Panky by the way Ding-Dong... all that boss stuff's kinda weird, just call me Panky ok?"

"Ok sir, Mr. Panky, no problema sir," said Ding-Dong smiling into the mirror, "Same like hanky-panky, huh?"

Panky smiled, said proudly, "You got it Ding-Dong, exactly like it."

The Datsun Cherry pulled up outside the Parc Hotel, a one star establishment at best. It was very close to Burgos Street where all the "girlie bars" were.

Panky looked out the car window and decided that Burgos was clearly not a daytime place. It seemed subdued, gloomy. The skyline was tasteless modernity: decades of plastic facades, faded and worn, tiny pointless balconies with shriveled potted plants and broken neon signs. The whole area a mismatched confusion of bars, clubs, condos and chemists; it felt sad and neglected in the cold light of day, but Panky wasn't bothered; he'd been told that Burgos Street came alive when the sun goes down. Every night: guaranteed.

Panky smiled, it seemed perfect, his kind of place. Looking around hopefully he got out with his bag, told Ding-Dong to wait for him while he booked in and got some more pesos.

No problema, Ding-Dong was happy to be of service; the meter was still running and the traffic was getting a little lighter now.

Panky entered the Parc Hotel, casually strolled up to the front desk, boots squeaky on the cracked tile floor. He grinned at the sleeping receptionist stretched across the desk snoring; close by slept a young guy in a blue and white uniform, slumped in a chair, a pump action shot gun balanced precariously across his knees.

Panky looked around: dull magnolia walls scuffed by years of worldly luggage, faded, crooked paintings in cheap dusty frames, a giant antique aircon gasped and wheezed in the corner, a plastic potted palm sat wilting in the heat. This was it, the full splendour of the Parc Hotel. It seemed fine to Panky, more than adequate.

He slammed his hand down hard on the bell and both guys jumped from their slumber. Their sleepy eyes confused but instantly ready for service.

"Good morning sir!" said Rommel; his voice was delicate, lisping slightly and feminine, his name evident by his crooked ID.

"Good afternoon Rommel," said Panky checking his watch, "I'd like a room for the night and I need some pesos if you..."

"No problema sir!" Rommel said quickly, pleased at the prospect of making a little extra on the exchange rate. He pushed the registration book towards their latest guest and passed him a leaky ball pen. Rommel had soft manicured hands like a girl; his fingernails were pink and glittery. "Passport please... sir." Big smile now from Rommel.

"My passport?" said Panky, $300 in his hand.

"Security sir," said Rommel. The big sweet smile was still there, his soft gentle eyes were fixed on the money, "Is company policy," he added. Rommel eased the money politely from Panky's hand as he signed the book and slapped his passport on the desk. Rommel, still with the big smile, handed him the room keys and a fist full of pesos. "Have a nice stay sir; if you need anything, and I mean *anything* just call me."

Panky wasn't sure what Rommel was getting at; despite his macho name he was obviously as gay as Christmas, as camp as Baden Powell. "Maybe you could charge this up for me? I forgot my charger, left in a hurry," he said, passing his mobile phone across the desk, "But don't lose it... please, I'll be in very big trouble without it, ok? Very big trouble."

"No problem sir, it's very safe... we're very security conscious here sir."

The mere mention of security and the young guy with the shotgun rose slowly from his seat and stood casually to attention; he smiled with spray-starched pride, shining brass buckles and badges.

Rommel took the phone, put it under the desk. "Maybe you're looking for a nice girl sir?" said Rommel with inquisitive eyebrows and a salacious knowing smile.

Panky turned slowly, grinned and headed out towards Ding-Dong.

Outside Panky leaned on the Datsun, looked down at Ding-Dong and pulled two 1000 peso notes from the wad in his hand, handed them through the driver's window, "This is for you Ding-Dong."

"Jesus and Maria!" said Ding-Dong looking up, "No, no… too much sir, 500 plus tip only! I cannot take all this, it would not be right!"

Panky wasn't taking no for an answer. "It's ok, you deserve it," he said, "You didn't try and rip me off did you? Besides you're a good man. Go and buy the kids some milk or something… you know they need it."

Ding-Dong took the cash, eyes welling just slightly with tears, his prayers answered for a day or two.

Panky smiled and said, "Give me your number, maybe I'll see you around… if I need you, I'll call ok?"

"No problema Mr. Panky sir, no problema, just call my cell phone," Ding-Dong handed him a dog-eared business card, "Any time, night or day… and God bless you my fren."

The old Datsun coughed and spluttered its way along the street, Ding-Dong's skinny arm waved goodbye through the window and his eyes said thanks again in the rearview mirror.

Panky strolled back into the Parc Hotel. He welcomed the prospect of a shower, but it was low on his list of priorities. Smiling he banged his hand hard on the bell again.

Rommel and the young guard jumped up startled as before, deja vued from their dozing positions.

Panky said: "Rommel, maybe you can recommend a good bar, what I need is a lot of cold beer, some quality whiskey and some female company." Panky stressed the word female and Rommel smiled.

FOURTEEN

It was early evening and still fairly quiet in "Fat Willies" bar. The place was dark and predictable: heavy red velvet curtains at the entrance, booming bass line music from the speakers, a long bright back lit bar, a rainbow of coloured bottles, half a dozen girlie bartenders, slow smiling service in short skirts. Huge flesh filled mirrors lined the walls, the perennial stage offered an array of young girls: the buxom, the bulimic, the lithe and the languid, exotic temptation for every taste.

Panky liked the place immediately, full of promise. He sat alone smoking a cigarette, finished his fourth beer and knocked back another shot of whiskey. The lines of coke he'd snorted in his room earlier had cleared his head, sharpened his perspective. The long journey and the hallucinations were long forgotten now; he wasn't losing the plot, he was feeling good and looking for some action.

About fifty girls danced on the stage, giggles and smiles, teeth white in ultra violet light as predictable r'n'b droned from giant speakers; the willing, hopeful girls shook their credentials and resumed their nightly routine.

Panky looked around. Across the room in a thick Marlboro cloud sat four fat Americans in tee shirts, shorts and trainers: middle-aged cornpone peckerheads laughing loudly, celebrating their return to Asia. Panky watched the macho guys telling tired old war stories; boastfully recalling the past, thirty-five years ago they were kids that won a ticket to Nam and now they laughed about it with apparent ease. Panky sneered and looked away. Close by in the crimson shadows he watched Japanese men in business suits sitting with skinny girls on their corporate laps; lustful eyes and wandering hands combined as the girls cavorted playfully. Samurai honour and sensibility had clearly taken the night off.

Panky looked around some more and smiled, smoked and drank some more, his eyes finally drifting back to the girls on the stage.

Over to the far side of the bar in a dark wrap around booth sat three British lads, drunken eyes full of arrogance, staring around, looking for something. Cheap beer on their breath and malice on their minds— hooligan mentality and obvious to Panky. He'd seen it all before and too many times. What's with that tired old Bulldog mentality? What is it with Brits abroad?

Panky was deep in thought, the music droned and the girls continued to dance. Slightly mesmerized he watched the fifty sweet young girls bouncing to the sounds, gyrating with abandon, young brown eyes promising and promiscuous. Lovely!

Then the hooligans started chanting.

Panky glanced over at them, smiled at the predictability of it all. He knew exactly what was going to happen, it was only a matter of time.

"Here we go, here we go, here we go!"

Oh good they're going, thought Panky as he knocked back another whiskey, tried to block out the sound. He stared at his glass, thought it was a shame

Chris couldn't make it, so much catching up to do… ten years was a long time, a lot can happen in ten years. People change, right? But Panky understood the situation, he understood the concept of "family obligations"; ok, maybe he didn't really *understand* them… but he had heard of them. His mind drifted some more as the Mamasan approached him, heavy make up matching her physique, a warm alluring expression. There was little doubt that *she* knew what men wanted; despite her vintage she still had nice eyes, almost sexy, but she was way too old for bikinis, way too old for the stage. She reached his table and smiled, her cool hand brushing purposefully against his arm, a venereal veteran.

"Americano?" she said, her voice oiled and oozing.

"British," Panky said returning the smile.

"You look for nice girl huh?" she said with fluttering lashes, a sweet suggestive sparkle in her eyes.

"Maybe."

The Mamasan looked over at the hooligans; calm displeasure replaced her warm sensuality.

Panky followed her stare and echoed her displeasure.

The chavvy hooligan types were working themselves into a frenzy, the corporate Japanese were leaving with grateful bows and polite smiles, the four Americans had moved to another table. The room suddenly felt like a snake poised to bite; felt like a coiled spring. It felt ready.

Panky looked over his shoulder at the disturbance, thinking: I can smell trouble a mile off. And he could, it was a talent he'd had since he was ten years old, since he was eleven he also had the talent to avoid it! Until recently that is, recently things had been different… he wondered if it was because he was getting old? He didn't like thinking about it.

The Bulldog boys were chucking beer around; their chants getting louder. "Get your tits out, get you tits out… get your tits out for the lads!"

Highbrow stuff thought Panky as he swallowed more beer and lit another cigarette.

The boys started chucking ice on the stage. One of the young girls slipped, fell flat on her back, legs kicking in the air, instant tears; small screams of concern and confusion rang out from the other girls.

Across room the boys laughed themselves stupid. It didn't take much.

Panky stared at them, hated their ignorance, their obvious lack of respect. Did these silly British boys have no compassion at all? Did they really think these sweet young girls enjoyed the abuse they were paid to endure? Did they really think the girls liked the rough drunken groping and probing of the mainly old men that paraded in and out every night? Smelly old guys, Viagra dependant. Panky had had almost enough, but decided to try and relax, he'd only been in town a couple of hours, it wasn't even his problem.

An ice cube shattered on the back of his head.

Suddenly it was his problem. He was almost pleased. Why not have a few words with the boys? Calm things down a little, he thought. Panky hated bullies; he had for as long as he could remember, even before the bizarre incident with Chris' dad. He had always believed that you've got to stand up to them, if you don't the bullies win and no one wants that. He sniffed the cocaine residue from the back of his throat and felt it burn. Nice.

He got up, turned and walked slowly towards the boys, very casual, checking them out one at a time. Saw three British hooligans beered up and belligerent. The big one in the middle at the back of the table was the obvious leader, the two smaller wiry lads his sidekicks. The big guy wearing a red stretched tee shirt, Bruce Lee in flight across his chest, the sidekicks in stylish football shirts proclaiming their weekend affinities. Football fucking hooligans, thought Panky.

As Panky got closer to their table he felt a powerful rush of adrenalin, his throat felt dry and constricted and his heart pounded frantically, he felt pleasure and more than a little justice in his intentions. As he got closer he noticed a heavy wooden bar stool standing to one side, nodded his head slightly telling himself that things were under control; things were going to be ok, he'd been here before and lived to tell the tale. He reached their table and the noise and laughter abruptly subsided. Three young hardened faces stared at him, drunken fighting eyes looked into his, shoulders turned, bodies poised, ready to attack.

"All right lads?" said Panky with a friendly tone, smiling, looking at all three of them but casually. "Do us a little favour, settle down a bit, it's early right? You're giving the British a bad name."

The boys exchanged glances. Who the fuck is this? The big guy at the back with the cropped hair snorted in disbelief. The boy on the left stared arrogantly at Panky, said, "Lads? Us? Fuck off granddad! Their laughter filled the air as they lifted their bottles and drank some more. The boy on the right didn't want to be left out, he said, "Yeah, fuck off you old hippy or Bruce'll use his karate on ya, innit!" He glanced at his leader for approval and got it; the leader made a couple of Kung Fu type noises, threw a couple of punches in the air. The boys laughed some more, loud and confident in their strength.

Panky remained expressionless, puzzled. What did they mean granddad? And who's an old hippy?

The boy on the left spoke again, eyes alight with the prospect of violence, wanting it to happen, "Yeah, fuck off before we give you that facelift you've been saving up for!"

Panky said nothing, didn't even blink.

Bruce the leader sat back proud, chuckling as his boys pulled cutthroat razors from their back pockets. Sharp blades flashed in the flickering light.

Panky threw up his hands quick and defensively, his eyes said: Not for me thanks, and he backed off slowly.

The boys roared with laughter and swallowed more beer; a clear victory for them, another win and away from home this time.

Out of sight and quickly forgotten Panky walked towards the heavy wooden barstool. He picked it up by the rungs andfixed it tight and rigid into his arm: his right arm was now two foot longer, with a five pound solid piece of wood at the end. A formidable weapon for sure and one he'd used before, Panky thinking: Justice delayed is justice denied, right?

The boys were loud, still celebrating their recent success, oblivious to Panky's retraced steps, his quiet return. He spun around fast with the stool locked firmly in position, gaining maximum impact. The boy on the left lifted his eyes as the seat smashed into his face with a sickening *whack*! A bone-breaking crack and splattering blood filled the air, the boy's head flew backwards shattering the glass panel behind him, he slumped forward across the table. Done. One down.

Fat Bruce sat shocked with wide eyes as he coughed in disbelief and sprayed beer into the air.

Panky slashed the bar stool back through the air in the opposite direction, gaining momentum, no hesitation, one determined movement, split second timing and accurate. The boy on the right was taken totally unawares, still shocked at what happened to his mate, shocked by the sudden attack, by the unexpected violence, still looking at Bruce for direction. *Whack!* The bar stool met its target, blood and teeth this time, glass shattered and showered as before. The boy slid groaning and bleeding under the table, glasses and ashtrays smashed onto the floor. Done! Simple. Two down. Then virtual silence: Panky stared at Bruce.

The music was still droning in the background, the girls on the stage were still dancing and adoring themselves in the mirrors.

Panky and Bruce were far away in another dimension, locked into another more violent world, adversaries poised with pumping hearts, eyes fixed and staring, waiting for the slightest move.

Panky smiled, thinking: Laugh that off fat boy.

Bruce looked at the bloodied stool in Panky's hand, glanced at his fallen friends, saw Panky's determined face and realised he was stuck behind the table and a very easy target.

Panky smiled.

Bruce let out a loud, guttural Kung Fu scream and punched wildly into the air, strong well-practiced gestures, a small warning of what was to come. Then he grunted and lifted the table. Faced with adrenalin strength the bolts pulled easily from the floor, glass smashed around Bruce's feet as he threw the table to one side and took his position—ready to attack. Ready to avenge.

Panky stood ready too, bar stool firmly in position as Bruce high kicked and punched his way towards him, guttural screams filled the air. Panky just stared ahead, silent, conserving energy, awaiting the inevitable.

Bruce was not happy; he was pretty fast for a fat bastard, obviously good at that Kung Fu stuff, but he didn't like the look on Panky's face: Panky looked like he was enjoying every minute of it. It seemed obvious to Bruce that they'd picked on the wrong guy, but he kept going, it was too late to stop now.

Panky dodged punches and high kicks with remarkable ease. Bruce was giving it his best, harder kicks and punches, spinning screams of anger and frustration, more punches, but nothing connected. Panky expected him to get exhausted pretty quick—all that weight, all that shouting and showing off—and of course he did. Bruce was red faced now, a street fighting beetroot gasping for breath, a beetroot punching the air.

Panky started to shout, trying to taunt and confuse. "C'mon fat boy use your karate… use your karate!" Panky stepped away from more punches; ducked and dived like a well-trained, well-seasoned boxer. He held the stool rigid, spun to gain power, aimed for direction and *whack*! The stool hit Bruce on the side of the head, not full impact but hard enough; he staggered, his balance briefly gone.

Panky sidestepped and spun again shouting, "Use your karate, use your karate!" And then *whack*! He hit him again. Nice shot! Bang on! Panky went for the kill. *Whack*!

Bruce suddenly stopped in his tracks, blood trickled down his sweaty fat forehead, his big hands were still raised, but his legs bent like rubber, his vision obviously gone. He sank slowly to the floor and collapsed into a fat heap. Done. Three down. Sorted!

Panky stepped back and looked at the damage, thinking: Not bad, shame Chris wasn't here, it would've been fun, like the old days!

The girls were still dancing and preening, the music continued to play as if nothing had happened, everyone but Panky oblivious to the blitz and mayhem. The four rednecks glanced over briefly and continued their boring war stories, feeling safer in the past. But the word was out. The Mamasan came out of her office eyes wide with horror, hands raised to her painted mouth, clearly shocked, not sure whether to laugh or cry or just call for the cleaners.

Panky put down the bloodied stool, walked quietly towards the exit, turned, smiled and waved at the Mamasan, thinking: Fuckin' karate experts! Football hooligans, bunch of tossers!

FIFTEEN

Panky had been in 'Mike Hunt's' bar just long enough to discreetly snort a couple of lines of coke in the comfort room and buy some Viagra and condoms from the vending machine. He returned to the bar, bought a couple of drinks, sat down at a table and stared at the girls on the stage. His eyes were bright with anticipation; he licked his lips and grinned like a pampered tomcat. He wasn't really looking for guidance or advice, but when the fat man sat next to him he felt he was about to get some and he was right.

"Nice girls huh?"

"Not too bad," said Panky, noticing the heavy layers of wobbly man flesh through the fat man's gaping shirtfront, noticing the hairy puffy pink folds.

"I guess that's what you're looking for, right? A nice girl?"

"Maybe."

Big fat smiles from the fat man.

"No worries, we've got 'em all here mate, you want it… we got it… good selection and clean too, mostly," he said confident and friendly.

Mostly clean, thought Panky, that's reassuring.

"Got some fresh ones just arrived from the province, they don't come cheap if you know what I mean, cherry girls never do, do they?"

Panky wasn't too sure if the fat man was trying to be witty or not. It was hard to tell. He was a 350-pound

Aussie, minimum 350, probably more; he was in his late fifties and red faced, puffing and sweating despite the cool air from the aircon. He seemed harmless and friendly enough, but Panky had never liked salesmen, he always felt they were trying to sell him something.

'Mike Hunt's' was much the same as the previous bar, only bigger, brighter and busier. On stage sixty or so pouting dancing girls paraded with numbers on their brief bikinis, smiles bright in ultra violet light once again, smooth silky flesh moved rhythmically and enticing; boobs bobbed gently, buttocks bounced gracefully and testosterone wafted through the air. The place was good. The only real difference was the music; to Panky it was a major improvement. Billy Idol sang 'Hot in the city', a flashback to the early 80's', another ominous and appropriate number.

Panky stared at the stage checking out the numbers. Quite a cosmopolitan crowd, thought Panky, a host of men keen and shamelessly drinking their way through the night, smiling, almost drooling with delight: the female form a feast for hungry eyes. A typical scene: primitive with primeval intentions. Some things just never change.

He swallowed some beer and looked back at the stage ignoring the fat man; numbers 68 and 69 looked pretty good to Panky… from a distance.

"Forget numbers 68 and 69 mate, they're geezers!" said the fat man.

Panky looked again at 68 and 69, couldn't believe it! From a distance they looked so good, better than good, much better. Maybe he did need a little advice after all?

He looked across the table at the 350-pound wobbly Aussie, sipped another beer and listened as the guy continued.

"Ribs out, silicon in, plumbing sorted, plenty of hormones and Bob's your uncle!" The fat man laughed, puffed as his face reddened and he rolled his eyes comically, "Or should I say Bob's your auntie!"

It was a good line, well practiced, Panky actually laughed into his beer. "Strictly for the weirdo's mate, those two!" the fat man continued, "But see number 7… she'll…"

Panky looked at number 7 who was well aware that the boss was doing his stuff; she smiled and wiggled her ass playfully, pushed out her small breasts and then stuck out the longest tongue in the universe. It was truly amazing!

The fat man whispered into Panky's ear.

Panky could imagine it; initially it was a wonderful prospect, then he realized the girl was a professional; her tongue had probably worked its wonders on a nightly basis for God knows how many years. His expression quickly changed to one of disgusted as the consequences sank in. The fat man was reading his mind, it wasn't difficult, "So don't kiss her then mate," he said chuckling as only fat people can, his ample chins waggling in unison. "So, look at 26!"

Panky looked for the number, caught the eye of a stunning girl, a trim golden body with long flowing hair, red pouting lips beckoned as she posed. Phew!

"Now 26 is good mate, she's got…" the fat man whispered again, his furtive behavior suggesting these girls really had secrets.

Panky listened and looked at 26.

"It's true mate… two of 'em," the fat man exclaimed, "…see for yourself!"

Panky looked again but couldn't believe it. Two? Really? He didn't think it was physically possible, wasn't really sure if it were something he'd enjoy anyway. Two for God's sake!

The fat man continued: "Now numbers 12 and 13 are special, real close if you know what I mean."

He looked at 12 and 13, gyrating close together, hands moving skillfully over each other's bodies, loving every minute of it. It may have been a quick decision—possibly even hasty—but Panky had done enough window-shopping, he'd nearly had enough to drink. He nodded approval to the fat man and with a wink the girls were off of the stage and strolling towards him with big smiles. Panky's smile was big too as they draped themselves around him, soft warm perfumed skin in his face, tongues teasing his neck and his ears, hands inside his shirt caressing his flesh, teasing his nipples. Phew!

The waitress brought more whiskey for Panky, one for the fat man, cocktails for the girls—no one had ordered they just came. Panky didn't care, he smiled, clinked glasses with the fat man and they knocked back their drinks. He smiled at the girls and lit a cigarette, exhaled a cloud of smoke and looked up, the fat man was gone.

"Hi handsome what's your name?" asked number 12 running thin painted fingers through his tangled curly hair.

"Me? My name's Jack Daniels! Call me Jack."

The girls looked at each other and giggled as they caressed his body; four dark eyes guaranteed satisfaction, guaranteed an amazing night.

"Hi Jack!" purred number 13; her hands caressed his inner thigh, her tongue licked slowly across her pink pouting lips.

A few minutes later, back in the Parc hotel, things were going well.

Panky's room seemed different now: the lights were low, with the jazzy muzak from the radio came a laid back ambience, the cooling air hung heavy with the essence of nubile and even the shadows were hot and provocative.

Good time to relax and have a few drinks, thought Panky. An aperitif or two maybe? Panky was on his second glass of beer now and with just a little encouragement the girls were down to their underwear, dancing slowly together, looking good, very good. To Panky's eyes it was Christmas day and Easter all in one: soft red beckoning lips, small pink darting tongues, keen and curious; unblemished flesh, firm young buttocks easing from side to side with the soft music; portentous tiny snatches of pubic hair peeking out through tiny lace knickers; sweet young breasts gently bobbing with every giggle. Phew!

Panky padded over to the refrigerated mini bar and opened the door. He needed another drink and quick. "Ok girls what're you having?" he said, "Let's get this party started!" His face was flushed and glowing in the bright cool light of the mini bar. "Whiskey, Tequila, Gin, beer... whatever you want! Cigarettes?"

The girls stood arm in arm swaying gently to the music, looking a little coy now, very possibly younger than 18.

Number 13 said, "Cigarettes and alcohol, we no like Jack... Mamasan she say bad habit!"

Number 12 nodded in agreement.

Panky thought they were kidding.

Number 12 said, "We like Coca cola and candy!" The girls looked into each other's eyes, giggled and shared a well-practiced high five.

Somewhat dismayed and just a tad disappointed, Panky threw them some candy.

As they picked it up off the floor he crossed the room and handed them both a can of coke. The girls ate the candy like starving kids, slurped noisily at the coke cans.

Panky sat on the side of the bed watching, amazed at their hunger, the sweet naivety. He pulled off his boots, slipped off his clothes, threw them on the floor in a heap and put his wallet, his watch and his ring on the table next to the bed.

The girls looked over at him with big brown eyes; they slowly and seductively licked chocolate from their fingers. One of them burped and they both giggled.

Panky smiled, raised his glass and swallowed some beer, he was a little uncertain of what to do next. He had a pretty good idea of course, but where the hell do you begin?

Number 13 ran her hands over her friend's body and gently undid her bra; it fell to the floor revealing beautiful small brown breasts, her nipples were erect already. She looked down at them and giggled as though it had never happened before.

She walked over to Panky and grabbed him by the hand.

"You need shower Jack, you so stinky!"

Panky felt sure she was right, with a big smile on his face and a growing bulge in his Calvin Klein's he followed her into the bathroom.

As water splashed, playful shouts and screams emanated from the bathroom Number 13 pulled a small brown envelope from her bra, poured it into Panky's beer and swiftly stirred it with her finger.

Eventually Panky and number 12 came out of the shower wrapped in once fluffy white towels, engulfed in a billowing cloud of steam.

The girls were smiling and finishing their cans of coke as Panky crossed the room and swallowed the last of his beer in one decisive gulp.

"You're boss says you're kind of close," he said as he put down his glass.

"Sure we are Jack," the girls said in unison looking into each other eyes, giggling more than ever.

"I think this is going to be a night to remember!" said Panky as he stepped out of his underpants and admired his erection.

The jazzy muzak continued to play, the girls stood smiling, and caressing each other's firm adolescent bodies.

Panky smiled his biggest smile and once again the girls giggled playfully.

SIXTEEN

When Panky eventually woke up he had no idea where he was. This came as no big surprise as he rarely knew where he was when he first woke up. The surprise was the heat and the noise. The mad, blaring noise came from the TV; the cartoon channel was on full volume. *FULL*.

Tom and Jerry were kicking the shit out of each other, the same as they had been for the last forty years or more; there was hooting and revving in the background too; a cacophony of angry traffic with that strange chaotic intensity that Panky had heard before. The heat too was intense. The room was as hot as a pizza oven and Panky was gasping, he could hardly breathe. Brilliant sunshine crept in through the holes in the tattered curtains; bright rays of dust motes seemed to hang in the air like torch beams, like Star Wars weapons. The room felt surreal, felt claustrophobic.

Panky's first thought was to scratch the inside of his throat, he wanted to claw at it with his nails, wanted to stop it feeling like sawdust and peanut shells, wanted to stop the dull drumming sensation in his head, the phasing in and out, the gut churning nausea. He wanted to stop that a lot, but what he really needed was a drink. With sticky eyes he tried to focus on the room, trays of half eaten meals were scattered around, big ginger cockroaches feeding on scraps. One clung to the wall, fluttered its thin ginger wings. There were candy wrappers and empty coke cans everywhere.

He tried to stand up but could only stumble, so he stumbled over to the mini bar and opened the door. The light lit up his weary gray face as he squinted inside in disbelief. The disappointment was immediate: the mini bar was totally empty! Not even a fuckin ice cube! Panky stood as straight as he could. He looked around the room searching for clues. Confused and bewildered he scratched his head with one hand and his balls with the other. He vaguely remembered two girls, young girls and the multi chinned face of the fat man.

He looked at the nightstand beside the disheveled bed. Oh no! Like the girls, his watch, his ring and his wallet were gone! He scanned the room, realised his clothes and his boots were gone too! All that remained were his scruffy jeans and there was nothing at all to drink! For fuck's sake! Panky sat on the bed thinking: This is a dream right? I'm still asleep and it's a dream, it's a Third World fuckin' nightmare.

SEVENTEEN

Rommel and the guard were actually awake when
Panky stumbled down the stairs, when he staggered
towards the reception desk. Rommel was wearing
cinnamon coloured lipstick and gold hoop earrings; his
pink shirt was knotted above the waist exposing his flat
brown stomach and his pierced navel. On the stool next
to him Shotgun Boy, the guard, was wearing his
favourite sneer, holding an antique Colt .45.

Panky stood sweating at the desk, naked apart from
his scruffy jeans; his eyes wild and his expression
troubled; he watched them put down their cups and
stare at him open mouthed.

It was their afternoon coffee break, weak instant
coffee sat in chipped cups on the desk, the sweet sugary
smell rising with the billowing steam made Panky more
nauseous than ever. He slumped across the desk and
started to explain his predicament—he was pretty calm
at first. Rommel and Shotgun Boy didn't seem too
bothered; they seemed more interested in their coffee.
Between hot noisy slurps, Rommel said he didn't see
any girls leave with Panky's stuff, uh-uh not a thing,
but of course it was always possible that he'd fallen
asleep, that did happen sometimes. Rommel blew
gracefully at the steam above his cup, asked Shotgun
Boy, but he'd seen nothing either.

Panky said maybe he'd dozed off too, Rommel said
yeah it was possible they did work long hours. Panky

heard a soft theatrical gasp. He saw Rommel's lashes flutter, saw his painted nails dance at his cinnamon lips: he'd suddenly remembered something: Panky coming back drunk, arm in arm with two young girls. *Very* young girls, he added with a small sneer, he looked over at Shotgun Boy, grinned and said he hoped that Panky hadn't broken any laws. Panky wanted to squeeze his Adam's apple and watch his eyes bulge.

Panky sighed and smiled, said ok, let's call the police.

Rommel and Shotgun Boy fell about laughing.

Rommel said yeah—great idea; tell them to look for two young girls with dark hair and brown eyes, easy to find in Manila, ha ha ha!

Shotgun Boy was holding his sides, tears running down his cherubic cheeks.

Panky couldn't really see the humour, didn't find his desperate predicament *that* funny, felt like slapping them both, teaching them some manners. He considered the idea for about twenty seconds, decided it wouldn't help. He said, "Ok guys, no problema lets get this sorted… give me my mobile, my cell phone."

Rommel and Shotgun Boy just fell around laughing again, Rommel camping it up, slapping his thighs, stamping his tiny feet.

Panky felt weak and helpless like a car crash victim—he looked like one too. He lay across the desk with his arms outstretched, fists opening and closing, his forehead flat on the desk; wild eyes pink and sticky, breath sour and fetid. But he wasn't angry, not yet; but he was frustrated, very. He looked at Rommel; their eyes were level through the sweet steam of his coffee. "Rommel… please, I need my cell phone."

Rommel smirked at Shotgun Boy before he spoke, "Sorry sir," he said limp wristed and suddenly lisping, camper than ever, "Company policy is company policy, you pay your bill you get your cell phone, there's nothing else I can do."

Now Panky *was* angry, he hated the way Rommel suddenly lisped, hated the way he said 'company polithy'. What the hell was that all about? "Look Rommel you fucking Nazi," he shouted, "If you don't give me the cell phone I am totally fucked ok? Understand? Tot…al…ly fucked!"

Rommel and Shotgun Boy exchanged glances.

"What don't you understand? Huh?" said Panky trying hard to ease up a little, "You give me the cell phone, I make a call and then I'll get the money to pay you… it's easy, right?"

"The meals alone were $100," said Rommel as he flicked through some papers, "the complete mini bar works out at…" he checked the figures, " $75 not including the additional cans of coke and the candy bars… plus two days rent, that's another $90 and of course the late payment charge." Rommel grinned sweetly at the guard, "We're looking at about $300 minimum, plus tax, service charges and of course our tip."

Panky stood erect at the reception desk; ran his fingers through his tangled hair, tried to shake the cobwebs from his brain. "Look," he shouted as he banged his fist on the counter, "Watch my lips… if I can't use my cell phone I can't get the money, do you understand?"

"Calm down sir, please!" lisped Rommel stepping back slightly and nodding to the guard.

"Calm down?" bellowed Panky pacing to and fro hands thrust deeply into his empty pockets, "What do you mean calm down? I am calm! You want to see me not calm, huh? Keep giving me that 'company polithy' bullshit! C'mon try it!"

Shotgun Boy put down his coffee, slid off his stool behind the desk and picked up his old shotgun, he pointed it at Panky's face and cocked it.

The cruel, cold metallic click spoke a thousand words, in a hundred different languages.

Panky stopped pacing, stood silent staring at the darkness of the barrels; a double darkness like tiny round Ray Bans but deadly.

Rommel said, "What I mean sir... is calm down and get out!" He looked at the guard and they both smiled. "Go away and come back when you've got some money and *then* you can have your cell phone... *and* your passport... sir."

Panky continued to stare down the barrels of the shotgun, he'd forgotten all about his passport.

"Otherwise we'll call the police and they'll arrest you," said Rommel, his pretty hands on his slender hips, the bitch tone back in his voice again.

"Arrest me for what?" said Panky, eyes still firmly on the shotgun.

"Depends what we tell them... sir!"

Shotgun Boy smiled and nodded stupidly.

Panky stared down the barrels of the old shotgun.

EIGHTEEN

Panky sat on the pavement outside the Parc Hotel, naked apart from his scruffy Levis, smoking his last cigarette, thinking: Well, here I am 10,000 miles from home and totally fucked! Not fucked like I expected to be fucked… but *fucked* fucked!

The afternoon sun was hot and relentless; the traffic grid locked and noisy. Panky sat and gazed around, clueless on what to do next. He watched ragged, dirty street kids point at him and laugh hysterically, their faces distorted and crazy, plastic bags full of solvent held tightly in their dirty hands, inhaling with mad enthusiasm. He watched them running wild and frantic through the busy streets, unwanted children hooked on glue at ten, fighting constant hunger with cheap drugs, getting thinner and madder as their empty days ticked by. Phew! Street kids ran hysterical through hooting traffic, Panky sat for an hour or two, watched puzzled pedestrians stare at him in disbelief.

He watched the traffic some more. He noticed two young girls slide out of a taxi, pay the driver. They looked good, well-dressed and sexy, stylish office types in tight skirts and white blouses. Nice, thought Panky, very nice. Maybe they'd see him and offer help? Maybe they'd save him?

The girls glanced across the street at him and smiled, giggled together.

This is it! he thought. His heart raced madly, his smile grew hopeful and he waved, but the girls just laughed and turned and entered their office.

As they vanished from sight their taxi pulled away, thick black smoke pluming from its rusting exhaust. Panky sat dejected, watched the yellow battered Datsun Cherry fight its way back into the traffic. He looked at the door of the cab, shook his head and looked again. He saw the words 'Ding-Dong' scrawled in red letters.

He stood up panting as the taxi gained speed and pulled away slowly. It was Ding-Dong for sure! Panky started to run as fast as he could, the hot sun in his face, the scorching pavement tingled his feet as he chased through the traffic, he dodged Juicy Fruit and Marlboro vendors. He kept running.

Pedestrians and drivers stopped and stared. The crazy looking, half naked foreigner sprinted through the hot dusty streets screaming "Ding-Dong, Ding-Dong, Ding-Dong!"

Panky kept running and screaming, gaining ground, winding his way around cars, ignoring the stares from bewildered old ladies, running hard, gaining ground and doing good. Then *bosh*! His foot found a deep pothole and he tumbled to the ground. He fell hard on his face, tasted the road, blood streaming from his nostrils. He grabbed onto the nearest car, ignored the exhaust fumes in his face, the heat of the metal on his fingers and pulled himself back onto his feet. He watched the Datsun pull away in the distance. He couldn't give up now, no way; the battered cab and its weary old driver were his only chance of survival. He wiped the blood from his face with dirty fingers and continued running, shouting "Ding-Dong, Ding-Dong, Ding-Dong!"

He could still see the car as he sprinted along, as he continued to run, getting closer and closer. He was going to make it!

The Datsun stopped abruptly at traffic lights, Panky ran faster than ever, convinced this was his only chance; dodged more vendors, wiped the streaming blood from his face. He made it to the car and collapsed on the hot tarmac road gasping. His dirty bloodied fingertips curled over the open window, he slowly pulled himself up onto his knees, panting hard and desperate; blood streaked his face, sweat soaked his hair, stuck to his unshaven face. As Panky's laboured breath filled the cab Ding-Dong turned his head towards the window, studied Panky's face, saw the blood and the sweat, heard his panting exhaustion.

Their eyes met.

Panky smiled, wiped his face and sniffed at tears of joy.

Ding-Dong smiled too. He said, "Hey British, Mr. Panky! How you doing my fren? You havin' a good time?"

NINETEEN

Panky sat in the back of the Datsun Cherry, naked apart from his jeans, almost pleased to feel the springs in his arse again.

Ding-Dong watched him in the rear view, saw him wipe the blood off his face.

"They even took the condoms and the Viagra!" said Panky his hands trembling, his voice bitter like a jilted groom.

The traffic slowed to a halt, Ding-Dong's eyes went back to the rear view. "You looking very weak Mr. Panky," said Ding-Dong, "When you last eat my fren?"

Panky had no idea; he shrugged and shook his head.

"We Filipino's... we lub to eat!" shouted Ding-Dong above the incessant traffic, "We stop, we eat, ok? Filipino hospitality!"

"Yeah, sure," said Panky, "I could murder a cold beer and some cigarettes!"

Ding-Dong revved the engine, swerved out of the traffic and hammered through the shadowy back streets, screeched around corners and hurtled headlong through a gaggle of pedestrians; he seemed to know the streets real well. Panky guessed he was hungry too.

The Datsun pulled up noisily outside a makeshift car park, Ding-Dong wrenched on the handbrake.

The car park was surrounded and protected by cyclone wire and a slouching uniformed kid with an ancient shotgun and a sleepy face. Panky just had to smile. Row upon row of hot dusty cars sat shimmering in the heat. Beyond them, at the back of the compound, sat a scruffy old caravan; from the serving hatch the noise of frying and chopping and coughing escaped in waves, it escaped with the steam and the smoke and the heat.

Ding-Dong waved his hand in the air, told Panky that the drinks were on the way, he said the food was excellent, very well priced too, terrific value.

Panky said he needed a cold beer and a cigarette.

They sat at a plastic picnic table in scorching sunlight, litter all around them, watching skinny cats and dogs hissing and pissing and begging in the hot gray gravel among the cars, sad eyed hungry strays, hopeful for scraps of anything.

Panky continued to explain his dilemma, sweat on his brow, fiery sun in his eyes. Ding-Dong sat nodded and grinned; he was a good listener.

A couple of cars started their engines, hot fumes and noise wafted across their table. Panky had never dined in a car park before, the idea had never really appealed to him. He coughed and grinned and smiled across the table at Ding-Dong as he waited for his beer. He watched a couple of scabby dogs humping frantically just a few feet away. Nice appetizer!

A stocky, sweating Chinaman strolled slowly from the caravan in a diminishing cloud of smoke and a violent fit of coughing. His once white apron was multicolored like an artist's smock; his tattered shorts were greasy and frayed above his hairy varicose legs. He put a beer and a dusty can of Coke on the table, ambled back to the caravan without a word.

Ding-Dong smiled, opened his Coke can with a *pssst*.

Panky picked up his bottle of San Miguel and despite its warmth took a massive gulp. He swallowed and let out a huge sigh of relief. Phew! What a morning, or was it afternoon? He had no idea. Despite the location, the heat, the fumes, the scabby cats and dogs and the ongoing canine fornication, Panky was feeling pretty good now. Things were looking up. Ding-Dong was a total hero and in Panky's eyes he was doing a real good job: beer, albeit warm beer, cigarettes *and* transportation were quite a step up from earlier in the day. The only problem now was getting some money and getting the phone back. Panky finished his beer.

Ding-Dong got his mobile phone out of his pocket, it was old, as big as an infant's shoebox, but it worked and he dialed. The first couple of calls didn't seem to bring much joy. Ding-Dong tried again. "Op o naman," said Ding-Dong into the shoebox, "Hindi Americano, Breeteesh, Breeteesh!" Ding-Dong smiled, nodded, gave Panky the thumbs up and waffled on incoherently in his native Tagalog. "Hindi! Hindi!" he said, "Hindi, my good fren Mr. Panky… very good fren, very good." Ding-Dong smiled again, switched off the shoebox and put it back into his pocket. "Ok na!" said Ding-Dong, "Walang problema, no more problem… let's eat!"

Bang on cue the Chinaman walked out of the caravan with a large metal tray of food, coughing in the smoke and steam like before. He sauntered up to the table, face glistening and deadpan, sweat trickled from his brow, ran down his unshaven chin as he casually crashed the tray onto the table. Ding-Dong looked delighted and ordered more beer for Panky, asked the Chinaman for a glass of ice this time, told him, with just a touch of authority, that foreigners hated warm beer. The Chinaman said nothing, just pulled a bottle of San Miguel out of his shorts pocket, wiped it on his apron, explained curtly that they had no ice today—no ice!

Panky eyed the food suspiciously and Ding-Dong smiled hungrily.

Panky looked around, he could smell something, something bad, very bad; he didn't know if it was the food, the waiter, the wildlife or what. It was a *very, very* bad smell, like methane gas or dying rats. It made Panky want to gag, but he knew he couldn't. He didn't want to insult Ding-Dong; the old guy had been such a hero.

Ding-Dong smiled hungrily as the Chinaman wandered off lighting another Marlboro; he coughed and spluttered his way back to the caravan kicking and cursing at stray cats and dogs.

Panky didn't want to eat it was that simple. He didn't even want to look at the food, but he didn't want to offend his only friend, his saviour. That wouldn't be right—where the hell would he be now without Ding-Dong?

With big eager eyes Ding-Dong stuffed a handful of steaming rice into his mouth and chewed noisily. How could Panky refuse? It would be so rude. He knew that in some countries not eating was the ultimate insult, Ding-Dong had done so much, he deserved more than insults, a lot more. Panky watched him swallow, grab another handful of rice and shovel it into his mouth as if some kind of culinary race had just begun. Panky smiled, drew heavily on his cigarette and exhaled a lungful of smoke into the air.

"You must eat!" said Ding-Dong chewing and swallowing, just a few grains of white rice stuck to his dark chin, another hot handful of rice poised ready for consumption.

Panky grimaced, clapped his hands together in burst of phony enthusiasm—he'd rather eat cardboard.

"What are we having then Ding-Dong?" His smile was slightly nervous, just a tad forced; he just *had* to eat, the last thing he wanted was to get left sitting in the car park watching the dogs shagging among the cars. He just had to eat, there was no way out.

Ding-Dong grabbed another handful of rice, shoveled it in his mouth and stood up. "This," he said chewing and pointing to one of the silver trays, "This is chicken intestine, grilled to perfection." Ding-Dong picked up some thin white intestines, splashed them into a small bowl of the blackest soy sauce and garlic and shoved them into his mouth with the rice. Yummy!

Panky glanced at the silver tray, puffed on his cigarette, took another swig of his warm beer.

"You no like?" said Ding-Dong grabbing some more, repeating the process. Loving it.

Panky shook his head, "Uh huh."

Ding-Dong pointed to another silver tray, a large crispy steaming fish, tail and head still in place; the fish's dark deadeye stared up at them.

Panky would have bet good money that the fish was staring right at him, but he didn't have any money so he grinned at Ding-Dong and waited for his words.

"And this pish," said Ding-Dong wiping the soy sauce and rice from his chin, "Is bery, bery sarap… tasty… you say in English, de ba?"

Panky nodded yes, not sure of what 'de ba?' meant, guessed bery meant very, watched as Ding-Dong pulled out the fishes exposed eye, popped it open between his crooked yellow teeth, sucked out the juice, crunched what was left of it and swallowed it.

"The eye is the best, mas sarap… ver…y tasty" said Ding-Dong as he munched happily and slurped from his warm can of Coke.

Panky flicked away his cigarette butt, tried his best not to look shocked or disgusted.

Ding-Dong continued to eat noisily, pointed to another tray, picked up a fluffy orange ball, popped it into his mouth and chewed. "One day old chicks," he said."

Panky looked confused, wiped the sweat from his brow and lit another of Ding-Dong's cigarettes.

Ding-Dong explained: "You get baby chick, ok?" Panky nodded. "Only one day old, ok?" he chewed some more, "Then you cook, dip in batter, deep fry to perfection," he said proudly as he swallowed.

Panky swallowed too, it was the only way he could stop himself from gagging.

Ding-Dong continued as he pointed to the next tray, "This is balot, very famous dish of the Philippines."

Panky looked at the duck egg. It looked harmless enough; an egg is an egg, right? Ding-Dong picked up the egg, cracked the end of the shell on the table, tipped it into his mouth and sucked out some juice. "Balot," he said, "fertilized duck egg, boiled…"

"To perfection?" asked Panky.

"Correck! And ver…y good aphrodisiac." said Ding-Dong pleased that Panky was following with such interest. He removed the shell, took a large bite out of the egg. "The crunchy bits are just the bones," he said, "And the beak." He held up the egg so his new friend could see the evidence, "The feathers are hard to swallow, you spit them out, ok?"

Panky wanted to spit but just smiled and smoked.

"You no like?" asked Ding-Dong.

Panky said nothing, just pointed to the next dish.

"This one sweet sour meat wid vegetable, you like?" asked the old taxi driver. Ding-Dong heaped some onto a plate of steaming rice and Panky smiled. It looked good.

Panky took the plate, cautiously sniffed its steaming contents and smiled at Ding-Dong who was nodding enthusiastically, looking delighted. Panky was happy now, relieved. Not only did the sweet and sour smell good, but it also looked good and fresh: tangy sweet pineapple, crisp red and green bell peppers, thin slices of red onion, tiny chunks of fresh garlic and small pieces of meat in a sticky sweet orange sauce. Sarap naman! Simmered to perfection! He threw his cigarette away, started to eat with a plastic spoon and fork; he was starving, couldn't even remember the last time he ate.

Ding-Dong continued to eat with his hands, smiled happily as he watched his new friend tuck into the meal.

Panky had forgotten all about the bad smell, the bad smell that filled his nostrils, turned his stomach, but as he continued to eat he caught another pungent whiff.

Ding-Dong saw him sniffing and laughed. "That smell," he said, "is Durian, ver...y famous fruit of the Philippines, ver...y famous. Ok, yes... very bad smell... but the taste so beautiful, forget the smell, and eat the fruit."

"Ver...y sarap?" asked Panky.

Ding-Dong laughed at the humour, nodded enthusiastically as he ate.

Panky declined the famous pungent fruit, continued with his sweet and sour. The Durian smell was worse than disgusting, much, much worse. Panky found it hard to describe, methane gas perhaps, rotting flesh maybe... death row underwear... He smiled to himself as he ate, proud of his imagination. Panky'd never actually smelled rotting flesh or death row underwear, but he was pretty sure that's exactly what it'd be like. He held his breathe and continued with his sweet and sour. He pulled a small bone from his mouth, looked at it suspiciously, thinking: It's just a bone Panky; you eat meat you get bones, relax and enjoy. He casually threw the bone to one of the skinny scabby dogs nearby; it was gone in seconds, swallowed. The dog looked sad and pathetic, what was left of its fur was sparse and scab ridden; its skin was black and pink, riddled with sores and weeping lesions. Yuk! Panky looked away.

Ding-Dong chewed his mouthful of rice and fish head, "You like dog huh?"

Panky glanced at the pitiful dog cowering among the cars, waiting amongst the litter for another bone, hopeful, desperate for anything. "Don't mind 'em," he said wiping the tangy orange sauce from his chin.

"You eat much dog in England?"

Panky laughed, "No Ding-Dong, call us traditional, but in England we only eat pussy."

Ding-Dong was in instant fits of laughter, he loved Mr. Panky's sense of humour, slapped his hand on the greasy table as he laughed. "You only eat pussy, ha! I like that... you funny, rude but funny guy Mr. Panky," he said and he laughed some more, slapped his hand on the table again.

Panky swigged his warm beer and watched Ding-Dong laughing. He liked Ding-Dong a lot, enjoyed his company and why not? Where the hell would he be without it?

Ding-Dong wiped his eyes and his mouth on his arm, "So this first time you eat dog, huh?"

Panky looked at his nearly empty plate, then at the scabby, skinny dog cowering low in the gravel and litter. He spat a mouthful of sweet and sour dog into the gray gravel between his bare feet. The last thing he wanted to do was offend Ding-Dong, but he had to spit...he just had to!

TWENTY

Panky sat in the back of Ding-Dong's cab and finished his cigarette; he sighed heavily, took out his mobile phone and dialed Chris' number. It rang.

Chris was sitting in his garden by the pool, playing with his kids and having fun.

Clara still wasn't speaking to him, but he could handle that, it had happened before and like all marriages, it would certainly happen again. Chris' biggest problem was that Clara wasn't one to argue, she didn't think it was right in front of the kids; her weapon when disagreements arose—and it wasn't very often— was complete silence.

It drove Chris nuts. Clara knew it did. That's why she did it.

The kids ran and swam and dived and screamed around the pool, they were having a lot of fun. Chris sat watching. He just loved being a dad, loved being called daddy.

Clara sat silent in the shade, watched the fun from behind her Ray Bans.

Over on the table Chris' phone rang. Clara and Chris looked over at it in unison, like it was a bomb about to explode. They turned back and looked at each other. The phone continued to ring.

Chris stood up, walked over to the table and picked up the phone. "Hello?"

Clara scowled in the shade; she knew who it was, she'd been expecting the call.

Chris: "Hello?"

Panky: "Hi, it's me!"

Chris: "Hey Panky, how's it hangin' geezer? ...How's Manila?"

Panky: "Un-fuckin'-believable, that's how it was!"

Chris: "What d'ya mean?"

Panky: "Long, long story mate... if it wasn't for my friend Ding-Dong the dog eater, I don't know where I'd be. Look sorry to be so direct but I need about $500... right now!"

Chris: "$500! For what?"

Panky: "Don't even ask mate... like I said... long story."

Chris: "No probs, I'll send Boy my driver; I'll send $600 just in case, ok?"

Panky: "Terrific, I owe you one geezer."

Chris: "D'you think I'd say no?"

Panky: "Never crossed my mind."

Chris: "Just wait for Boy, ok; he'll call you once he's in the city."

Panky: "Cheers geez, later."

Trying hard not to smile too obviously, Chris switched off his phone and looked around the pool, then around the garden; apart from the gawky tall coconut trees rustling in the breeze, it was totally quiet.

He was all alone.

Clara had left with the kids as soon as he'd said, 'Hey Panky, how's it hangin'.'

TWENTY ONE

Panky sat in the back of Chris' new Range Rover as Boy drove them carefully through the city. They were heading south towards a cooler climate, cruising towards green trees and tranquility, getting away from the bustle, the pollution and the people. Panky was glad. He sat silent enjoying the cushioned comfort and the aircon; naked still apart from his jeans, but he didn't care. He gazed out the tinted window, watched towering billboards zip by and felt a corporate attack on the senses: McDonalds, Ford, Levis, Caltex, Colgate, Pizza Hut, Unilever and Kentucky Fried filled the sky with colour, filled it with a beckoning blur. God bless America.

Boy looked into the rearview, said, "I think you got a friend for life with Ding-Dong, Mr. Panky."

Panky smiled, "Oh, for sure," he said and Boy smiled back. Panky had given Ding-Dong $100, considered it a just reward for saving his life, thought it was a bargain.

Ding-Dong sat in his old Datsun Cherry and cried openly, wiped the tears from his face, said it was far too much, said he couldn't take a month's wages for one days work. But Panky insisted, so they shook hands and with tears in their eyes and smiles on their lips they went their separate ways. Panky promised that whenever he needed a cab he'd call Ding-Dong, night or day, regardless of where he was going. He promised and Ding-Dong believed him. They were frens.

Panky loved the Range Rover, loved the luxury, the 'new car' smell, the soft leather seats, the cool comfort. He was styling! He was gasping for a cigarette too, but noticed the 'No Smoking' sign and decided against it.

Boy glanced again into the rearview, looked at his passenger and grinned. When Boy had eventually found Mr. Panky he was more than a little surprised to see him in such a state, in such a mess: practically naked and penniless, the guy didn't even have shoes. Boy thought it was funny, decided that Mr. Panky was quite a character, 10,000 miles from home and the guy didn't even have luggage, not a change of underwear, not even a toothbrush. You had to see the funny side. Just before Boy started his journey north, Chris had casually mentioned that his friend had had a few problems in the city, but he didn't elaborate, so Boy didn't ask. It wasn't his place to ask questions, but it was hard not to be curious.

And Clara had taken him to one side and told him to watch out for this stranger, said she was sure he'd be a problem, one way or another.

Boy glanced into the rearview: he seemed harmless enough. So far anyway.

TWENTY TWO

The two huge men walked straight through customs ahead of the crowd without a hitch, no questions asked, just courteous smiles; just strolled through, easy.

Fortunately for them they left the plane via the first class exit, quickly got ahead of the herd in coach, ahead of the hoi polloi. It was all part of traveling in style, having a little class, the men agreed on that and smiled together feeling like celebrities. They cruised through passport control, then through the VIP channel—again without a hitch. They looked impressive in their Italian suits, silk ties perfectly knotted, expensive shoes polished like mirrors: executives for sure with attitudes to match.

As they strolled along they filled the air with expensive colognes and carried bulging bags of duty free: vodka, scotch and cigarettes. The big guys looked happy, they were enjoying their trip already and they'd only just landed.

The airport was cool and bright, more modern than they'd expected.

As they strolled along they looked behind them, saw the noisy anxious masses from coach rushing toward arrivals, rushing towards the conveyor belt like crazy ants.

The 'executives' stayed cool and calm and ahead of the crowd. With a click of the fingers and just a touch of arrogance, they got some kid to pick up their designer baggage. The kid puffed and grunted as he loaded it onto his trolley, smiled as he pushed it along in front of them. They headed towards the exit and the heat and the chaos outside.

The biggest guy eased his shirt collar away from his huge neck a little, feeling the heat already despite the aircon; his partner strolled alongside smiling, oblivious, too busy catching his image in the mirrors, too busy feeling stylish and smart. They got their visa stamps without question or comment and headed towards their awaiting limousine. It was all so easy. They were pleased their boss had good contacts.

A uniformed driver loaded their bags into the limo; they climbed in and sampled the cool luxury.

The guy with the big smile opened the electric window, tipped the kid five dollars and grinned as he danced around and hopped with jubilation, the kid nearly dying of happiness.

The big guys were laughing quietly as the limo pulled away. They had good reason to laugh; everything had gone extremely smoothly, no one had even looked at their passports.

The limo driver turned and said, "Welcome to the Philippines, Mabuhay!" and in the cool comfort of the back seat their laughter grew.

They cruised through the heavy traffic towards Manila and the laughter continued to grow. They were having a great time. It was their first trip to Asia and it was all expenses paid. Boris Morozov and Vladimir Brodsky agreed that without a doubt and whatever happened, this was going to be a trip to remember.

TWENTY THREE

Boy was quiet and in control as always. The Range Rover cruised silently at 180 mph.

Panky sat in the back feeling comfortable and relaxed; at last he felt safe, all his troubles seemed a long way behind, he was longing to see his old friend Chris.

The difference between the city and the countryside was amazing, gone was the smoke, the noise, the pollution and the people; just wide open spaces and trees and fields and clear blue skies. It was beautiful, almost breathtaking.

Boy looked in the rearview mirror. "Your first trip to the Philippines?" he asked.

"That's right," said Panky.

Boy just smiled and concentrated on driving.

Panky watched rice fields, coffee plantations, rows and rows of pineapples zip by; saw massive gray Carabaos like prehistoric beasts of burden ambling along; saw leather skinned farmers and waving kids at the edge of the road, saw tall purple mountains in the distance. Wow!

The journey continued in silence, Panky stared out of the window, soaked up the scenery.

After about an hour Boy glanced into the rearview. His passenger was barely awake.

"Time for your video sir," said Boy.

"Video?"

"Yes sir."

Panky had noticed the TV in the car, saw it when he first got in; thought it was a cool idea, perfect for kids on long journeys. He was more than impressed there was a video too.

A second later the video clicked on.

Two young giggling children appeared on the TV screen: two kids up close to the camera, having fun and pulling faces. The smiling kids moved away and Chris' tanned face appeared, his short-cropped hair was almost blonde now from the sun, his huge smile and his cleft chin were just the same as ten years ago. He'd hardly changed at all, Panky couldn't believe it. Sitting there by the pool relaxed and grinning, Chris actually looked younger than he did in Amsterdam.

"Hello geezer, how's it hanging?" said Chris smiling on the screen.

Panky smiled too, so pleased to see his friend after so long, so pleased to be back with his old "Partner in grime." The geezer looks so fuckin healthy, thought Panky, what's wrong with him? And he did, Chris looked great; he still had that "don't fuck with me" kind of look—Panky was pleased about that—but he looked happy with it; he looked contented. And his teeth looked so white.

Back on the screen, Chris said, "I thought you were never gonna make it, how the hell are you?"

Panky smiled like it was his birthday.

"As you can see I'm doing ok, I'm coping *quite* nicely," said Chris with grin.

Panky was amazed at everything: Boy the driver, the new Range Rover, the TV, the video, the beautiful children, the casual poolside chitchat and of course the beautiful girls cavorting in the background. He was amazed and dying to get there.

"Last time we were together, I didn't have a pot to piss in, remember?" said Chris.

Of course I remember thought Panky, how could I possibly forget?

Chris continued: "Life's rich tapestry and all that, geezer? Life's ups and downs, mostly ups just lately… luckily. A lot's happened believe me Panky."

Panky believed him and felt a momentary pang of envy, he wondered sometimes, but not often, what the whole family thing was like, wondered if he'd ever experience it.

"I can't wait to see you mate, so much to tell you."

Panky couldn't wait to listen.

"Don't worry about the Philippines it's an amazing place, really… the people here are fantastic."

Boy smiled.

"You should be here in four or five hours, depending on traffic… but you're in good hands, so don't worry."

Boy smiled again, nodded his head slightly in agreement, as always things were under control.

"Have a drink if you want one," said Chris, "have a couple… there's Chivas, ice in the refrigerator… help yourself… please, but no smoking in the car or my wife will kill you."

Boy smiled again, and again he nodded his head slightly. She would for sure, Clara loved the 'new car' smell; wanted it to stay that way for as long as possible.

"See you soon mate, take it easy geezer," said Chris as the video ended and the screen went blank.

Panky sighed, saw Boy's eyes in the rearview and said, "It's true Boy… really… last time I saw Chris he was single, forty five years old, had about $400 in his pocket and the clothes he was standing in."

Boy concentrated on the road and said nothing; it wasn't his place to pry.

Panky looked at the suit hanging in the back of the car, it obviously belonged to Chris. He opened the jacket, noticed the Armani label and felt the quality of the material. Nice. Life's rich tapestry indeed he thought. Chris had obviously made a shit load of money and Panky was dying to find out how—dying to find out.

"So, Sir Chris make good money in Philippines, huh Boy?" asked Panky. Knowing Chris as he did there was no way it was anything legal… no fuckin' way.

Boy smiled. It wasn't his place to give away secrets either.

It must be *very* nice to have money, lots of money thought Panky, but I'd hate to be looking over my shoulder all the time.

TWENTY FOUR

Boris and Vlad sat in the sprawling reception lounge in Makati's Shangri-La hotel. The place was opulent and impressive; the five star air was cool and clean, it felt European; there were beautiful artworks on the walls and tasteful, quality furniture all around. An orchestra was playing Vivaldi on the 1st floor balcony.

The Russians didn't expect anything like this, not in a third world country; the Shangri La was amazing by any standards.

Boris and Vlad over tipped the pretty waitress and almost smiled when she brought the drinks to their table.

They sat sipping their Canadian Clubs and eating fistfuls of garlic peanuts, looking around, taking it all in. In unison they sat back in overstuffed armchairs and relaxed, listened to the soothing melodic sounds of the orchestra.

Boris watched as a multitude of guests wandered around the cordon bleu restaurants and the overpriced gift shops. He thought perhaps that he and Vlad stood out a little with their dark suits and their Ray Ban sunglasses, thought that maybe, compared to the people around them, they looked a little sinister and of course he was right. It wasn't just their immense size—they were easily four or five times bigger than the average Filipino—and it wasn't just the dark suits bulging with muscle or the short-cropped hair and facial scars that made them stand out. The real problem, thought Boris, was their husky Muscovite accents. In reality of course, the accents themselves were fine, but as Zoltan had instructed, they were using Canadian passports.

They sounded about as Canadian as Rasputin's dad.

"Do I sound Canadian to you?" Boris asked Vlad.

Vlad just sipped his drink and grinned, didn't feel the question deserved an answer.

"I didn't think so," said Boris, "And we cannot change our voices... correct?"

Vlad just grinned again.

"Maybe we need to change our image, we need to blend in, ok?"

Vlad said, "Ok," and they drained their glasses, stood up and sauntered heavily toward the gift shops and peered into the windows.

It didn't take them long to find the shop they were looking for.

They tried on a selection of casual wear, limited of course by their size and bulk, and finally decided on identical Hawaiian suits; lightweight threads with colourful floral prints. Something different, something tropical.

Boris was keen on the tropical look, wanted to see how it felt, wanted to see how he looked with such a drastic change in style—he hadn't worn short trousers since he was eight years old.

The assistant assured them that the suits they chose looked fantastic, said the material would give a little once it had been washed, that they shouldn't worry if the outfits felt a little tight across the arms and chest at first. That was perfectly normal she said.

Boris picked his favorite colour; the pattern was white sampaguita blossoms on a bright red background.

Stylish and tropical just like you wanted, the assistant said nervously but with a smile.

Vlad wasn't too sure which colour looked best on him, finally decided on the turquoise. The blue almost went with his eyes and he liked that.

The Russians stood side by side in their new suits and checked themselves out in the large mirror. Vlad did a twirl, but Boris declined; they both grinned and agreed with the assistant, they did look fantastic.

The only problem they had now was their shoes: size twelve Oxfords looked kind of silly with Hawaiian shorts. Even Boris knew that.

Their next stop was the shoe shop.

They were lucky the young assistant told them, there were only three pairs of size twelve's in the entire store. Most Filipino men wore size seven or eight, nine at the most she added looking up, smiling nervously at the two huge men.

The Russians left the shoe shop and wandered back to the reception lounge wearing their new colourful suits and their leather sandals, carrying their old ones in trendy designer carrier bags.

They sat down at the same table as before, ordered more Canadian Clubs and grinned at each other feeling cool and tropical, because it was still sunny outside and because they felt they added a certain anonymity, they decided to stick with the wraparound Ray Bans. Vlad said why not? Ray Bans look good with practically anything and Boris agreed.

The Hawaiian suits did appear a little tight across the chest and around the biceps, but they looked ok-ish.

The leather sandals looked pretty good too, went well with the outfits. It was the long dark woolen socks that looked a little out of place.

The assistant spotted the problem immediately, but didn't have the courage to mention it. She'd never seen anyone quite as big as the two men before, found them hard to understand. They had the strangest Canadian accents she'd ever heard.

Boris and Vlad sat drinking and relaxing, feeling stylish, swallowing peanuts.

Afternoon slowly became evening.

"I think the women here are amazing," said Vlad flushed with alcohol, beaming at the waitresses, peanut mulch in the gaps between his teeth.

"They're small that's for sure," said Boris without emotion, "Not really my type but nice and easy to throw around."

Vlad laughed into his drink, beckoned a waitress and ordered some more.

Boris picked at his teeth, knocked back his Canadian Club and said he was feeling good about the trip so far, very good.

Vlad said "Yeah, we can have some fun here I think."

Boris sipped his drink, said he felt good about the situation too, said he knew they could easily resolve the problem, said that Panky should be easy to find, he stood out like a sore thumb anywhere, even in Amsterdam.

Vlad chuckled with Canadian Club confidence and agreed that the job should be easy. He sighed and looked around, things were going good so far; he'd never seen Boris quite so relaxed, quite so at ease, the change of scenery was obviously good for him.

Boris smiled his twisted little smile and drank another Canadian Club: he secretly yearned for vodka but said nothing: incognito was the order of the day and he knew it.

So the Russians sat drinking in their sampaguita suits, with their wraparound shades firmly in place.

Big smiles and flushed complexions.

Whether they actually blended in any more than before was debatable.

An hour or so later, after several more drinks and about a kilo and a half of garlic peanuts Boris' cell phone rang.

He answered it.

Boris: "Err…yes… hello?"

Zoltan: "Boris, it's me."

Boris: "Hey, we're here, what's up?"

Zoltan: "Any problems?"

Boris: "No, no problems."

Zoltan: "Ok, just keep me informed… and remember *little brother*, I want no more *'moments of weakness'*… ok?"

Boris: "Ok…ok, no problem."

Zoltan hung up and Boris switched off his phone, put it away and grinned at Vlad.

"Zoltan seems in a good mood," he said.

"It's because we're gonna find this Panky," said Vlad, "Because we're gonna get the money, take it back to him… that's why he's happy Boris… is a lot of money not to have."

"You're right," said Boris nodding gently, remembering the old days in Moscow, "Is a lot of money not to have."

Vlad nodded a little too, thinking: Sure it's a lot of money not to have. He remembered the old days, the hardships they'd endured. He remembered the constant hunger. He remembered Moscow. How could he forget it?

After the dissolution of the Soviet Union things had been good for a couple of years, very good, but eventually there was nothing left, nothing left to steal and no one worth extorting except other criminals. It was a miserable existence. Times were very hard. Going out to eat was practically impossible, even for someone with Zoltan's connections. The food shortages were a major headache and the big guys loved to eat.

They struggled by on the revenues from the gambling machines that Zoltan had in all the tourist hotels and the money they made from buying and selling foreign currency on the black market—the Fartsovka business. Zoltan doubling his money over night with the foreign currency, which was ok for a while, but it wasn't enough. It wasn't nearly enough. Suddenly they became a lot more solvent, were able to consider a move to Amsterdam, to greener pastures. Some said that Zoltan made his money flooding the market with low-grade heroin, that he imported it direct from contacts in Pakistan, had it cut and cut and then cut again. Others said that the money was made when he organized the theft of some fourteenth century Byzantine artifacts, sold them to a collector in Switzerland. Word was the icons came from one of the churches nestled 'safely' in the Kremlin, that Zoltan delivered them to Switzerland personally. But that was all rumours. In Moscow at the time the only thing there wasn't a shortage of was rumours.

Vlad looked back and remembered being hungry a lot of the time. He smiled and exhaled a little air from his nostrils, thinking: Hunger's something you never forget. If he never saw Moscow again he'd be happy. He'd be very happy.

The Russians sat in their tropical suits and continued to relax, continued drinking Canadian Club, swallowing large handfuls of peanuts. They were lovin' life: the cool five star ambience, soothing classical music from the balcony, cordon bleu food and lots of it, excellent service, basically surrounded by Third World luxury and splendour. Everything was just perfect and once they'd finished their drinks they were off for a sauna and a massage.

Vlad smiled at Boris.

Boris returned the smile. It was hard not to smile.

Vlad said, "So tomorrow, we go find him... and then..."

"And then we find out where the money is and we kill him, slowly, is easy!" said Boris raising his glass and snorting a little air as they laughed together.

TWENTY FIVE

The Range Rover cruised past the beautiful Lake Taal and Boy prompted Panky to take a look at the volcano in the huge lake.

"It's the eighth wonder of the world," said Boy, "Or that's what they say." He looked at his passenger in the rear view, the guy was looking drunk, wasted, had dribble in his stubble, his eyes were red rimmed and puffy. "Well worth a look," said Boy without much enthusiasm; he knew that there was a good chance his passenger wasn't listening and probably couldn't even focus. He doubted if he could hear at all, all that Chivas he'd drunk. Man, could this guy put it away!

Panky screwed up his eyes and tried to focus, it wasn't easy.

The Range Rover turned right, headed inland toward undulating countryside and a veritable sea of coconut trees shimmering and swaying in the cool coastal breeze. A small mountain range stood splendid in the distance, all purple and green and tipped with light fuzzy clouds.

If Panky had been able to see clearly, he would have agreed that the view was truly magnificent.

The car cruised slowly through the quiet country roads, through the tree lined winding lanes and passed a number of small villages. They passed bungalows and bamboo huts set back slightly off the road; children pumped water by hand, wizened old guys strolled with

Carabaos and goats, some had colorful fighting cocks under their arms. They passed chattering mothers in gossiping groups and toddlers played happily in the street, small glowing bonfires smoldered every few yards, billowing hazy gray smoke filled the air and distorted the pinkest of sunsets.

Panky missed it all. The Chivas had really done the trick.

Boy glanced into the rearview mirror; saw his passenger looking gaunt and pale and drunk. He looked worse than ever.

Boy just kept driving. He wasn't 100% sure, but he had a pretty good idea that Clara didn't really approve of this oddball character. He was pretty sure that she didn't really want him to visit. He thought it was strange, but Clara seemed to hate Mr. Panky despite the fact that they hadn't met. Maybe she knew something that Boy didn't? But hey, thought Boy, all that personal stuff's out of my hands, I'm just the driver; all I want to do is get the guy back to the house.

Panky coughed and spluttered.

Boy looked in the rearview mirror. "You known Sir Chris long?" slurred Panky, not quite sure why he'd said 'Sir Chris' or why he was striking up a conversation at all, he could barely speak.

"Yes sir," said Boy, "I work for Sir Chris over five years now... he's says I'm best driver bodyguard he's ever had!"

"Driver *and* bodyguard? He needs a bodyguard?"

"Of course," said Boy, "This is the Philippines, but don't worry, I used to be special services!"

Panky grinned and wondered what the hell he'd let himself in for and as the journey continued he fell back to sleep. The snoring didn't really worry Boy, but when Panky started grinding his teeth the radio just had to go on.

It was dark when Panky finally opened his eyes again and stretched and yawned, he was dying for a cigarette and his mouth felt like sandpaper and peanut shells, gazing into the dark night he said, "So it's not guns, goons and gold here any more?"

"No sir," Boy looked into the rear view and chuckled, "They're still here... the guns, the goons *and* the gold... but that's a phrase from the old days."

"So what's it like here now then," asked Panky and Boy explained 'what it was like' in detail. Somehow he managed to keep a straight face and said everything that Chris had instructed him to.

"So let me get this straight," said Panky sounding a tad anxious, "It's ok here... apart from erupting volcanoes, earthquakes, hurricanes, floods, typhoid, hepatitis A and B, malaria, coups, revolutions, communist rebel attacks, assassinations and riots?"

"And kidnappings!" said Boy with a smile.

"And kidnappings!" said Panky exhaling nervously. Panky almost finished the Chivas in one gulp, and then he took out his cigarettes, opened the packet and sniffed the contents.

Boy watched in amazement but said nothing. He looked into the rearview mirror, said, "You ok sir?"

"Yeah, fine," lied Panky, his face was pale and green; his eyes were red above purple blue bags like old bruises. He kept seeing those two punks, Sid and D.K., those dead kids... he kept seeing them again. He was having flashbacks again, not good! He'd be there soon, panic! Hello thought Panky, nice to meet you Clara, please excuse me while I have a quick cocaine induce paranoid hallucination.

The radio playing was 'The Passenger' by Iggy Pop, another flashback from the past.

Panky wondered why every single song he heard just lately seemed so significant, so appropriate. He shook his head, wondered if it was all some kind of conspiracy.

"You sure you're ok sir?" asked Boy.

"Fine," said Panky, "fine!" But he didn't look it; he was getting greener by the minute.

Boy watched him drain the last of the Chivas in one feverish gulp and wondered if it was a good idea.

"I'm just… just a bit… just a b…" And then *whoosh*! Panky threw up all over the car; a massive exorcist type projectile hurtled across the front seat and covered the dashboard with a huge *splash*.

Boy pulled the car to the side of the road and stopped. He turned and looked at Panky who was heaving, gasping and retching… and then… *whoosh*… another stomach full of foul smelling orange vomit covered the Armani suit. Totally covered it!

Panky wiped the vomit from his mouth with the white head rest cover from the front seat, at the same time managed to pour the final drops of Chivas onto the floor of the car.

Boy opened the windows and said, "That's… a very bad smell sir… what the hell did you eat?

"Dog mostly Boy," said Panky with a thin smile on his pale green face, "But don't worry, I didn't eat a whole one!"

TWENTY-SIX

It was a cool clear night at Chris and Clara's, the moon was high and full, bright stars filled the sky like thrown confetti. In the surrounding jungle, cicadas made their vibrant electric noise, an orchestra of a thousand tiny drills, a high low undulating wall of sound; crickets tried their best to compete. Despite the early evening, deranged roosters screeched their pre dawn chorus from rustling treetops. The house was large and tasteful, a neo colonial design: white walls and a pitched red roof. It looked impressive, imposing in the glare of the spotlights with its balconies and terraces, trees and exotic plants all around. There were spotlights on the swimming pool too, clear blue water shimmered and glistened silently.

Chris and Clara sat by the pool in reclining chairs and silence. Clara had hardly spoken since Panky's last phone call. It was driving Chris nuts and she knew it and she was pleased.

Chris sighed with frustration and looked over at the pool, looked at the young girls swimming around having fun—the girls were maids, gardeners, cooks and ya-ya's. It was Clara's idea that the staff was all female and young; she enjoyed the company she said and Chris found it hard to complain. He didn't mind watching them relax, didn't mind it at all. As always, one girl in particular caught his eye.

A sudden *whoosh* from the pool broke the silence. Mai Ling came rushing to the surface gasping for air; her body was lean and tanned. She climbed gracefully from the water and as she shook her hair a million tiny droplets seemed to catch the spotlight, shone like gems against the darkness of the night.

That's how it seemed to Chris anyway. He suddenly realised he was staring again. He turned and grinned hopefully at his wife, but once again—as expected—she ignored him.

Chris looked at his watch, sighed again heavily and said, "Well... he'll probably be here soon." He said it as if they were waiting for the postman to arrive.

Clara stood up and strolled slowly towards the house, "How wonderful for you both," she said with just a hint of bile and venom, "I'll be in *my* room."

Chris smiled, knowing he was onto a loser.

"It's *our* room silly," he said trying his best to sound like nothing bad was happening, like this bizarre stranger turning up wasn't going to rock their world or bring an end to their domestic bliss.

"It was," said Clara as she strolled towards the house.

TWENTY-SEVEN

As the Ranger Rover approached the house Chris saw its headlights, heard the familiar *hoot hoot*, the harsh metallic clang of the tall gates on the flagstone drive. He looked over; saw the guards holding the gates open, saluting as the car pulled up the driveway toward the garage.

Panky had finally arrived.

The windows of the car were all open still; Panky's weary face framed by the rear window, the stench of orange vomit, tangy and acidic lingered heavily— essence of dog.

Panky stared out of the window astonished by the grandeur of the house. Astonished too by the guards with their uniforms and Armalite rifles; astonished by the grounds with their trees and manicured lawns, by the glimmering swimming pool and especially astonished by the bevy of young girls playing in the water. Nice. He liked it here already.

Chris saw his haggard face framed in the car window; saw his tired eyes blinking and bewildered, saw his hair wild with neglect, his stubbly chin. It was good to see him again. Chris smiled, stood up and crossed the lawn towards the car with his arms open wide, thinking: Shit... he looks rough... what the hell happened?

Panky slid out of the car, naked still apart from his jeans and staggered towards Chris with open arms and his biggest smile, thinking: God, Chris looks so healthy... what the hell happened to him? How come his teeth are so white?

As Panky shuffled over towards his old partner he had a quick flashback. He saw Chris on the TV screen again, smiling and looking cool, saying: Have a drink if you want one, have a couple... there's Chivas, ice in the refrigerator... help yourself... please, but no smoking in the car or my wife will kill you. Panky remembered that Chris' wife liked the new smell of the car; she wanted to keep it that way. He looked back at the Range Rover, saw the open windows, the spray of orange vomit on the paintwork like go-fast racing stripes; saw it trickling still, seeping off the sills of the window, cold and congealed. He turned back from the car and walked over to his old friend, smiling, thinking: Hmmm, not the best of starts.

The guys stood eye-to-eye grinning. They coiled their arms around each other, laughed, shared a lingering man-hug and laughed again and finally dried their eyes. It was seriously emotional. Ten years is a long time.

Chris and Panky strolled arm in arm through the garden, sat by the pool and looked at each other in silence. Neither guy able to find the words he really wanted to at first, both clearly shocked, speechless by their sudden new reality.

Panky lit a much-needed cigarette; his hands were trembling.

A pretty uniformed girl brought Champagne and cool crystal glasses to their table.

Pop! Chris poured, they clinked glasses and swallowed the ice-cold nectar: it was dry and crisp and bubbly. It was perfect.

Between sips and slurps the conversation resumed. Panky smoked with a passion, gesturing wildly with his hands as he explained about his problems on the journey: the vomit, the dog, the car park restaurant and his hero Ding-Dong. He didn't mention his disastrous night on Burgos Street or the problems in the girlie bars, all the shit that went down, decided it would probably be wise to save that story for later, didn't want to appear lacking in street smarts, not to Chris. They talked about everything and nothing, anxious and excited like kids.

Another bottle went *pop*! More champagne. Their raucous laughter and the clinking of crystal glasses echoed around the garden. They were getting into it. Bacchus would be so proud.

Chris fumbled awkwardly with another cork and Panky's eyes wandered across the garden. He saw crouched flickering images by a candle lit grotto; saw a small group of girls on their knees, rosaries around their fingers, prayers on their lips, saw the tranquil figurine face of the Virgin Mary staring down at the girls, heard the cool gentle sound of running water. To Panky it was a rare and hallowed vision and to him the soft religious words created a strange devout energy.

"Hail Mary, full of grace, the Lord is with you,"

"Blessed are you among women and blessed is the fruit of your womb, Jesus,"

"Holy Mary, mother of God, pray for us sinners now and at the hour of our death, Amen."

He couldn't help but stare. The prayers seemed to reach a new intensity, they grew louder, more fervent, the girls praying harder now as candles flickered eerily in the gathering breeze. Panky listened and watched in awe.

"Hail Mary, full of grace, the Lord is with you,"
"Blessed are you among women and blessed is the fruit of your womb, Jesus,"
"Holy Mary, mother of God, pray for us sinners now and at the hour of our death, Amen."

The solemn pretty faces of the girls looked distorted with the insistence of belief, soft sweet lips moved in sync with their pious incantations, their eyes were clear and white and wonderful, the words were getting louder and louder. Four soft holy young voices chanted in unison:

"Hail Mary, full of grace, the Lord is with you,"
"Blessed are you among women and blessed is the fruit of your womb, Jesus,"
"Holy Mary, mother of God, pray for us sinners now and at the hour of our death, Amen."

It was all too much. Panky turned and watched Chris struggling with another cork; the passionate prayers were still rising in intensity, filling his head and clouding his thoughts. It was a bit scary; the words seemed directed at him and him alone.

Suddenly the prayers stopped.

Panky looked up; saw the young girls staring at him, glaring, sacrosanct hands clasping beaded rosaries.

They were looking him right in the eyes: right in the eyes. His body trembled slightly. To Panky it was eerie, eerie and weird.

Pop! Chris finally opened the bottle.

Panky was more than happy to turn and smile and offer his glass.

"Champagne!" slurred Chris, stating the obvious as he poured.

Panky lit a cigarette and exhaled into the night sky. He looked over at the grotto but the girls were gone! Silence now from the grotto, just the trickling water, nothing to see but flickering candlelight and the image of the Virgin Mary. Weird or what? It was like they'd never been there. Panky sighed heavily, swallowed his Champagne in one swift gulp and poured some more.

"What a place…" he said, wondering if what he'd seen was real.

Chris grinned; he looked a little drunk already.

Panky looked a little sad as he spoke, "Sorry I look like shit and smell about the same… like I said what happened in Manila… a long story… I… err…"

Chris was either not listening or didn't care, he was used to Panky, knew what he was like and always expected the worse, "So how's the *real* sin city then? How's Amsterdam? Mad as ever?"

"Oh yeah… mad as ever," Panky wondering how to change the subject. He didn't want to even *think* about Amsterdam, he'd put all that way behind him, he didn't want to dwell on the negative, the carnage, the dead kids, not now. He didn't think Chris really needed it but he smiled and said, "More Champagne geezer?"

Chris offered his glass, "I don't really drink any more," he said flatly like he was reminding himself about it, "Can't handle the hangovers."

"Or the memory loss!" said Panky with a grin as he poured, recalling the fact that after any given drinking session Chris never remembered a bloody thing; whole nights, days too sometimes, just gone; blacked out and forgotten. Often it was just as well.

"Come on I'll show you around." Chris stood up and swayed across the lawn with the Champagne in his hand, grinning back at Panky. "C'mon!"

Panky followed him gazing around still, taking it all in, still amazed by the beauty of everything. That was the moment he first saw Mai Ling. As she climbed gracefully from the pool, her smile was full and confident, her eyes were wide and inquisitive, she was pert and tanned. Panky thinking: Whoa! Stunning. And Panky *was* stunned, he felt like he'd been tasered again. He stood with his mouth slightly open trying hard not to pant and give himself away. Mai-Ling smiled at him, grabbed her towel and ran off towards the changing room at the back of the pool. As she ran she looked back and smiled some more. Wow what a picture! Panky was spellbound. He ran to catch up with Chris, hoping with every step that the girl was real.

Neither of the guys saw Clara looking down at them from the balcony upstairs. She was lurking in the shadows, watching their every move, and catching pieces of their conversation. She really didn't like seeing her husband looking *so* happy, *so* overjoyed to be with his 'partner in grime' after *so* long and drinking *so* much again already. Humph! She wasn't at all impressed with the way Panky looked either; the guy was practically naked. Clara hiding in the shadows thinking: Just look at the state of him! OK, he looks a bit like Colin Farrell but so what? And so obviously lusting after Mai-Ling just minutes after his arrival, Clara was not impressed! Despite what Chris had said she couldn't see a good side to Panky, she doubted there even was one.

The guys swayed drunkenly arm in arm towards the house, Chris looking elegant in his white cotton trousers, the matching shirt with the Chinese collar—casual hippy chic, designer expensive and Panky still naked apart from his jeans. Chris led the way holding his breath slightly. He hoped that in the morning he'd remember to explain to Panky the need for deodorants and after shaves in tropical climates, but he guessed that he'd probably forget. As they plodded along Chris was thinking how weird it was that Panky smelled of vinegar and damp dog, he even caught a whiff of smoldering plastic. He was curious, but didn't like to ask.

As they ambled along some more, Panky saw the interior of the house through a large sweeping archway. An impressive mixture of ethnic artifacts and Victorian antiques filled the room; the lights were soft, the walls the color of warm butter; half a dozen tall green potted palms sat in Chinese vases, the furnishings and fabrics too were warm with natural, earth colors: cinnamon, orange and purple, gold and russets and reds; bamboo, mahogany and rattan, polished and shining. The art nouveau and the native blended well; elegant porcelain stood delicate against intricate Chinese screens; Rossetti's pale, ghostly wife staring blankly at fat smiling Buddha's; the antique overhead fans turned quietly, whispered a quiet breeze through long gossamer curtains. The room felt cool and comfortable, it was subtle, stylish and welcoming. Nice.

As they entered the house Panky felt the soft Persian rug beneath his dirty feet. This isn't bad, he thought, this isn't bad at all.

Chris looked drunk, flushed with excitement as they clambered through the room dodging chairs and dainty plant stands. Chris came to a sudden halt, beckoned Panky to fill his glass. "Here's to us!" said Chris with drunken enthusiasm, "Partners in grime!" "The boys from the brown stuff!"

"Partners in grime!" said Panky with a chuckle.

They clinked and drank some more.

"God we had some fun didn't we?"

Panky gulped his drink and said, "We sure did..."

Chris grabbed his arm, dragged him across the polished wooden floor to a large wall decorated with photographs. A photographic testament to Chris' life, past and present. Chris was swaying to and fro; his crooked smile was drunk and wet. He pointed to a picture of a young Filipina: smiling on graduation day, dressed proudly in her gowns, yellow and black. She had beautiful eyes; she looked sweet and naïve but dark and sultry, an exciting combination. "That's my wife Clara," Chris slurred proudly, "It is... really..." and then he added, "*And* she loves me!" Or at least she used to thought Chris as he laid his outstretched hand against the wall and propped himself up. Standing was getting difficult.

"She looks so young... and beautiful," said Panky swaying slightly, amused at Chris so drunk already.

"Only way to go Panky… really… Asian women have got the right attitude mate, they have really… they actually like looking after their men! They do! They actually *like* it!"

Panky nodded his head gently to show he understood and looked at the girl. She was one of the ones praying at the grotto; the one leading the prayers, or at least that's how it seemed to Panky.

"Yeah ok…" continued Chris, wiping dribble off his chin, "You might think she's a bit young, but what's 20 years nowadays? Hey? It's nothing, right?"

Panky grinned, it was ok by him. He took the Champagne bottle from Chris and gulped at the bottle.

They stumbled along a little more, and their eyes focused on a very different picture. It was a newspaper clipping dated 1979; the front of some dirty little tabloid with a half page photograph of three punk rockers, three wild, crazy looking kids: an 'all action' photograph yellowed and torn.

"Fuck me!" said Panky.

"Ha!" said Chris, "Bet you didn't expect to see that bad boy?"

Chris was right. The photograph was something Panky had long forgotten; something he never expected to see again.

"How'd you manage to keep a copy? Must be thirty years old, more than!" Panky thinking: *Bad boy*? That's a bit American.

Chris just grinned. They swigged the Champagne from the bottle and stared at the front page: the title read, POLICE RAID ILLEGAL PUNK ROCK PARTY!

"That…" said Chris, "*if* you remember, was our misspent youth—it sounded like yoof—course I kept a copy…" Chris hiccupped and belched and continued, "All pimples and political angst weren't we?"

Panky was surprised but he actually remembered it well, an important night in the history of punk rock. It was a great, great night. 'The Cure' playing back up for 'Siouxsie and the Banshees' in an old warehouse in South London, but the Banshees guitarist sprained his wrist somehow, couldn't play, so Robert Smith from the Cure took his place. He played brilliantly, knew every song. Robert Smith was a genius, a fucking hero; he saved the whole event. Panky stared at the photo and remembered back: Chris, Panky and a girl called Lola, totally wasted, standing crushed in the crowd and loving every minute of it. He remembered too, the seething youthful mass, the pogo-ing up and down among the strobe lights, remembered the three of them jumping around like their lives depended on it, gob and camaraderie in the air. The music was loud and anarchic: mad jangling guitars, passionate nihilistic vocals, pounding drums, all screeching and blasting from the stacks of giant speakers. Panky remembered the three of them, just kids, inseparable and wild: Lola only sixteen but looking so much older, manic black make up, smeared red lipstick. She wore a black leather jacket, heavy with a thousand silver studs, the shortest tartan mini skirt, eighteen holed Dr Marten boots and ripped black fishnet stockings—she was styling. Her raven spiky hair was almost blue, her ripped black T-shirt tried in vain to hide her breasts. At sixteen Lola was quite some punk.

Panky remembered it all so clearly: Chris with amphetamine eyes, cropped peroxide hair and black strapped bondage trousers, his chest naked beneath his jacket; laughing and drinking and jumping around, so excited. He saw Lola making a toast, holding up her warm can of beer and shouting: "Here's to Sex, Drugs and Rock and Roll... and dying before we're middle aged!"—She never actually said as much, but Chris and Panky knew she was terrified of ending up like her mother: a single alcoholic with four kids, aged thirty-two. He saw Chris holding up a can and shouting: "Yeah and here's to... continued unemployment... and to the curse of poverty!" Chris staring at Lola as she crushed a beer can beneath her Dr Marten boot. He remembered it all so clearly. Panky saw himself too: standing in the thick of it, grinning, yelling: "And here's to the fucking Cold War, the bomb and the Russians!"

It was then that a fat middle-aged photographer ran up to them and with a flash, snapped their picture and ran away, headed for the door. Seconds later the police arrived in force, crashed the place and pulled the plugs. Silence and darkness, then chaos and screams, walkie-talkie voices crackled and dogs barked and bit. The police swarmed the building, kicked the fuck out of anyone in their path. Panky remembered that they weren't too big on human rights back then, not with punks or miners anyway. It was quite a night. Hard to forget.

Chris swigged Champagne, slid slowly down the wall saying: "Remember how paranoid you were about the Russians?"

Panky looked away from the picture thinking: Yeah, funny that.

"Times have certainly changed haven't they?" slurred Chris.

Panky grinned, thinking: Not for me they haven't mate, and purleeeeze don't go on about the Russians.

Chris sighed audibly. "We've come a long way haven't we Panky?"

Panky smirked, "Yeah, about 10,000 miles."

Chris was slowly sliding down the wall still, but he hadn't seemed to notice, he said, "No… I'm not talking about miles Panky, I mean as people… as men."

"Not me," said Panky with a throaty chuckle, "I'm in limbo, my life's the same as it's *always* been… the only difference… I take more drugs… that I get for free… and I always, always, wear a condom with strangers!"

"With strange women, I hope," said Chris almost on the floor now—seemingly unaware or beyond caring.

"Well yeah, of course, strange women," said Panky with a grin, "And talking of strange women, I wonder what the lovely Lola's doing now?"

Chris's eyelids dropped a little and his face saddened. "Not a lot Panky I'm afraid… she died Christmas '92."

"Oh fuck,"

Chris stared into the bottle searching for words.

Panky looked up and said, "Drugs was it?"

"Well yeah… kind of…" Chris looked emotional, "She fell off a chemist's shop roof Christmas night, breaking in… you know, looking to steal a fix, landed among a group of festive carol singers."

Panky wasn't sure if he should laugh or cry.

Chris continued, "Interrupted 'Good tidings we bring,' from three stories up... slipped on the icy slates, landed in the snow, smashed her skull to pieces. The carol singers couldn't fucking believe it!"

Panky didn't know what to say, he felt for the words but couldn't find them; had that strange reality check when you hear about a friend who's dead, sad for them of course, but scared just as much for yourself, reminded that no one lives for ever, reminded it could happen today or maybe tomorrow. "Tragic or what?" he said, it was the best he could do.

Chris was on the floor now, feet propped up against a chair so he couldn't slide away on the polished floor, feet scrunched up in a nice Persian carpet, still hanging on to the Champagne bottle, "Tragic for sure," he said and grabbed the chair and pulled himself up, grabbed Panky's arm and lead him toward the stairs. They dragged themselves upstairs, plodded breathless towards the top, "She had the best tits didn't she? What a waste," said Chris.

"Fantastic tits!" said Panky with a huge smile, "Fantastic... both of 'em! Nipples like chapel hat pegs!" and they laughed together sharing their grief the only way they knew.

Once at the top of the landing Chris put his finger to his mouth like drunks often do and went, "*Sssshhh!*"

Panky got the idea immediately. He was real quick sometimes

Chris stumbled over to Panky, put his hands on his shoulders and felt the grime of the last twenty four hours on his palms, pulled his friend towards a bedroom door and said, "Oi, come here, look at this."

The door was wedged open with a giant Winnie the Pooh. Inside the room, bathed in the softest of night lights, slept two young children: faces cherubic and innocent, snoring quiet and melodic.

Panky felt a sudden rush of emotion, smiled at the scene as he gazed around aimlessly, grinning, feeling happy for Chris. His eyes drifted slowly to the floor, dismembered Barbie Doll's lay naked, scattered on the carpet, arms and legs akimbo, skinny plastic chicks lying among the Lego with thin smiles and piercing blue eyes; over in the corner Batman and Robin stood ready for action, muscles pumped but their mouths firmly sealed: they saw nothing—or at least that's what they're saying. Panky looked away thinking: Ah, the innocence of youth.

He looked back at Chris, grinned some more. The guys stood either side of the bedroom door, Chris grasping the frame to keep his balance. 'London Bridge is falling down' played quietly, a tinkling tune in the background. Chris said, "Who'd believe a nutter like me'd end up with beautiful, healthy kids like these, hey? Who'd fuckin' believe it?"

Panky smiled, happy for Chris and his obvious joy.

"I count my blessings every day Panky, every fuckin' day!" said Chris getting louder, swearing more as he slid slowly down the wall. "It's all part of God's plan Panky. All part of the Big Geezer's plan."

Panky stood and watched Chris slide towards the floor again, thinking: Oh Oh! Here we go! I thought this was too good to be true.

Chris stared drunkenly at his kids and tried to wipe the dribble off his chin.

Panky thinking: What's with all the 'blessings' and the 'God's plan' stuff? The Big Geezer?

Wiping the dribble on his designer shirt, Chris said, "These kids are nothin' short of miracles Panky!"

Clara was just along the corridor, quiet in the shadows in the doorway of her bedroom—listening to the conversation. She stepped back into the room, wiped her puffy eyes with a damp handkerchief, smiled and sighed heavily: she was pleased with Chris the proud father, but hated to see him so drunk. She was far from impressed with Panky's conversation; talking about that dead girl's nipples! Dreadful!

Chris pushed himself back up the wall, looked Panky in the eyes, held his hands out like a mad Baptist preacher, glanced up to the heavens and continued, "Believe me Panky, really, these kids are nothin' short of miracles!" Sliding down the wall again he added, "But they're noisy little fuckers in the morning!"

The following morning by the pool, in the harsh early morning sunlight, the guys sat at the same table as the night before, surrounded by exotic plants, colourful flowers and hungry insects.

It was as though they'd never moved, but the Champagne and the previous night's ambience was long gone. The morning brought breakfast and fragile constitutions.

Panky sat slumped in a cushioned chair smoking a cigarette, the sun in his pink, puffy eyes; his throat like sandpaper and peanut shells again. He was clearly hung over, but he still looked better than when he'd first arrived. Much better.

Before they finally went to sleep, Chris let Panky choose some clothes, some bathroom stuff, and toiletries. He explained the need for deodorant, told Panky it was essential, daily. He explained about the tropical climate, the humidity, said you sweat like a pig on a stick if you're not careful. He knew it was late, but he also knew he'd remember nothing in the morning. Panky said, "Sure… no problema, I'll try anything once." So the following morning, once Panky was fully awake and he'd got his bearings, remembered where he was, he sampled them all and put on the clothes. He looked good. He looked younger and smelled better too. He was wearing an old black t-shirt, it was loose and limp, the red logo faded beyond recognition; the shorts he wore were army green, old and comfortable; they looked good with the battered Converse pumps. The shave had taken at least fifteen years off him, no more thick stubble with all those flecks of gray; his hair was combed and shiny. He smelled sweet and expensive. Like Jekyll and Hyde, it was quite a change.

Chris sat with shaking hands and heavy eyelids, looking confused, sounding almost breathless; he was panting. He told Panky he remembered pouring the Champagne, remembered talking a lot, but that was about it. He didn't remember much else, said it was all a bit of a blur. They'd talked a lot the night before, or at least Chris had, Panky listened mostly. He was dying to ask Chris how he'd made so much money; he was *dying* to find out, but he never really got the chance. He could wait. There was no rush. He was going nowhere, he had nowhere to go.

Despite his drunken state, Chris'd explained about the Philippines, how things were here. Told Panky how friendly and carefree the people were, said they were always happy and laughing, rarely serious about anything, even important things like which side of the road to drive on. Chris told him that the Spanish had run the country for hundreds of years, then the Americans colonized it, the Japanese took over for a while during the Second World War and then the Americans took it back again. A very colourful history: the Chinese always the ones with the money regardless of politics. Chris explained too, that most Filipinos worshipped America, believed in the American dream, considered the States a country of wealth and opportunity, a place where someone could get ahead. Anyone. But Chris didn't stop there, he went on and said that life in the Province was simple, easy too and cheap, nothing much to do really—nothing much to spend your money on either.

"So what do you then? Where do you go?" asked Panky, thinking he'd die of boredom in about a week, staring at coconuts not much of a challenge.

"What do we do?"

"Yeah... what do you do? You know... on a social level, what do you do for fun?"

"We don't do anything," said Chris with a smile, "Not now, not any more Panky... we're parents now." Chris explained in detail about his orchids, his bonsai, all the different fruit they grew in the garden: pineapples, calamanci, mangoes, grapefruit... more than 12 different types of banana here in the Philippines, he said; they grew black pepper, coffee, even chocolate.

Fascinating stuff, thought Panky, *if* you're a gardener, a vegetarian or a weirdo. What he really wanted to know about was the dosh, the money. How the hell Chris had managed to make so much? What had he been up to?

A pert young girl brought two huge English breakfasts on a tray; put them carefully on the table. She smiled and sashayed quietly away.

Chris and Panky sat staring at the food. They looked at each other and tried their best to smile. They turned a pale green at roughly the same time.

But Panky felt brave, felt he had to show a little appreciation and after much thought he lifted a fork full of crispy, greasy bacon up toward his open mouth. His hand was shaking but somehow the bacon made it inside. He chewed slowly, forcing a smile.

Chris sat up slightly and made the sign of the holy trinity with his trembling hand, said:

"Bless us oh Lord for these thy gifts that we receive from thy bounty…"

Panky couldn't believe it! He nearly choked on his bacon. He wasn't too sure what to do, eat the bacon, get on his knees and put his hands together or run and fetch a bible. This was all very new to him. Very new. He hadn't prayed since he was seven, well, not out loud or in front of people.

"Through Christ our Lord, the Son, the Father and the Holy spirit… Amen." Chris looked up towards the heavens.

Panky chewed his bacon slowly, wondering what to expect next, watched Chris stare at the food and gently shake his head, heard him exhale deeply and empty his pious lungs.

The plates were massive and full: eggs, bacon, sausages, fried tomatoes, mushrooms, fried bread, fried onions; Heinz baked beans, bubble and squeak, buttered toast and half a pint of hot, sweet tea. Phew!

With trembling fingers Chris picked up his knife and fork; he peered across the table through the steam of his sweet tea and said, "Us Westerners… take too much for granted Panky."

Panky looked up and grinned finding it difficult to swallow the bacon, imagined broken light bulbs scratching and slicing at the sandpaper and peanut shells in his throat.

"A lot of people here," said Chris, deadpan and still panting slightly, sweating profusely, "Wouldn't eat this much in a week… really… we should thank God for our good fortune Panky… we should praise the Lord."

Panky grinned again, felt his face blushing; the shards of bacon were half way swallowed, but he wasn't too sure if he could actually speak. He looked at Chris thinking: Yeah, ok, why not? Thanks God. He nodded as he tried to swallow. Despite the religious stuff, Panky thought things were looking up: good company, clean clothes, hot water, all sorts of bathroom stuff—some things he'd never seen before—a great location, top food and plenty of alcohol. Not a bad start. The young girls splashing around the pool in their bikinis didn't look too horrible either. He finally swallowed his bacon and smiled. He'd pretty much forgotten his problems—the most recent ones anyhow—he'd put them behind him, he was good at that, but he *was* a bit concerned about Chris, a bit concerned about his religious fervour. What was *that* all about? Was he serious or putting him on, having a laugh? Panky wasn't sure. A lot can happen in ten years. The only thing he was really sure about was he wanted to make a good impression with Chris' wife, the wise and beautiful Clara; the one with the passionate eyes. He hadn't seen much of her so far and he hoped that she was ok, hoped she didn't mind having a stranger in the house; hoped she liked him. It was important that she did. He wasn't here to rock the boat; he didn't want to spoil things for Chris and his family. No way.

TWENTY EIGHT

Vlad and Boris sat in the Shangri-La hotel eating breakfast. The restaurant was full of morning sunlight and hungry guests. It was five star quiet—the tiny sound of silverware on porcelain, the rustle of financial papers, cool conditioned air. The décor was subtle, a perfect example of native chic, very up market: tall glass walls filled with sunlight and reflections, natural stone and exotic greenery, clear water running over clean pebbles, and wind chimes. Soothing sights and sounds. The Russians hadn't really noticed, weren't the kind of guys that got excited about interior decorating, as far as they were concerned the service and the food were excellent and that was good enough.

They'd decided to wear their Hawaiian suits again, had them washed and pressed over night and wore their Ray Bans again during breakfast. Keeping up the image, trying hard to blend in again.

"I'm going to the C.R.," said Boris getting up from the table, glancing at the mess he was leaving behind, "The toilet," he said, "that's what they call it here."

Vladimir grinned and watched Boris stroll heavily across the restaurant, saw his Hawaiian suit still tight across the shoulders, around the biceps, saw a few people notice his enormous size and stare at his long black socks with the brown leather sandals.

People who didn't know better grinning at Boris' socks over breakfast.

Vlad's phone rang. He answered it.

"Yes… hello?"

Zoltan: "Vlad, it's me, where's Boris?"

Vlad: "Err… he's in the C.R., the toilet… he just left."

Zoltan: "Ok listen; I know you're new… new to the business… a rookie…"

Vlad: "Sure…"

Zoltan: "And I know you've had a few problems settling in, made a few fuck ups… I know that and maybe one day I can forgive you? …maybe…but first I need you to do something for me…"

Vlad: "Hey, Zoltan, no problem… whatever you need, you got it!"

Zoltan: "Ok, ok, relax… I want you to keep a very close eye on Boris for me… I want…"

Vlad: "You want no more '*moments of weakness*'?"

Zoltan: "Exactly!"

Vlad: "Don't worry… this job will be quick and easy, then we're straight home… no problem, I promise you."

Zoltan: "Ok, just don't let me down Vladimir…"

Vlad was going to say goodbye, thanks for the vote of confidence, I won't let you down, stuff like that, but Zoltan hung up.

Vlad smiled anyway. He was doing ok now for a rookie, helping *the* boss, watching the boss's brother for Christ's sake! This was his chance to prove himself. Things were going to get better for him he could feel it.

Vlad put his phone away, sat quietly at the table looking at the mess Boris had left behind: egg yolk splashed across the table, a scattered mountain of bread crumbs, ketchup all around, half a cup of coffee still steaming in the saucer, nibbled sugar cubes. Boris wasn't big on etiquette.

Vlad sat back and smiled at passing girls like some toothpaste commercial on TV, a smile so big his gums were on display. A fixed smile like major-league superstars, phony like Hollywood. But it seemed to work, girls were smiling back. No one was more surprised than Vlad.

Boris plodded back from the C.R., padded slowly towards the table, eyeing Vlad with his super grin. He sat down with a grunt, straightened his Ray Bans.

Vlad was beaming, clearly excited, "While you were in the toilet… some girl… and she was cute I promise you… she asked me where I was from, came over to the table and just asked me."

Boris slouched in the chair looking across the glass-topped table, through the yellow flowers, passed the menu, above the breakfast remnants into Vlad's eyes. "And so what did you say?"

Vlad said, "From Canada of course."

"Good!" said Boris. He was pleased his rookie partner was picking things up, not before time.

Vlad started to giggle. He tried hard but he couldn't control it, his face turned red, flushed with effort.

Boris looked at him, raised an eyebrow.

"Sorry Boris, but I have to laugh," said Vlad, "This girl… you have to see the humour…"

Boris smiled slightly, adjusted his Ray Bans and waited for the punch line.

"The girl, she said that I sounded Canadian… she used to live there she said… really… told me as soon as I spoke she knew where I was from…" Vlad wiped his face with a serviette and continued to speak through his laughter, "She asked me was I from New Brunswick?"

Boris and Vlad laughed together quietly and then eye-to-eye they chuckled and snorted across the table. The laughter grew as they watched each other's faces, watched each others rising, falling shoulders. It was a deep contagious laughter, the type that grows and grows, comes from nowhere and takes control. Tears were falling from behind their Ray Bans; they slapped their huge thighs trying hard to contain themselves, laughing so much now that it hurt. People were looking over.

"We need some guns Boris," said Vlad trying hard to stop, trying hard to catch his breath, looking his partner in the eyes again, wondering if he should mention that Zoltan had called, the humour tainted now with just a little fear as he chuckled helplessly.

"Yes… yes we do," said Boris, wiping his tears away, but still laughing, "We do need some guns!"

TWENTY NINE

Panky and Chris sat by the pool at their table. They'd both made a hopeless effort at eating breakfast, so much food wasted despite Chris' prayer. Chris was scanning the table now thinking: What a sin. Which of course it was.

The pool glimmered in the heat, a soft warm breeze rustled the palm fronds gently and the early morning roosters cock-a-doodle-doo-ed as though their lives depended on it.

Panky smiled slightly, pretended the roosters weren't doing his head in. He found it hard to believe they made that noise all the time. Dawn chorus... forget it! This went on 24/7; they even did it at midnight! Relentless cock-a-doodle-doos, it was mind numbing.

Chris grinned at Panky. Panky smiled, thinking: If noisy roosters are my biggest problem, I'm not doing so bad, right?

Chris stood up slowly, his eyes still tired, his face pale green still, fragile looking. He said, "I've got to take some flowers to the chapel, I promised Father Paul... I'll see you in a couple of hours, ok?" He pulled a roll of money out of his pocket, put it on the table in front of Panky and said, "A bit of pocket money..." He winked at Panky, grinned through his pallor.

Panky shaded his eyes from the sun, smiled gratefully and watched Chris turn and walk away. He wondered if Chris was taking the piss again, Father Paul, the flowers and all that.

Over his shoulder, walking away slowly, Chris said, "And don't forget, you are *not* in Amsterdam, ok? You're a foreigner and it's obvious... got that?"

Panky grinned at the lecture and the lecturer.

"If you meet anyone," Chris continued, "just treat 'em with respect, they're big on that here..."

"Of course," said Panky. Why wouldn't he?

Chris continued to walk away slowly, then turned again as though he'd forgotten to say something, "And don't be surprised if they ask you lots of questions, don't be shocked if they think you're rich... it's just like that here, Ok?"

Panky smiled, looked over at the pool, at the sun on it.

"And everyone will think you're American," he said, "But don't worry about it! ... Just make yourself at home!"

Panky looked up and over to Chris, but he'd gone. He sat by the pool and looked around: no gardeners, maids, houseboys or ya-ya's, no screaming kids either; the place so quiet now, even the demented roosters were taking a break. He smoked a cigarette and watched the pool. He looked around the empty garden and wondered why David Hockney spent half his life painting empty swimming pools. How weird was that? Why bother?

He stared at the sky. It was blue and cloudless, the same as before.

The warm breeze caressed him gently and he sighed at its touch. Warm air sweet and thick with coffee blossom, jungle birds chattered in the distance;

everything seemed so easy, so laid back. The place seemed so peaceful, the warm air so soothing. Panky was bored.

Suddenly Mai-Ling appeared: there she was strolling alongside the pool in her micro bikini. Looking good! Looking real good! Panky sat up, watched her walk, watched her taut brown body get closer and then closer still. She was definitely the girl from the night before, Panky was sure of it; the subterranean Goddess, the one that smiled at him. She was real! Panky smiled, his heart missed a beat.

Mai-Ling smiled back and blushed, but just slightly. As she walked past her eyelids almost fluttered.

Panky was sure he could hear her breathing. She looked amazing as she sashayed across the patio; casually glancing back at Panky she smiled again and then finally disappeared from view. Panky was utterly and totally smitten. Smitten: it was that simple. Smitten and desperately in need of a cold beer.

After a few more minutes' tranquility and basking in the morning sun again, he was bored again. The girl had gone and he needed a beer, a cold one, maybe two, possibly more. Panky thinking: It's been quite a morning *and* the girl is actually real. Good reason to celebrate. He stood up and wandered towards the garage, saw a Honda SUV parked there. As he got closer he felt sure the keys were inside. Chris had said 'Make yourself at home,' he remembered that clearly. If he was at home right now, he'd been going out for a beer for sure, not only was breakfast over ages ago, but the girl was real *and* she'd looked back and smiled at him again. That had to mean *something*. Right?

He opened the driver's door of the Honda, the keys swayed and rattled slightly for him. Good stuff.

The car smelled good, smelled feminine and cared for, it was probably Clara's. Panky hadn't forgotten he wanted to get on with Clara, hadn't forgotten he wanted to create a good impression; he'd take it easy for sure. He could be a very careful driver when he needed to be. He slid into the driver's seat, adjusted it to fit his hairy white legs. He smiled into the rear view and started the engine, borrowed Converse pumps eager on the pedals. The engine roared, the wheels spun, stones from the driveway flew through the air and bounced off the metal garage doors—the noise sounded like some desperate getaway. Panky knew it wasn't a good start. But it reminded him that he was probably in Clara's car, a new one at that; whatever he did, whatever happened, he had to take it easy. He didn't want to upset *the wife*.

The Honda screeched and hammered towards the guardhouse, Panky saluted the guards as they quickly opened the gates and stood to attention. They were obviously surprised to see the Honda being driven so recklessly; they saluted back with confused grins and wide eyes. Panky laughed out loud as he headed towards the nearest bar, a cloud of dust swirling in his wake. Despite Chris' weirdness and the prayers and everything, he was having a great time, and now that breakfast was over he was dying for a beer or two.

He drove slowly through the jungle, through the quiet village streets. He looked around, felt himself pushed into the past, pushed into a simpler place and a simpler life. It felt different and it felt good. He wasn't sure why.

The trees were a hundred shades of green, thick along the roadside, coconut, banana and mango. He saw a fire tree too, flickering bright clusters of red and orange, glowing there in the sunlight; the air was still sweet with the scent of morning blossom. The journey continued, he saw small gray, block built bungalows with bright painted roofs stood back off the road, bamboo huts too, thatched and rickety and rustic. He saw gardens bright with exotic flowers, orchids hanging from trees, their texture delicate, fragile like fine silk, a smell like patchouli and Chinese pears breezing in through the window. Nice.

As he drove along slowly he peered down a small ravine, saw a mother walking alongside the white rushing river, clear bright water cascading over rocks and boulders. Half a dozen children followed the woman, small kids hopping from rock to rock, boulder to boulder with childish practiced nonchalance; the mother looking behind from time to time, keeping them in line as she balanced a large plastic bowl on her head and carried a bag of clothes in her hand. They were off to do the washing. The children skipped and laughed and jumped and they sang as they moved along, clear waters gushed and foamed beside them. The kids and the river suddenly vanished from view replaced by heads of yellow corn bending in the breeze, tall and ripe and ready. The Honda then slowed at a rickety wooden bridge, seemed to crawl across nervously. Panky hanging out the open window and suddenly looking down a much bigger ravine. An anxious look grew slowly on his face; tired old timbers creaked as the Honda edged its way along. Then the road again: trees and fields of coffee, endless rows of pineapples, gawky tall coconut trees swaying in the sky. Panky trying to enjoy the view, take it all in before it got boring.

He continued to drive carefully through the quiet streets until he saw a sign that said, 'Cold Beer'. The place was a ramshackle hut, the weathered sign above the door said 'Bongs Bar'. Panky smiled. Perfect. He laughed out loud again, swerved the Honda across the road and pulled into the makeshift car park in a twisting blanket of dust. Bongs! Thought Panky, Ha! It had to be an omen.

He turned off the engine, pulled up the handbrake and slid out of the car, his shirt stuck to his back despite the aircon. He lit a cigarette and looked around, verdant jungle in the background, as always, the blue sky and intense heat still the same. Perfect time for a cold beer. Before he entered the bar he pointed the car key toward the car and pressed the little button. There was a high tech bleep and a click as the doors locked in unison. Panky stood staring at the Honda, felt a weird sensation; the high tech car locking experience seemed so incongruous, he wasn't sure why. He buried the keys in his pocket and headed towards the door of the bar, he looked through the unglazed open window into cool darkness, heard the blades of an old ceiling fan turning, calling out for lubrication.

He walked up the timber steps, pushed open the squeaky bamboo door. Inside—except for around the bar—the place was just a few candles away from dark, it was a hundred percent bamboo through and through; the floor was red clay smooth as a cue ball, flattened by decades of drunken feet. At first the only sound was the old, old ceiling fan squeaking away, trying it's hardest to keep working.

Panky entered, saw Bong the proprietor slumped across the bar, heard his snoring, heard the flies buzzing around his head among his nasal exclamations, saw the dazzle of fluorescent light reflected off a big old refrigerator back there behind the bar. He saw a long line of empty whiskey and brandy bottles up high on a shelf, testament no doubt to a hundred drunken nights and a few dusty souvenirs on top of the refrigerator: a small green plastic statue of Liberty, a chubby smiling Buddha, J.C. high on the cross in his usual pose, a faded picture of the Beatles cut from some old magazine, proudly framed forty or more years before, and finally he noticed the 'I heart Reagan' sticker on the door of the fridge, a political blast from the past.

A small pink skinned scabby dog lay curled up on the floor in the corner by the bar, it opened one eye and growled showing pointed yellow teeth; the small but vicious growl the only sound apart from the snoring, the flies and the fan. Panky shuffled forward slightly, feeling decidedly thirsty, more determined than ever to have a beer, but the scabby dog growled and stopped him in his tracks. With his eyes fixed firmly on the mangy beast he coughed theatrically and said, "Any chance of a cold beer?"

Bong opened one rheumy eye, sat up slowly and smiled showing Panky his gums, his lack of teeth. "Hey Americano," he said, "Welcome… welcome, cold beer no problema, take a seat my fren." The old guy gestured towards the table; seemed genuinely pleased to have a customer, happy to have some company apart from the little dog with the pointy teeth.

Panky pulled up a rickety bamboo chair, sat down at a well-used bamboo table and finished his cigarette.

Bong got up slowly, yawned and wiped the sleepiness from his face. He turned and shuffled toward a shelf, reached up for a dusty bottle of beer, wiped it casually on his moth eaten vest and gave Panky his best smile. Panky smiled back.

Bong opened the bottle with his plastic lighter. *Pop*! He returned to Panky's table, stood the bottle and a sad plastic beaker in front of him next to two huge watermelons.

"Nice melons, madam," said Panky, with a Vaudeville smirk, rubbing them with his sweaty hands and lusty enthusiasm.

Bong kind of gazed at him, not certain what to say, no wanting to lose his only customer.

Panky grinned at the lost humour and picked up the bottle anxious to pour, immediately felt the temperature of the bottle. He smiled and said, "Err... sorry... a cold beer?"

"A cold beer!" said Bong, "Ha! I'm sorry my fren... you want cold beer, no problema... I unnerstan, for a while huh?" As Bong turned away Panky looked around the bar, he saw old faded bunting, red, white and blue, hanging limp from the ceiling laced with cobwebs, remnants no doubt of a long forgotten celebration, the ghost of good times gone hiding among the gloom. Again he saw the souvenirs on top of the ref, shining almost in the bright fluorescent light, an incongruous mixture of imported kitsch, finally his eyes rested back on the two huge watermelons sitting there on the table.

Bong was stooping low beside the scabby dog, one hand held open the lid of an old plastic icebox; the other removed a large lump of ice from inside. Bong looked up and smiled.

Panky watched him shuffle over to the high shelf and remove a large plastic jug, the ice gripped hard and dripping now in his other hand. He coughed and blew the dust from the plastic jug, moved back to Panky's table still smiling, showing his gums again. Eager to please, he removed a sharp shining machete from the sheath at his waist, preceded to chop the ice into slithers; most of it fell into the jug. The small tinkling sound of ice-cold gems seemed to fill the bar. Bong lifted the bottle, recklessly poured the beer over the icy slithers, smiled at his only customer. "Cold beer na!" he said proudly.

Panky stared at the old plastic jug and looked up at Bong trying hard not to look shocked or surprised.

"How's dat my fren?" asked Bong.

Panky looked again at the jug, watched the one hundred percent foam swirling around madly. He smiled at Bong; there was nothing else he could do. "Perfect!" he said, remembering Chris' words, trying to show the old guy some respect, trying to look grateful as he poured warmish foam into the chipped plastic beaker.

"You have vacation here my fren?"

"Yep, that's right," said Panky taking a sip, wiping the warm white foam from his lips. "Americano, coreck?"

"No, no," said Panky trying the foam again, "British!"

"Oh British, I like British," said Bong—it sounded like Breeteesh, like Ding-Dong and for a split second Panky wondered about his old mate, wondered what he was up to. "British poun' bery strong huh?" said Bong, as he walked back behind the bar. His eyes were suddenly wide and bright, the topic of money obviously of some interest to him.

"Apparently," said Panky sipping again at his warm foam. He still had no idea about the Breeteesh poun', hadn't even seen one in over a decade.

"You mus' be very reech come all this way for vacation, huh?" said Bong, leaning on the bar, lighting a Marlboro red, coughing like a cancerous old cowboy in the glow and the smoke of the match.

"You know Sir Chris...?" asked Panky pointing up the street toward the route he'd taken.

Bong's face filled with pride and he stood straight, "Sir Chris... of course," he threw out his arms dramatically, "He my good fren'... he come here after church drink many melon juss with me... my good fren' Sir Chris, good, good fren."

Panky sipped foam, thinking: After church? Melon juss? What the hell? Maybe Chris wasn't taking the piss after all? Maybe he wasn't just having a laugh? Maybe he had joined the God squad? No... thought Panky, no... not possible.

"He have Filipina wife Sir Chris, no? Berrry beautiful girl, an' berrry beautiful children too huh?"

Panky nodded as he lit a cigarette, giving the foam a chance to settle down a bit.

"You look for nice girl here in Philippines?"

Panky watched Bong coughing into his cloud of smoke and said, "Maybe."

Bong winked and grinned like he had a secret; he turned and banged on the door of the bamboo-serving hatch on the wall at the rear of the bar. "Maybe you like my cuzin... Honey Girl? Huh? Maybe you like her?"

Panky grinned, checked out the foam as Bong slapped his hand on the wall, small tapping sounds sending a secret signal.

"She like foreigner... berrry much," he said, "She good girl... birgin too!" Bong was clearly proud of his cuzin and her birginity.

Panky was intrigued, wondered how she'd compare to Mai-Ling.

The serving hatch opened, Honey Girl stood there, smiling.

Panky was amazed, lost for words; he reached for the foam and poured, his eyes fixed on Honey Girl's somewhat enigmatic smile.

Bong grinned and nodded, keen to see Honey Girl fixed up with a wealthy foreigner.

Panky gulped foam and stared into her eyes.

She giggled coyly, snorted a little air, her face neatly framed by the bamboo-serving hatch. Honey Girl easily weighed 200 pound, *easily* and that was a kind, wild guess. It was hard to tell as only her head and chins could be seen. Her acne was not excessive, but it was clearly apparent, fortunately for Honey Girl it didn't stand out any more than her thin black wispy moustache. She seemed a cheerful, happy girl though, standing there posing, showing off her thick nasal hairs, her crooked teeth.

Panky thinking: God, no wonder she's a birgin, but saying nothing, just smiling, wiping the foam from his lips again. Bong smiled proud, the hatch slammed shut and Honey Girl plodded back to the kitchen to her greasy pots and pans. Panky smiled at Bong, words failed him. The bar was quiet now. "Not so busy today?" said Panky.

"Is ok my fren," said Bong.

Then the convivial atmosphere changed completely, went from day into night like the click of a switch. Candles flickered and shadows danced as two swarthy macho guys stepped through the squeaking entrance door. The guys looked serious and said nothing; they just walked in and sat at a table away from Panky, waited in the settling candlelight.

Bong reached up and took two bottles of beer from the shelf, opened them with his plastic lighter, *Pop!* *Pop!*, and then sauntered over to their table.

Panky looked over at the machos, saw their muscles and machetes; a lifetime of scaling gawky trees and lowering heavy bundles of coconuts was obvious. The guys looked tough; their muscles were pumped and tight, biceps like baseballs, blue veins like baby snakes and taut leather skin. Their attitude seemed somber and for some reason slightly malevolent. The machos paid with a handful of coins and said nothing, just sipped at their warm dusty bottles.

Bong walked back behind the bar, settled back into his slouched position and lit another cigarette; his cough like syrup and glue.

Panky smiled again at Bong, he seemed a nice old guy. Panky was pleased business was picking up for him.

"This best bar for ten miles, it's true my fren… hey, you like Karaoke? You must like Beatles huh, you Breeteesh right?"

Panky grinned: he hated Karaoke. Hated it like no smoking long haul flights, like grafting Customs

154

officials, like karate experts, bullies and bar girls that rob your stuff. He said nothing.

"Maybe Tom Jones huh?" asked Bong, "Crispy Junior he come soon, he berrry good, berrry popular."

Panky sipped from his beaker, got a little beer this time and lit a cigarette to celebrate, thinking: Crispy Junior, now that's some name. He looked over at the machos saw them lighting their Marlboro's, filling the air with blue gray smoke.

Bong lifted his eyebrows, whispered confidentially, "Crispy Junior berrry entertaining..."

Panky wasn't sure what Bong was trying to imply.

Bong looked over at the machos, chuckled quietly and wandered off to the kitchen.

Panky and the machos were alone in the candle light, smoking and silent. Panky looked over at the guys and smiled, they ignored him.

The beer was a disaster: the foam was cold now, but tasted dusty and bitter, tasted of plastic. Panky stood up, wandered behind the bar, grabbed a bottle of Fundador brandy off the shelf and returned to his seat. He opened the bottle, sniffed the contents suspiciously and filled his beaker, thinking: Now that's more like it. He drained the beaker and filled it again.

The machos looked on without interest. If Panky wanted a drinking competition he was out of luck, tough as they appeared the machos could not hold their liquor, certainly not as much as Panky; even on a good night a couple of beers and they were done. It was a genetic thing.

The squeaky bamboo door opened slightly reminding the drinkers it was still daylight outside; Crispy Junior edged his way carefully into the bar.

He looked at least ninety-two years old, maybe older, his skin was dark and wrinkly like a nicotine tortoise; he was painfully skinny, had the eyes of a blind man and the big white smile of a born entertainer. He pulled at an old tarpaulin at the side of the bar, revealed a Karaoke machine. He grabbed the wire, plugged it in and smiled at his audience of three. He connected a microphone and switched it on. The room filled instantly with high-pitched feedback, harsh white noise and loud; sounds like electric seagulls, sounds like a car crash followed by silence. Crispy Junior took out his scratched aviator sunglasses, slid them on casually, held the mike in both hands and looked over at the TV screen. His mouth was moist and ready; his lips trembled with anticipation. He looked kind of odd in his skin tight t-shirt, his tight black nylon flares were swollen and worn at the knees, held up by a white patent belt. He cleared the phlegm from his throat and spat majestically over his shoulder as the song began. Familiar sounds filled the bar; they took Panky back to his childhood. Crispy's fans considered this song his anthem. It was an all time favourite. Crispy Junior sang his version of 'The Green green Grass of Home' by Tom Jones.

He sang it very, very badly—sometimes with feedback, sometimes without. He got a lot of the words wrong too, but it didn't seem to bother him. To Crispy Junior the words were not important; it was the feeling that mattered, the emotion; he was almost professional. His moves were extremely fluid; his skinny hips gyrating rhythmically, grinding to and fro, it was a remarkable achievement for someone so old.

Panky swallowed some brandy and poured another, he was getting into it, having fun, this was better than the X Factor rejects. Not only that but he had a nice little buzz going from the brandy and the foam. A nice little buzz. He looked over at the deadpan machos still smoking and silent, not even speaking together.

Crispy Junior warbled and strutted.

Panky grinned and lifted his glass, made a toast to the silent machos, a gesture of good will, showing the locals a bit of respect just like he'd promised Chris. They just stared at him.

As the ancient entertainer tried a couple of high notes, Panky winced and giggled, hammed it up a little for the machos but they still ignored him. Ok, the poor old guy was a tad sad but the situation was still funny, how could they not laugh? Their faces remained expressionless, for some reason they seemed to like Crispy Junior. Panky just had to laugh and why not? he wasn't being cruel, he was just having fun, right? The trembling gyrating hips of the singer alone were hilarious; forget the high notes and the wrong words. He drank another brandy and chuckled to himself as he glanced at the machos again. Their deadpan faces made Panky laugh even more; couldn't they see it was funny? Didn't they have a sense of humour? Too tough and rugged to let their hair down a little and have some fun? The place and the singer seemed weird, almost surreal. Panky wanted to share the humor, wanted to laugh with somebody; wanted to share this crazy moment.

Crispy Junior's faltering voice filled the room.

Panky's laughter continued to grow, but somehow he managed to hold it in, his shoulders moved up and down, he spilt a little brandy as he poured another, couldn't stop the laughter.

The machos suddenly turned their attention from the decrepit singer and stared at Panky. For some strange reason their glares were angry, the sweat on their dark faces shining in the flickering candlelight.

Panky was a little drunk now; half the bottle of brandy had gone. He raised his beaker to salute the machos, showing his respect again; he then made silly drunken faces showing his contempt for the singing, pointed to his ears and shook his head, screwed up his features, held his nose and pulled an imaginary toilet chain, like saying: Wow! This guy stinks, but it's funny, right?

Crispy Junior continued singing as the machos stood up in unison; they put down their warm beers, stamped their cigarette butts out on the smooth floor and moved slowly over to Panky. They did not seem happy at all. Panky had no idea why.

Panky watched them as they moved slowly toward him scowling in the candlelight. Panky thinking: Ok, so what the fuck's going on here?

Crispy continued to warble passionately in the background, strutting his stuff, wiggling his skinny arse.

The machos stood close to Panky's table now and stared down at him. He could smell the garlic, tobacco and beer on their breath. He was tempted to say, "The Listerine's are on me guys," but he looked at their eyes and decided against it.

Without a single word of warning, the biggest guy pulled his machete from the sheath at his waist. Z… *zzzing*! It was a sharp dangerous noise; the same sharp dangerous noise Panky heard in every pirate movie he'd seen since he was a kid. Suddenly the shining blade was at his throat, it felt sharp on his Adam's apple. Panky now thinking: Shit, I never saw this one coming! The two swarthy guys stared down at him, violence set deep in their black eyes; their mouths seemed brutal and were quivering, the smell of sweat and testosterone filled the air. Panky gulped audibly.

"So, you no like the way our father sings huh? You theenk is funny?" said the biggest macho twisting the blade slightly.

Panky looked into his black macho eyes, saw hatred, blood and brutality.

Not to be outdone by his older larger brother, the smaller macho stepped forward slightly, *Z...zzzing...* his two-kilo machete shone in the tremulous candlelight, looked as sharp as a surgeons scalpel.

"Your... f... father," stammered Panky, "He's... he's... err..." For once in his life Panky was *totally* speechless. He looked at the machos and gulped, felt the cold steel against his throat and instantly sober.

"He, he... what?" asked the smaller macho and then slashed his machete through the air and sliced one of the large green melons completely in half.

Z...zzzing... Thwack!! The melon split perfectly into two; that cruel melon redness suddenly there, shining, seeping like an open wound, seeds and juices oozing onto the bamboo table, glistening.

Panky felt the sharp blade on his Adam's apple, felt it quiver slightly. Oh Oh! Suddenly the blade went *Z...zzzing... Thwack*!! And split the other melon in half, more sparkling sticky redness, more oozing on the table, another ominous red image slashed into existence. Panky gulped and tried to clear his throat as the blade swiftly returned to his quivering Adam's apple.

Crispy Junior was oblivious of the ensuing violence, still singing his lungs out tunelessly, still dancing like a drug-crazed chicken, tossing the microphone stylishly from one hand to the other. He'd picked up some terrific moves over the years.

Back behind the bar the door to the kitchen opened and Bong suddenly appeared carrying a tray of food, Honey Girl was close behind him, looking large and voluptuous, lumpy, blushing slightly at the prospect of meeting the foreigner. She'd applied a little make up; she was eating a loaf of bread.

Bong and Honey Girl were smiling happily until they realized what was happening, until they saw the blade at Panky's throat, the angry eyes of the macho brothers. Bong was shocked. Honey Girl gasped and spat out her bread.

Panky's body sank slightly as he sighed with relief.

"Putang ina mo!" yelled Bong moving out from behind the bar, "Putang ina mo!"

Panky sighed again and smiled just slightly as the sheepish machos slid their machetes back into the leather sheaths at their sides. Panky didn't know what 'putang ina mo' meant, but as a phrase it seemed to be effective and he was pleased.

"Ano ba yan?" screamed Bong as he moved toward Panky, "Ano ba yan? You do this to my customer in my bar? Are you some kind of crazy?"

Panky wasn't sure, but guessed that Bong wanted to know what the hell was going on. He was right.

"You know this guy best fren of Sir Chris? You know that? Huh?" said Bong waving his hands about theatrically, "Is this how you show our guest Filipino hospitality? Is it?"

The brothers stood open mouthed, hung their heads and shared fleeting guilty glances. The last thing they wanted to do was upset Sir Chris—sure he was only a foreigner, but he was well connected, very well connected. Sir Chris was not the kind of guy you fucked about with. It was that simple.

The biggest macho stepped back a little before he spoke; tears of frustration welling in his eyes. "But theez... foreigner..." he said and then spat on the floor as though the word tasted bad, "He theenk our poor helpless father sing funny, he has no respeck for Crispy... we jus teach him respeck!"

Bong put the tray on the bar, moved forward and the machos backed off a little more. "And this surprises you?" said Bong advancing and sounding shocked.

The macho brothers shared looks of confusion, stepped back some more.

"Everyone thinks Crispy Junior's singing is funny, you didn't know this?

The machos shared a puzzled glance as Bong continued, "I hate to shock you, but everyone thinks his dancing is funny too!"

Heads turned. All eyes on Crispy Junior now as he stomped and strutted his way towards the end of his anthem, giving it his all, sweat and tears in his eyes, dried white spittle on his thin red lips.

Bong stared at the guys; their eyes were sad and repentant, they waited for Bong to continue, they knew he would and he did.

"Maybe if you had the brains or even the balls to explain to him that he is NOT Tom Jones..." Crispy was one on knee now, fingers splayed, hands trembling like bats, rheumy eyes looking up to the heavens. "...Then maybe, maybe he'd stop doing this? De ba?"

Bong spoke mostly English for Panky's benefit, he was confidant the brothers had a pretty good idea what he was talking about, but didn't really care either way.

Crispy Junior hung his head with professional pride as the song finally ended, wrinkly hands still shaking, hair matted to his forehead with sweat, nylon flares thick with the dust of his performance.

The brothers stood either side of Crispy Junior, wrenched the microphone from his skinny grip, carried him carefully through the squeaky door into brilliant sunshine.

Bong grinned, rolled his rheumy eyes.

Panky knocked back a large brandy, lit a cigarette and inhaled.

Bong looked over at Panky, grinned and laughed almost silently; he snorted a little air from his nostrils, slowly shook his head and raised his hands like a Yiddish grandmother as if to say: Don't look at me I just own the place.

Panky looked across at Honey Girl; she was acting coy, fluttering her eyelids, casually finishing her loaf of bread, small crumbs in her moustache. Panky gave her a furtive glance; decided she was at least two hundred pounds. He looked back at Bong again, grinned as if to say: No thanks, she's not *quite* my type, and swallowed the remains of his brandy.

Bong smiled and said, "Ha! You theenk *this* performance is something, forget it, you should have seen him when he thought he was Elvis!"

Honey Girl remembered and giggled through her bread, her eyes filled with laughter and memories, her substantial bulk quivered and contorted with humorous thoughts. She smiled, coughed and then spluttered, the bamboo hut seemed to shake slightly, the small scabby dog opened both eyes and looked around; her burst of hilarity percolated deep inside—Bong and Panky could almost feel it.

She pulled the loaf from her lips, let out an enormous belt of laughter and a shower of soggy breadcrumbs filled the air.

THIRTY

When Panky finally stepped outside, the sun filled his eyes and made him dizzy. One small step out of the door, he was sweating and exhausted. God it was hot! Leaving hadn't been easy. Bong apologized non-stop and insisted they eat together before Panky continued his journey, said he'd prepared some special local dishes, some delicacies. When Panky heard the word 'delicacies' he immediately thought dog, looked around to see if the scabby little creature with the pointy teeth was still there, but he hadn't moved, he was still curled up at the bar dozing. He opened one eye, growled and showed his pointy teeth again as if he knew someone was thinking about him.

Honey Girl stood quietly in the background opening a large bag of chips, still trying her best to be coy and alluring, bread crumbs on her ample bosom.

Panky stood at the bar and said, "Thanks but…" and explained he had a delicate stomach, lied and told Bong the doctor advised an alcohol only diet. So he finished his brandy, shook hands, dumped a handful of notes on the bar and he was out of there.

He drove the Honda through some quiet villages, wasn't too sure where he was going, but was keen to get away from the madness. After a mile or so, and with that 'culture shocked' look still firmly on his face, Panky pulled the car over to the side of the road and pulled up the handbrake. He needed a rest, a few minutes solitude. He sat in the car and sighed heavily, he felt exhausted. The last few days hadn't exactly gone smoothly. First there were the hallucinations on the plane: those violent images reminding him of the problems he'd left behind; Amsterdam and all the shit that went down flooding his mind, leaving him feeling tortured and guilty. Phew! Panky thinking: What the hell *was* that all about? Cocaine psychosis or what? It wasn't his most relaxing flight ever either: twelve hours in economy is a long time under any conditions—the wine and beer had helped, but not much. He wasn't sure if it was just paranoia, but he had a feeling the flight attendant had it in for him, he didn't know why. Maybe it was what he'd said about high altitudes and the effect on women's ovaries. He wasn't sure, it was meant as a joke. And then there was the grilling at customs, that heavy 'donation' thing at the airport, Mrs. Piranha Smile. Now that was unexpected *and* nerve wracking. The prospect of cavity searches and Asian jail time did not appeal, not one bit. Later he'd had his little 'confrontation' with the hooligans: disrespectful bully boys, pulling blades on him like that for no real reason. Kids nowadays, what's wrong with them? Sorting them out had been easy, a pleasure; someone's got to teach them right from wrong; someone's got to educate them, right? Panky figured he was helping; a good spank is better than therapy sometimes. Straight after that he'd had the problem with the girls, lost all his money, his phone and everything, *another* fucking nightmare. More grief from the younger generation; Panky couldn't understand it; they had no respect at all some of them. Being saved by Ding-Dong was definitely a high point, despite the springs in his arse. But then he'd eaten the dog and puked all over Chris' new car: not the best of moves, not exactly a great start. Then of course, once he finally got to the house, there was Chris and Clara to handle. Chris with that mad religious stuff. Was he serious or having a laugh? Panky still wasn't sure; it was hard to tell. He'd hardly seen Clara apart from the time she was praying by the grotto. She didn't exactly look overwhelmed by his presence, she didn't seem exactly overjoyed to see him, not even a smile. He wondered why? Maybe it was something Chris'd said? Maybe Chris had told her about their adventures in Amsterdam? No, he wouldn't mention that, not to his wife. He wasn't stupid. And finally the melon slashing shit, the unexpected 'attack' by Crispy Junior's macho boys. Phew! So far things hadn't been easy, so much for getting away from it all! He didn't even want to consider all the poverty he'd seen and how sad that had made him feel. He didn't even want to go there…

He sat back and enjoyed the cushioned comfort of the sweet smelling car, savoured the aircon, took a few deep breaths and calmed himself down. What he really needed was a smoke, so he pulled out his papers and his stash from his pocket and proceeded to skin up, started to make a big fat joint. That's what he really needed. He sat rolling a spliff, chuckling quietly, thinking: Well, I guess it's nice to meet some local people.

He decided that the 'green, green grass of home' was exactly what he needed. Luckily the girls in the hotel hadn't found his stash; he'd have been surprised if they had because he kept it in a very private place—it was way too pungent to smuggle externally. He opened the car windows, moistened the spliff with his tongue, lit it and inhaled as deeply as he could. Aaahhhh! Time to relax. He exhaled and the car filled with a dense pungent aroma, smoke billowed through the open windows and Panky sat peaceful and mellow, still chuckling quietly to himself about Crispy Junior's performance. A vision he'd remember forever. He took another deep puff on the joint and watched a small stainless steel jeep drive by.

The two guys in the jeep were in their forties, wearing t-shirts and Levis, baseball caps on backwards, Che Guevara handsome and unshaven. They looked tough and they eyed Panky suspiciously. Their jeep had stickers on the front windscreen: Real Men Pray and Pro Gun at the bottom, across the top a much larger sticker said, "The Beatles".

Panky couldn't help but notice, they had holsters strapped to their shoulders, inside the holsters sat big handguns. Panky looking, thinking: Hmmm.

The jeep cruised past the Honda: the Honda with smoke pouring out the windows. The driver turned, looked at his brother and said, "Americano?" His brother nodded slightly, yes, he agreed.

Panky hid the joint out of sight as the jeep went by.

The guys looked over at him as they cruised past.

Panky feeling stoned and paranoid already, thinking: Ok, and who the fuck are you guys? He sat and smoked and watched the jeep disappear into the distance. Sighing heavily, he relaxed again, clicked on the stereo.

"Watching the Detectives" by Elvis Costello and the Attractions boomed a heavy bass line from the speakers, another trip back to the distant past. Panky loved the song and turned it up loud, thinking: all these old classic punk songs, Sam T Coleridge eat ya heart out!

The Honda seemed to rock slightly with the sounds of the music, dense smoke billowed from the windows and Panky sat happy and relaxed; this was exactly what he needed, a well-earned break. He was too involved in the music, too preoccupied by the spliff to notice the jeep hammering back along the hot dusty road towards him. He sat mellow in a haze of super skunk, fragrant or what? The pulsating music filled his mind, carried him back to his adolescence; fleeting snapshots of his youth: girls, gigs, and ganja, a long, lingering blur of nihilistic pleasure; sex, drugs and decadence. The party that lasted forever!

When he opened his eyes he was shocked to see the jeep hurtling over bumps towards him, a spiraling cloud of dust in its wake, the sun gleaming reflections off the polished silver body, off the windscreen; bright reflections slashing like angry blades. The guys in the jeep looked tougher and more intimidating as they got closer. Panky thinking: Jesus Christ what now?

The brothers in the jeep were Perfecto and Procopeo Morales—also known as Ecto and Peo. The jeep pulled alongside the Honda and the brothers pulled out their handguns.

Panky turned the key, revved the engine into a frenzy and screeched away; he had no idea why or where he was going but it seemed like a good idea to get away. The guys looked heavy and had guns. What the hell? Panky spun the Honda around and careered along the road, *fast*. The jeep was behind him now, but it was getting more distant by the second, getting lost in a swirling blanket of pale dust. Panky grinned, thinking: No competition, eat my dust! He threw the Honda around a tight corner and screeched rubber; he pulled hard on the steering wheel, turned quickly onto a dirt road and floored it! He was flying! The road was full of bumps and potholes but the car handled it well, the tires stuck to the bumpy road like shit to a blanket. After a minute or two he checked out the rearview mirror and slowed down a fraction. His pursuers had gone, his heart was beating fit to burst, but they'd gone.

"Watching the Detectives," boomed from the speakers still.

Panky puffed on the spliff in his mouth and grinned. He looked in the mirror again, nothing! He slowed right down, cruised along feeling hot and tired, wondering if his heart could take all this. He looked in the rearview mirror again. There they were again. Shit! And they were hacking along, flying over bumps, defying gravity, the guys looking meaner than ever, the passenger aiming his big handgun, gritting his teeth.

The chase continued, both cars lifting into the air, crashing back down again, tall coconut trees zip zipped by, shadows and sunlight flickering across their windscreens, flashing like sharpened steel. Panky was scared. The Honda hit a boulder, swerved and mounted the side of the road. Panky held on tight, pushed his foot hard on the gas, did a hundred and eighty degree turn and hurtled onto a bigger smoother road gaining some speed and just a little distance. He wrestled with the gear stick and pulled away, but the jeep was still there, still behind him. As he glance into the rearview mirror again he lost control slightly, mounted the side of the road again.

This time he was not so lucky. The bumper clipped a small bamboo hut, women and children *screamed* and chickens *squawked* into the air, a fluttering cloud of feathers swirling among the screams. Panky glanced out the side window, just a quick look as he dropped a gear and gained some speed. The bamboo hut was in pieces: demolished. Children cried; villagers stood with hands to their open mouths, shock and horror on their faces as they watched the chase in the shimmering distance. Panky kept his eyes on the road ahead and floored it. He was losing them again, he almost laughed with relief. But why were they after him? And who the hell were they? As he hacked along madly he looked ahead, saw a young boy standing in the middle of the road leading a huge gray carabao, a skinny young kid holding the massive beast burden on a thin strand of rope. Panky tried to slow down, but the kid and carabao were getting closer. Behind him the jeep was catching up.

Elvis Costello still singing about detectives and shooting and Panky seeing the boy's eyes wide with fear and disbelief, getting closer and fast, seeing the kid in his tattered clothes, bare feet caked with mud, a bright young face dripping with sweat, getting closer and closer still. Panky looked in the rearview mirror and slammed on the breaks.

Rubber screeched and burned on the concrete road, blue-black smoke peeled from the tires, a bitter smoldering stench filled the air, thick plumes rushing past the Honda like steamers in a storm.

The boy and the carabao stood watching the Honda, watching it get closer and closer and then closer still. Behind the Honda the silver jeep was gaining ground; its occupants looked dangerous and fiercely determined. Screeching tires and Elvis Costello's voice competing for Panky's ears.

With brake pads burning rubber the Honda skidded and slid, twisted from side to side and then slid some more. The kid and his charge weren't far away now; the Honda was almost upon them. Anxious to avoid what was clearly inevitable, the young boy dropped the rope, leapt to the side of the road and rolled through the tall grass and sunflowers. The front bumper of the Honda hit the carabao horns and hit them hard; hit it as it stooped to chew on some weeds.

Bosh! Time stood still. Silence.

The kid lay amongst the foliage open mouthed. The carabao just stood there, frozen.

The Morales brothers pulled up behind Panky's borrowed car with a screech of tires, they jumped out, handguns aimed, ready for action.

The carabao just stood there, didn't even blink.

Panky held onto the steering wheel. Waiting.

The front windows of the Honda were open. Two handguns eased their way inside, got close to Panky's head. It was his turn to stay frozen now and he did. Two triggers went *click* as the guns were cocked in unison and edged closer to Panky's head. He didn't move. He didn't dare. Sweat ran down his face and Elvis Costello finally stopped singing. Panky still had the joint between his dry lips, he'd forgotten all about it.

The boy lay at the side of the road expecting violence and death, expecting shots and a victim: the boy was local, he knew the Morales brothers, knew how they worked. The carabao's long pink tongue darted from its mouth and licked the bumper of the Honda but no one really noticed. No one caught sight of that final symbolic act.

Panky, the Morales brothers, the boy and the
carabao gazed around in the brilliant sunshine, in the
tangible silence.

With a sad blink of his eyes and just the smallest of
grunts, the carabao fell sideways onto the road. Dead!
A seven hundred kilo collapse.

Panky slowly turned his head, very slowly, left then
right. He looked down the barrels of the guns; saw the
triggers cocked and ready. Fear crept through his loins,
his gonads felt like garden peas, frozen ones; his mouth
fell dry like cotton wool; his pulse raced like a rabid
greyhound, his palms practically gushed with sweat. He
swallowed hard, head spinning, blood pounding in his
ears, he felt dizzy and scared.

"Hi Joe!" said a calm, slightly panting voice.

It was Peo Morales. He didn't like foreigners much,
especially Americanos. Peo Morales pointed his
handgun at Panky's head, "I said... hi Joe!"

Panky's eyes drifted slowly towards the voice.

The guy looked rugged and weathered, strong like a
farmer, but serious and menacing; hatred and maybe a
little revenge for the carabao swimming in his small
black eyes. Panky didn't know what to do. Thinking:
who the fuck are these guys? And then he realized: it
was the Honda that had caught their eye and not Panky.
This was Clara's car right? Clara the wife of Chris, the
rich British guy, right? *That* was the story. They were
kidnappers after Clara not Panky and to Panky it
suddenly seemed so obvious.

"Hi," he said grasping at straws, scared to smile or
even grin, "Kidnappers right?"

The gunmen laughed together. In unison they said
"Kidnappers!" and then they laughed some more. Their

jovial uttering left and right seemed to seep through the windows and echo through Panky's head. The barrels of the guns swayed slightly with the merriment, but they were still in Panky's face.

"No, not kidnappers," said the brother, Ecto Morales, still chuckling, "Much worse than that Joe... we're the police. Get out of the car and spread your legs, don't try anything stupid."

Panky eased slowly out of the Honda, did as he was told and put his hands on his head—it seemed like a good idea. He was keen to show some respect.

Peo Morales stepped up to their captive, pulled the forgotten spliff from his dry lips and smelled it. He said, "Tut, tut, tut... marijuana Joe... big trouble."

Ecto put a strong hand on Panky's shoulder, spun him around, pushed his face hard into the dust on the side of the car and kicked his legs further apart. "This not your car... huh?" Ecto whispered into Panky's ear.

Panky said, "My friend's car... well his wife's, I think... no, it's not my car, officer."

The cop searched Panky, lifted his passport, his roll of cash and his stash out of his pocket, looked over at his brother and said, "Tut, tut, tut..." and shook his head in gentle dismay. He opened the passport and flicked through the pages, "Son of a beech jus arrive from Amsterdam!"

Peo Morales was also tutting loudly, shaking his head in disbelief. He moved over to the captive and spun him around; slipped the landing card out of the passport his brother was holding and held it in Panky's worried face. "You don't unnerstan drug trafficking punishable by death here in our country?"

Panky could see the landing card, could see the "WARNING: DEATH TO DRUG TRAFFICKERS" statement in bold print at the bottom of the page. He'd seen it before, he remembered the time clearly, but decided to stay silent.

"So you bring drugs from Amsterdam, you sell them to our children, huh? Make some easy money here?" said Ecto.

Panky wanted to say: No of course not, you've got it all wrong. And he wanted to weep openly and beg for clemency, but once again he decided to keep quiet.

Ecto checked out the passport some more. "Humph, so you're Breeteesh, huh? Mister... Panky Wellard," he said and he looked at his brother and smiled. "Panky Wellard? This is really your name?" The brothers grinned. "Is some funny name, no?"

Panky grinned back and thought of Ding-Dong. Touché.

Peo's red baseball cap was keeping the sun off his neck, but small beads of sweat were running down his face and settling in his moustache, he got closer to Panky the gun still pointed at Panky's head. "Hey Breeteesh, I hear everyone is reech in your country now, is dat correck?"

Panky's dizziness was getting worse, his throat was dry with dust, he was finding it hard to speak, his throat seemed gripped by hot steel fingers, he was about to respond when Peo spoke again. "But do you know the Beatles...?"

Panky couldn't believe his ears, he screwed up his features hoping it would help, maybe give him some idea what to say: The Beatles...?

He coughed and said, "Sure, I know the Beatles…" then added, "I grew up listening to The Beatles."

The cops lost their smiles. Ecto spoke, "This is not the question, my brother's English not good? Do you *know* The Beatles?" Ecto grinned, but his brother was shaking his head slightly. "Ok, ok," said Ecto quickly, realising his mistake, "Do you know Paul McCartney and Ringo Starr?" He'd forgotten about the tragic demise of John and George.

Panky wasn't sure if these guys were serious or joking. He stood dizzy, the sun blazing in his eyes; sweat running down his face, a large anxious knot in his stomach. "No… no I'm sorry, I don't," he said.

Ecto unrolled the roll of cash he'd lifted from Panky's pocket, notes fluttered in the breeze. "This a lot of money to carry aroun' in your pocket."

Peo looked at the notes, "Maybe three or four months wages for us… is only pocket change to you, huh?"

Panky looked at the guns still pointed at his head and decided to keep quiet.

Ecto grinned at his brother, "So you don't know Paul and Ringo, huh?"

"No I don't… not personally, I'm sorry." Panky thought he'd try a different approach; remembered Mrs. Piranha Smile, at customs, figured it was worth a shot. "Look, officers… why not just keep the money? It'll pay for the damage, pay for the cow and everything… it was an accident, I just arrived, I'm really sorry!"

The cop's faces went from casual miffed to distinct and irrefutable anger.

Panky watched their expressions change; he wasn't pleased with the result. He'd obviously said the wrong thing.

The cops stiffened their arms; thrust their guns closer to Panky's face. Peo said, "Are you suggesting we are corrup...? Putang ina mo! You son of a beech! We're officers of the law... does that mean nothing to you?"

Panky thinking: Oh shit! Right approach, wrong cops!

Peo paced up and down looking seriously pissed off, "Maybe you hear bad theengs about the Philippines? We cannot just take your stinking money... who you theenk we are my fren? Huh? We uphold the law... you unnerstan? We don't break it..." He handed Panky his passport and cash, but put the stash in the pocket of his jeans, turned and smiled again at his brother.

Panky decided to keep quiet.

The brothers slid their handguns back into their shoulder holsters and for the millionth time in just a couple of days Panky gave a small dry sigh of relief.

Ecto moved closer to Panky, slid $200 from the money in his hand saying, "Ok, we take just $200 for the damage to the stall, the chicken you kill, you unnerstan?"

Panky said nothing.

Peo moved closer, took $300 and said, "An' $300 for the carabao you kill, if that's ok wid you?"

Panky nodded with enthusiasm. It was fine by him. No problema.

A small group of young boys had gathered; they stood watching the action with big eyes and dirty faces; amazed as the cops took large quantities of American dollar bills from the strange looking foreigner. This was better than TV. The skinny kids stood in line wide eyed and excited, they were dressed in scruffy ragged shorts, only one had shoes, one wore a t-shirt, it was tattered and faded, it said: "New York Knicks". The boys had never seen so much money before, to them it proved what people said was right, all Americans really are rich. Man, just look at all that money!

Ecto slid some more notes from Panky's sticky hand saying, "And the woman, the boy, will probably need medication, no?" Peo nodded, his brother was right. "So we take $100 more for medication, Ok?" Panky said nothing, just swallowed.

Peo came back, took another $300 from the diminishing wad, saying, "And $300 for possession of narcotics… an out of court settlement, is ok?"

Panky looked at the boys, watched them giggle at his dilemma.

Ecto took another $100, "We mustn't forget $100 for the speeding and reckless driving…"

Peo took the final $100 bill, "And of course… $100 for disturbing the peace."

Panky's sweaty hand was empty now, still trembling slightly.

"You best fren of Sir Chris, huh?" asked Ecto.

Panky was visibly shocked; he nodded a feeble yes and offered his weakest smiled. He heard flies buzzing around the dead carabao.

Ecto continued, "This much we know already my fren…" The brothers were smiling big time now, nodding happily, like men who'd found the Yamashita treasure.

"Mam Clara, his wife? She ask us keep an eye on you... make sure you have no problems here," said Peo, trying his best to keep a straight face.

"You can go now," Ecto said, "Welcome to the Philippines my fren, Mabuhay!"

Panky turned towards the Honda, still not quite sure what the hell had happened.

"Just one thing my fren..." said Peo, grinning as his brother Ecto tried hard to keep a straight face.

Panky turned reluctantly and looked the cop in the eyes.

"You drive carefully now, huh?" he said still grinning and reaching into his pocket for his cell phone.

THIRTY ONE

Panky drove carefully back to the house wondering all the way if he'd been set up or not. He really wasn't sure.

When he reached Chris' house he pulled up to the gate and hooted. The guards saluted, opened the gates and Panky pulled slowly into the driveway; didn't want anyone thinking he'd been thrashing the car.

He parked the Honda in front of the garage, jumped out, slammed the door and checked the vehicle for damage. Looking around furtively, he spat on the bumper, polished it with the bottom of his borrowed t-shirt, removed a little carabao dribble. No problem, good as new!

He crunched his way across the gravel path, sat at a table by the pool, let out a massive sigh of relief, lit a much-needed cigarette and stared at the Hockney pool scene.

A few minutes later Chris appeared, clearly ready to go out somewhere, clapped his hands together said, "So… ready for the world's best beach Panky?"

"Sure," said Panky, as Chris sat down and joined him at the table.

"See you took the Honda for a spin, have a nice drive?"

Panky said, "Yeah… wonderful."

"The people here are fantastic here aren't they? So friendly."

"Oh yeah… fantastic. Very understanding too," said Panky, exhaling heavily, not sure whether to elaborate or not. "Chris, there's something I should tell you…" he said.

Chris grinned and held up his cell phone. "I know all about it! News travels fast here. Bong called me to apologise, just don't mention it to Clara, ok? Don't want her getting the wrong idea do we? She might think you were nasty taking the piss out of poor old Crispy Junior, I'm sure you were just having a laugh, right? He is pretty unusual."

Panky promised to say nothing, told Chris he didn't mean to be disrespectful, said it was all a bit of a culture shock. It was bad enough that Clara would find out about the car chase and his introduction to the Morales brothers, the cops. She'd hear about that for sure. The more he thought about it, the more convinced he was it was her idea. He still hadn't said hello to her; still hadn't been introduced.

Chris pulled a wad of cash from his pocket, laid it on the table.

"A bit more pocket money?" asked Panky.

"Yeah… why not?" said Chris grinning as his old friend picked up the money, pushed it casually into his borrowed shorts.

Chris grinned, "I hear Honey Girl's got the hots for you?"

Their eyes slowly met and they laughed together like they always had, until tears ran down their face.

"She's a birgin you know?" said Chris and they laughed some more.

"Can't think why?" added Panky wiping the tears from his eyes.

Chris stood up, said, "Come on geezer, let's go…"

He strolled towards his Mercedes van, sandals crunching on the gravel. Panky followed.

Panky reached the vans open door and looked inside; saw Boy the driver and Mai-Ling, the girl from the pool, sitting up front and saw Clara and the kids sitting there in the back.

Chris stood behind him, "This is Clara my wife… the boss," said Chris and laughed, "… and of course, our beautiful children."

Panky smiled, thinking: Chris was right the kids are beautiful. Clara looked great too with her sultry smile and passionate eyes.

As Chris and Panky climbed into the Mercedes, the air was cool and the atmosphere icy.

Panky smiled and thrust out his hand, ready to shake, but Clara ignored it, saying curtly, "I've heard such a lot about you Panky."

"All good I hope?" asked Panky as he sat down.

Clara said nothing.

Chris closed the door and the van pulled away.

THIRTY TWO

As Panky and Chris lay on sun loungers at Pacoma beach, the sun beat down relentlessly from the cloud free sky and crystal blue waves lapped almost silently on the powder white shoreline. Nice.

Chris looked good stretched out in the heat; he looked tanned and healthy; in total contrast Panky was the whitest person on the beach, skin like low fat yoghurt. The beach was unusually busy; maybe two dozen bodies lay scattered like some semi-erotic battle scene.

Chris sipped his melon juice as Panky swigged another beer.

In the distance Mai-Ling, Clara and the children played happily by the warm waters edge.

Panky watched Mai-Ling's every move, as always she looked stunning.

Panky lay flat on his sun lounger glistening with factor fifty lotion, "So where's the gear then," he whispered to Chris.

Chris turned his head, "The gear?"

"Yeah, you know... the gear... the stuff... I want to spin one, I want to skin up, get one together... you know... make a joint... build a spliff... I've had a hell of a day so far, believe me, I really need to relax.

As Chris sat up sweat and lotion trickled down his tanned muscles, shone in the sunlight. He looked Panky in the eyes.

"You're kidding, right?" Chris looking puzzled, thinking: How much more relaxed can you possibly get?

Panky sat up straight and fast, a look of concern pasted across his face, "Course I'm not kidding, come on geez, don't mess about… I'm dying for a smoke… dying…"

Chris grinned bemused, "Hate to tell you this Panky… sorry mate, really… but I don't do all that stuff any more."

Panky stared at Chris waiting for him to crack up laughing and pass the stash, but Chris just sat with the sun in his eyes, stared at him blankly.

Panky thinking: Come on… he's joking right? He must be.

"Now *you're* kidding, right?" said Panky.

Chris held the blank look and shrugged slightly.

"You…?" Panky laughed because he had to, "YOU… don't smoke any more, that's impossible… no not impossible… ridiculous!"

Chris grinned sheepishly. Simply put, his life had changed.

Panky was close to emotional, "But I know you geezer, you always smoke… right? You always have!"

Chris shook his head from left to right, a clear and obvious no. He slurped his melon juice with his eyes fixed on Panky, waiting for some kind of reaction.

Panky drained his bottle of beer in one swift gulp; "Oh I get it…" he looked around furtively, "Too up market now are we? Hey?"

"What d'you mean?" asked Chris, "I'm not with you…"

With mischievous eyes Panky held his hand to the side of his mouth; guiding the words directly to Chris he continued in a stage whisper, "Controlled cocaine habit is it? Got some dosh now haven't you? A bit of the old folding stuff and you've gone up market, right?"

Chris stared in disbelief.

Panky smiled big at the prospect, clapped his greasy hands together.

He whispered, "Excellent, I could handle a few lines of marchin' powder."

Chris grinned, "There's no such thing as a controlled cocaine habit Panky, you should know that... we tried it in Amsterdam, remember?"

It was Panky's turn to stare blankly.

He looked so sad and pathetic Chris nearly laughed, he said, "Look... geezer... sorry to disappoint you, but I'm a reformed character... I'm a dad now, ok? I'm as clean as a whistling cliché. "

Panky looked shocked, ran his fingers through his curly hair and exhaled. He said, "You mean I've traveled all this way, like 10,000 miles to see my old "partner in grime" and you've gone straight on me? You're kidding me, you must be... It's a joke!"

Chris' tone was like his eyes, apologetic. He said, "It's not a joke Panky, I'm deadly serious."

"Un-fucking-believable," said Panky, "Un-fucking-believable!"

Chris sighed, "I'm a role model now Panky, I take my parental responsibilities very seriously... being a dad's a major commitment! Really..."

Panky looked emotional, tears almost welling as he tried to speak, "But Chris... a beach like this deserves to be smoked on," he whined. He looked down at his glistening pink body and wiped the sweat from his brow with the back of his hand, "I thought this was all too good to be true…" He lifted his bottle to his lips, but it was empty, "You'd better get me another beer mate and quick…"

Chris lifted the last cold one from the icebox and passed it to his emotional friend.

Panky shook his head sadly, lit a cigarette and opened the beer. He grinned at Chris, but his grin was more sarcastic than grateful, much more. As he drained the bottle noisily he noticed a group of young Filipinas wandering by in the heat, their boom box was playing the old classic "Peaches" by the Stranglers. Appropriate or what? thought Panky as he heard the chorus. He was beginning to worry about all these musical trips to the past; it was starting to seem like more than just a coincidence.

Chris stood up, "I'll err, go and get some more beer then," he said, his eyes were downcast and guilty as he turned and tip toed off across scorching hot sand.

Panky licked his lips and stared lustfully as another group of young girls sashayed by. Their bodies were brown and oiled, curvaceous young girls flaunting their newfound sexuality. The air was full of sweet, sultry aromas: musk, coconut oil and essence of nubile. Nice.

Panky enjoyed the fleshy distraction, but could still hear The Stranglers fading into the distance. The notion of a musical conspiracy left him feeling confused and a little paranoid.

He shook his head trying to loose the paranoia. He focused on the girls, as they strolled by some of them were looking back at him, giggling and smiling, clearly interested and hopeful; the prospect of getting involved with a foreigner and eventually escaping to a land of opportunity—*any land*—was high on the girls 'to do' list.

Totally unaware of his new 'meal ticket' persona, Panky sat back and grinned and winked lecherously. What a beach! A host of semi clad young buttocks, firm and tantalizing teased his eyes and stretched his imagination. Phew! Maybe things weren't so bad here after all? Panky sat staring, almost drooling, at the varied array of exotic female form. He wiped the sweat from his brow and adjusted his shorts again.

He didn't see Clara return from the shoreline and sit behind him, he had no idea she was right there. Panky sat oblivious to her close proximity, groaning and licking his lips, tongue like a lecherous wolf, sighing. He was miles away in a fleshy fantasy world, a world full of heat and lust, a world full of sweat and physical improbability.

"I hope you're having a good time?" said Clara quietly.

Panky jumped and quickly turned to face her, thinking: Oh my God, she must have heard me groaning, she must have heard me! "Oh, yeah… wonderful, it's very nice here, beautiful… what a beach, what a view!" he said, just a little anxiously, his pink face turning a slightly darker shade.

Clara's smile was thin and tight on her face; she hated the way he was lusting after anything that moved, anything even remotely female, girls half his age and younger. She sat thinking: These British men, so obvious, so typical.

"What-a-view," repeated Panky, "It's not like this where I come from you know," he said, wondering where this conversation was going, hoping he could keep it civilized.

"I'm sure it's not," said Clara with a little authority, "You'll see a lot of beautiful young girls here in the Philippines." She emphasized the word *girls* and paused for effect, the thin smile still tight on her face, "Of course, at your age, it's ok to look… but don't even *think* about touching." Clara smiled, but only to herself, pleased with her words of warning and their delivery. Succinct, she thought.

Panky looked around casually, avoiding Clara's gaze. He saw smooth brown skin in every direction, young hot flesh, smiles so curious and probably willing. He grinned and turned back to Clara as she spoke.

"Do you know what happens to middle aged men that mess with under aged girls here," she asked, her eyes a little fierce now and scornful—loving every minute of this. "Do you know what middle aged men get when they're caught corrupting minors?" she asked.

Panky cracked a smile; wasn't sure what she meant, didn't really consider himself as middle aged—although of course he was and had been for some years. He shrugged.

Clara smiled. "Go on guess…"

"Err… ok, let me see," he said, "What do middle aged men get… when they mess with young girls…? Err?"

Clara clarified her comment, said, "Under aged girls… under aged."

Panky smiled broadly, "Ok, under aged girls… err… no idea!"

"Oh come on Panky, think," purred Clara.

He was happy Clara was talking to him at last but couldn't work out what she was trying to say, he didn't want to appear rude or obvious, maybe she was getting to like him now? Maybe she was finally seeing the better side of him? He suddenly looked inspired, raised his hand like a ten year old, he said, "I know... I know..." He said it so proudly. "Erections, right? They get erections!"

"No, not erections Panky," said Clara sighing with disappointment, getting up and walking away—bored with her little game now. "What they get is the death sentence," she said as she wandered off, sneering just slightly over her tanned shoulder, "The death sentence!"

Panky mouthed the words as Clara ambled back to the shoreline. "The death sentence!"

He couldn't believe it!

A few minutes later Chris returned with more beer.

"All right geezer? Having a good time?"

"Oh yeah," said Panky adjusting his shorts, "fucking marvelous!"

The afternoon went by slowly and peacefully, the sun blazed down with a vengeance and Panky drank more and more beer. His body went from pale pink to very, very bright pink.

Chris, Clara, Mai-Ling and the kids sat under a huge parasol not wanting to damage their skin beyond repair—Chris liked a few hours in the sun, but knew his limitations.

Panky seemed oblivious to the power of the tropical sun; he just lay there with his skin cooking, surrounded by an army of empty beer bottles. Every chance he got he smiled at Mai-Ling. He tried to be discreet but he wasn't. As he continued drinking beer, his eyes became glazed and pink; eventually they matched his skin.

"Careful you don't get sunstroke sir," said Mai-Ling, smiling and unsure of why she even cared.

Panky sat up and smiled at her concern, he stretched and yawned, wiped the sweat from his shiny pink brow and stood up.

Swaying only slightly he said, "You're right, I need to cool down. Thank you." He squinted at the glimmering blue horizon, turned, grinned and ran hotfoot toward the sea. As he hopped along, he looked back and smiled, happy to see everyone watching his moves.

Chris, Clara, Mai-Ling and even the kids expected his exit to get theatrical, expected him to exaggerate his every quick step in the hot sand and of course he did; hamming it up all the way, waving madly and pulling 'hot sand' faces, making the kids laugh out loud.

He finally made it to the shore and dipped his toe into the warm water, turned and waved at the giggling kids. They liked Uncle Panky as they called him; he was fun to have around. It was then that he focused on two teenage kids buried in the sand, bodies buried up to their scrawny necks, sun tanned faces, eyes distorted by sunlight, two solitary heads poking out of the sand, smiling like guillotined trophies. Panky looked again. He couldn't believe it!

It was Sid and D.K.! The kids from Amsterdam! The dead ones!

Panky blinked madly, shook his head and looked again. Oh yes, it was definitely them! He'd forgotten all about his hallucinations on the plane, he'd put them out of his mind, blamed them on the stress and the pressure of Amsterdam, blamed them on the violence and the carnage he'd witnessed before he ran away. The mayhem, all the dead bodies! He just stood and stared. His body trembled.

"Careful you don't get sunstroke, sir," the buried heads said in comic unison, bloodied, gory faces, mimicking Mai-Ling perfectly.

Panky screamed and ran into the water as fast as he could. Bubbling white foam cascaded through the air and with a huge splash he vanished under gently rippling waves.

Chris stood up and shaded his eyes from the sun, looked out to sea. At first he was concerned, Panky *had* drunk a lot of beer, but he guessed it was just the shock of the water or maybe a crab or something had bitten him. It was a pretty loud scream whatever caused it!

Chris, Clara, Mai-ling, *and* the kids, looked out to sea unsure of what to expect.

Panky's pink face surfaced, coughing and spluttering; he looked at the two heads in the sand, saw a couple of young Filipinos grinning at him, chuckling together, surprised at the foreigners over reaction— surely he'd seen people buried in the sand before?

Panky spat salty water back into the sea and sighed with relief. He floated and stared at the pure blue sky, listen as his breathing slowed, watched his chest rise and fall with every breath and wondered what the hell was happening to him. It was hard not to feel a tad concerned, even for him, a die-hard hedonist!

As he continued to float he looked around and saw an old Banca boat anchored nearby. A group of boys were queuing up, taking it in turns to dive off into the deep water. They were noisy and excited, having a lot of fun. Panky, keen to forget his recurring hallucinations and cool down a bit, swam awkwardly towards the boat, climbed up the outrigger and crawled onto the swaying deck gasping for breath.

The boys clapped and cheered his arrival, pushed him almost to the front of the bustling queue.

Panky stood on wobbly legs and watched the kids dive into the clear blue depths, watched as they 'bombed' into the water making Hiroshima clouds of warm white spray. It was a lot of fun. Panky was ten years old again. His pink body looked odd, misplaced, among the small, dark boys in the queue. His crooked drunken smile looked strangely permanent in the sunlight, a beach boy wino with twisted vision and swirling consciousness. He chuckled as his body swayed with the boats momentum; he shuffled slowly forward with the queue, unsteady on his feet.

Finally it was Panky's turn; he edged forward, stood precariously at the side of the Banca and smiled at the disorderly line of playmates behind him.

The boys jumped and cheered and clapped their hands as he belly flopped and splashed into the depths of the ocean. Despite his distinct lack of style, he plummeted headlong through the water... *whoosh*... His pink body twisted, turned with an awkward, spastic grace as he went further and further down. A million tiny bubbles rose gently to the surface.

He was totally unaware that his head barely missed the sharp ragged coral. As he turned and floated slowly back to the surface, he was suddenly engulfed in a cloud of colourful fish. Time stood still as he watched them drift slowly away, shining in kaleidoscopic wonder. Down there in the clear depths, down deep beneath the water he witnessed a silent new world, an amazing world of color and coordination, vivid and unreal like some surreal aquatic trip.

A huge stingray swept passed below him, huge fins like brown spotted wings silently projecting it along, graceful and majestic; coral swayed like exotic plants in a sudden breeze, weird and wonderful anemones sat like baby aliens waiting to be fed. The silence was palpable and pure; the colours were clear, bright and animated.

Panky surfaced with popping ears and running nostrils; the boys with their dark faces and their white, white smiles cheered joyfully as he climbed clumsily back onboard and pushed his way to the head of the queue. Panky wanted more. It was amazing.

He stood once again poised to reenter his brave new world; the boys patted him on the back, shook his hand and urged him on, laughing. His eyes were hazy, full of alcohol, but his intentions were clear as he dived back in and cut through the water. *Whoosh.*

Chris and his entourage stood up again, watched as he took his second plunge. They knew he was drunk and their looks of concern were justified.

Once again his head barely missed the coral.

As he rose once more to the surface, saw fleeting groups of colourful fish; he marveled at a Puffer fish; saw a solitary Stonefish, deadly and awesome, watched it giving him the eye.

As he continued up towards the surface, he heard the boys 'bombing' into the ocean; their laughter muffled and distorted, echoed like cries of confinement.

He climbed onboard again, jumped the queue and dived.

Whoosh.....

Down he went; the dive was hard and sleek this time, buoyed by newfound confidence.

Whoosh!!

Down he went, further and further down, hurtling fast towards the ragged coral.

Mai-Ling, Chris, Clara *and* the kids, stood on tiptoe looking out towards the Banca. They'd watched his third more powerful dive and shared silent looks of concern. He'd been down there much longer than before—much longer.

When his head smashed into the coral he was pondering the beauty of this silent subterranean paradise, lulled into a false sense of security by alcohol and graceful aquatic beauty. The sudden impact was a total shock. *Total.* A hazy diluting shawl of fresh red blood surrounded and floated up above his flaccid form as he began to surface; his lungs expelled their bubbling contents and mixed with the hazy redness of his blood.

The boys on the Banca stopped silent as the thin cloud of blood reached the surface.

Seconds later came Panky's lifeless body.

Clara saw the boys stand peering over the side of the boat; she stood and ran towards the sea. She dived in perfectly and swam quickly towards Panky's floating body. She swam fast and accurate, her arms powered through the surface, legs kicking hard propelling her along.

Chris and Mai-Ling shared an emotional glance and looked back out to sea; both amazed at Clara's strength and determination—they were shocked that she'd actually bothered. Chris secretly delighted that maybe Clara had finally seen some redeeming features in his oldest friend and hoped he wasn't dead

When Clara finally reached Panky she twisted his body and turned his head out of the water; she stretched out her arm, put a hand under his chin and gasping, she struggled back to the shore.

The small boys stood silent on the edge of the Banca, amazed at the fate of their erstwhile companion.

Mai-Ling and Chris ran to the shore, waded out as far as they could.

Clara was getting closer and closer, her panting breath seemed the only sound for miles. She released Panky's chin from her grip, Chris and Mai-Ling dragged him quickly to the shoreline.

Mai-Ling gave mouth to mouth, seemed determined to help save him.

Clara crawled on all fours through the shallow water towards her husband, exhausted. She stood and wrapped her dripping arms around him gasping for breath; her eyes were wide with fear and expectation. Had she saved him? Would he live?

A small crowd gathered as Mai-Ling pinched Panky's nose and breathed and listened, breathed and listened. She pumped and pushed his chest and then breathed and listened some more.

After a while, and to the crowd's amazement, Panky coughed and spluttered. He puked water onto the sand, gasped and panted like an overweight marathon runner, long strands of snot dangled from his nose. He'd made it!

The gathered crowd sighed and gasped in unison, they clapped quietly and solemnly, showing Clara and Mai-Ling a little appreciation.

Panky lay on the sand in a twisted fetal position; coughed, spat, gasped and gagged. He attempted to stand but collapsed into a quivering pink heap, unconscious.

Mai-Ling crouched by his side, touched the sticky thick blood oozing from the wound hidden in his hair.

She looked up into a crowd of dark curious faces. "We'd better get him to a hospital!" she said, displaying the blood on her fingers.

Clara was standing on the edge of the crowd, hands on hips, still flushed and panting, dripping wet. Her voice rose above the morbid, curious murmur, "A hospital? I don't think so Mai-Ling, not a hospital, straight to re-hab!"

THIRTY-THREE

Panky was back at Chris and Clara's house lying in bed unconscious.

Chris, Clara and Mai-Ling stood around the bed in the cool, darkened room with the Doctor they'd called, and looked down at him in silence. The only sound apart from the roosters outside in the garden was the motion of the overhead fan and the mad jazz buzz of the air con.

Mai-Ling stood and stared at Panky with a genuine look of concern; her bedside manner was calm and professional. Mai-Ling knew the Doctor, they'd met before a few times and although he hadn't said as much, she was confidant that Panky would be ok once he'd taken his medicine, once he'd spent a few days taking it easy. Her only *real* concern was that if the fever persisted he might get delirious and fall out of bed. The Doctor nodded professionally, said it was unlikely but yes, of course, it was possible.

Mai-Ling stood by the bed, listened intently and took mental notes; she was confidant that things would be ok. She had a plan.

The Doctor smiled at Chris, Clara and Mai-Ling; he was a kind man, expensive, but kind.

"He's tough," the Doctor said, as he put his stethoscope and blood pressure pump back into his leather bag, "Don't worry, he'll be ok."

Clara's eyes moved from Panky to the Doctor, "And the good news Doctor?"

When Panky finally woke up he had no idea where he was, absolutely no idea; but that was nothing new and it came as no major surprise to him. The big surprise was, he was strapped to a bed and couldn't move, not an inch, he could barely wiggle his fingers. Whoa! Despite the brightness creeping in behind the long dark curtains he was cold too, freezing cold; his lungs felt shriveled like walnuts, his body was trembling. What the fuck was going on?

He lay there with darting paranoid eyes, trying to work out where he was and just as importantly why he was strapped down like some kind of prisoner? He lifted his head slightly; saw his arms and legs strapped tightly to the bed, thick leather straps. Like it or not he was going nowhere.

He laid his head—which was pounding—back onto the pillow and listened to the roosters outside, listened too to the quiet hypnotic rhythm of the overhead fan, the mad jazz aircon and tried to remember what happened. It wasn't easy and after a while despite his fears and a world of confusion he drifted into a deep sleep.

When Mai-Ling came back into the bedroom to check on Panky he was still fast asleep and snoring peacefully. It was night now. She turned off the air-con, switched on the lamp on the dressing table and opened the curtains to the balcony; a warm breeze of sweet night air filled the room.

The night was full of jungle sounds: cicadas, crickets and frogs buzzed and chirped and croaked creating a tremulous wall of sound; delicate fireflies danced in the night's gentle darkness, glowing beams of light, like silent tiny fairies. Jungle tranquility.

Mai-Ling smiled at Panky as he mumbled and snored, she decided that Clara was right, he did look a bit like Colin Farrell, not only that but he looked ok now too, thank goodness; thankfully her prayers had paid off. She wondered why she was so attracted to him; maybe he brought out the nurse in her? Was that it? Did she want to help him, give him the sense of purpose, the sense of family that Chris had found with Clara? Mai-Ling knew that family life was different in Europe, less traditional, more independent than the Philippines because, certainly in the majority of cases, the '*granny state*' had replaced the real sense of family, the dependence on it; she'd discussed it with Clara and often and they'd agreed it wasn't a good thing, but the British considered it progress. But maybe it wasn't that at all, maybe it was because she'd always had a thing for English guys, so different from their American counterparts, more polite, a more subtle kind of cool. Just like the guys in Spandau Ballet: Mai-Ling was a serious fan years ago and oh how she'd dreamt of going to see them in concert in London when she was a teenager, back in the eighties, bizarre because at the time she couldn't even afford the jeepney fare across Manila and didn't even own a passport.

Mia-Ling smiled at her thoughts, her nostalgia; she looked across the room at Panky and hated the way he was grinding his teeth, decided it was probably a stress related thing and of course she was absolutely right. She gently bathed his face and neck with warm soapy water, careful not to wake him; took his temperature which was still high but ok, checked the straps were tight, kissed his forehead like a mother would a small child and quietly left the room humming 'To cut a long story short' by Spandau Ballet.

Panky opened his eyes and realised that day had become night; he'd obviously been asleep for a while. His eyes darted around the room, he noticed that the curtains were now open, the air-con was off and the lamp was on, there was no doubt that someone, at some time, had entered the room. But where the hell was he? And what the hell was going on?

He lay there for what seemed hours, but was probably only a few minutes. He tried hard to remember. Nothing! He couldn't remember a bloody thing.

He looked out at the clear night sky, saw a million bright stars and wondered what the time was. Outside in the distance he heard rooster's cock-a-doodle-do-ing, but he knew that it didn't mean much. Ok, he thought, the demented rooster night shift! That must mean that I'm in the tropics, and probably in the Philippines. He grinned thinking: Ok, that's good! Relax! Take it easy. A series of snippets and snapshots rushed through his mind, gushing like a waterfall. He started to remember things. Faces came first, people's eyes, pained expressions. Chris, Clara, Mai-Ling, the kids on the beach. They were waving, watching him dive off the Banca! He remembered that. His thoughts started to flow more quickly. The bevy of young girls on the beach, oiled and smiling, parading up and down, staring, smiling at him and giving him the eye! He remembered that for sure, how could he possibly forget? He remembered dying for a smoke too, a beach like that deserved to be smoked on. He remembered those words, recalled the bitter disappointment, the shock, and remembered drinking untold beers as compensation. Then he heard the echoing *whoosh*. Remembered the bubbles rising up towards the bright distorted surface of the ocean, remembered that silent almost eerie underwater world, the bright colors, the tranquility, the beauty. The sharp coral slicing into his flesh, blood all around him like a cloud of red smoke, he remembered that. Then floating, floating up to the surface, spluttering, puking and gasping on the sand in a trembling heap. Whoa!

Panky laid his head back on the pillow, the pillow was drenched with sweat, but despite the cooling moisture it was soft and comfortable. He could cope with the smell it was his. He closed his eyes. He felt so tired and he felt so alone.

As Mai-Ling entered the room again and tip-toed quietly across the bedroom Panky stirred sleepily, he opened one sticky eye and watched her movements. She was looking good. He turned his head slightly, through the open balcony doors he saw clear blue skies and glimmering sunlight, not a cloud in sight. Shadows moved through the lofty palm fronds with the breeze, they looked huge like dampened feathers, he could smell coffee blossom, a pure sweet smell, and the sweet oily flesh of coconuts; heard a small chorus of birdsong, light and almost musical in the distance. As always, it was a beautiful morning.

Mai-Ling walked over to the bed, checked the straps and said, "Hi! Didn't want you falling out."

Panky smiled and as Mai-Ling got closer he wondered how bad his breath was. His head still throbbed and pounded, his skin felt stretched across his skull, tight and taut.

Mai-Ling stooped down and wiped his brow, "The Doctor said your liver is competing with your brain for vitamin B…"

Panky grinned, confused.

"Your liver's winning, easily," she said, as she adjusted the bedclothes, "You need lots of rest and lots of vitamin B… otherwise you might start hallucinating… we wouldn't want that, would we?" Mai-Ling picked up and opened a bottle of pills, poured a glass of water from a tall crystal decanter.

Panky grinned again as he watched her.

"Too much alcohol apparently… among other things," she said as she put two tablets between his lips, washed them down with some sips of water.

Panky coughed as he swallowed and then smiled, "I like hallucinations," he said weakly, "but I've never had 'em for free before."

Mai-Ling forced a smile. She picked up the remote control for the TV, put it in Panky's hand and wrapped his fingers around it loosely. "Don't want you dying of boredom do we?" she said. She put the bottle of vitamin B on the bedside table, looked Panky in the eyes, smiled, turned and quietly left the room.

Panky closed his eyes and let out a major sigh of relief. So things were fine after all. The paranoia was, as always, just paranoia! Ok, he *was* strapped in the bed, and for some reason Mai-Ling *had* locked the door behind her, which seemed odd, but he was in good hands. If the medicine worked he'd be up and about in no time.

He considered a quick visit to Bong's bar for a couple of glasses of foam, thought it might be fun to see how everyone was doing, but first he had to get better. He couldn't believe it was the alcohol causing the hallucinations! Could not believe it! Sure, he'd had a few drinks over the last few days—too many to count, but what's new? It's not as if he was a trembling alcoholic, vomiting in secret, hiding bottles of booze so no one discovered the truth, no way! No "My name is Panky and I'm an alcoholic." He was just a social drinker and that was where it ended. Ok, so he had an active social life, long hours, and lots of drinks. But what can you do? He didn't see it as a problem. He was ok now, he was safe and thankfully the hallucinations were finished, done with, a thing of the past. He sighed and pointed the remote control at the TV. It came instantly to life and splashes of colour lit the room as he surfed the tube.

First there was a Japanese game show: no thanks, *flick*, 'The Sound of Music' dubbed in Korean: uh-huh, *flick*, golf: I don't think so, way too exciting, *flick*, hungry crocodiles floated on the Discovery channel: not for me, *flick*, Dorothy and the Munchkins singing in Chinese: no way, far too trippy: *flick*. He went from channel to channel to channel. Nothing. There were hundreds of channels too, or that's how it seemed, but there was nothing he wanted to watch.

He chuckled quietly, shook his head in mild disbelief and continued to *flick* through the channels, thinking: I can't believe it's the alcohol! I just can't believe it! I *might* start hallucinating! Ha! Now that's a funny one. *Flick, flick... flick.*

He continued to chuckle without sound, screwed up his eyes and stared at the screen, saw a wide-eyed priest raving in the pulpit; saw his stiff white collar against worn black cloth, like a crooked fallen halo. The priests face was red and full of angst, old but fiercely animated. His thin pleading hands moved dramatically through the air, his eyes looked frightful and strange, piercing and fanatical. His shrill dry voice boomed from the TV's speakers, his ominous words echoed around the room...

"If you do evil and reject the Lord... he will bring upon you disaster, trouble and confusion... in everything you do!"

Panky stared at the screen, didn't like what he saw or what he heard, but he watched some more, for some reason he was curious. The holy man's words poured from the speakers like sacred water and splashed around the room...

"Disaster, trouble and confusion... in everything you do! Until you are quickly and completely... destroyed!"

The priest's ranting and raving was building to a dizzying holy crescendo, dry spittle stuck white to his thin withered lips. His thin nervous finger pointed accusingly towards the screen. It pointed to Panky. The priest's anxious words seemed destined for Panky's ears alone. Panky was gasping now, wide eyed in a cold sweat; visibly shaken by this sudden outburst of religious fervour; shaken by the personal accusations. He'd had enough, he pointed the remote and with a *flick* another channel appeared. But it was the priest again.

Panky was confused, *flick*, he moved to another channel.

The camera panned for a close up on the priest, his eyes were red and wrinkled, decades of sinful confession had clearly taken their toll, his expression was tortured and tired, exhausted. It seemed that only now after years of dogged devotion he'd finally seen and heard enough, he'd finally realised that the writhing line of sinners was endless and he couldn't deny it. His barrage of holy vernacular continued...

"I am burning... burning with fever and I am near death!"

Panky was shaking now, thinking: For fuck's sake! What's going on? He was panicking, trying desperately to change the channels, wanting to loose this blithering priest and his sanctimonious predictions. *Flick*, the priest was still there. *Flick,* and there he was again, raving in the pulpit, his face red and fearful, his words cutting and slicing, worming their way into Panky's mind...

"I am worn out and utterly crushed, my heart is troubled and I groan with pain!"

Panky squirmed in his straps, squirmed hard and desperate, he wanted to get away and fast. The manic priest and his words were too close for comfort, way too close; the speech had gotten personal, it seemed directed at Panky and at him alone. It was frightening and he couldn't move, he couldn't stop the words, couldn't stop them. He shook his head from side to side, closed his eyes as tight as he could.

The voice of the priest suddenly disappeared. It was gone and the room was silent again. Outside birds sang songs that lifted and lingered on the breeze.

Panky gave a huge whispering sigh of relief. He laid still for a while, his eyes still tightly shut and tried to calm down; gradually his breathing slowed, went back to normal and his trampoline heart stopped bouncing in his chest. Phew! He opened his eyes.

And there they were in all their gory glory, Sid and D.K.: the two dead kids from Amsterdam. They were leaning over the bed grinning, smoking huge spliffs, and flicking ash on the bedclothes. Their faces were thin, splattered with blood and dirt, decaying and twisted worse than before, their wounds oozed and wept, their crazy laughter spilled like butchered entrails.

Panky turned and twisted his body desperate to escape, but he was going nowhere. He screamed and screamed and screamed, but there was hardly a sound.

THIRTY FOUR

Chris and Clara sat at a table by the pool waiting for breakfast to be served. They were silent and serious, their earlier conversation had covered a lot of ground—neither of them had heard Panky's feeble screams from the back of the house. Chris hung his head slightly, looked up at Clara with sad and guilty eyes.

"But he's my oldest friend," said Clara, mimicking Chris perfectly, "We were kids, punks together, we went through a lot of shit together in Amsterdam… we were close… like brothers," Clara smiled and continued—she knew she was doing well, "Don't worry babe, you'll like him… really… he's Catholic!"

Chris said nothing; knew anything he said would be ignored and worthless.

"As soon as he arrived you were drunk," said Clara scowling, "You probably don't remember a thing, do you?"

Chris shook his head slightly; she was right of course—as always. He remembered opening the champagne but that was about it.

"I heard you laughing about a dead girls' nipples, a dead drug addict to be precise, if I'm not mistaken?"

Chris vaguely remembered telling Panky about Lola's sad demise, how she fell off the roof and landed on the carol singers, he looked up and decided not to dwell on the subject.

"Even before he gets here he needs money.... not exactly a great start is it?"

Chris kept his head hung low, sad guilty eyes fixed on his wife.

"Six hundred dollars for God knows what... in the girlie bars!" Clara was getting into it now, knew she was on a winner. "Then he vomits half a dog all over the new car—it'll never smell the same—and then pukes the other half all over that nice Armani suit I bought you! Lovely!"

Chris was going to say something in Panky's defense, decided against it.

"And then he insults that poor old man Crispy Junior—the one who thinks he's Elvis, sorry the one who thinks he's Tom Jones—*then* he upsets Crispy's boys, nearly gets himself killed... chopped to pieces, and *then*... he terrifies the local community with *my* car, *my* new car... demolishes the only vegetable store for about five miles and kills most of their chickens!" Clara paused for breath, but only briefly: "And *then* he kills Tatay's carabao, nearly kills that poor young boy that looks after it, and *then*... he gets busted for possession of narcotics, reckless driving and disturbing the peace," Clara stood up, put her hands on her hips and stared at Chris, raised her voice slightly, she still hadn't finished: "And *then*... he gets so drunk and sun burned he nearly drowns himself, costs us a fortune in medicine and Doctors bills... not too bad for the first day! I know this Panky's your oldest friend Chris but why?"

Chris stared off into space. What can you say? The worse thing about it: it was all completely true and as for exactly why Panky was his oldest, most cherished friend, Chris didn't want to explain it all to Clara, he wasn't proud about his past, the things that had happened, the problems with his dad and what Panky had done.

When Panky woke up that morning, the first thing he saw was Mai-Ling tidying the room. For a change he knew where he was almost immediately; a comforting and somewhat unusual start to the day.

Mai-Ling stood across the room cleaning a cutthroat razor, looking cool in her starched white uniform. When she'd finished she put the razor back into a small leather case, put the case into a draw. She turned and looked at her patient.

Panky was looking over at her. They exchanged smiles.

She walked over to his bed, untied the leather straps and wiped his brow. "You were out for three days," she said as she rinsed the face flannel in a bowl of soapy water, wiped his brow again, "Three days…"

Panky said nothing. He wasn't sure about anything any more; he wasn't sure what were dreams, nightmares, hallucinations or reality. He had no idea, but he did know where he was, which was refreshing.

"I knew you'd get delirious, that's why I strapped you in," said Mai-Ling.

Panky smiled revealing a gap in his top front teeth; for some reason two teeth were missing. He looked comical and old.

Mai-Ling looked at him, "That reminds me, didn't want you to swallow this." She handed him a plastic pink denture, it looked old and uncared for, the teeth almost yellow like some ghoulish Halloween trick.

Panky smiled revealing the gap and his gums in their entirety. It was quite a gap.

Mai-Ling smiled, tried hard not to laugh at his pained demeanour, she'd seen yellow dentures before it wasn't a problem, she seen gapped tooth people too: nurses saw a lot of bizarre stuff.

Panky's sad smile was a picture, a Kodak moment for the brave.

Mai-Ling leaned over and passed him a hand mirror.

Panky held up the mirror, popped the denture back into his mouth in one practiced move. Ten years vanished from his face in seconds, the humourous visage suddenly gone.

Mai-Ling stood by the bed waiting for some reaction; he had to be pleased his face was back together.

Panky peered into the mirror and froze, his face turned white, his hands trembled and tears filled his eyes. He gasped! He sat up suddenly, shocked and open-mouthed. He couldn't believe it! Could not believe it! He was completely bald. Totally fucking bald. Not a single hair on his head, not one and for some weird reason he was wearing striped pajamas, like some old man, like some poor old invalid! Striped pajamas for God's sake! What had they done to him? Was it all part of some cruel experiment? He looked, gasped again at his reflection, shook his head and looked again. Maybe he was having a nightmare? Maybe he was hallucinating again already?   He couldn't be sure, but his thick curly locks had gone, all of them. His pale pate shone slightly with fresh sweat; his heart thumped in his chest, blood seemed to rush and fill his ears, he was dizzy.

"Where... where's my hair? What's going on? What happened to my hair?" he sounded breathless and bewildered, lost and confused.

"I'm sorry," Mai-Ling said, "but we... I... I had to."

"I can't... I can't believe it," said Panky feebly, still clearly shocked, "My hair... my hair's all gone." He let the mirror fall onto the bedclothes and looked down. "It's bad enough that I'm wearing pyjamas... what's *that* all about? Am I eighty years old now or what? Have I been asleep for three days or thirty five years? Am I dying here or what?"

Mai-Ling could see the fear in his eyes; she tried hard not to laugh.

"No... you're not dying, you had twenty eight stitches in your head, that's all," she said, "I had no choice, anyway it suits you... you look younger."

Panky eased his fingers gently across his head, felt the stitches and understood. Twenty eight stitches wow! That was good, probably a record. He'd never had that many before—not all at once anyway. Panky thinking: She said I look younger! OK, now that *can't* be bad!

Panky gave Mai-Ling his biggest smile, beckoned her over to the bed, got her close and whispered in her ear. "I should tell you" he said, serious and dramatic, looking around furtively, like the furniture was listening, "That my grandmother... on her... on her deathbed..."—Mai-Ling smiled sadly—"She told me that... if... and *only* if, a beautiful girl called Mai-Ling ever saved my life... I should marry her straight away... immediately, without hesitation! That's what she said." Panky looked totally sad, eyes like a sick puppy, "Those... were her final words."

Mai-Ling's face stayed close to Panky's, she blushed, looked thoughtful before she spoke. "You're joking aren't you? It's a joke, right?"

Panky held her hand and gazed into her eyes, her softness seemed to penetrate his flesh, seemed to pump life back into his body. For one precious moment he said nothing, just gazed into her eyes, breathed deeply and calmly, squeezed her hand. "Yeah... of course I'm joking," he said, "My grandmother's still alive, at least I think she is, haven't seen her for decades," he grinned and chuckled quietly, "But you are beautiful, very and we are both single and..."

"Clara warned me about you," Mai-Ling said, pulling away from his grasp—just a little reluctance there. She walked across the room with a curious smirk planted on her face, she obviously liked this guy and she knew that he knew it. She talked to Clara a lot about foreign guys, she'd learned a lot.

Panky sat up, swung his legs out of the bed and exhaled, tired from the sudden exertion. He stood unsteadily on the cool marble floor and looked around. He grinned at Mai-Ling and started to stretch his weary body; arms and legs pumped and extended, his head touched his knees, up and down, back and forth, arms and legs akimbo now, working those muscles, stretching and panting. He did about two hours Tai Chi in a couple of minutes and finally stopped.

"Talking of Clara," he said, "I'd better go and apologize, can't be certain, but I don't think she was too impressed with my first day's behavior!"

Mai-Ling smiled knowingly.

"Not a very good start," said Panky, "First impressions and all that... you know?"

Mai-Ling smiled again. Yeah, she knew.

Panky walked through the house in his striped cotton pajamas, out onto the patio, into the bright morning sunlight.

He smelled cut grass, watered plants and sweet, sweet coffee blossom; birds were singing in the trees; the morning air tasted fresh and new. Nice.

Clara was sitting at a table on the patio overlooking the pool, eating breakfast, dressed in a colourful sarong, brown shoulders looking warm in the sun. There was pan de sal and fruit on the table, the fruit looked fresh, colourful and delicious, hot black coffee steamed in a mug that said 'I luv mom' in big red letters.

Panky pulled up a chair and sat next to Clara, his face was pale, pink and sheepish, his scalp was shiny and white, his ears seemed much bigger than before.

"You can join me if you like," said Clara sarcastically as she threw him a fleeting glance.

Panky knew he should've asked first, cursed himself silently. He said, "I'm err... I'm sorry about... about everything... I really am."

Clara looked up from her breakfast and stared at him. Clara with her deadpan morning beauty.

"And err... thanks for... thanks for saving my life." His words sounded mechanical and forced, a little uncertain.

Clara held her stare, her voice was cool and controlled, she said, "That's ok Panky... even *I* couldn't stand by and watch you drown." Clara grinned slightly, almost laughed at the honesty of her words, but she stifled the emotion and looked Panky in the eyes. She said, "Anyway, that was three days ago, I've calmed down now… let's just try and forget all about it, shall we?"

Panky shaded his eyes from the sun, gulped audibly as he nodded a feeble yes and grinned.

"I guess this place does take a little getting used too," Clara added, "It must be…" she searched for the words, "It must be quite an adjustment after a decade in Amsterdam?" Her eyes were on Panky as she ate a small piece of grapefruit; her smile was thin and curt.

Panky wasn't sure if it was the situation or the sharpness of the grapefruit.

Clara blew gently, sipped her coffee, she smiled before she spoke. "I did it for Chris anyway… not for you… he loves you like a brother, probably more," she smiled again, "I can't begin to think why, really."

Panky lowered his bald head as Clara continued, he was sure she still hated him. He was certain of it.

"As a good Catholic I like to think that all *good people* deserve a second chance, don't you Panky?" she said popping a grape into her mouth with Cleopatra nonchalance.

Panky looked up and smiled. Cool, maybe she didn't hate him?

"I'm just not sure if you're actually a *good person* or not," she added, "It's very hard to tell."

Panky lost his smile, stared blankly at the fruit on the table, decided not to say anything about melons, however firm.

"I hope you thanked Mai-Ling," said Clara, she paused for thought, "For some very strange reason she seems to like you."

Panky wasn't sure what to say, decided to play safe and keep quiet.

Clara stood up and gazed blankly at the glimmering pool.

"You can thank her today," she said, "We're going on a boat ride; we're going to an island, ready in 10 minutes, ok?"

Panky said, "Sure, no problema."

"And don't worry, no diving today Panky… I promise."

Panky wasn't sure what to say. He wasn't sure if Clara was serious or having a laugh.

"By the way" she said turning, walking away, "Nice hair cut, you look younger… cleaner!"

Panky wasn't too sure if it was a compliment or not, younger, fine, but cleaner, what did that suggest?

It was the perfect day for a boat ride. The old Banca boat's outriggers crashed and slashed through the waves sending a sheen of clear foaming water high into the air, filling it with soft sounds, pale rainbow colors. The Captain stood in the sunlight, dark and tanned, rigid at the helm, his face was weathered and the color of cigars, his eyes were wide and alert, full of maritime experience. He looked out at the calm, but rippling blue horizon and the old Banca cut and whispered its way through the South China Sea. Behind them in the boats bubbling wake, bright shining silver fish jumped out of the water and flashed into the air, dived in and back out again, gracious, liquid momentum, silverfish sparkling, dancing like mercury against a solid blue sky and back there at the stern the put-put-put of the engine mumbled hypnotically.

Ahead they could see the white dot of the island getting closer and closer, the tops of the coconut palms and banana trees changed slowly from a bright verdant blur to something more vivid and alive, hot sun reflected from the powder white sands of the shore and shimmered.

Panky and Chris sat together on a makeshift seat, shirts off, the sun and the sea in their faces—Panky's borrowed baseball cap protected his shining pate, NYC in bold white letters. Opposite sat Clara and Mai-Ling, bikini clad and beautiful, shaded by a colorful parasol, laughing together at something the guys had missed. They laughed and squealed together as warm clear water sprayed across the boat and soaked them. They were having fun already; the day had hardly begun.

As the island got closer they hung their heads over the sides of the boat like excited kids, saw a colourful world of coral and darting fish below their distorted reflections, silent shapes and gilled animation a feast for their eager eyes.

The island loomed beautiful, verdant, deserted. Perfect white sand glared and glistered, welcomed them to paradise. Not a footprint in sight. Nice.

The boat cruised shallow waters and gushed its way towards the shore. Crunching stones and sand and shells echoed through the old damp timbers of the boat, announcing their arrival to the sea birds circling and hovering above.

The gangplank splashed into the water. The heavy anchor plopped to lower depths. The Captain helped the ladies off the boat, led them through warm shallow water to the gently lapping shoreline.

The Captains' mate carried the large picnic hamper down the gangplank with practiced muscular ease, placed it safely on the beach, smiled and flashed his white teeth at the ladies.

Panky and Chris wobbled down the gangplank, nervous novices, arms out for balance, darting eyes anxious all the way. Clara and Mai-Ling watched, giggled at their wavering lack of style.

The Captain touched the peak of his cap, told them he'd be back later.

The mate retrieved the heavy anchor; the engine came back to life and the boat put-put-putted away, disappeared into the shimmering distance.

Panky looked at happy faces full of achievement and anticipation; they'd made it and a peaceful day in paradise lay ahead. Good food, cool drinks and special company; a day to cherish and remember, a day of tranquility, a day of friends and lovers. That's what Panky wanted anyway.

Clara looked up towards the line of trees swaying in the distance, checked out the sun, chose a place to camp. She looked relaxed, happy like Panky had never seen her before.

Panky thinking: Maybe she's finally buried the hatchet. It was hard to tell.

The guys carried the large wicker hamper. The girls struggled with bags and blankets, laughing all the way.

They made camp.

Once they'd finished getting organised, Panky said, "We're going to find some firewood, see you later."

Clara and Chris looked up as they emptied the hamper, Chris said, "Ok, see you later, purleeeeze be careful."

Mai-Ling and Panky wandered slowly into the heat blurred blue and white distance, walked apart and silent, sharing stolen glances like teenage kids on a first date. Their bodies seemed drawn together, getting closer with one step, moving apart again awkwardly with the next, grinning at what was happening; their hands, like their eyes, seemed out of control; inadvertently touching, fingers drawn together like strange fleshy magnets, each small touch another sentence in their story, they both knew it and were pleased.

Eventually they sat silent on the sand, stared out over the sparkling blue horizon, seabirds overhead like a screeching serenade swooping around; silver strips of sunlight on the blue water, intense heat. Panky lit a cigarette, exhaled a cloud of smoke, twisted his NYC cap in his hands and then played quietly with the shells and stones that lay around his feet.

Mai-Ling looked at him, "Hey, relax."

"Relax?"

"Yeah, relax, you know..."

Panky grinned awkwardly, blew a plume of smoke, "Old people relax Mai-Ling... I've got too much on my mind to relax." He drew heavily on his cigarette, liked saying her name and smiled. "I have heard about relaxing though... like cross stitching and crochet, right? It's for old people isn't it? Sad, *old* people, jigsaw puzzle people... and basket weavers?" he said, laughing, hoping she didn't hear 'basket cases'.

"Why you so worried about getting old?" asked the nurse.

"Am I?" asked Panky genuinely surprised.

"Maybe I'm wrong; that's how it seems..."

Panky interrupted, "Hey, maybe you're right, maybe 'old' does scare me... I like young, I always have, it's fun, right? you can do things… you can make mistakes when you're young—no one minds, they expect it. It's different when you're old, life gets too serious."

"So how old are you? If you don't mind me…"

Panky thinking: At least twenty years older than you sweetheart, maybe twenty five. "Truth is Mai-Ling I'm nearly… nearly fifteen…" he coughed and looked as coy as he could, "I'm fourteen and three quarters actually, tall for my age."

Mai-Ling laughed, stared at him briefly then fell silent.

They stared at the horizon, watched the sea birds circling noisily above; saw them swoop down diving for fish. They sat silent; sharing furtive glances, smiles and sighs. The afternoon slid by like ice cream in the sun.

"Do you like it here?" asked Mai-Ling.

"What's not to like?" said Panky, "Beer's five dollars a case, cigarettes are two packs for a dollar. How bad can that be? I've got a lot on my mind, lots of problems. But I love it here, really I do."

"Problems?"

"Yeah… problems." said Panky, standing up and skimming stones across the water, trying not to feel corny.

"Old problems or new problems?"

"Oh… both."

They remained silent again for a while; the silence wasn't awkward it was just there and Panky skimmed more stones across the water.

"So Mai-Ling, you a psychiatric nurse or what?" he asked.

Mai-Ling chuckled slightly, her turn to look coy, "No, I'm not…" she said, "But when did this all begin?"

Panky grinned at the answer, "Can't be sure… at birth I guess, I was nine months premature."

Mai-Ling laughed again and stared at him.

"You're a funny guy Panky!"

"Funny ha ha or funny peculiar?"

"Funny ha ha," replied the nurse.

"Is that good or bad?"

"Don't worry… it's all good," she said with a smile.

Panky sighed with relief, flicked his cigarette into the sea and wished he hadn't—not an ashtray for miles.

Mia-Ling asked Panky how long he'd been friends with Chris, Panky said since junior school, since they were about six years old, about a million years. She asked him how come they were so close and he said they just were; they'd been through a lot together.

Mai-Ling could see in Panky's eyes and hear in his voice that Chris was so much more than just some old friend he hadn't seen for a while.

Panky went on to explain how Chris' dad used to treat Chris and his little sisters: the beatings, the threats, the intimidation, knocking one of the girls down with a savage back hander just for wearing make up on one occasion and although Chris' dad had never actually hit his mum, how he'd kept her scared, practically terrified, day and night for years, made her life a nightmare. Panky explained that Chris' dad, Mick Taylor, was an ex-paratrooper; he'd served in Korea when he first joined up, he'd seen some action too and he loved to drink and fight every weekend. The guy was a local heavyweight, was never known to back down to anyone or lose a fight; most people were at least wary if not scared of him, especially when he'd been drinking. Panky said that one day he saw Chris' dad chasing Chris around their small garden trying to hit him with a leather belt, apparently Chris had looked at his dad the wrong way during an argument, a case of dumb insolence, a punishable offence according to Mick Taylor. Panky said he shouted and told Chris' dad to leave Chris alone and he did, he left Chris bruised and shaken and turned and chased Panky down the road and through the town, shouting abuse and trying to thrash him with the belt – public displays of domestic violence were perfectly acceptable in small towns in the early seventies.

Mai-Ling sat quiet and amazed, she'd always thought of the UK as a more civilized place.

Panky went on to say that it was outside Mick Taylor's local pub that Panky, aged twelve, had turned and punched Mad Mick –as they called him –on the jaw and knocked him clean out. The best punch –and probably the luckiest for everyone concerned –that Panky had ever thrown. No one could believe it, especially all the drinkers watching the commotion through the pub windows and cheering on Panky. Bizarrely, no one ever saw Mad Mick Taylor after that day, he completely disappeared, vanished; some say he got blown up in Angola a few years later whilst serving as a mercenary, but no one was really sure. Panky told Mia-Ling he hated bullies, asked her not to mention the story to Chris or Clara, said it wasn't something Chris or Panky were particularly proud of despite Chris' mum being over the bloody moon and Chris' sisters celebrating by rushing out and buying loads of make up from Biba.

Mai-Ling smiled, she'd heard all about Panky and what had happened with Mad Mick Taylor, Chris explained it all one night when he was drunk and Clara was looking after the babies, Chris probably didn't remember a thing. Mai-Ling hadn't mentioned it to Clara, thought it best not to get involved in other people's history, she wanted to change the subject, "You must have had a lot of fun in Amsterdam… you and Chris?"

Panky's face lit up with memories, grinned like a manacled masochist. "Of course… it was a crazy. We were crazy, completely broke, but we had the most fun ever, really we did. We were inseparable, me and Chris," he paused for thought, "Batman and Robin meets Laurel and Hardy… on drugs."

Mai-Ling moved closer, rested her head gently on Panky's shoulder. It felt like it belonged there. It felt good. They stared at the blue horizon, silent again for a while.

"What did you do in Amsterdam? What kind of job?" asked Mai-Ling not too sure what to expect as an answer. She knew the truth already, from Clara, she'd heard so much about Panky, but she wanted to hear *his* version.

"What did I do?" Panky paused and decided to be honest, "I was a… I was a dealer."

"Oh a dealer, really? Cards or cars?"

"Drugs," said Panky, "I was a drug dealer, I can't deny it."

Mai-Ling pretended to look slightly shocked, was going to raise her hand to her mouth, but didn't want to over do it.

Panky smiled at her, added, "It's different over in Amsterdam Mai-Ling, it's *all* totally legal—well, ok, some of it's *all* totally legal," he laughed, "What good are rules if you can't break 'em occasionally?"

He grinned, stood up and lifted a large piece of driftwood—big as a small tree almost—onto his shoulder, "Come on," he said, "any more of this and you won't like me any more…"

"Who said I like you?" asked Mai-Ling, hoping she hadn't blown her cover and made it completely obvious that despite his problems and issues that she thought Panky was a complete hero.

He grabbed her outstretched hand and pulled her up.

They walked back to Chris and Clara smiling, hand in hand. Neither of them knew exactly what had happened, but they both knew something had.

The glowing remains of the campfire sent blue gray plumes of smoke spiraling high into the clear blue sky; the smoke smelled sweet against the salt air and the sun beat down relentlessly.

Chris, Clara, Mai-Ling and Panky lay sprawled on tartan beach blankets, content and sleepy after their lavish barbeque. The plates and bottles and bones were cleared and packed away.

It was time to kick back and do nothing.

Before the meal began everyone told Panky exactly how they felt, spelled it out for Panky in no uncertain terms. Chris, Clara and Mai-Ling, all three adamant that he shouldn't drink, avoid alcohol completely they said, just for a few days at least. They reminded him of what the Doctor had said.

Of course he agreed, he said they were right, said he'd be foolish to have a relapse and spoil such a perfect day. He said two or three glasses of wine were all he was going to have, four maximum! Maybe five, he said with a smirk, *if* the sun stayed out. He promised faithfully and added with some authority, that most Doctors actually recommend red wine, on a daily basis! He said red wine was practically medicine, good for the blood *and* the circulation, and anyway he'd taken a double dose of vitamin B, just to be safe.

So after they'd said their prayers and thanked the Lord, they ate and drank to excess: oysters Rockefeller, fresh plump prawns and mussels thick with garlic and butter; giant spare ribs and t-bone steaks sizzled and spat on the open fire. Nice. The sweet smell of smoldering wood mingled with the tangy aroma of herbs and spices; the hot juicy fragrance of slow cooking meat filled the air and tantalised their taste buds, salads and bread and cheeses sat to one side, the choicest of wines flowed freely. It was a beach blanket banquet. They were silent and joyful as they ate.

Long after the meal the wine continued to flow, cool crisp Beaujolais fruity, light and refreshing—Panky said nothing; just kept drinking, praying silently that he'd be ok.

Clara put down her glass, rubbed sun tan lotion onto Chris' broad shoulders.

Mai-Ling shrugged, glanced at Clara hoping for approval and said, "Oh well," and did the same to Panky.

The guys shared satisfied glances, sipped their wine and stared across the glimmering horizon.

Clara and Mai-Ling looked happy and relaxed, flushed slightly by the wine as they massaged their respective men.

Like a lost balloon the afternoon drifted by quietly. Eventually Panky turned and looked at the girls behind him, when he spoke he sounded a little drunk—four or five glasses, yeah! "We're sitting around a campfire, right?" he said, slurring just a tad.

The girls nodded with deadpan faces, wondering what to expect.

"So... it must be time for a fire side story? Right?"

"So tell us what happened to you in Makati," said Clara in a flash, a wicked grin quick on her lips.

Panky glanced at Mai-Ling.

Shit. He'd forgotten all about Makati.

THIRTY FIVE

The fat manager in Mike Hunt's girlie bar in Burgos Street, Makati, was sitting at a table near the bar sweating profusely; looking flushed and nervous, looking scared. Sweat trickled down the fat folds of his face, his jowls glistened in the semi darkness and fear and foreboding filled his beady eyes.

Boris and Vladimir were sitting across the table looking huge and menacing; they were still trying hard to blend in, still wearing their Hawaiian suits and their Ray Bans.

They'd had a long conversation with the fat man; they'd asked him lots of different questions. Was the bar insured against fire? If so, for how much? Were the hospitals good in Makati? Was the fire brigade quick in responding to emergencies? How on earth did fire engines get through all the traffic? Simple questions.

Beyond the atmosphere of their table, the bar was business as usual. The DJ played 'Hot in the city' by Billy Idol, endless girls cavorted on stage and a few lonely men sat grinning at them. It was still quite early, the place was quiet.

Boris flicked his Zippo open and shut, the flint sparked with bright ominous potential, he smiled exposing his bad teeth.

Vlad sipped vodka and watched the girls.

The fat man sat opposite sweating in silence. He wiped his fat face with his handkerchief, grinned and said, "Forget numbers 68 and 69 fellas… they're geezers, blokes… you know what I mean? They're men."

Boris flicked his Zippo, sparks reflected in his dull gray eyes, his teeth looked yellow in the ultra violet light; he seemed strangely entranced by the Zippo and its potential. He continued to stare at the fat man.

The fat man sat silent again, sweated some more.

Boris looked across the bar at numbers 68 and 69, moistened his top lip with his tongue. He didn't care what the fat man said—they looked ok to him, looked just about perfect.

The fat man wiped his face again, nervously continued his pitch, "R… ribs out, s… silicone in, plumbing sorted, plenty of hormones and B… Bob's your uncle… or should I say B… Bob's your aunt…" He laughed and rolled his eyes; his laugh was gingerly and pathetic.

The Russians sat deadpan, not really caring, not even sure what he was on about.

Boris flicked his Zippo; Vlad sipped his vodka, eyes on the 350-pound manager. Boris and Vlad said nothing, just stared at the fat man, watched him sweat. They were having a great time.

"We'll take numbers 12 and 13," said Vladimir eventually, "they're the ones Rommel recommended, the ones from the hotel."

Boris nodded, knocked back his vodka and told a passing waitress to get more and to be quick about it.

The fat man pointed towards the stage and clicked his chubby, sausage fingers.

Numbers 12 and 13 jumped down smiling and joined the guys at their table.

Vlad thought they looked a bit small and thin but good enough despite their age. He said nothing as they draped themselves around him and caressed his substantial muscles.

Boris got his vodka, a large one, sat back, sneered and played with his Zippo again.

The fat man added some diet coke, knocked back his whiskey and sighed heavily. His hands were trembling, the ice in his glass made a faint nervous noise.

Boris pulled a photograph from his pocket, shoved it under the noses of the two young girls. It was Panky and Leary Katz, the photograph he'd ripped from the wall in the houseboat—it seemed like eons ago, but it wasn't.

The girls looked at the photo and then at Boris, back to the photo and then at Vlad, back to the photo and then at the fat man.

The fat man nodded, he wanted the girls to speak up.

The girls looked at the photo again. "Yeah, that's him!" they said, wide eyed and excited.

The fat man wiped his jowls and sighed like only a 350-pound man can, a faint look of relief covered his chubby face like a sudden rash.

Boris finished his vodka in one decisive gulp, put away his Zippo and grinned at Vlad.

Number 13 said, "Ok guys, this is easy… you pay… then we say!"

The girls giggled, delighted at the prospect of easy money, blind to the consequences.

Vlad smiled and blushed slightly as their soft hands went back to his muscles, wandered around the inside of his shirt, tweaked his nipples.

Number 12 smiled and thrust out her pert breasts before she spoke. "Him, his name Jack... Jack Daniel... we know where he go..." she said, pointing to the photograph. "He talk too much, he so stinky... you give us money we tell you where he go... no problema!"

Boris and Vlad smiled and stood up.

Boris beckoned two girls from the stage, told them it was time to leave.

Vlad nodded and said, "Ok, let's go."

The girls giggled at the prospect, they'd never seen such big guys before, they were curious.

The fat man didn't ask the guys for money, the drinks and the girls were on the house.

As the Russian hit men left with four of his best girls and an unpaid tab, the fat man wiped his face with a sticky bar towel—his handkerchief was soaking.

THIRTY-SIX

The sun was glowing orange and slowly sinking; it seemed to be melting, almost dripping into the horizon with the shimmering force of its own heat; around it the sunset was wild and beautiful like shards of glass, diminishing shades of pink and crimson.

Low tide lapped lazily against the pure white sand and left a gentle sibilant whispering in the air. The sea glimmered, shone like a fading dream.

Chris, Clara and Mai-Ling sat around the bonfire still waiting for Panky to speak. They wanted to hear a story, their eyes made it obvious.

The bonfire continued to glow, sent blue gray plumes of smoke billowing up high towards the faint, pale ringed moon.

Panky sat smoking a cigarette, shooting glances at the three of them, searching hard for the right words, caution on his lips for once.

He gulped at his wine glass, puffed heavily on his cigarette and said, "No… no, no… I don't think so, no stories about Makati." He looked around awkwardly, finally fixed his eyes on Mai-Ling and smiled slightly.

Clara sipped at her wine, looked over at Panky and grinned mischievously.

She said, "Ok Panky… we'll forget Makati, for now anyway. Why not tell us a story about the 'Partners in grime' instead?" She sipped at her wine again, eyebrows high with anticipation.

Panky glanced at a nervous Chris as Clara continued.

"A story about your adventures in Amsterdam," she said with calm enthusiasm. "Chris hasn't really explained what you did, you *'Partners in grime'* and I'm, well, I'm just curious... I *am* his wife." Clara gave a smile that could melt a pacemaker; her eyes looked huge and hopeful. "I'm sure you can understand, can't you Panky?"

Panky looked furtively across at Chris.

Chris' eyes screamed: No, no no! His biggest nightmare looming there before him, Chris thinking: She doesn't need to know Panky; just keep quiet, purleeeeze... she just doesn't need to know!

Panky smiled—it was the smile he always used when he felt completely trapped.

He tried to remain calm, but it wasn't easy. The endless flowing wine had taken its toll; he was dying to tell a story! He didn't care which one it was; he had hundreds of them.

Clara's smile, like her eyes, was sly and cunning. It seemed impossible to refuse.

She sipped her wine and stared at Panky knowing he'd just love the chance to appease her.

"Come on Panky... don't be shy," she purred, "Please..."

"No, I'd better not, I like it here... and it's our misadventures rather than adventures believe me!" he said with an anxious smirk.

He glanced over at Chris who was sitting with his knees up tight into his chest, his hands wrapped around his head like a fetus trying to block out the noise of the heartbeat.

Chris turned slowly towards Panky; eyes like a headlight rabbit.

Despite the smoke from the bonfire, Panky smelled fear in the air, Chris' fear.

"Please... Panky," said Clara, her voice sultry and servile. She looked at Mai-Ling and gave a discreet wink.

"Come on Panky," said Mai-Ling, "Chris won't mind, will you Chris?"

Chris' arms fell from his head in a swift defeated move. He picked up his glass gulped his wine and looked out at the sunset.

Panky said, "I would but those days were kind of err... they were kind of sordid," the reluctance to elaborate was thick in his throat.

Chris was no support, staring off into space, gulping his wine.

Clara and Mai-Ling stared at Panky, watched his resilience ebb slowly away like the sun slipping below the horizon.

"And anyway, it's ancient history," said Panky defiantly, lighting a cigarette.

"But we love ancient history, don't we Mai-Ling?" said Clara, quick as a fox, her voice urgent yet whispering.

Mai-Ling sipped her wine, looked up and nodded yes.

Panky pulled on his cigarette, looked over at Chris for help; he was turned away lost in the remains of the sunset.

"Ok... 'Partners in grime' it is!" said Panky, with a clap of his hands and just a touch of false enthusiasm. The houseguest was clearly beaten.

Chris turned, stared at his oldest friend and let out a massive sigh; he was clearly beaten too. He reached over for another bottle of wine and opened it.

"So…" said Panky, "Phew! Where do I start?"

All eyes on Panky now, he stared at his knees and searched for the words.

"Ok, me and Chris…" he said and coughed nervously, "Well, you know we always say we've been through 'a lot of shit together'?"

Clara and Mai-Ling nodded yes.

"Well it's absolutely true… we have… literally."

Clara sat grinning, eager to learn the facts. Chris had never told her *that much* about his 'Partners in grime' adventures. Of course, like any husband, he'd let a few things slip over the years, especially when he used to drink every day, but he'd never really gone into specifics. Clara just loved specifics.

Chris was still turned away from the group, staring off into the distant horizon.

"No, Panky… please… not *the* story!" he shouted, "Spare me! Please! His voice sounded distant and pitiful.

Clara was quick to respond, "Ignore him he's drunk… carry on please… we're listening… the story."

Chris groaned and swallowed more wine, thinking: Dignity? Who needs it anyway?

Mai-Ling and Clara got closer together ready to listen. All ears and grinning.

Panky continued he didn't want to disappoint Clara. Not now, nor Mai-Ling.

"Well… about ten years ago, me and Chris were broke, I mean real broke… almost destitute… this I should add… was just before Chris left me all alone and came here to make his fortune. Right Chris?"

Chris groaned again, said nothing.

"Anyway, we needed some work… we *really* needed some work, *badly* needed some, anything and we tried so hard, we really did, but there was nothing about… nothing at all, zero, and then somehow and God only knows how, I managed to get us jobs at Schipol airport."

Chris turned looked his wife in the eye, groaned and turned away again. Embarrassed.

"So, we've got to go back about ten years… ok? Because, folks… that's when it all began…" Panky hamming it up big time now and clearly having a great time.

Clara and Mai-Ling were waiting and eager.

"Yes, it's…..the infamous adventures… of the 'Partners in grime'," he said with outstretched arms and open hands. He said it proudly, with a deep serious voice as though he was announcing some Oscar winning movie. He grinned at his audience.

Mai-Ling and Clara edged towards the fire slightly; they huddled together and smiled back at Panky. It was getting cooler now; the sky was slowly getting darker.

Panky looked at his audience of two—he couldn't include Chris—and continued.

"Schipol airport… is one of, if not, *the* biggest and busiest airport in Europe," he said waving his hands about like airplanes for effect, "It's a glorious sprawling monument to modernity, all glass and steel and concrete… a high grade, high tech, futuristic beast…"

Panky looked around furtively as though the trees or the fish in the sea were listening, rubbed his hands together and continued in a dramatic stage whisper, "But deep below the surface it's got a secret, very sordid life." He paused and looked over at Chris who was still staring off into the early evening sky, mumbling incoherently like a lost cause. Panky decided to leave him alone and continued on. He was telling the truth; how bad could that be?

He coughed dramatically and continued in a slightly more natural tone, the stage dramatics were over, he'd set the scene and he'd done it well. "It's important to remember that about fifty gazillion passengers arrive at and depart from Schipol Airport every single day and the two of us were smack bang in the thick of it, Chris and me... Partners... 'Partners in grime'... and believe me, it's quite a story, it really is!"

THIRTY-SEVEN

Ten years or so earlier....

The gent's toilets in Schipol airports arrivals lounge was incredibly clean. The long echoing room gleamed and shined, it smelled fresh and untainted; a sea of lustrous white tiles. The sparkling chrome fixtures and the mirrored walls caught the harsh brightness of the fluorescent strip lights and sent it radiating back to its source. Natural sweet forest fragrances and industrial bleaches mixed and blended, a bittersweet aroma filled the warm conditioned air and soft jazzy muzak oozed from the ceiling speakers like warm treacle on a summers day. It was a very classy toilet.

A row of white hand basins sat gleaming in the shining jet-black counter, Panky and Chris stood up against them staring at their reflections in the tall shining mirrors. They both seemed lost, deep in thought. Behind them the endless phalanx of cubicles sat still and silent, doors ajar; they too smelled sweet and shone with a luminous glare.

Panky and Chris drew soap from bright chrome dispensers and washed their hands in silence.

Chris did not look happy. Next to him in mocking contrast Panky wore a small crooked smile and his mischievous eyes shone brightly.

Both guys were clean-shaven now, looking smart in their starched blue pin striped shirts, in their pleated blue trousers. Panky's curls were tied into a small ponytail with a rubber band; Chris wore his hair in his typical short-cropped style. They both looked smart and professional, but tired.

Panky dried his hands on a paper towel; put it carefully in the garbage can. He picked up a pilots cap from the shiny black counter, grinned at Chris in the mirror and put the cap firmly on his head. He turned and marched up and down in front of the mirrors: Hitler impersonations reflecting as he marched, goose-stepping, saluting, and hamming it up. Making quite a show with just one cap, a salute to John Cleese. He did look really funny, but for some reason Chris wasn't laughing.

Chris ignored the goofy goose-stepping and with a surly, sarcastic grin continued to wash his hands. He was tired, getting fed up with Panky's endless antics, sure, he loved the guy, of course he did, they were like brothers, but it was 3 a.m. and Chris was bored and exhausted. Chris leaned closer to the mirror, rubbed his dark tired eyes, pulled on his lower eyelids, looked inside as if he expected to find something strange or unexpected lurking there. There was nothing.

From one of the cubicles behind them a hands free high tech toilet flushed, the powerful sound of gushing water bounced off the tiles and echoed around the room.

Panky turned and grinned at his reflection in the mirror, gave a final phallic stiff armed salute, clicked his heels together and stopped goose-stepping. He removed the cap quickly, returned it to where he'd found it and stood next to Chris again shoulder to shoulder up against the counter.

He removed a cigarette from his pocket, lit it and smoked as he looked at his tired but relatively dapper reflection.

Chris stood gazing into the mirror, dazed, looking a little confused, sighing and groaning.

A tall Dutch pilot appeared from one of the cubicles, the heels of his black leather shoes clicked importantly on the clean tiled floor announcing his approach. He was smart yet macho in his pale blue uniform; his friendly face was pink, pale and confident. He grinned at the guys as he towered above them and washed his hands. He put his cap firmly onto his stylish blond head and sauntered out through the door, heels clicking.

Chris continued to wash his hands; steam rose up and shrouded the mirror, partially blurring his reflection.

"I fuckin' hate this job!" he said fixing his eyes on Panky in the mirror, "Fuckin' hate it! ... I don't know how I let you talk me into it?"

Panky posed in the mirror, left and right profile, checking out his new look.

"Chris, it's simple," he said, "How many times do I have to remind you? We needed the money! And anyway it's not *that* bad!"

Chris turned off the tap, sneered into the mirror.

The guys turned in unison and padded over towards two cleaning trolleys: brushes, cloths, fluids, toilet rolls, dustbin liners and detergents sat like silent weapons.

Chris sighed heavily.

Panky smiled at him.

They each picked up a bright red apron from their trolleys and put them on with clockwork precision. They stood in the sparkling silence and tightened the strings around their necks and waists without looking. It seemed like something they'd done a hundred times before. In white 'go fast' lettering, emblazoned across the front of the aprons it said 'Eeeezzzzzee clean'.

Chris and Panky grabbed their respective mops, finished polishing the white tiled floor as they backed their way out towards the door.

Panky seemed happy with his menial task, handled the mop with an enthusiastic flourish, had quite a professional rhythm going on, but Chris was slow and cumbersome, looked pissed off beyond belief. "Hey! You gotta see the funny side of it," said Panky mopping away happily.

"Thanks for the advice," said Chris, as he mopped, "Your words of guidance make things so much easier… it's mind numbingly boring Panky, but you need a mind to realise it."

Chris stopped mopping, stood erect and spat on the floor that Panky just mopped and smiled his biggest smile.

Panky stopped mopping, looked at the gob and frowned.

"Hey! You gotta see the funny side of it Panky," said Chris, with a broad, sarcastic grin.

The guys laughed together like the old friends they were and mopped their way into the next day.

They were toilet cleaners now, had been for a couple of weeks. Panky thought they might as well make the best of it, why not? They were 'Partners in grime' now, he loved that phrase, and at least as far as *he* was concerned, the adventure had just begun. They wandered through the massive, practically empty airport, pushing their trolleys ahead of them.

It was quiet now; the place seemed bigger, brighter than ever and they chatted and smiled at the occasional girl as they meandered across a huge expanse of floor. They knew that as long as they kept moving they looked busy and that was good; every night between toilet blocks they strolled around for as long as they could; the endless floors seemed to be crying out for a polish, but they managed to ignore the cries.

To Chris it was a tedious, thankless job that never ended. He looked sour faced and despondent as he struggled along with his rattling cart, dirty water splashing about all over the place. Chris could've been happier, much happier, easily—it was clear to see. But Panky was loving life. He looked upon the place as a vast and colourful playground and as they plodded along with their carts he kept reminding Chris that the airport was a fantastic place to work, said it was full of exciting opportunities, a place where all sorts of crazy stuff happened. Panky went on and on and on about it, but his friend wasn't listening.

Chris didn't care too much about Panky's 'positive view' on things; he was fed up with hearing about it. But to Panky, the job was never dull, how could it be? There was always some new kind of madness going on somewhere, plus, and most importantly, it was a chance to see life from a totally new perspective.

To Chris it was tedium personified. It was smelly too. Like sniffing around the arse hole of humanity Chris said.

Panky disagreed, he said people would be amazed if they knew what went on in airport toilets—and of course he was right. They'd be amazed; they'd be mortified; especially with the airport toilets just a few minutes away from Amsterdam's red light district. Plus, Panky also kept reminding Chris, the money was good, really good. If they worked weekends and the graveyard shift and did overtime, even after taxes the money was excellent. Panky kept saying, "What's wrong with spending your life in toilets if the money's good? Someone's got to do it? Right?"

Chris didn't reply. He just wasn't a toilet person.

But despite Chris' initial reluctance the 'partners' worked every chance they got: late nights, early mornings and long, long weekends, they didn't care. It was a working sleeping couple of months, and they'd come to terms with it. They had no choice.

"It's a temporary sacrifice, not a strategic fucking career move," said Panky and he was right, a sacrifice driven by looming destitution, driven by the simple need for a little money.

Of course, the guys both knew that you *can* get by fairly easily without money in Amsterdam, *if* you know the right people—God knows they had and for months—but like any city full of vice and temptation it's not so much fun when the only thing in your pockets is your hands.

Like most wonderful opportunities the job had its drawbacks, had its risks. They'd often have to get up at 3 a.m. and walk through the eerie darkness of the ghetto—the ghetto where they lived—to get to work. The infamous Biljmer, concrete jungle personified, the very place where the 747 full of jet fuel crashed into the neighbouring tower block while Panky was watching 'The Antiques Road show' on BBC TV, bar-b-qued hundreds of poor –mostly immigrant– people. It was a high-rise, high-risk sprawl: especially risky for a couple of white boys. It took about 5 minutes to get to the bus stop if you were quick—if you were lucky.

They knew it was a dangerous place to be at such an ungodly hour, a very dangerous place, everyone they knew had warned them, but they didn't seem to mind, didn't seem to care. They seemed unconcerned, wandering around in the partially lit passageways, among the twenty storey tower blocks, graffiti and litter, desperation all around; it didn't seem to bother them.

So they'd plod towards the bus stop, their early morning spliffs numbing the pain of it all, grinning at mad junkies as they ambled along, laughing at strung out muggers lurking brutal in the bushes, hiding in acrid shadows, huddled in hallways—bottom-feeding predators looking for some action. It didn't seem to worry the 'Partners in grime' a bit. In fact they seemed strangely excited by the prospect of some real and sudden violence, seemed exhilarated by it, like they wanted shit to happen. It wouldn't have mattered much if they did care—if they were scared, because they had no choice, they had to work, it was a money thing. If the bus was leaving at 3 a.m. they had to be on it.

So they'd stroll through the cold early morning, the breeze bitter on their sleepy faces, toothpaste breath spiraling ahead of them strangely animated against the orange street lights and they'd march towards the distant sanctity of the bus stop. There they'd wait patiently for the womb like warmth and the safety of the bus.

Once aboard the bus, the routine was simple: head for the back and doze until they got there. They agreed it felt weird being the only white boys on the bus, the minority, two white faces in an ocean of black and brown ones. One of the wasted white boys always clutching a wrinkled plastic bag, clutching it like a ravenous street person; their boring meager sandwiches wrapped carefully, smelling like farts: eggs every day.

Once there they'd don their uniforms, stock up their trolleys and they were off. Off into a world of toilet bowls, strange sickening smells, sanitary napkins and anal deposits. Chris always complaining about the arrivals blocks being the worst, always saying how much he hated arrivals. Always saying he wasn't sure if it was the 'cordon bleu' food, the copious amounts of alcohol or just the altitude that turned people's stomach contents into a potent mixture of diarrhea and napalm. Maybe it was the combination of all three? It was hard to tell. Once off the long haul flights untold passengers would make a wild dash for the toilet and explode in gratified unison. Many of the passengers had clearly never seen such high tech toilets before, many of them made it abundantly clear they were used to little more than a hole in the ground. Some even stood on the seats and shat from a distance and that's not easy.

Panky kept reminding Chris to look beyond the job and consider the perks, because the perks were good. The best perks Panky had ever had. He really liked the perks. To him that's what it was all about, the real excitement was in all the drugs they kept finding and God only knows they found a lot! They learned a lot in their first couple of weeks in the toilets. They learned fast like street people do. It seemed that loads of passengers 'considered' smuggling drugs out of Amsterdam and 'considered' was the key word. Some did it successfully, but fortunately most failed.

Chris and Panky witnessed dozens of people being dragged off for cavity searches and shakedowns—great fun to watch—remorse and regret in their frightened eyes. Ha! But when push came to shove the majority of 'would be' drug smugglers would get half way there and then bottle it, they'd chicken out.

And where would they dump their stash once the paranoia had set in? In the airport of course.

And where in the airport? In the toilet, where else?

But it wasn't all fun and games. Oh no!

Dragging half dead junkies out of the toilets in departures was a regular recurring headache.

The pathetic sight and sickening smell of faeces and vomit covered junkies was never the biggest of laughs! No perks there! They agreed on that!

The 'Partners' agreed too, that they'd never forget the kid they found early one morning slumped on a toilet bowl, a needle stuck in his scrawny riddled arm. The kid maybe twenty-five at most, looking at least a hundred years old—maybe more, looking like the world had betrayed him, maybe it had? His head titled backwards in the flickering gloom of the cubicle, red veined eyes rolled back into his head like he'd been dead for hours; saliva and vomit like tiny twisted streamers hanging from his crooked useless mouth.

Chris and Panky jumped in unison, both gasped out loud with shock when the kid suddenly jerked towards them, blinked his tragic eyes and mumbled, "Leave me!"

They did as he asked—they left him. That wasn't much of a laugh.

The problem was that anyone could hang out in departures, anyone, some people even lived there. One guy slept in the toilet every night for months, curling up around the bowl, newspaper for a pillow, but he was easy to handle, no trouble at all, never left any mess, always smiled at the guys and said hello, how ya doin'? Thanks for giving me a break guys, thanks for not turning me in. One day he explained to the guys his mother was a Moroccan whore and his father a French alcoholic, he said it with laughter in his eyes. They liked him, admired his honesty.

But after a while even Chris didn't mind handling the burnouts and the low lifes, it was just another part of the job. Like cops and robbers, you got used to it.

But the 'Partners' never got used to finding endless bags of grass and hashish. Perks. They were finding so much stuff they didn't have to buy any. They were constantly wasted. To the guys it was the weirdest kind of heaven, they were never quite sure if any of it was real or if it was just some crazy dream they were sharing, they used to pinch each other and laugh hysterically. They had tons of little plastic bags full of stuff to smoke, tons of them, so much so they were giving it away. They were even paying the rent in the ghetto with what they found; their Persian landlord was perpetually wasted.

Things were looking up. Things were working out.

Early one morning Panky was hurtling along on his trolley, laying across the top among the dustbin liners and the cleaning agents, arms and legs stretched out like a wounded star fish, a born again juvenile stoned out of his mind with mops and buckets and bottles rattling in his ears as he hammered through the departures gates, a manic look pasted across his face.

Chris was in the distance pushing his squeaky trolley, still looking pissed off and tired, still fed up with Panky's antics, dirty water splashing out of his buckets onto the floor as he trundled along, Chris not noticing or caring.

Panky was way ahead and gaining momentum. He was moving and fast!

Chris watching, thinking: If he runs someone over they'll be dead for sure! But he couldn't help crack a smile as he watched Panky getting faster and faster and faster, like some crazy twisted arrow, heading straight for the next toilet block to be cleaned, hacking and rattling headlong towards the open door.

The airport was always quiet at this early hour, Chris heard Panky's voice echo across the expanse of floor ahead of him.

"I just love the smell of toilets in the morning!" he shouted madly as he sped towards the fluorescent glare emanating from the open toilet door. The trolley clattered along at astonishing speed, Chris saw it ease through the doorway and vanish into the toilet block with a harsh resounding crash. He then heard an echoing clang, twisted metal on ceramic tiles and uncontrollable hysterical laughter from Panky! Panky was a fucking lunatic and Chris loved him.

One night Chris and Panky sat in the departures toilet block. They sat up on the counter with their backs against the mirrors, aprons off and spliffs alight. They'd thrown out a couple of sleeping vagrants, regulars who didn't argue, put the Cleaning Keep Out sign on the front of the door, locked it and were taking a break. It wasn't the nicest place to be on a Saturday night, especially before they'd done the cleaning, but it was the last block on the shift and they were tired. What can you do?

They sat against the tarnished mirrors among discarded hand towels and litter and smoked and giggled like schoolboys as desperate anguished passengers rattled on the toilet door bursting for a piss. They both had dustbin liners hidden away under their carts, bags full of goodies, their night's findings.

"So what've you got then?" Chris asked Panky.

Panky exhaled a billowing cloud of super smoke, slid down off the counter, lifted his bag off his trolley and opened it.

"Well… strictly on the drugs side of things," he said, in his earnest and serious TV anchormans voice, "I've got eleven bags."

He held them up for Chris to see and continued, "Mostly super skunk, way too smelly to smuggle externally."

Chris grinned. Not too bad!

"Plus four bags of hash and…" Panky dug deep into the bag, "… a nice big lump of Moroccan, zero zero if I'm not mistaken!"

Panky held it up.

Chris was impressed.

"I found it just sitting in an ashtray, in the bar," said Panky, his face riddled with wonder and disbelief. "Plus… I found twenty grams of Mexican speed… ariba, ariba," he held up the bulging plastic bag full of dirty white crystals, "And a big bag of pills." He held the bag up high like a proud fisherman.

Chris lifted an eyelid, whoa… maybe it was ecstasy again? Big money!

His partner preempted him, "I don't know what they are yet… but I'll try a couple when we get home, I'll let you know!"

Panky clutched his plastic bin liner lovingly; his face was flushed with success. He'd had a pretty good night.

Now it was Chris' turn to show and tell. But it wasn't all drugs that they found. Oh no! Between them they found untold treasures of a far more sexual nature too, things from the ruder side of the red light district. They found hundreds of porno mags, hundreds, mostly in good condition, just a few with the pages stuck together; dildos were two a penny, some used and slightly hairy, others in pristine condition—the only box they'd ever seen was the one they were purchased in. They found flaccid inflatable women, wicked leather bullwhips, nip clips, clit zips and sweat stained latex lingerie. They even found a selection of knob enlarging pumps.

They'd often sit back and laugh, amused by the thought of getting caught red handed smuggling a knob enlarger out of the country, caught by those serious faced fuckers in customs.

But it wasn't just weird erotic gadgetry either; they found a cornucopia of clothes, shoes, hats, umbrellas, books, empty wallets, photograph albums. You name it, they'd probably found it. A never-ending supply of pre-flight flotsam and jetsam, intimate bits and pieces of people's lives: the lost, the neglected, the forgotten and the discarded.

Chris finished his spliff, flicked it onto the floor among the litter, and slid down off the counter. He strolled towards the seemingly endless row of cubicles and pushed the doors open one by one, a dull thudding sound echoed around the dirty toilet. Chris' practiced pace and timing was perfect, finally all the doors stood ajar.

"Are you ready geezer?" asked Chris, with rare enthusiasm.

"Always ready mate," said Panky, with his familiar mischievous grin.

The guys stood together at the first cubicle, peered inside with hopeful eyes.

"Go on then," said Chris.

Panky entered the cubicle, jumped up and stood on the toilet seat with his back against the wall, looking out at Chris watching him. He put his hands above his head and carefully ran his fingers along a small unintentional shelf above him; at a stretch he could just about reach.

The shelf, or the space, enabled the cubicles fluorescent strip light to be changed.

If you knew about it, it also provided an excellent hiding place.

"Anything?" asked Chris, as Panky slid his fingers carefully along the shelf.

"No… nothing," said Panky as he jumped down and stepped out of the cubicle. His tone was serious and professional now like a bomb disposal expert, "And luckily no more hidden syringes!" he said.

It was Chris's turn next; he did cubicle number two, same ritual, same moves, exactly.

Chris jumped down and stepped out of the second cubicle.

"Zero, zilch, nada!" His voice was deep and serious too, like an FBI agent or someone on C.S.I. It was a game they always played, it made searching more fun.

Panky tried the third stall, back against the wall, boots planted firmly on the seat, fingers on the ledge, Chris' hopeful eyes watching his every move.

"Hello, hello... what have we got here then?" said Panky with his arms in the air, fingers moving carefully along the ledge. His voice was normal now; the silly voice game was over. They'd found something and it was looking big! Time for serious.

Panky's eyes were full of mischief, mayhem and delight as he pulled the long package carefully off the shelf.

Chris stood open mouthed, arms akimbo, eyes full of anticipation.

Panky jumped down, stepped out of the cubicle and held the package gently, but firmly in both hands, like an injured bird.

It was the size of a half baguette, wrapped carefully in newspaper, taped tightly with gray ducting tape, the type kidnappers and serial killers use.

Panky looked at the package carefully.

Chris grinned.

"It's wrapped in today's newspaper," he said to Chris, "So it hasn't been here long."

The guys just stood there and stared at each other.

Chris said, "Come on then geezer, let's get the fucker open!"

They rushed over towards the jet-black counter and laid the package down as carefully as you would a newborn babe. Their faces were flushed and expectant in the mirror; the air full of sweat and testosterone, thick with anticipation.

Panky took a switchblade knife, a flick knife, out of his pocket and clicked it open, the thin metallic click echoed around the room like the sound of a broken stick.

The 'Partners in grime' stood silent and still, looked at the parcel, then at each other.

"Go on then! Do it!" said Chris.

Panky edged forwards, the bright steel blade shone in fluorescent light. He looked back at Chris.

"Go on!"

The blade slid into the package with ease, sliced through the tape and paper without a sound. Panky looked at Chris with wide eyes and gulped audibly. Chris looked back at Panky, expelled the air from his lungs slowly.

Crystal white powder trickled from the parcel onto the jet-black counter.

Chris and Panky stood speechless; big eyes, open mouths and panting hot breath.

Panky looked away from the package and stared at Chris, "Go on, try it… but not too much, it might not be coke."

Chris smiled, "Looks like coke to me!"

"Me too mate, but you never know… just watching your back geezer."

Chris grinned, licked his index finger, dipped it into the spilled powder, tasted it and smiled like he'd just lost his cherry.

"Nose candy or what?" he said, pulling a twenty-guilder note from his pocket, rolling it up with precision, "Someone's in BIG, BIG trouble!"

Panky said, "Yeah, and it's probably us!" They laughed together and snorted huge lines of coke with casual expertise.

Chris was sniffing and gagging and swallowing, "Bolivian fuckin' marching powder or what? he said, "This stuff's the dog's bollocks."

Panky watched as Chris panted and wiped the cold sweat from his brow, said, "This shit's so good its scary, it's so good... it *needs* cutting."

The guys laughed, slapped each other on the back and did some more.

With their heads down busily snorting their enormous stash of Bolivian mood enhancer, neither of them heard the toilet door open.

Neither of them heard the footsteps quietly approaching, neither of them saw the small anxious Greek guy called Dimitrious poke his head around the tiled corner. They didn't see him watching as they filled their cavernous nostrils with copious amounts of coke, giggling like loons.

Dimitrious peered around the corner, his face full of panic and terror, he was sweating buckets, looking wired to the max; in his hand was the passkey he'd stolen earlier from a trolley left parked in the bar. He was a sneaky character and he looked it.

As the anxious Greek watched the guys doing his coke, his blue eyes turned wild and his breathing got increasingly laboured. With his black stubble, his balding pate and his numerous shiny gold earrings he looked like a traveling gypsy. A lost travelling gypsy.

Dimitrious inhaled deeply, puffed out his chest and turned the tiled corner. He stood in the harsh fluorescent light, watched Chris and Panky as they wiped their noses and fooled around.

The Greek pulled a large commando knife from his waistband and shouted, "Give me my coke you son of bitches!"

The guys looked up at Dimi's reflection in the mirror, slowly turned around to face him. They couldn't believe it. How did the fuck did the guy get in?

Chris had coke and a big stupid grin all over his face, he couldn't stop sniggering and sniffing.

Panky sniffed, turned his head, looked at Chris and laughed. He couldn't help it!

Chris looked straight ahead at the wired looking Greek, saw him hold up the big commando knife, saw him wave it menacingly.

Chris turned his head slowly and looked at Panky with a 'what now geezer?' expression, wiped his face, removed the coke and the grin.

"Give me the fuckin' coke or I'll cut your throats, rip out your hearts and shit on the milk of your grandmother's breasts!" bellowed Dimi, slashing the blade around viciously, showing how he'd do it, making it glisten and shine in the fluorescent glare.

Panky chuckled and stared the little Greek in the eyes, thinking: Ok, so the guy's small and theatrical, but he's still got a weapon, but has he got the balls and the ability to use it? Panky stared him in the eyes some more, thinking: The guy's a joke, he's not even close to threatening, he's not even holding the fucking knife properly.

Chris looked at Panky and then back to the Greek.

"We were just about to hand it in," said Chris, sniffing again, wiping the residue from his left nostril.

Panky looked at Chris and nearly laughed out loud, the way he said it, all that innocence in his voice, all that powder in his nostrils. Funny as fuck!

Panky and Chris stood frozen waiting for the little guy to make his move; he didn't really look a problem, but who knows? A big knife can do a lot of damage. Chris and Panky had seen it happen a couple of times and it wasn't nice.

"So… you're gonna shit on the milk of our grandmother's breasts are you?" said Panky, with a tone of total disbelief, "What's *that* all about?"

The scatalogical Greek looked down at his trainers, embarrassed, "It's err, it's a Greek thing," he said, obviously not too proud of his choice of words. He grinned as if he was sorry.

Chris and Panky relaxed. Neither of them had to say the guy's a clown and a loser, they both knew it. It was instinct.

"Give me the powder mother's fucker!" the diminutive Greek suddenly shouted, waving his blade about, trying to sound scary.

Panky and Chris tried hard to hold back their laughter.

Dimi suddenly lunged forward.

Chris and Panky backed off a little, still grinning.

"Look you fucking toilet cleaners," said the knife wielding coke mule, trying his best to sound tough and frightening—it wasn't working. He shouted, "If I don't catch the next flight to Athens I'm a dead man… ok? You got that? I'm a dead man!"

Panky looked at his partner and smiled. Ok, now the Greek had definitely blown it. Wrong words. Not only was he looking for sympathy, but sweat trickled from his furrowed brow, his hands were shaking like a carp out of water, his eyes were welling up like he was about to cry—these were not the qualities of a hardened street fighter.

Panky's shoulders moved up and down slightly as he giggled quietly.

Chris saw him laugh and he knew what would come next. He'd seen it all before, so he wiped the coke off his top lip, gagged hard on the residue in the back of his throat and waited quietly for Panky to make his move.

Panky held up his hands, "Oi Zorba! Chill out man… put the blade away, take the coke, we don't even like the stuff!"

Chris gagged this time on stifled laughter, made a strange noise in his throat like tearing sackcloth.

"I mean it," said Panky, "Take it man, it's yours… hey, we're sorry, just put the blade away, ok? We're, err…we're…"

"We're pacifists," said Chris, with a smile and a wink and a sniff.

The Greek lowered the knife and his eyes. He moistened his lips, smiled with naïve arrogance. He stepped forward towards the guys and the big parcel of coke behind them. On his very first step forward Panky lunged at him, and hammered him with two beautiful punches. *Whack*! The first punch was on the nose, breaking the bone and splitting the flesh; blood sprayed into the air, covered the crazy Greek's face in seconds and gave him a dark and sticky devils mask. *Whack*! Another punch followed instantly, a great left hook, fast and accurate, right on the jaw. Knocked the guy unconscious, smashed out two or three of his teeth, split his gums top and bottom. His legs turned to rubber and he dropped to the ground, a bantamweight loser in a heavy weight contest.

Panky and Chris shared a quiet moment; shook their heads sadly in phony remorse, looked at the Greek slumped on the floor in a bloody heap. Out for the count.

Panky grinned at Chris but didn't say a word. He kicked the knife out of harms way, picked the Greek up by the seat of his pants and his collar and dragged him casually towards a cubicle. He grinned broadly at Chris as he threw the Greek inside the toilet like a sack of potatoes. He locked the door, put up an Out of Order sign and sauntered back towards the coke, wiping his hands together and smiling like nothing had happened.

Chris was back at the counter already, snorting some more coke, laughing like a madman. He looked up at Panky with big shiny eyes, giggled stupidly, passed him a twenty-guilder note and then snorted some more.

When Panky had finally done snorting, he looked up, wiped the residue off his nose, smiled and said, "No one... and I mean no one, shits on the milk of my grandmother's breasts!"

THIRTY-EIGHT

Back on the beach, it was cooler and dark now. The wind was scattering thin yellow clouds fast across the face of the moon, stars shone high in the sky; the only sound was the tide lapping gently on the shore, the water whispering through the sand, the occasional crackling ember from the bonfire.

Panky, Clara, Mai-Ling and Chris sat much as before. Chris was curled up in a ball in the sand, clutching his wine bottle.

Clara and Mai-Ling sat stunned.

"I said the story was sordid didn't I?" Panky said proudly.

Clara and Mai-Ling smiled politely, sipped their wine.

"Now of course not every day was that much fun, if only... most of the time it was just mop until you drop," said Panky, "And then back to the ghetto for a kip, a sleep..."

Clara and Mai-Ling smiled politely again, sipped their wine again. They were both a little shocked.

"We found two hundred and fifty grams of primo marchin' powder... cocaine," he explained, "The stuff was so good that we had to get it cut! Our mate Jason said it was the best coke on the streets and that's saying something in Amsterdam."

Mai-Ling and Clara weren't too sure what he was on about now, so they said nothing.

Chris just lay in a heap.

"We sold half of it that night and stuck the rest up our noses!" said Panky, like a boastful athlete. "It seemed the only sensible thing to do," he added, "And what a month that was, I can tell you!"

Mai-Ling and Clara grinned a little empathy, sipped their wine and stared at the bonfire.

"But… that was the beginning of the end for the 'Partners in grime'" Panky said sadly, "The beginning of the end… You see, every day we took more and more coke, we had so much of the stuff it was hard not to, impossible. And every day we promised, promised, promised ourselves…" said Panky, spanking his hand on the blanket for emphasis, "We promised each other that as soon as it was gone, that would be it… we wouldn't buy any more! No way!"

Clara and Mai-Ling smiled, sipped and stared.

Panky looked across at Mai-Ling, saw the shadows of the fire flickering and highlighting the contours of her face, she looked amazing.

He wondered if he should end the story before he dug himself into a hole. Maybe he'd already done it, he wasn't sure. He was drunk so he continued: "So after about a month, when it was all gone…"

"We went straight out and bought some more," shouted Chris from the shadows.

Panky smiled, pleased that his partner was back. He'd missed him.

"I hope you ladies understand that we *had* to snort what was left… what we didn't sell," said Panky, "We *had* to snort it… we just had to, it was a gift from God! Even Chris said so!"

Clara and Mai-Ling looked over at Chris who had turned around to face the fire now.

"I didn't say it was a *gift* from God Panky! I said it was a warning from God!"

Clara and Mai-Ling smiled, looked relieved.

"Talk about funny stories," said Panky, totally ignoring Chris, standing up and swaying a little, "There was me, Chris and this fat girl from Birmingham…"

Chris said, "I think we'd better get back now guys… I think we've had enough stories for one day?"

THIRTY-NINE

The journey back was quiet and uneventful, except when Chris slipped drunkenly off the gangplank and fell into the sea. He was a little shocked and very wet, but he was ok.

Once the Banca boat had docked safely, they unloaded all the picnic stuff and stepped back onto dry land. They paid—and over tipped—the Captain and his mate; thanked them for a job well done and all agreed it had been a wonderful day. Memorable. Everything Panky had hoped for.

On the way back Clara phoned Boy to collect them and he was at the dock, waiting with the Range Rover and a big smile.

Boy knew some short cuts, so getting back to the house was quicker than usual. It was quiet too, almost silent, apart from the snoring and the grinding of Panky's teeth. Everyone seemed exhausted.

When they eventually arrived, Chris and Panky slid out of the car and agreed that a nightcap before bed was both essential and an excellent idea.

"Come on, let's go to my den," slurred Chris, dressed now in old khaki shorts and a ripped black muscle shirt, looking totally disheveled and more than a little weary, "I've got some Chivas needs drinking."

Panky was keen and right behind him.

They stumbled through the house.

Panky thought the idea of a grown man having a den was a little odd, but he said nothing.

Chris and Panky had a den when they were twelve years old that was the last time Panky had been in one, he wasn't too sure what to expect.

But the den was pretty cool: comfortable sofas, Persian rugs, exotic plants, a massive TV, a stereo with giant speakers, a DVD player, a computer system, a very well stocked refrigerator, an espresso machine. State of the art everything. Impressive.

Panky couldn't help but notice an array of colourful L.P. covers hung in neat rows across one wall, framed in black; they caught his wandering eye as soon as he staggered into the room. He wasn't sure if it was because of their 'Long Player' size, but for some reason they seemed dated, seemed a little tragic.

Panky cracked a smile, tried not to feel old. He saw photographs and tabloid clippings too. What had once seemed controversial and exciting now looked faded, sad and tame. Nevertheless there it was, a shrine to punk; the distant past in fading pictures—Chris and Panky's past—their misspent youth. More than thirty years ago. It made Panky's head spin. Phew! A sudden flood of memory. He screwed up his eyes, tilted his head slightly, tried to focus on the vivid display. He swayed and sighed heavily as the artwork screamed at him from the wall, as it gouged at his tired eyes and jangled his nerves. All he wanted was a nightcap. He didn't expect all this emotional shit. He stood ponderous and philosophical. It was a rare moment.

He looked at the album sleeves and smiled drunkenly at his erstwhile heroes: The Sex Pistols, The Clash, The Damned, The Stranglers, The Cure, The Ruts, The Slits, The Fall, The Boomtown Rats, The Undertones, Crass and Generation X. Dark and ominous names from a dark and ominous era.

Panky stared at the album covers, thinking: First-generation TV kids. That's why we were punks, kids with no future; we saw so much on TV and no one even realised. He blinked and looked back at his childhood, thinking: growing up with the horrors of Vietnam on TV night after night wasn't easy, and then there was Charlie Manson's gang, how scary was all that stuff for little kids? Those Helter Skelter eyes! So much for hippies and the love generation? And every night the media cheerfully reminded us that the bomb could drop tomorrow or maybe the next day, or maybe the day after that. Where exactly did "make love not war" fit in? Panky thinking: we had nuclear holocaust on our lips, Big Brother on our minds, 1984 was just around the corner and we were shit scared about the future— George Orwell and Margaret Thatcher had a lot to answer for. No wonder our generation was confused, he thought, we'd gone from counter culture revolution to disco. That's quite a leap.

Panky jerked from his late night reverie, looked over at Chris who was propped up against the wall with the bottle of Chivas clenched in his hand. Panky watched him staring at the shrine to punk, saw his eyes in some distant trance, saw him smile almost sadly.

Chris smiled, wondered where they'd all gone: the punks, the bands, the vinyl revolutionaries, the crazy kids ripped on speed and warm beer, the kids that dreamed of anarchy, kids with nothing to lose. Where were *they* now? Chris took a swig from the Chivas and belched, he'd seen Sting on Oprah telling everyone what a great shag he is now despite his age and his baldness, he'd watched Bono prancing around saving continents single handedly—far out and good for Bono—but where were all the others? Where were the rebellious punks that hadn't become respectable, middle-aged household names? Where were The Mekons, Scritti Politti, The Buzzcocks, and ATV?

Chris took another swig, passed the bottle to Panky and let out another enormous belch; he preferred to keep the memories of the past out of his head, too much turmoil, and way too much anguish. He was too old for all that now. The shrine to punk was purely decorative, just for show; it wasn't there to make you think. The world was a different place, thought Chris; it wasn't much better, but at least it was different.

So with both the future and the past unresolved, Chris and Panky slumped down into the cushions of the large sofa, sighed deeply in unison and chuckled together. Their tired drunken eyes said: Fuck the past, there's nothing much you can do about it anyway, not then and certainly not now. They drank more Chivas.

The room was peaceful, cool and comfortable; ideal drinking conditions, they finished half the bottle with ease.

Panky said: "You know, it's weird being straight all the time."

Chris: "What do you mean... all the time?"

Panky: "You know, *all... the... time...*"

Chris: You've only been here four days, that's not exactly all... the... time... is it?"

Panky: "All right then, it's weird being straight for four days."

Chris: "Four days... yeah, that's quite an accomplishment? You must be kind of proud?"

Panky: "Course I'm proud."

Chris: "But hang on... if I remember correctly... on your first day here, you got stoned and just a little drunk and then busted, all within an hour of leaving the house... so I guess that day doesn't really count? Does it?

Panky almost grinned.

Chris continued: The *next* three days, and again tell me if I'm wrong, please, but the next three days you were either unconscious or asleep... right? So I guess they don't really count either do they?"

Panky raised an eyebrow, swigged on the Chivas.

Chris: "So I guess what you're really trying to say, is that its strange being straight... today?"

Panky wasn't sure whether to laugh or be indignant.

He said: "Well it is, it's strange but nice... it's different... but it's ok. I can handle it, I'm surprised."

They sat in silence for a while. The night breeze filled the room from the open balcony doors, the moon was pale and yellow; crickets and cicadas did their noisy thing, filled the room with distant electric pulses. The guys continued to drink, enjoying the quiet and the Chivas.

Panky wanted to ask Chris how he'd made his money. He was still dying to find out, but decided maybe it wasn't the right time. They were too drunk. He wanted to explain to Chris what had really happened in Manila too, the problems with the girls and all that, but he decided to save it. Wait for a better time for all that too. Maybe though, maybe it was a good time to tell Chris why he was there, tell him about all the death and disasters in Amsterdam; but then again maybe not—so many maybes.

He grabbed the Chivas from Chris and swallowed a mouthful. Sometimes it's just best to say nothing.

Chris was sprawled out on the big cushioned sofa, dirty bare feet up on the glass-topped coffee table, between the Buddha's and the candles. He sighed, looked up and said, "Panky… I've got a confession to make." Truth was Chris wanted Panky's confession, wanted to know all about what happened in Amsterdam. Wanted to know why Panky had run from the place he loved so dearly. Basically Chris wanted the dirt; he thought that preempting the situation was a good idea, thought it might get the ball rolling.

Panky grinned and rubbed his hands together, he loved confessions, plus Chris was very drunk, so it could be a good one.

Chris continued in a sad confessional tone: "I've become Americanized dude, I mean Panky!"

Panky wanted to laugh and if Chris hadn't looked so sad he would've.

Chris said: "I couldn't help it… I'm sorry Panky, but everyone here just loves America… they're mad about the place, they think it's heaven…they all want a taste of the American Dream."

Panky was close to laughter, but he didn't have the heart. Chris seemed so worried, seemed so affected and serious. Panky let him continue.

"I call a lift an escalator now, Panky… I do really, I can't help it… I call the fucking pavement the sidewalk… I do! I call autumn fall, I call a full stop a period, and the boot of the car's a trunk and it gets worse Panky, believe me, much worse... I even know what a semester is!"

Panky tried his best to keep a straight face; listened as Chris rambled on, tried his best to look sympathetic.

Chris carried on, explained his problem some more: said that instead of saying twenty he said twenny now, couldn't help it! Tomatoes were tom-ay-toes, sweets were candy, petrol was gasoline and nappys were diapers. He called his family guys—it didn't matter that two of them were female—and worse, he called his wife and his daughter honey pie and pumpkin, called his son big guy or big fella, even though he was small. It was never ending, half the time he sounded like John fucking Wayne. He said he was so embarrassed, said he even sat in his LayZeeBoy and watched Oprah four times a week, eating Oreos and Doritos, drinking Snapple.

"Hey, don't worry about it, I watched Oprah once," said Panky, "It doesn't mean a thing! Fuhgettaboutit! Capiche?"—Sounding like Joey from 'Friends' now.

Chris wiped the tears from his eyes, wondered if Panky was taking the piss or not, wondered if he'd like a knuckle sandwich, a quick smack in the mouth?

They sat in silence and drank more Chivas.

Panky lit a cigarette, still not sure if Chris was putting him on, busting his balls, or as he preferred to say, having a laugh. But he was pleased he hadn't mentioned The Lord yet and prayed they'd avoid theology altogether.

Chris held his head in his hands, looked distraught.

Panky thinking: Maybe living in this jungle seclusion's affected him? Chris's small problems seem so blown out of proportion, way out. Being Americanized isn't such a bad thing, as long as you don't take it too seriously—half the world loves America, more than half—as long as you don't start square dancing or chewing Red Man tobacco it hardly matters. Who really gives a fuck? Poor Chris seemed like he was bent out of shape for nothing. Panky sat quiet and thought about things for a while, wondered if these so called 'confessions' were some kind of set up. Maybe Chris's confessions were preemptive? Could be the next confession Chris wanted to hear was Panky's. But then he thought: No, Chris just isn't that sneaky; he's not like that.

Chris looked up, "Panky?"

"Yeah," said Panky, looking him in the eyes, passing him the Chivas—not much left now, the nightcap nearly over.

"Can I ask you a question?"

"Sure…"

"Why are you here?" asked Chris.

Panky looked up, "Good question geezer and come to that why are any of us here, right?"

Chris said, "No, I mean, why are *you*, *here*?

Panky smiled, snatched the remains of the Chivas and lit a cigarette. Ha! He was right! Chris *was* that sneaky.

The room was silent apart from the jungle orchestration, cicadas getting real loud now, sounding like a million tiny dentist drills, undulating, electric; in the distance local dogs were baying at the pale moon, like mad wolves.

Panky swigged on the remaining Chivas, smoked his cigarette, "Do you really want to know?" he said.

Chris was about to say: Yes, of course I want to know, when the door flew open and *crashed* against the wall. Chris and Panky turned quickly in unison, watched Clara and Mai-Ling tumble through the door and fall into a heap just inside the room.

The girls where loud and giggly, clearly drunk. They lay sprawled across the polished wood floor, a mass of tangled golden limbs, arms and legs everywhere, bright young faces still aglow from the day on the beach. The lipstick smeared across their mouths looked sexier than ever, their hair was wild and tangled. They were drunk, silly and curious, yet they still both looked amazing.

Panky staring, thinking: Nice, a little girl on girl action. Chris staring, thinking: Hmmm.

Clara looked up at the guys with big eyes and smiled. She teased the top of the bottle of champagne she was holding with her tongue and took a sip; despite the bubbles, she didn't spill a drop. Her smile was warm and full of fun, full of promises.

Chris and Panky stood up slowly and looked at the girls. They were looking good, awkward yes, with their arms and legs like fighting spiders, but still looking good. Their crooked smiles were soft, full of embarrassment; faces flushed with champagne. They stood side-by-side and brushed themselves down trying their best not to laugh.

Chris looked shocked and glanced at Panky in disbelief.

Panky just shrugged, exhaled through his nose.

Chris and Panky both thinking: Ok, so they'd been listening at the door, big deal, they were drunk and having fun. The big question was how long had they been listening, what had they heard? Maybe the even bigger question was—what were they hoping to hear?

Chris smiled at Clara; looked in her eyes and immediately knew what the girls were up to. "It looks like we *all* want to know why you're here Panky," said Chris.

The girls shared a furtive glance and giggled quietly, giving away their secret.

Panky sighed heavily.

The girls padded across the room, sunk themselves deep into the sofa opposite Chris and Panky. Waiting.

All eyes on Panky again. He said, "Are you sure you want to know?"

The silence said: Yes, of course we want to know.

"It's kind of…"

"Sordid?" purred Clara as she passed the champagne to Mai-Ling. Both girls grinned, but said nothing. They liked sordid now, thought it was fun.

Panky thought the champagne seemed good for Clara, she'd lightened up, she seemed playful. He looked around, Chris was wearing an expectant grin, he was drunk and ready for anything; the girls sat with big eyes and bated champagne breath. Panky had no choice and he knew it. He coughed and cleared his throat, "Ok then, I hope you're sitting comfortably?"

His audience waited.

"Phew! Now this *really is* quite a story… way beyond sordid, I promise you. It all started less than a week ago… it seems like a fucking life time, excuse my language, but it's less than a week. Ten o'clock Monday night was when the shit *really* hit the fan, but everything *started* going wrong Monday morning, very early Monday morning and when I say wrong, I mean very, very wrong... I can't be one hundred percent certain... but this is what I *think* happened, ok?

Chris, Clara and Mai-Ling nodded ok. They were listening.

FORTY

It was Sunday morning about 11.10 a.m. when Panky finally made it to work. He was late as usual, but it didn't matter. He was the manager of a coffee shop called 'The Other Twilight Zone' in Amsterdam's red light district, along the Warmoesstraat, down there among the bars and the restaurants, not far from central station, in amongst the action. It was a small, but popular place, the atmosphere was mellow and relaxed, the music didn't make your ears bleed and fortunately they didn't get too many tourists. It was a cool place too, arty, but not pretentious, the staff were good at their jobs and fun; they sold quality drugs at fair prices and always offered discount on bulk orders. The word was they sold some of the best super skunk and hash in the city. You could buy other, illegal stuff too, if you knew who and how to ask, that's where Panky came in. The place was a little goldmine and Panky often wished it were his.

It was the perfect place for Panky to work and most days he loved it: the hours were reasonably flexible, the food and drinks were good, plentiful and free, he put all his favourite punk classics on the juke box, plus he got the chance to put a few deals of his own together—bigger deals, under the table stuff, illegal, but well worth the risk.

Panky stumbled and crashed through the entrance door and the bell on the door rang noisily announcing his arrival. He looked up and saw Leary and Carol. Leary Katz—infamous American chemist—worked as the barman, sold the hash and the weed too. Carol van Eyke—voluptuous Dutch girl—was the waitress, did the food and drinks, sold hash and weed too when they were busy. Leary, dressed as always in a Grateful Dead T-shirt, and Carol stood against the bar in a thick haze of smoke and stared up at the TV hanging high on the wall. They stood motionless and silent, intent on the screen, ignoring Panky's dramatic entrance.

Panky sauntered towards them, took a spliff from the bar and lit it. Leary was a good friend of Panky's; over the years they'd done some great deals together; they'd made a lot of money and wasted it all. Easy come, easy go. Panky always said that having a chemist on the team was more than useful and Leary Katz certainly knew his chemicals. When it came to recreational drugs he was an expert, he was also very hands on when it came to testing samples, basically Leary was a party animal and that was another reason he got on so well with Panky. Leary was from New York originally, visited Amsterdam for a two-week vacation a decade ago and just decide to stay, said he liked the place a lot, said it was a lot of fun. Carol, the waitress, was in her twenties and loved every aspect of selling drugs, she thought her current job description looked funny on her resume. She wasn't too sure if her experience would help much when it came to future career moves, but she didn't really care. Panky liked Carol a lot; a team player he called her, always happy and always happy to help out. People liked Carol; she had a great body and did well on tips. Carol, Leary and Panky were quite a team.

The coffee shop itself was like most other coffee shops in Amsterdam: a long thin smoke stained room with a bar at the end, seats along the walls on the right, a long counter for rolling joints on, tables and chairs along the left: a simple layout that worked. The décor was plain and unassuming except for the tall green plastic aliens that aligned the wall between the tables, a gimmick from when the coffee shop first opened. Calling it 'The Other Twilight Zone' seemed ok-ish, but the luminous green aliens weren't really necessary. No one really ever noticed them.

Panky leaned against the bar and smoked his spliff, watched Carol and Leary staring up awkwardly at the TV. He was about to speak when Carol and Leary turned in unison, each had a finger held vertical to their lips, saying: "*Sssshhh!*" Panky got the message, grinned and looked up at the TV.

The picture flashed away from the respectable cap toothed anchorman to a complete contrast: two mug shots. The mug shots of two glum looking adolescents, holding up their identity numbers with nicotine fingers, sneering at the camera; retro punks with spiky dyed hair, acne and attitudes. The youth of today.

The anchorman continued his voice over: "Police are still searching for two young boys, D.K. Bartholomew aged fifteen and his sixteen year old brother Sid missing since…"

Panky started to speak, but Leary and Carol turned in their cloud of smoke and said: "*Sssshhhhh!*" again. So he did. He smoked his spliff, took Leary's cold beer from the bar and finished it, wishing he hadn't been so late as usual, wishing he knew what the news story was all about and why his friends were so interested. Leary and Carol just standing there silent and gazing, heads tilted back at an uncomfortable angle, glued to the TV like never before.

The anchorman continued: "There maybe some connection." Then a more familiar face replaced the kid's mug shots; it was their mother Judy, she was a punk too; she looked a little prettier than her boys, but just a little.

The anchorman said: "Thirty one year old Judy Bartholomew from Brixton, London died on her way back to the U.K. yesterday aboard flight number 197A from Amsterdam. Authorities cannot confirm the cause of death as yet, but believe it may be another drug related incident."

Leary and Carol turned and looked at Panky who was behind the bar now getting another beer. They sat silent on stools at the bar looking shocked. Panky sat down and faced them, sipped his beer, finished his spliff, slowly shook his head and looked as shocked as his coworkers. Judy Bartholomew was one of Panky's girlfriends, another slightly crazy but fun loving girl. Leary and Carol knew her well, they couldn't believe she was dead and their glum faces proved it.

Carol looked up and said apparently Judy'd died from swallowing condoms full of cocaine; word was she'd swallowed more than anyone else in the history of drug smuggling. "She wasn't even that big," said Carol, tears welling in her stunned blue eyes.

Panky sighed heavily, drank some beer and lit another spliff. Things weren't going too good for him just lately, the drug trade seemed to be getting harder by the day, far too much ducking and diving involved for someone his age. More than ten years in the business now and it seemed like a lifetime; like most other exciting jobs it soon became routine, the glamour faded quicker than a politicians smile—people like Judy didn't make it any easier. But Panky's biggest problem was his recent dealings with the Russian mob; he owed them a lot of money, $100,000 to be exact, it seemed they were fed up with waiting. He leaned across the bar grabbed a bottle of Chivas and took a large gulp.

"You got problems too?" asked Carol chewing on her fingernails.

"No, not really," lied Panky, he was pretty sure the Russians were going to give him a bit of pressure, was expecting it to happen any time. Panky grinned thinking: Surely after all the deals we've done together they know I'll pay; I'm just a bit late that's all. It's nothing personal for God's sake. "I didn't even know Judy had any kids," said Panky snapping out of his reverie, exhaling a huge cloud of smoke.

Carol and Leary stared at him across the bar.

"Hey!" Panky said raising his hands defensively, "This has got nothing to do with me I promise you; I stopped selling her coke weeks ago... she was getting way too crazy!" Panky held up his hands defensively, "I'm innocent," he said, "I promise you... I'm completely innocent!"

7.15 a.m. Monday morning and the sun peeking out of the clouds on the horizon, throwing thin glimmers of light across the cold dull brown water of the North Sea. D.K. and Sid Bartholomew were in the bar of the super ferry going from Harwich, England to the Hook of

Holland; going on to the city of Amsterdam by train. The boys were on a mission.

D.K. and Sid were punk rockers, retro punks as their mum called them; both had spiky dyed hair, wore bondage trousers with chains and straps and black studded leather jackets, both boys were big for their age, looked older than they really were, never had a problem buying drugs or alcohol anywhere.

Sid was playing on the 'Flesh eating Zombies' arcade machine, holding the big real looking gun with both hands and killing Zombies with every shot, shooting everything in sight. He was very good, every time he killed another Zombie the screen in front of him filled with dripping blood.

His brother D.K. sat a few feet away at a table looking bored, throwing peanuts in the air, catching them in his mouth like his mum had tried to teach him; most of them were falling on the floor, but he didn't seem too bothered.

D.K. gazed around aimlessly chewing the few peanuts he'd managed to catch and smoked another cigarette; his spotty face a picture of adolescent angst; the spiky blue hair and the heavily pierced eyebrows didn't do much for him. As always, he had his Walkman on and loud, maximum volume. He was listening to the Clash again, 'Guns on the roof' this time, a song about death, guns, revolution, all that stuff. It sounded violent and vaguely paramilitary. It was one of D.K.'s favorites.

D.K. and Sid were from a dynasty of dysfunction, fourth generation benefit dependent and proud; a couple of unplanned rough kids who'd never seen their fathers and never really wanted to, whomever they were.

They'd learned how to be punks from their mum and their grandma at a very early age, the two women thought it was 'dead funny' having a couple of punk toddlers. As a result D.K. and Sid had grown up wild and uncontrollable, that's what their probation officer and the social workers said anyway, last time they saw them both, that was months ago now, but nothing much had changed. The boys were still a problem.

Sid watched a lot of action movies, you could tell: he stood relaxed in a perfect shooting posture, a cigarette clamped between his crooked yellow teeth; holding the big replica gun steady, closing one eye as he aimed, breathing steady, squeezing the trigger not pulling it like on TV. Every time he shot, he hit another Zombie, every time he hit another Zombie the screen turned red with blood again. Sid loved it. Thought it was the best machine he'd ever seen.

Escaping from England had been easy. "A piece of piss innit," Sid said, and as always young D.K. agreed with him. When they came on board the ship the night before, they'd sat in the bar drinking a few beers and smoking untold cigarettes. Sid said it was fun shooting Zombies, said he was having the time of his life. D.K. said, yeah, killing Zombies was a riot. Unlike Sid, D.K. wasn't much of a shot, he preferred playing on the slot machines, didn't seem to care how much he lost.

Later that night in the bar they watched themselves on BBC1 TV, saw their mug shots, heard the plastic faced anchorman explain how they got away from the authorities, from the social workers, from all the people at the child care department. They laughed until tears ran down their faces and their stomachs ached.

D.K. sat at his table bored now with the journey, dying to get to Amsterdam, dying to see a bit of action.

Sid was chuckling madly, blasting away at the Zombies, and taking no prisoners, still killing everything in sight. He blasted another Zombie's head to pieces and looked over at D.K. as the blood slowly trickled down and filled the screen.

"I fuckin' hate Mondays," said D.K. turning off his Walkman, picking a handful of nuts off the floor, throwing them up and catching a couple in his mouth, "I never go to school on Mondays anyway," he said.

Sid was relaxing while the blood filled the screen again, lighting another cigarette, coughing like a pro, grinning at his little brother.

D.K. yawned and squinted, picked at his nose, saw the early morning sun creeping in through the portholes and the heavy metal door, saw the sun catch and reflect off the studs on Sid's leather jacket, heard screaming gulls diving wildly for flotsam.

"You never go to school period," said Sid, "Or should that be a semi-colon?"

D.K. slouched back in the chair, put his large Dr. Marten boots on the table and tried hard not to look confused. He wasn't too sure what a semi colon was, but didn't want to ask, thought it might be something in your arse like a prostrate, but wasn't sure. He said, "Oh, that's fuckin' funny that Sid... *really* fuckin' funny. It's great havin' a brother that's such a smart arse."

Sid grinned some more, coughed a little as he stood waiting for the Zombies to start their attack.

"So smart arse..." said D.K. "When we gonna get there, then? I'm dying for a proper smoke."

"I told you," said Sid, ducking and diving, aiming and shooting now because the Zombies had appeared again, "We're nearly there... you'll be sitting in a coffee shop smoking some wicked weed by eleven o'clock, ok? I promise."

D.K. stared at the ashtray full of peanuts and ground his cigarette butt into the carpet, he'd been asking how long 'til they arrive for quite a few hours now. He knew it annoyed Sid, that's why he did it, but he also knew that if Sid said he'd be there by eleven that he'd be there by eleven. Sid was a good brother and he always kept his promises. D.K. looked at the clock and smiled despite the fact he'd started feeling nervous, a bit edgy; his stomach had butterflies. He said, "D'you really think it's up to us though Sid?"

Sid shot D.K. a glance, looked suddenly angry, stared over his shoulder as the Zombies went down, cigarette smoke in his face. "Of course it's up to us you fuck wit..." Sid looked around before he continued, wanted to make sure no one was listening. "It doesn't matter if he meant to do it or not does it? He killed our muvva and it's payback time... ok? Don't worry it's gonna be easy."

D.K. looked nervous, stopped messing with the peanuts, puffed hard on his cigarette butt. When he spoke his voice proved he wasn't sixteen for almost ten more months. "But d'you think you can really do it?"

Sid spat out his cigarette, crushed it into the carpet with his size ten Dr. Marten boot; the smell of burning carpet thick in the air for just as second. "Of course I can do it!" snarled Sid aiming and shooting, getting a couple more Zombies, the screen filling with blood for about the twentieth time. "It's easy D.K., easy... it's like shooting fuckin' Zombies innit?" Sid laughed; the sound was manic, marred with the prospect of violence and bloodshed.

D.K. bit on his fingernails and continued to look nervous.

Sid looked over his shoulder again and said, "Anyone can pull a trigger D.K.," He shot another Zombie just to prove it and grinned at his little brother's nervousness, "I just need you for a bit of back up."

The youngest punk sprawled himself across the table among the empty beer glasses and the peanut shells, even though he didn't see his mum that often he really missed her already, couldn't quite believe she was dead. He looked at Sid's confident face, watched the way his big brother stood and held the gun and never missed. D.K. sighed deeply, coughed and spat a large glob of phlegm into the ashtray, gazed around aimlessly, listened to the gulls screeching like starving lunatics outside.

Sid was looking at the screen and feeling good, still holding the big gun even though all the Zombies were dead now.

Six words appeared on the old game screen...
GAME OVER... THE TOP KILLER IS   ?
Sid was laughing out loud as he typed in the three letters, S... I... D.

About 7.25 a.m. on that same Monday morning Panky wandered through Amsterdam's red light district. The sun's weak rays streamed through the gaps between the tall old buildings, dappling Panky with pale sunlight as he staggered through diminishing shadows. He was heading home after an emotional night. He'd finished the bottle of Chivas without much effort and smoked spliffs until his lungs wheezed, but still didn't feel any better.

After the news about Judy the long hours in the coffee shop seemed tedious and torturous, like waiting in the dentist for a root canal, but Panky didn't know what else to do or where else to go. He sat gloomily with Leary and Carol avoiding the BBC news like a hat full of spiders, watching the Discovery channel, learning stuff about crocodiles and how they lived, useful stuff to know if you live in Amsterdam.

Around 5 a.m. he was tempted to open another bottle of Chivas, *really* drown his sorrows and get *totally* shit faced, but Carol and Leary suggested he go home, suggested he try and sleep. It was good idea, one he hadn't considered. As he stumbled through the empty narrow streets towards his houseboat he caught glimpses of his rough and rumpled reflection in the sex shop windows, chuckled quietly to himself like drunks do, laughed at the fleeting glimpses of dildos and other such gadgets and gimmicks. The sex aid scene seemed silly in the cold light of day, without the neon lights, the girls in the windows, without the crowds of anxious men, the lustful darkness of the night. It seemed puerile and pointless.

He continued along the old cobbled street scratching his head, rubbing his stubble and puffing hard on his cigarette, wondering if he should have had more than just a couple of lines of coke before he left. He'd needed something to help him make it home that was for sure, just lately even the best recreational substances didn't seem to have the right effect. He didn't know if it was too much or not enough. It was hard to tell. Maybe he was just getting paranoid? Maybe he was just getting old? Maybe he was getting old and paranoid? It was hard to tell.

Panky looked over his shoulder again as he weaved and wobbled along, his eyes were red and anxious, the bags underneath like fading bruises. As he moved along he gazed around at the familiar ancient city, at the tall thin tenements; amazed that he'd managed to survive so long in such a crazy fucked up place. He turned a corner and stepped onto a small elegant footbridge that crossed the canal, the water looked cold and uninviting, green and murky. White gulls with black eyes like robbers, squawked overhead, the salty morning air tasted sharp in his parched throat. He continued on, coughing and spluttering, shaking his head, hoping he'd make it home. He staggered over the bridge, eyes screwed up against the early rays of sunlight. Once across he bumped into a couple of parked cars, mumbled incoherent curses, crossed the road and somehow made it to the other side. He bounced off the wall of the empty church, had to steady himself in case he collapsed. He was pretty wasted.

Every fifteen steps exactly he turned around to make sure he wasn't being followed. He timed it. He was nervous, expecting heat, expecting grief from the Russians any time now. He looked again; was sure someone was following him, watching him; had that feeling, but the streets were quiet and empty, just a few stray cats hanging around, early morning tranquility.

But Boris and Vlad weren't far behind. They'd been following Panky ever since he'd left the coffee shop. Despite their significant bulk the Russians were nimble on their feet; their faces were bright and pink with cold, the collars of their big dark coats turned up against the chill morning air. They ran and dodged and hid behind parked cars.

Finally with a huge sigh of relief, Panky made it to his dilapidated houseboat. He stood at the top of the gangplank and looked down. He saw timbers dry and flaking, losing their paint; the small dirty window with its cracked glass; the incongruous sign that said 'Home sweet home' and the steep flight of steps that lead down to his battered refuge. It looked a long way down.

Vlad and Boris crept silently behind parked cars, got closer to the houseboat, watched Panky holding onto the handrail, saw him stand at the top of the stairs. The Russians were smiling.

Panky breathed deeply, squinted at the sun in his eyes again. He looked down and felt nauseous, felt dizzy. It looked a long way down, steep and dangerous as always.

Vlad and Boris shuffled along, got a little closer, keeping cover and keeping quiet. Vlad pulled a 9mm Glock with a fitted suppressor from inside his coat. The blue-black metal of the gun felt cold and lethal in his hand. He smiled at Boris, crouched next to him behind an old BMW. Boris smiled his evil little smile and nodded approval.

Vlad aimed the gun.

Panky stood at the top of the stairs feeling hesitant and wary. He didn't know why, it was one of those feelings, a survival thing.

Vlad aimed and squeezed the trigger. Fired four almost silent shots in quick succession.

Panky saw everything in slow motion, the sudden burst of wood and splinters on the handrail, years of paint and varnish like heavy dust motes spiraling up through the early morning air. He saw another burst high in front of him on the deck like a small explosion, a puff of dust and tiny wooden fragments filled the air like some small-discoloured cloud. He had no idea what was happening, no idea. He shook his head in disbelief, swayed precariously on the top step. It was only when the third bullet whizzed passed his ear that he realised someone was shooting at him. Panky thinking: *Fuck, fuck, fuck!* … As another bullet zipped passed his ear. Without hesitation he threw himself headlong down the steep flight of stairs, arms lashed tightly around his head, spastic legs twisted and aimless. When he landed he smashed through the heavy wooden doors at the bottom and lay there in a heap. Out cold. The blood from his face dripped down onto the dirty floor, mingled darkly with the broken glass and fragments of splintered wood.

If the Russians were planning to come and kill him, they wouldn't find it too difficult.

Sid and D.K. sat on the train heading for Amsterdam.

It was 10.05 a.m. Monday morning and they were nearly there.

Sid was sitting quietly reading 'Guns and ammo' licking his lips with silent anticipation, chain smoking cigarettes, gobbing on the floor. D.K. stood plucking manically at his 'air guitar', singing along to the song on his Walkman. His mumbled lyrics sounded tortured and vague. The Walkman's volume was on full, like some hopeful kind of barrier trying to keep the world at bay. It seemed to be working.

Despite their age and the No Smoking sign, Sid and D.K. drank warm weak beer and smoked endless cigarettes as the train hurtled noisily towards Amsterdam.

A tall Dutch ticket collector wandered along the corridor calling for tickets, walked straight passed their carriage with a solemn almost paranoid demeanour, gave the boys a quick furtive glance. He didn't care if they had tickets or not, it made no difference to him; so what if they smoked and drank beer, no one had complained, not to him anyway. It was early Monday morning, way too early for problems with crazy looking British kids. He mumbled something in a thick throaty Dutch voice, hung his head slightly, sighed and kept walking.

The boys were excited about seeing Amsterdam for the first time, seeing it for themselves. They'd heard so much about the place from their mum; Judy had worked in the red light district for over ten years, totally loved the place, loads better than working in the local plastics factory she said. While their mum was away the boys stayed in Brixton with their grandma. Living in the crumbling sixties tower block with grandma was never that much fun, so high up you could open the window and almost spit on the clouds. The boys fucking hated it. The place so full of people, constant noise day and night, night and day, people fighting and screaming and dirt, litter, wall to wall attack dogs and dogs shit everywhere. They hated it all.

But it wasn't just the decaying environment that depressed them. Grandma had a lot of personal problems, being drunk and delusional was just one of them. But it wasn't *just* that…

Grandma was angry and bitter too, hated the fact that she was past it at forty five or 'left on the shelf' as she liked to call it—like an old tin of tuna.

Her life hadn't really changed much over the decades, still struggling by on benefits and a bit of money from her regular *so called* men friends, still wearing the same old punk clothes, still snorting low grade cocaine when she could afford to and speed when she couldn't. Poor grandma, she was so popular with the boys when she was young, someone once said that she used to be good looking when she was young, a great shag too, but it was hard to tell now. The boys doubted it. Grandma looked so much older than here forty five years despite her efforts to stay young and desirable: the bleached spiky hair, the thick powdery make up on her crows' feet, the heavy black mascara that clung like errant spiders to her eyes, the tattoos, the numerous facial and body piercings. Despite all that, she still looked older than forty five, much older. Her few remaining teeth were gray, yellow and crooked, her breath always heavy with cheap gin, hand rolled cigarettes and grass and her clothes like her body smelled old and worn and out of date. Poor Grandma felt that life had passed her by and that it was all down hill from here on and to a certain extent it had and it was.

The young retro punks were more than pleased to be leaving Grandma behind again, they laughed about her 'old-timers disease', wondered how long it would be until she realised that they'd actually gone, that they'd escaped once again. They'd wanted to visit Amsterdam ever since they could remember; their mum had told them so many stories about the place; told them how much freedom there was; how much fun she had, all the wild parties, all the drugs, the crazy people. But she wouldn't let them visit until D.K. was sixteen. She was strict like that sometimes.

The boys were obviously excited about the trip; you could see it in their eyes. So pleased to be getting away from grandma and the tower block, the smell of piss and cabbage, the stench of poverty and dogs shit. So pleased to be getting away from the chavvy hip-hop gangs that threw rocks and stones at them, taunted them about their crazy grandma and their acne. Pleased too to be leaving behind the relentless cops, cops who always stopped and searched them because they were different. The same cops that knew Judy, their mum, had some serious Amsterdam connections, the same cops that made fun of their poor old grandma and made stupid jokes about her problems. They were pleased to be getting away from everything. Running away had been an easy decision. D.K. wondered why they hadn't thought of going as far as Amsterdam before.

As the train clattered along Sid's face was full of thought, his young eyes full of delight, he sat with his feet up on the opposite seat; his Dr. Marten boots looking huge and menacing, keeping the other passengers away. He continued to read 'Guns and ammo', lips moving silently on the longer words as he struggled through the articles. He was trying hard to forget about grandma and the tower block, but it wasn't easy.

As the train continued its journey, the bright fleeting sun caught the shining gold of Sid's pierced ears and nostrils, it sparkled and it glimmered, reflected on the jagged peak of his bright red Mohawk. Sid was never one to worry too much about hair or the way it was cut, but he loved his Mohawk, he cherished its rebellious style, he tended and caressed it lovingly like a pet and every time he looked into the mirror he thought of Robert De Niro, Jodie Foster and Harvey Keitell, thought of 'Taxi Driver' and all that wicked killing. All that blood, the guns, all that desperate excitement. Sid smiled, thinking about murder and revenge.

D.K. was standing looking out of the train's big window playing 'air guitar'; his young face twisted and contorted with the effort. He looked out and saw trees, buildings, the expansive flat Dutch landscape flashing by, swishing past. The Walkman fell silent, the music stopped and D.K. stood still, gazing out, entranced. He smiled as a new song started to play, an ominous song that he loved so much. He knew every word, grandma had taught him the lyrics one day when she was speeding and couldn't sleep.

The train rattled along the track, Sid sat reading and smoking, drinking his flat warm beer. His little brother D.K. stared out the window feeling hypnotized by passing telegraph poles, singing the words to The Guns of Brixton, his favourite song ever, a song about guns and kicking down doors by the Clash, playing his imaginary guitar,

When Panky finally woke up or gained consciousness—he wasn't sure which it was—he heard nearby church bells ringing.

It was Monday morning, 10.30 a.m. exactly and as usual he was late for work. He lay on the floor for a while trying to remember what had actually happened, trying to put past events into some kind of order. It wasn't easy. He was cold and his body ached, he felt scared to move.

Rays of pale sunlight streaked through the broken wooden doors behind him, lit up the shards of glass scattered around the floor. Flickering streams of dust motes hung silent in the air. Panky groaned as he wiped the dust from his eyes. The blood that had trickled down his face and dripped onto the floor had dried now; the smell of it remained faint in the room, like rust. Moving just his eyes he looked around, not really knowing what to expect.

Turquoise bodied flies buzzed noisily around his head but he ignored them; light-footed cockroaches tip toed across the floor and stared at him. Crawling like a caterpillar and aching like a bastard, Panky slowly dragged his body along the floor, through the shattered glass, through the wooden splinters and the dirt. He peered inside the old houseboat. There was no one there. Good.

His ears filled with the sounds of cold canal waters slapping against the side of boat, mad screeching gulls and the distant rumble of traffic and trams. He tried to get up. It hurt. His eyes focused on his old white punch bag hanging there from the ceiling; his only witness to a million fights and a million successful bouts. He sighed deeply. He wasn't feeling very tough today, that was for sure.

As he strained to get up his mobile phone began to ring. He fumbled awkwardly through his pockets. He pulled it out, ignored the caller ID and answered it. "Fuck off!" he shouted and threw the phone across the room. Using his hands against the timbers on the side of the boat, and with more than a little effort, he managed to stand up. He stepped unsteadily across the room and stared into a broken mirror hanging on the wall. His face was like the room, a total mess; he looked totally fucked: his two top front teeth were missing (again!), wood chips and splinters were stuck in the curls of his hair, trickles of dried blood made his face look ghoulish, zombie like. He was tempted to laugh.

As he slowly edged towards the dirty kitchen sink a small legion of cockroaches scattered, their ginger wings and bodies were bright and shiny in the pale light from the dirty window. Panky grabbed a handful of utensils—including a large butcher's knife—from the bowl of the sink and dropped them noisily onto the adjacent counter. He turned on the tap and quickly washed his face. The water was ice cold. Breathtaking.

With water and diluted blood trickling down his vacuous face he looked around, he felt more conscious now, a bit more awake. He looked down on the floor and saw an empty coffee can and kicked it in disgust. He really needed some coffee. He shuffled over to the refrigerator and opened the door; saw nothing but the interior light, a brown apple core and an empty bottle of ketchup. Not good.

As he moved over to the eye level cupboards he coughed and spluttered, scratched at the splinters on his chest, rubbed his aching back. He opened the first cupboard door, desperate for coffee now; he was searching without much hope. He saw nothing, not a thing. The cupboard was completely empty just cobwebs and dust. He repeated the process time and time again, opening doors, slamming them shut, finding absolutely nothing. A dozen cupboards, and like the refrigerator every one of them empty.

Despondent and frustrated he slumped to the floor and lit his last cigarette with his Zippo.   He threw the empty packet toward the overflowing garbage can, but missed by miles. He reached down, picked up the coffee can and threw it across the room.

"I can't fuck believe it," he said to the flies and the cockroaches, close to tears and trembling, "Can't fuckin' believe it! My body feels like I've been hit by a train, I've lost my teeth again, there's no fuckin' coffee, I'm out of cigarettes and I think someone's trying to kill me!"

Slumped on the floor in a sad disheveled heap he puffed heavily on his last cigarette. Holding his head in his hands, with gray smoke spiraling lazily through his hair, dappled sunlight across his face and crap and destruction all around he shouted, "I do not fuckin' believe this! I do *not* need problems today! *Not* today!"

At that very same moment D.K. stared out the train window. He was playing his 'air guitar', mumbling incoherently.

Sid was reading an article on Uzi's, a twisted smirk planted on his face.

It was 10.35 a.m. Monday morning. In a few minutes they'd be arriving at Central station Amsterdam.

It looked as though Sid's promise would be kept, that they'd be sitting in a coffee shop having a proper smoke by 11 o'clock.

D.K. smiled as he continued to sing about getting shot on the pavement.

An off key prophesy perhaps?

Two anxious crazy kids: revenge on their minds, getting closer and closer to Amsterdam.

It was 10.35 a.m. when Panky finished his last cigarette. He was still slumped on the floor of the houseboat, still looking at the mess, still feeling part of it. He looked down at his shaking hands and mumbled, "I'm getting too old for all this!"

As he stood up groaning, he noticed two large lines of cocaine and a metal tube laying on a piece of broken mirror on the cluttered coffee table. Big smile. "The breakfast of champions!" he announced to the insect world as he sneaked over towards the thick white beckoning lines. He moved quicker than he had for quite some time, furtive glances all around. He picked up the tube and sighed with anticipation. "Maybe there is a God?" he said to a twitching cockroach watching him from the wall.

He slid the cold metal tube into his nostril. And then he stopped and thought for just a second: Who the hell leaves big lines of coke lying around and then goes out for the day? Even in Amsterdam? Who the hell had been here while he was out? He shrugged and decided it didn't matter. Still shaking slightly, he snorted both lines with professional nonchalance. He gasped and spluttered and rubbed his nose. It was good cocaine, very good!

He ran his fingers through his tangled hair and glanced into the cracked mirror on the old wardrobe door. He looked worse than ever: tired red eyes, pale purple bags, streaks of diluted blood still on his pallid unshaven face, the missing teeth, wood splinters hanging in his curly hair, cocaine residue peeping out of his nostrils. "Much better!" he said to his reflection with a toothless grin. He turned back to the coffee table, licked his finger, picked up the fragments of powder from the mirror and rubbed them on his gums. "Much, much better!" The cocaine had made him acutely aware of his surroundings, aware of his current and perhaps dire situation. He was totally lucid and stood panting with wide eyes, listening: old dry timbers creaked as the houseboat rocked gently with the tide; gulls screeched like murder overhead, trams rattled by in the distance.

Outside life seemed to be going on as normal. To the rest of the world it was just another Monday morning, but to Panky it was a big, big day. The problem was it hadn't begun too well. A sudden bitter surge of panic welled up from the pit of his stomach as he remembered his plans and what lay ahead. If things went according to plan he'd be able to get the rest of the money he owed Zoltan and finally get the Russians off his back. Make a large amount of money at the same time. *If* things went according to plan.

He really didn't need any problems. Not today.

Behind him at the far end of the houseboat a hand appeared from under the bed, it snaked through the pile of damp blankets strewn across the mattress. Someone was hiding there, but Panky hadn't noticed. The hand was slim and female, its fingernails red and chipped, it held a remote control. The anonymous hand pointed the remote at the big old TV on the floor.

Click. The big old TV came to life with a dazzling flash. The room suddenly filled with a sea of flickering colour, a surge of discordant music seemed to pour, gush almost from the TV's tired old speakers. It was

MTV playing a song from the past: harsh electric guitars echoed and screeched, a heavy bass line droned, hummed and blended with the drums, the lyrics were spat like venom. It was Public Image Limited.

Panky pushed his hands to his temples, spun around on his heels confused and bewildered. The TV was *so fucking loud*! The words seemed to bounce around the room before they finally filled his ears.

He puffed and panted and swirled around some more. Well confused. A severe hint of cocaine panic rushed through his mind, spiraling paranoia jarred his thoughts, pierced them like icicles. His eyes searched desperately for some small clue as to what was happening, but all he saw was Johnny Lydon's gaunt twisted features on the screen. All he could hear were Johnny's shrill and wailing words. It seemed that the coke was *really*, really good. He stood bewildered and panting—close to total panic.

Behind him at the back of the room Soozie's face slowly appeared from under the bed, peeking through the damp blankets draped across the mattress; first an eye, then another eye, then her red moist mouth; finally her face in its entirety. Heavy make up, cocaine eyes, nervous twitching lips.

Panky heard the small noise of Soozie's breathing, did a semi-pirouette and faced her eye to eye. "Who the fuck are you?" he said, gasping, but somehow strangely relieved.

Soozie pulled back the blankets and crawled out from under the bed and she stood up. Her legs were long and trim, shapely, her ample breasts hung heavy in black lace. She shook her peroxide dreadlocks slowly with good effect, stretched her long limbs, flaunted the confusion of black tats on her lily-white skin and almost smiled.

Distant erotic snapshots swirled through Panky's mind. He cracked a smile. It was Soozie for sure. Panky sighed heavily before he spoke, "Soozie, right? Oozy Soozie! I can't fuckin' believe it…last time I saw you Soozie, you were trying to come to terms with those difficult but popular old English phrases… *Drunken mistake*… and… *Go away*. Remember? Panky pulled the plug on the TV, killed the music. He pulled a bent pre-rolled spliff from his pocket and lit it with his Zippo. He needed a smoke and badly. He didn't expect to see Soozie again, not ever and he certainly didn't need her around today. Not today.

Soozie pushed out her most endearing features, pouted and stayed silent.

"So how come you're still here?" asked Panky, inhaling deeply.

She sneered and said, "How come I'm still here? Fuck you! How come you've just got back?" Her voice was New York nasal, like grating finger nails, harsh like Wall Street traffic. Soozie paused to adjust her sneer and pose a little. She said, "And how come three weeks ago, you were going to buy condoms and I haven't seen you since?"

Panky wanted to tell her that not coming home for three weeks was a hint, he wanted to explain that he'd had enough of her: enough of her leeching, enough of her freeloading, enough of her sticking about fifty dollars of *his* coke up *her* nose every day and enough of her being there. Problem was she either didn't get the 'not so subtle' hints or she didn't want to. God knows he'd tried to get rid of her nicely, but nothing seemed to work. So he left, walked out.

He moved over to the dirty window and tried to look out at the morning, he heard pleasure boats full of tourists cruising by, distant cameras clicking, voices yakking with excitement.

"Look," he said, still staring out, still facing the window, "I had a mad night last night, ok? And when I finally got home I think someone tried to kill me, *again*... I fell headfirst down the fuckin' gangplank, nearly broke my neck... you probably heard that didn't you?"

Soozie tilted her head, shook it slightly and yawned.

Panky turned, saw her checking her chipped fingernails. He smiled sarcastically, did a Siskel and Ebert, gave her the two thumbs up. "Thanks for all the help Soozie," he said, "Don't know how I'd've managed without you."

Soozie continued to pout and look provocative. It was something she was good at.

Panky tried hard to keep his eyes off her body, off her moist pouting mouth; he remembered how much trouble she'd caused him before.

He said, "Now look sweetheart, it's Monday morning, and it's *well* after 10.00... I've just regained consciousness, I can't find my teeth, I'm late for fuckin' work again—as usual—and I've got a *very* big day ahead of me, Ok? So I don't need any more grief from you, got that?"

Panky took a final hit from his spliff and tossed it into an old coffee cup. It hissed.

Sid and D.K.'s train was slowing down, pulling noisily into Amsterdam's busy central station.

It was 10.40 a.m. Their eyes were full of anticipation, full of youthful excitement.

Sid took the final drag of his cigarette and put in an empty beer can. It hissed.

D.K. was still staring out the window bug eyed, still singing the song about the Guns of Brixton.

As Sid and D.K. jumped out of the train and weaved their way through the noisy bustling crowds of Central Station, Panky turned from the dirty window of the houseboat and stood staring at Soozie. He pulled another twisted spliff from his pocket and lit it. He stood staring through the smoke, eyes full of contempt. Today of all days he wanted to get rid of Soozie and quick, but he knew from experience that with Soozie even the simplest of things were never easy—like any other leech she was hard to remove without doing damage, without spilling at least a little blood.

As he smoked his spliff he decided he couldn't be subtle this time. It just didn't fucking work. He'd have to go hard, he'd have to scare the shit out of her and do it good. He looked down at the floor and spotted his denture. With a brief, fleeting look of amazement he bent down and picked it up. He blew away the dust and the lint, and casually popped it back into his mouth. He wriggled his dry lips over the teeth, welcomed them back into his mouth and felt better immediately, felt about fifteen years younger. "Why don't you just do us both a big favour?" he said, still wiggling his lips slightly, pointing his thumb towards the door and the fragments of sunlight.

"Why don't you make me?" said Soozie, like the spoiled brat she was, still pouting and sulky.

Panky looked at her wondering how much more contempt he could get into his eyes.

"Fucking make me!" she mouthed silently.

He just stared at her, remembered their lustful times together.

Her silent words were full of heat and ambiguity, seductive, full of perversity and promise. Or that's how it seemed to Panky.

She licked her lips, stretched her lithesome body and thrust out her endearing features a little more.

Panky watched her every move, remembered what he saw in her. He moved over to the kitchen sink, eyes still fixed on his teenage tease, his erstwhile seductress. Juicy Soozie: the sycophantic nympho. He was thinking: Can't deny that she's looking good, in a sluttish, white trash kind of way. Tempting like a porno princess—definitely worth a shot, if only for old times sake. And Soozie *was* tempting, *very* tempting. One small sultry smile from Soozie, one small flick of that vicious pink tongue, one quick flash of those heavy jugs even a eunuch would be reaching for his condoms. Panky soon forgot his aching back, his untold cuts and bruises. He coughed and hawked the cocaine residue from the back of his throat, got a little buzz going. Nice. He turned on the tap at the sink, doused his face with icy water and glanced over his shoulder at his beautiful burden, thinking: Maybe a quickie just for old time's sake isn't such a bad idea? Just pop it in and see what happens?

Panky looked at her again and smiled, tried his best to look charming, pleased to have his teeth back. He turned and searched for his toothbrush; brushing his teeth would be the first step toward some minimal foreplay. Soozie might be a slut, a bitch and a parasite, but he was still a gentlemen. Eventually, there among the dirty plates, the cutlery and the soggy old bits of food, he found a tired looking—anonymous— toothbrush. He proceeded to hunt for the toothpaste. When he found it, it was empty, just a sad mangled tube. Empty like the coffee can, empty like the cupboards and the refrigerator. Everything was fucking empty; everything was used and probably by Soozie the promiscuous leech. Panky was not happy. Not happy!

With one broad sweep of his arm he sent all the stuff, the utensils and knives, all that kitchen shit, *crashing* onto the floor.

Soozie was shocked by the sudden violence. This was a side of Panky she hadn't expected, that she hadn't seen before. He'd always been such a gentleman, such a walkover.

Smiling like some drug-crazed jackal, Panky stooped down and picked up the large butcher's knife off the floor. The blade looked sharp and deadly; it looked lethal as it flickered and shone slightly in the dim morning sunlight.

Soozie watched him pick up the knife, saw him stare at the blade, saw him consider its potential. Panky suddenly looked mean and menacing. Soozie sat silent looking terrified, the pout had gone now, her shoulders had dropped, and her hands were beginning to shake slightly.

Panky lifted the knife above his shoulder and ran towards her plunging it wildly, screaming at the top of his lungs. He deserved an Oscar nomination. A Hitchcock psycho moment.

Soozie's screams were the loudest. The loudest Panky had ever heard.

Boris and Vlad stood in Beefo's the fully automated junk food paradise. It was 10.40 a.m. Monday morning and time for breakfast, the most important meal of the day. Both Russians had warm grease on their substantial chins, food bulging in their hungry mouths, cheeks like giant gerbils as they chewed on their warm synthetic food. They loomed large and menacing, savouring their cholesterol, their monosodium glutamate, their nitrites and their extenders. Yum! Boris and Vlad stood close to a large wall filled with small windows, their covetous eyes on the display of warm congealing snacks as they slurped and munched noisily. Beefo's was the latest in high tech fast food concepts and popular with vagrants, street people and beggars; popular due to the prices and speed of the service rather than the quality of the food. The place didn't have any staff out front—it didn't need any. All you had to do to retrieve a sumptuous offering was insert some coins into the slot by the window and remove the food of your choice. Fast food personified. Greasy and synthetic, but cheap.

Vlad stared beyond the popular little windows, looked through the serving hatch; saw a hairy knuckled chef working in the steamy clattering kitchen; watched him plunge a large butcher's knife into a hanging carcass, slice off a massive lump of cow; heard him coughing and hawking, saw him wipe the blood off his hands onto his once white apron.

Still chewing, Boris extended his arm and fed more coins into a slot in the wall. He grabbed at a thin crispy chicken leg, ripped at the flesh with his teeth, grinning like some ravenous wolf. "I guess your warning shots weren't too effective Vladimir, huh?" he said through his chicken with a taunting tone, "Zoltan, he called me and this vykovskyi, this Panky, still hasn't delivered the money."

Vlad sniffed and chewed, wiped the grease from his mouth with the back of his hand again.

"Two hours it's been," said Boris, "And still nothing." He pulled a small piece of chicken from between his teeth and stared at it before he swallowed it. "Zoltan is getting a little anxious," he said, "Is a lot of money not to have."

Vlad nodded, it was a lot of money not to have. He remembered the old days, the hardships they had to endure. He remembered Moscow and stared at his fifth hotdog suspiciously, sniffed at the gray pink meat before he devoured it in two bites. Chewing he said to Boris, "So now what?"

Boris dropped his chicken bones casually onto the floor, inserted more coins into a slot and grabbed at a portion of French fries. He added about a half kilo of salt and smothered them in mayonnaise from one of the huge dispensers near by. Munching on the warm sodden, French fries he said, "Zoltan told me we shouldn't get our hands dirty." He licked the mayonnaise from his fingers and his wrist, the irony escaping him. "So, first we send in the twins, the brothers Karamazov."

Vlad grinned knowingly, sniffed at the pale beef patty in his paw.

"They're the biggest nastiest street fighters this side of Siberia," said Boris stuffing another handful of fries into his mouth. With mayo on his lips he said, "And then we go, we deal with what's left, is not so difficult."

"Sounds good to me," said Vlad, wondering what to eat next, "But from what I've heard, the Karamazov's… there won't be much left to deal with."

Boris smiled showing the food in his teeth, wiped the mayonnaise off his lips with his fat greasy fingers and reached for a burger.

"Exactly Vladimir," he said, as he dropped some coins into the slot, "Exactly."

It was 10.42 a.m. and Panky was standing in the shadows of the houseboat, sweating now and panting, smiling sadistically. Sighing as though he'd just finished a tedious job, he dropped the large butcher's knife onto the floor. He turned and looked at his reflection in the wardrobe mirror: not good.

He walked over to the wardrobe, opened the door, retrieved an old camouflage parka and slipped it on; he then pulled out an old black silk scarf and wrapped it around his mouth and nose, pulled the hood of the parka over his head. Looking into the mirror he thought: Cool, I could be anyone. He stood staring at his reflection thinking that maybe something was missing, pulled an old pair of Ray Bans from the depths of the wardrobe and completed his new look as he slid them up onto his nose. He looked in the mirror again: Amazing, incognito or what? A slight touch of terrorist chic perhaps, but for Panky it worked. Sighing again like he'd just finished a mammoth task he looked down at the knife on the floor, then across the room at his swinging punch bag, its contents spilled silently from its multiple stab wounds, piles of sawdust growing on the floor. In the shadows behind the swinging punch bag sat a huddled and terrified Soozie.

"Just fuck right off Soozie, ok?" said Panky through the black scarf, "Got it?"

Soozie said nothing, couldn't speak through the tears, lines of mascara trickled down her face and made her look sad but clown like. As she sat there sobbing; shadows danced across her face and seemed to animated her fear.

"Look Soozie and listen carefully," said the now anonymous Panky, "The Russians are definitely after me… ok? If they come here… and there's every chance they will, you can be sure someone'll get hurt… so do yourself a big favour Soozie… got it?"

Soozie nodded and wiped the snot from her nose on the back of her hand. Yeah, she understood.

Panky left the houseboat, dragged himself awkwardly up the steep gangplank and walked into the midmorning sunlight, into the hustle and bustle of Amsterdam city.

Sid and D.K. strolled out of Amsterdam's Central station, satisfied grins across their spotty faces, bumped their way through the colourful crowds and headed straight for the red light district. It wasn't far.

As they ambled along the midmorning sun caught the sea of silver studs across the backs of their leather jackets, it seemed to linger there. Both boys had the word 'Brixton' at the base of their black jackets; despite their endless domestic problems they were still proud of their South London roots. Amsterdam's narrow cobbled streets seemed so full of wonder, offered such excitement, such diversity; sex on the left, drugs on the right and loud rock 'n' roll in D.K.'s headphones. The boys were having fun already just walking the streets, they were amazed by everything: the sounds, the smells, the myriad of oddball people, the general drugged up ambience and of course, particularly for a couple of teenage boys, the raw sexuality in the air and all the naughty girls.

They walked wide-eyed and open mouthed, like under privileged kids on a day trip to the zoo—gazing at the strange exotic creatures. They saw girls in their windows smiling at them, actually smiling, at *them*! Waving, beckoning too and proudly maintaining the oldest profession.

Sid was very impressed with the girls; they looked amazing to him, but first things first. They needed drugs, alcohol and guns. Gotta get your priorities straight, thought Sid, gotta stick to your plan if you want to succeed. He didn't actually have a plan as yet, nothing concrete anyway, but he was working on it and once he had one he'd stick to it for sure. The boys wandered along sucking up the ambience, sniffing at aromas in the air, big smiles splashed across their faces.

As always D.K. had his Walkman turned up to maximum volume, listening to one of his favourite bands: 'The Gang of Four', playing 'At home he's a tourist'. It seemed appropriate. D.K. suddenly stopped in his tracks, tilted his head back and looked up at a tall Teutonic blonde in her window; he was sweating now and breathless, eyes fixed on the girl as she beckoned him towards her. Her smile was big and luscious; her soft moist tongue brushed gently across her red lips, promised things that young D.K. had only dreamed of and read about in tabloid papers. D.K. thinking: Sick!

It was all too much for him; he wanted to run to her and lose himself in all that flesh. He had the money ready in his hand.

Sid grabbed him by the collar and dragged him up the street, ignoring his squirming protests.

It was 10.48 a.m. and they'd planned to be in the coffee shop by 11.00 a.m.

They'd be bang on time. Sid always kept his promises.

Boris and Vlad sat at a table in the club 'Esoterik'. The heat from the spotlights was hot in their faces; it was 10.50 a.m. Monday morning, time for a little pre lunch drink, an aperitif.

Apart from the barman and the weird looking stripper, they were the only ones in the bar—it wasn't exactly a daytime place, the club was underground in every sense of the word; it was dark and damp, had a sinister air, a very sinister air. The old brick walls were adorned with cobwebs and sadomasochistic accessories: chains and whips, handcuffs and dildos, leather and PVC outfits, blind folds and gags. Club 'Esoterik' was the netherworld of the Netherlands, a hardcore club; pain and perversity lurked in the sullen silence, hid behind blue velvet curtains.

The song 'Memories' by Public Image Limited suddenly bellowed from large high-stacked speakers, a lone spot light came on and just as suddenly the stripper came to life. Both weird and unexpected in the early morning silence. As she gyrated madly on the small circular stage, the dark wailing lyrics and screams seemed to circulate like swarming bees around her pale emaciated body. She danced wild—like a tripped out hippy—in the sudden strobe light, flashes like a paparazzi army all around her. The music was constant, relentless, and haunting. The pulsating flashes of light made her look frantic, dazed almost scared like she'd never done this before, her backstroking movements seemed robotic and bizarre; her huge blue veined breasts looked painful, silicon fit to burst; her makeup was thick and sticky, arachnid lids and lashes, just a wound for a mouth, that thin slash of red, a cynical sneer. She wiggled, wrapped tightly in see through plastic; breasts to ankles and tight; the track marks on her arms were covered, hidden by make up, but the ones between her toes were not. She kept dancing. She smiled and stared like the devil.

Vlad held a joint in his mouth, blew out smoke as he poured more vodka over the ice in the two glasses in front of him. He looked up and over at the skinny stripper, watched her dancing madly, decided she looked surreal, thought the 'sexy' see through plastic made her look like dancing leftovers, like she'd just rolled out of a giant lunchbox. Maybe she had, this *was* Amsterdam.

Boris shared flirtatious glances with the Lurch-like barman, smiling across the bar at him; the guy standing naked apart from his leather chaps and his body piercings, as gay as Christmas fairy lights but tall and gaunt with heroin eyes. Like the club, he too was scary looking, with a definite taste for violence in his lust. The guy was a homophobic nightmare; scars among the dark body hair: wiry thick hair, lots of scars and Nazi tats.

Boris snorted a line of cocaine off the old Formica table, sniffed, gagged a little, knocked back his vodka, and said, "Don't you just love this place?"

Vlad grinned, he wasn't too sure; either about the place itself or any connection it might have with the word love. The Lurch guy scared him and he didn't scare easy. He snorted a thick line of coke, gazed around at the torturous knick-knacks on the walls and wondered why? For some unknown reason the stripper threw her head back, laughed like a wounded hyena, and continued to dance madly.

Boris smiled at the barman again.

Vlad looked around aimlessly, felt uncomfortable and bored, this *really* wasn't his scene. He coughed, sighed a little at the tedium; it was almost lunchtime and outside the sun was shining.

Boris glanced at his watch, sniffed and smiled at Vlad.

Vlad said, "So... the brothers Karamazov, they should be there soon huh?"

Boris said, "Any minute now, Vladimir, any... minute... now... relax... enjoy..."

Panky slouched across the bar in the 'Other Twilight Zone' smoking a joint, quietly watching hazy sunlight pour through the big window down there at the end.

It was 10.55 a.m. Monday morning now and despite his traumatic start to the day he'd finally made it to work in one piece—considered it a good result. The warning shots from the Russians, the little 'tumble' down the stairs and the confrontation with Soozie hadn't given the morning exactly a leisurely start, but he'd put all that behind him.

The coffee shop was practically empty; as always Carol and Leary had everything under control, they were visibly shocked when Panky staggered through the door, only about an hour late, couldn't help but notice the splinters of wood in his hair, the streaks of dried blood on his neck, the terrorist garb he was wearing. They smiled and—as always—decided not to ask questions. Being only an hour late, for Panky, was still impressive for a Monday.

Panky went to the gent's toilet, put on a torn but clean black t-shirt, quickly washed his face and brushed some of the splinters from his hair. He looked better, but only slightly.

The red and green lights of the graphic equalizer came to life and a song started to play. It was Ian Dury and the Blockheads, a Stiff classic, 'Sex and Drugs and Rock 'n' roll'.

As he returned from the toilet he smiled, as far as Panky was concerned it was *the* punk anthem. He stood against the bar smoking, gazing at the sunlight looking haggard and tired. Carol and Leary joined him, sat on the other side of the bar and shared his spliff; chatted about nothing, avoiding the subject of Judy's death like a phone booth full of lepers.

Panky exhaled a large cloud of smoke and grinned; apart from his recent near death experience and Judy's complete death experience it seemed like a perfectly normal Monday morning. So far at least. "I hate to sound predictable," said Panky as he passed the smoldering joint to Leary, "But I hate mornings like this when nothin' happens and then all hell breaks loose."

Leary Katz sat in a haze of smoke, grinning, gently nodding affirmation, as always he was wearing one of his Grateful Dead t-shirts, a bright green one today, almost fluorescent—he had thirty three different ones. 'Got a T-shirt for every day of the month', Leary told Panky once, his voice proud and emotional—Panky just smiled and said nothing, confused with the number thirty three. 'That Jerry G was some talented guy Panky, believe me...' Leary said with dreamy nostalgic eyes, '*Way* talented, you know what I'm saying? I saw eighty concerts man, eighty! Even got a Jerry tie man, 100% silk too, none of that polyester bullshit... never worn it man, probably never will, but who knows, right? It's all destiny waiting to happen, you know what I'm saying dude? Am I right or am I right?' Panky smiled and nodded, he liked Leary a lot but sometimes he got a little lost in their conversations. *Way* lost! Leary leaned across the bar grabbed at a handful of bags of grass and hash, laid them on a tray next to a steaming black espresso and an ice cold Heineken. Leary grinned; someone was getting an early start.

Carol the waitress jumped off her bar stool lifted the heavy tray with practiced ease and a big smile and walked casually to the far end of the bar. Her two customers were sitting quietly at a table in dappled sunlight; she saw their faces, watched their eyes follow passersby, people in the street; she saw intrigue and wonder in their young eyes. To Carol they seemed new in town, inquisitive, still excited by everything, watching the world stagger by, so colourful and crazy. They'd made their choice from the 'substance' menu, from the hundred different samples of hash and weed on offer and waited for their order with stale, bated breath and eager expressions. Carol put down the tray on an adjacent table and served them. They looked familiar for some reason, Carol wasn't sure why. "Ok," she said with a big professional smile, "One espresso, one large Heineken, four bags of Super Skunk, two large bags of Northern Lights, four large bags of Red Lebanese, two bags of Thai Sticks and one packet of cheese and onion crisps." Carol reached for a bong and an ashtray, "And a bong and an ashtray!" she said, "That's four hundred and fifty guilders, plus my tip… thank you."

The boys looked up at Carol and smiled in unison. It was Sid and D.K.!

Sid handed her some money and D.K. stared at her magnificent cleavage.

The clock on the wall said 10.58 a.m.

As Carol took the money and headed back towards the cash register she looked back at the boys, sure that she knew them from somewhere, but she wasn't sure where: the sneers, the zits, the hairstyles, all looked familiar somehow.

Sid filled the bong and lit it. The boys smoked and drank and smoked some more.

D.K. said, "Sid?"

Sid said, "Wot?"

"So… that's definitely him is it?" D.K. staring up the end of the coffee shop now, focusing on Panky slouched across the bar, chatting and laughing with Carol and Leary, watched him pick up a newspaper and start to read it.

"Yeah," said Sid, "That's him… mum showed me photo's didn't she?

"D'ya really think it's his fault though Sid?"

"Don't be stupid D.K., course it's his fault! Where d'ya think she got all the coke from… the local fuckin' supermarket?"

D.K. stared at the bong, silent and thoughtful; he played with his empty crisp packet.

"Sid?"

"Wot?"

"You sure we can do this?" asked D.K.

"Course we can do it… its easy innit?"

Sid lit the bong again, spoke as smoke billowed from his pierced nostrils, "All we need is some guns and I've got that sorted," he said through a wafting cumulus of smoke.

D.K. watched his big brother smoke the bong some more, water bubbled like crazy as he sucked as hard as he could, filling his lungs with the sweet intoxicating smoke. He exhaled again deeply, filling the air all around them.

Sid continued talking in a proud, confidential tone; wanting to explain what was happening, wanting to show his kid brother that everything was under control.

"Mum gave me a number didn't she?" he said, "In case we ever came to visit; friends of hers innit? They can help us, ex KGP or something, fuckin' Russian geezers?"

D.K. listened intently, chewed his dirty fingernails and scratched his zits.

Sid looked around furtively and carried on, his face lit with enthusiasm, his conversation getting faster and more excited.

"Serious geezers mum said; get us anything we want if we got the money." Sid smiled and looked into his brother's frightened eyes, "And we've got the money haven't we?"

D.K. nodded, his eyes looked sad and young and tired. Yeah they had the money all right, all of mum's savings, the cash Judy'd made from all her previous smugglings. They found it in an old biscuit tin high up in Grandma's smelly kitchen, near the cleaning stuff, somewhere where grandma wouldn't look. It was the money their mother had put away for their orthodontic work.

Sid lit the bong again, the sound of bubbling water returned, smoke engulfed their table; filled their end of the bar like before.

The entrance door of the coffee shop suddenly flew open with a *crash*!

Sid and D.K. jumped at the sound, turned and watched as two huge Russians walked in, gazing around like they owned the place or had come with the money to buy it. It was the brothers Karamazov.

They strolled through the coffee shop in unison like they were joined at the hip; they were steroid massive with a cruel, dangerous demeanor: lips curled in arrogant sneers, cold marble eyes full of violent intent, short cropped hair dyed white, gulag tattoos, thick, thick necks and the blankest of blank expressions. Scary fucking geezers... like ogres.

Panky peeked over the top of his newspaper and smiled. He'd heard about the brothers Karamazov, it was them for sure. The biggest nastiest street fighters this side of Siberia, that's what he'd heard anyway, they certainly looked it. He was pretty sure they weren't hired for their social skills.

A little physical violence never hurt anybody, thought Panky, but these guys looked nasty.

The Russians sat down at a table and the bigger of the two clicked his fingers in the air for some service, his brother started to read the homo porno mag he'd pulled from his pocket.

Panky smiled, snorted at their naivety, at their arrogance as he silently witnessed the finger clicking routine—a routine hated by every hard working waiter and waitress in the world, a routine that almost guarantees you'll get your food or drink with at least a little saliva in it. Panky chuckled quietly behind his paper, signaled with his eyes for Carol and Leary to leave this one to him. He put down his newspaper, slid off his stool, came out from behind the bar and walked slowly towards them. "And what can we do you for?" he asked with a smirk.

The brothers grunted in unison, stood up slowly, faces still blank, but showing a few teeth now, marble eyes hard on Panky's face.

"We have... a little message... for you," said the one with the homo mag. He sounded like he was reading the words.

"From Zoltan," said the bigger one as he cracked a smile.

Without a word Panky suddenly lunged forward and fast, grabbed the smiling one by the Adam's apple, twisted the ample flesh and lifted the guy onto his toes. It wasn't easy.

At the same time, with his other hand and just as fast, he grabbed the balls of the other Russian and squeezed them in a vice like grip; squeezed and squeezed.

Both guys gasped, clearly shocked and helpless, neither of them used to being attacked by just one guy. They couldn't believe it; they couldn't move either.

The brother with his balls in a vice tried to speak, "This, you will regret…" he tried to say; his face almost purple now, tears welling in his eyes, sweat forming fast on his furrowed brow.

Panky turned and smiled at the silent brother, the one on tiptoes, the one trying hard to suck in air through his teeth, then he turned back quickly and head butted the bigger guy, the one with the purple face who'd given the silly warning. It was a perfect head butt, hard and accurate, the Russian's mouth and nose exploding together with the impact. The bone in the nose peeped through the flesh, teeth cracked and broke loose; fell out onto the floor in a pool of blood and saliva. Panky let go of the guy's testicles and the once arrogant Russian collapsed into a heap. The one on tiptoes was dizzy now from lack of oxygen, his face was flushed and distorted, eyes rolling, nearly blacking out, but Panky held on to his windpipe; held on tight as he moved closer to the guy on the floor.

Panky swung a heavy boot and kicked the prostrate guy hard in the balls. He shouted; "Fuck!" Then swung another kick and heard air wheeze out of exhausted lungs, "Right!" And then he kicked him again; heard his gonads crunch hard against his pelvis, "Off!" Satisfied that he'd done a fair job and pretty sure the Karamazov's wouldn't be trying anything else—at least for a while—Panky let go of the twisted Adam's apple, watched the huge guy slump into his seat, purple faced still, gasping for breath.

The strangled Russian held his neck as if it was broken and groaned quietly. He moved his eyes and looked up at Panky, curious if he should expect another onslaught, another attack. He decided the battle was over for now and moved towards his brother, tried to pick him up. The guy was heavy, a dead weight, it took time.

Panky stood back with Leary and Carol and watched, the three of them wearing their biggest smiles now. Panky's heart still beating so fast he could hear it thumping in his ears, wondered if Leary and Carol could hear it too.

The Russians got to their feet and scrambled towards the door.

"We'll be back for you vykovskyi," said the bigger brother looking back, spitting crimson pink saliva on the floor, "We'll be back… back with guns, we kill you!"

"Tell Zoltan to come see me the day after tomorrow," said Panky casually—he'd heard it all before, "I'll have his money by then, all of it."

Panky grinned at Carol and Leary and shrugged like saying: Oh well shit happens. With trembling hands he lit a spliff and poured himself a Chivas.

The groaning Russians tumbled out onto the street, into the sunshine.

Sid and D.K. sat smoking, watching it all happen. They sat open mouthed as Panky sprang into action, saw him take on the two massive gorilla types and still come out smiling. They couldn't believe it! The Panky guy was so fast, so much stronger than they expected.

Leary, Carol and Panky stood together against the bar.

"I think you're gonna have some trouble with those two dudes, man," said Leary.

"What Tweedledeeski and Tweedledumdski?" said Panky, "The fuckin' Soviet sisters? Let 'em try!"

"No, not the Russians dude," said Leary quietly, looking down the end of the bar at Sid and D.K., the boys sitting there still amazed, dappled by the broken sunlight, smoke spiraling around them, "Those two punks man, the punk kids... they're Judy's boys!"

Panky stood silent looking down the coffee shop at Sid and D.K., saw them staring back at him, sneering. Panky thinking: not today, please!

Carol nodded to herself; she knew she recognized their faces from somewhere; they were the kids on the TV, the runaways.

Sid and D.K. got up to leave, all eyes still fixed on Panky.

"Fuck me Sid," said D.K. nervously, as he edged his way towards the door, "This guy Panky's the business... we're gonna need some real big guns!"

D.K. sat outside the 'Rastamania' coffee shop in the midday sun, enjoying a cold liquid lunch and a couple of spliffs. It was 11.56 a.m. and D.K. was relaxing, the calm before the storm. He had a great view from where he was sitting, he could see it all: the tall old buildings along the canal steeped in history, warped and twisted with time; the prostitutes hanging out in their windows, teasing and laughing, doing their thing; the endless stream of pleasure boats cruising aimlessly up and down the canal taking the tourists for a ride, and the weirdest, strangest assortment of people D.K. had ever seen in his life. There were the bicycles too, thousands of fucking bicycles, bicycles everywhere.

D.K. watched a guy zoom along the pavement past his table on roller blades, so fast! The guy was practically naked, dressed in just a silver jock strap; silver glitter adorning his naked flesh, shining; the guy carrying a shopping bag and big cheesy grin. D.K. thinking: Now is that fucking weird or what? He then saw two gay boys strutting along in tight black leather trousers and shiny matching waistcoats, gay silver chains on their little leather caps, dressed like twins. Freddy Mercury fans maybe, possibly Burt Reynolds— the short-cropped hair and the handle bar moustaches giving away their little secrets. They were in their forties at least, maybe older, one was tall and thin, the other short and fat, the short fat one holding a small teddy bear, the
bear dressed in the same leather outfit, it even had the cap with the gay silver chains; he had it perched on his chubby open hand as they wended along with deadpan gay expressions. D.K. wondered where the hell they were going. To the vets for some teddy tests perhaps? Or a teddy bears picnic maybe… a gay one? D.K. chuckled, shoulders moving up and down as he smoked and gazed around aimlessly. He turned towards the coffee shop, saw Sid still on the telephone, talking and animated, looking pleased about something.

Eventually Sid walked back to the table outside and joined his brother, listened to his stories about the practically naked guy on the roller blades and the homo's with the teddy bear. Sid wasn't sure if D.K. was serious or taking the piss, decided that Amsterdam was a crazy place to live.

They drank cold beer, smoked some spliffs and ate shawarmas for lunch; laughing and joking around, chili sauce and garlic dip on their chins and on their breath. For a while they seemed like a couple of normal kids, tourists, innocent; larking around, messing about, making stupid comments about the oddballs walking by; a couple of young lads having a bit of fun, abroad for the first time.

Then a large black Mercedes pulled up quietly alongside their table.

Sid and D.K. looked at each other in mild disbelief studied their grinning reflections in the dark tinted windows of the limousine.

With a subtle buzz the driver's window opened and their reflections disappeared into the panel of the door. Brief words were exchanged.

The boys stood up and walked to the car; big smiles now as they climbed inside and lost themselves in leather luxury and cool conditioned air. It was the best car they'd ever sat in. Their delighted faces said it all.

The two big guys in the front turned, welcomed the boys with a grin and a nod. It was Boris and Vlad!

"Sorry to hear about your mother," said Vlad, his voice unusually serious and solemn, "To me she was a close friend, really." And she was. They'd met one night in 'The Milky Way' nightclub; Judy walked casually up to Vlad, told him she'd never done it with a really big Russian before and the romance blossomed from there. Judy asked Vlad if he was KGB 'cos the concept of secret service excited her. Vlad lied and said yes he was but keep it a secret. Vlad grinned at the punks.

Boris smirked and said nothing. He knew exactly how close Judy was to Vlad, he'd seen them at it; he'd heard the noises, the grunts, the groans, the screaming, and the squeaking bed. He'd watched it all through the crack in Vlad's bedroom door.

Sid nodded a little appreciation for Vlad's kind words, his eyes were glazed and bloodshot, *so* stoned; he knew they'd need a little pick me up to keep them going, need a little 'marchin' powder' to keep their minds clear, keep them focused on their mission. Sid sniffed, prepared his nostrils for the inevitable.

D.K. clicked on his Walkman, gazed out of the tinted window at nothing in particular, nodding his head to the spasmodic rhythm of the music; the song gave him his biggest smile. It wasn't just a classic track, it was their family anthem; it meant so much to him, made him think about his mum, the fun they used to have as a family whenever she was home: 'Damaged Goods' by 'Gang of Four' played loud in his ears, he mouthed the words silently as he nodded back and forth. Appropriate or what?

Sid sat staring at the Russians not sure what to say, he felt a bit nervous; he'd never actually bought any guns before. He'd never met a Russian before either, KPG or otherwise.

"So, what do you need?" asked Vlad.

"Two big hand guns for me," said Sid and he turned and looked at D.K. nodding to the music, "Very big hand guns… as many shots as possible… err… an Uzi… for D.K.," Sid smiled when he said that, considered his little brother's lack of talent when it came to shooting, an Uzi would more than compensate, "Err... about ten grams of coke... and that's it," he said clapping his hands together, grinning like he'd just bought a secondhand car.

Vlad and Boris nodded and smiled, no problem.

"Oh yeah, almost forgot... and lots of bullets," said Sid with a slight grimace, not sure if the bullets came with the guns or were an optional extra. He pulled a large wad of money out of his leather jacket and sniffed, looking forward to the coke already.

Vlad kept nodding and smiling, said, "No problem boys, you want it, you got it!

Panky glanced at the clock on the wall of the coffee shop, it was 9.56 p.m. Despite the brief moments of excitement the day seemed to last an eternity. Panky felt tired, drained, but he still had a lot to do and he knew it.

It was dark outside now; the red light district was finally coming back to life; people wandering through the bustling neon streets looking for fun; most of them eventually finding what they were looking for, whatever it was.

The coffee shop was crowded now; had a nice busy ambience going on: low lights, plenty of smoke, plenty of laughter, cosmopolitan chit chat a cacophony in the air, the cash register making its music in the corner. Commercially it was a good night.

'Warning Sign' by 'Talking Heads' tinkled from the speakers.

Panky was slumped across the bar looking exhausted, thinking: Now that's a funny little song. Another song that took him back to his youth—the band weren't exactly punk, but they were from that era. He lounged across the bar, watched Leary and Carol busily serving customers as he smoked a spliff, eyeing up the female customers, weighing out some hash. He had butterflies in his stomach. The big event would be coming come soon, real soon. In fact there were just a few minutes left before it kicked off and it needed to go smoothly, it needed to go without a hitch. Tonight he was doing his 'big deal', and hopefully making some 'big bucks', enough to get Zoltan and his boys off his back for good and still leave plenty to spare. Hopefully.

Just down the road, not far from the coffee shop a deaf old attendant sat by the door of a public toilet and waited for his customers to leave tips on his wooden platter. The old guy looked up at the clock on the wall, it ticked from 9.56 p.m. to 9.57 p.m.—it was a minute fast and always had been.

Suddenly the long tiled room echoed with harsh metallic sounds, cold metal on cold metal, guns being checked and cocked. The noise was dangerous, ominous, it had purpose. The sounds bounced around the room like bullets themselves; irrefutable deadly noises.

The deaf old attendant sat nearly asleep, one rheumy eye on his tips, oblivious to the sounds.

Sid and D.K. stood among the graffiti in adjacent cubicles with the doors propped open; they were both facing the toilet, facing the wall in front of them; the studs on their leather jackets caught the bright fluorescent light, illuminated the word 'Brixton' at the bottom of their jackets. Sid was holding two large handguns and smiling: two slightly used 9mm Glocks that each held seventeen hollow point bullets. Perfect.

He held the Glocks up to the light, admired their potential, smiled at them proudly like recently won trophies, shoved them into the waistband of his trousers, stooped forward holding a rolled up bank note and snorted two huge lines of cocaine from the top of the toilet cistern.

D.K.'s boyish voice rose from the depths of the adjacent cubicle.

"Sid?"

"Wot?" asked Sid with his usual aplomb.

"What's a semi colon?"

Sid nearly laughed.

"Not now D.K., I'll tell you later," he said sniffing, "I promise."

D.K. seemed satisfied with the response, figured it probably wasn't the best time for a chat about semi-colons—whatever they were.

With serious eyes and a slightly nervous expression D.K. checked and loaded his Uzi like Sid had showed him, once again cold metallic sounds bounced around the room like bullets. D.K. then stooped forward and snorted two huge lines of coke from the top of toilet cistern. He sniffed and wiped his nose, slid the Uzi into the bright yellow plastic carrier bag he'd pulled from his pocket and raised his left hand up into the air in some defiant kind of pose.

The two young punks turned, spun in perfect unison, wired to the gills, armed to the teeth and ready for action. Ready for mum's revenge.

Panky was leaning across the bar still smoking a joint, checking out more female tourists, giving them his friendly smile, saying "Hi, how's it going?" to a few of the regulars, sipping his large cold Heineken. On the surface he looked pretty relaxed.

The song 'Warning Signs' continued to tinkle gently from the speakers: the vocalist's words were robotic and repetitive, strangely foreboding.

Panky looked around the bar and smiled; he loved the place when it was buzzing like this, he liked the atmosphere, people laughing, chatting, having a good time. At times like these selling drugs was a lot of fun.

Julia, a huge guy with thick dark curly hair like Julia Roberts, sat at a table with his friend Jimmy smoking a few spliffs and enjoying a few cold beers. The guys were Panky's mates from London, both in their 30's and street wise geezers. They were dressed like football supporters: hats, scarves, t-shirts, all the gear.

Panky looked over at them, gave them the thumbs up. They smiled back. Things were going ok. It was nearly time.

Julia and Jimmy were smuggling Ecstasy into England. Panky had it all arranged.

They had ten thousand tablets each, taped to their legs and thighs with thick gray tape—the strong tape like kidnappers use. Once taped up, the tablets were covered over with tight spandex cycling pants, a pair of jeans on top of that. Simple.

Panky spent a couple of hours that afternoon briefing the guys; got them sorted as far as taping the tablets to their legs was concerned, made sure they did it right. Luckily, Julia and Jimmy were experienced, they'd done a few runs before; they'd taken hash and coke back to England hidden inside their cars, never had a problem, made some good money too. Panky told them smuggling the E's wasn't much different to the hash or the coke, not really; it was just hidden inside your trousers instead of a car. Same meat different gravy, said Panky, shouldn't be a problem. All they had to do was get back to England, meet another old mate in Soho, exchange the tablets for cash and the job was done: A piece of piss, Panky said, nothing to worry about. Panky's profit, after expenses, was thirty thousand pounds—nearly fifty thousand dollars! —A lot of money for a day or two's work and a little bit of planning, the rest of Zoltan's money and then some. Enough to get the Russian's off his back for good, tidy up his houseboat and maybe even enough for a holiday and a bit of a break from everything.

Initially Julia and Jimmy were keen, but cautious. "Easier to search your trousers than a car," said Julia, and of course he was right. But once Panky explained about the benefits of dressing up like football supporters and mingling with the crowds, the guys laughed and laughed, said it was a great idea and sure to work. The police might be looking for knives, razors and knuckle-dusters, but they wouldn't be looking for designer drugs, would they? Not on people coming back from a major sporting event. Weapons? Sure. But not drugs...

Julia and Jimmy were leaving for the ferry real soon; they had a train to catch just across the street, had to be at Central station at exactly 10.15 p.m.

Panky's only real concern was getting more heat from the Russians; he'd pay them as soon as Julia got back from England with the cash, he'd told them that already, a few times, but obviously Zoltan didn't trust him, thought he was up to something. Panky had considered offering a part payment; he'd had most of the money ready for a while now, but knew from experience that Zoltan was an all or nothing kind of guy. So fuck it, Zoltan would have to wait a little longer; it was as simple as that.

Panky slouched across the bar, exhaled a huge plume of smoke and smiled at a young Scandinavian girl who was staring at him. Wishing he wasn't quite so busy, he sipped his beer and looked over at Julia and Jimmy laughing together, enjoying themselves just before they left.

Things were going ok, so far anyway.

Vlad and Boris sat in the front window of 'Vincent's' restaurant directly across the street from 'The Other Twilight Zone'. Despite their bulk they could hardly be seen behind the fancy lettering painted on the big window. They were obscured by the logo that said 'Vincent's' in bold yellow, the colour of Vincent's sunflowers.

Boris looked at his Rolex copy; it was 9.58 p.m.

Boris and Vlad could see the coffee shop perfectly, could even see Panky lounging across the bar smoking another spliff, eyeing up the females, sipping his Heineken.

Boris said, "He looks relaxed," and Vlad agreed, considering he knew that sooner or later they'd be coming to get him, he did look relaxed.

The two big Russians liked the restaurant a lot; they were enjoying themselves; wasn't too often they got the chance to eat somewhere as stylish as 'Vincent's'. They knew it was a classy place when they booked the table so they'd made the effort and dressed up a little, both in elegant three piece suits; dark double breasted jackets full of muscle and brawn, matching silk accessories, red and blue ties and handkerchiefs, shoes polished like mirrors. Despite the scars and the close-cropped hair they looked smart, almost respectable; like two muscle bound stockbrokers, sitting at the table flexing their biceps and triceps, chatting about next year's projections over steak and a few good bottles of wine. They sat at their table staring out the window, silent now, watching, but relaxed about it. The meal was excellent and finished, cigars accompanied their fourth bottle of wine, they were waiting for the brandy and the coffee, the after dinner mints. Boris's plan was simple. Wait. Wait and then at the perfect moment storm into the coffee shop, stick their guns in Panky's face and demand the cash. They knew he had most of it now, he'd told them, a few times, so it had to be there somewhere, had to be close by. Panky wasn't stupid enough to leave nearly a hundred grand just lying around his houseboat. No way.

Boris touched the gun under his jacket, made sure it was there. He couldn't believe Panky had given the Karamazov's such a beating, couldn't believe the damage he'd done, the guy was obviously much stronger than he looked, faster too.

Zoltan was shocked too. His message to the Karamazov's was simple: leave the rest to Boris and Vlad, stay away from the coffee shop, don't take it personally, keep away.

Boris and Vlad sat at their table smoking Cuban cigars waiting for their coffee.

"The Karamazov's seemed a little unhappy I think," said Vlad.

"Hmm, upset maybe, in pain for sure," said Boris staring across the street deciding to go in just after ten o'clock. It seemed a good time.

"That Panky can dish it out pretty good" said Vlad.

"Yeah," said Boris, "He can."

Vlad sipped his coffee, "You think maybe we should kill him... all this hassle?"

"Why not?" Boris smiling as the waitress brought the coffee. "Maybe he'll have some electrical problems, maybe his little coffee shop will catch fire? Maybe his houseboat will too? Boris chuckled, smoked his cigar, and said, "Who knows these things, anything could happen?"

Vlad nodded his head in agreement, sipped his coffee thinking: Shit, bet my suit ends up smelling of smoke again.

Sid and D.K. left the public toilet at 9.58 p.m.

The young brothers walked briskly through the bright busy streets towards 'The Other Twilight Zone'. D.K.'s Walkman was on full volume. 'Judy is a punk' by 'The Ramones' was playing, a tribute to his mum. He held back the tears, but it wasn't easy.

Sid was walking with his head down and sniffing, his pace fast and determined; he held his guns tightly under his jacket, ready.

D.K. followed along behind trying hard to keep up, his Uzi held tightly in his sweaty hand, hidden in the bright yellow carrier bag. The boys looked mean and totally wired, they dodged bicycles, shoved their way through the crowds.

They entered a dimly lit alleyway, nearly there now. D.K. caught up and moved alongside his brother, looked up at him as they paced towards the coffee shop; the alleyway smelled of pizza and piss, red and green lights shone on their faces.

"Sid?" said D.K. as they marched along side-by-side, picking up the pace a bit.

"Wot?"

"Can I ask a question?"

"Wot?"

"Aren't you nervous Sid?"

"Me… nervous? You kiddin'?"

"Wot, not even a bit?"

"A bit yeah, natural innit? But no more than when I first kissed a girl…"

"Wow!" said D.K., "I've never kissed a proper girl."

Sid stopped abruptly and stared at his little brother, "But you've tried, right?"

"Oh yeah," said D.K. with a smile, "Course I've tried."

Sid grinned at his little brother, he'd let him do the big blonde later, but first they had a job to do, a mission to complete.

They walked the rest of the way in silence holding tightly onto their guns.

Boris and Vlad were still sitting at their table finishing their coffee and cigars when a taxicab pulled up across the street and parked outside 'The Other Twilight Zone'.

They sat silent in a cloud of Cuban cigar smoke sipping at brandy snifters as the Karamazov's lumbered out of the cab and pushed their way into the coffee shop.

It was 9.59 p.m. when Boris and Vlad casually looked out of the restaurants big window and it was only then that they realised what was actually happening.

Thick cigar smoke swirled gently around the table, hung in the flickering candlelight, it veiled Boris's florid face, gave him a vague ghostly appearance. He looked across the table at Vlad, shook his head and sighed deeply making the candlelight dance on their faces.

Boris said, "This is not a good situation Vladimir, not good at all." He touched the Beretta inside his jacket for reassurance. He was pleased he was armed but not really sure what to do next; Zoltan had told the Karamazov's to keep away, leave the rest to Boris and Vlad, but they clearly hadn't listened, because they were there in the coffee shop now with the door closing behind them.

Vlad said, "So what do we do? Call Zoltan?"

"No," said Boris, "Let's just wait… see what happens."

At 9.59 p.m. Panky stubbed out his spliff and knocked back another Chivas. The coffee shop was buzzing.

'Warning Signs' was playing still, sounded to Panky like it had been playing all night. It was a great night; the place was rockin' in a mellow kind of way. Panky had even got the mobile number of the cute little Scandinavian girl. Things were going good.

Then the door came open with a *crash*!

It was the Karamazov's. Back as promised and probably armed.

Panky didn't even flinch as the gorillas hobbled through the door. The smaller brother had his nose in some splint cum bandage affair, his eyes were purple turning yellow blue and puffy, his lips were swollen and split, teeth clearly missing.

Panky smiled at him, chuckled under his breath as the wounded ogre sat down at a table, nearly laughed out loud, wondering if his nuts were in a splint as well?

The bigger brother looked pretty much normal, but clearly couldn't speak, couldn't utter a sound. The bruising on his throat was noticeable even from a distance.

Again Panky looked across at their table, smiled and nodded a slightly arrogant hello to the bigger brother and tried hard not to laugh.

Julia the longhaired football enthusiast/smuggler stood up, wandered towards the bleach and graffiti of the gent's toilet. He seemed pretty wasted, didn't seem too sure on his feet.

Jimmy heard Julia giggle as he stood up, as he steadied himself on the marble topped table.

Panky hadn't told his smuggling buddies about his little 'tussle' with the Soviet sisters, didn't want to worry them unnecessarily, didn't think there was much chance of the guys from the gulag coming back so soon. Panky told his mates to get drunk before they left for the train station, explained that it was natural for *real* sports fans to be pissed out of their heads after the match, whether their team won or lost. So without too much effort Jimmy and Julia got into a few free beers.

Carol strolled from the bar, took the order from the battered Russians. The smaller brother gave the order and his brother seethed silently.

Panky nearly laughed out loud again when they ordered Campari's. Fucking pussycats or what?

They stared at Panky with vengeful eyes as they waited for their drinks.

Panky stared back thinking: Come on then bastards, if you're gonna do it, do it. His eyes then drifted through the haze of smoke beyond the two injured gorillas, beyond all the people at the tables chatting and having fun, beyond all that. He focused on the big window at the front of the coffee shop. He couldn't believe what he saw!

Sid and D.K. were standing there looking totally wired, staring at him like they were completely crazy. Their noses almost on the window, warm breathe steaming on the glass.

Boris and Vlad put down their cigars, knocked back the rest of their brandy and ordered two more, told the waitress to hurry and make them doubles. Their faces already flushed with alcohol, glistening with a thin film of perspiration; it seemed hot now in the candlelight, their breathing suddenly seemed loud, laboured across the table, amplified. Their expressions were blank and helpless.

Boris and Vlad could see the word 'Brixton' shining on the back of their jackets, silver flashes reflected from the streetlights.

The boys stood statue still and stared through the big glass window.

Boris looked at his Rolex copy: 9.59 almost 10.00. Time stood still. Or it seemed to.

Vlad looked across the table at Boris, "I think maybe we fucked up a little," he said.

Boris said, "I think Vladimir… maybe you're right for once."

Panky stood behind the bar staring at Sid and D.K.

The song 'Warning Signs' stopped playing, the amicable hubbub of the coffee shop seemed to diminish and fade. To Panky the place was practically silent now. He looked through the coffee shop beyond the Karamazov's, beyond the crowds of customers and stared at Sid and D.K.

The biggest Karamazov brother looked at Panky and realised that he wasn't focused on them at all. The fear etched on his face wasn't because of them or because of what *they* were going to do; it was because of something else, something further away in the distance. Wincing with pain the Russian slowly turned his head, saw the two young punks staring through the big front window, recognised them from earlier that day in the coffee shop.

Sid and D.K stood still and silent, adrenaline and cocaine in their wide young eyes, breath still hot and steamy on the glass.

Panky stared transfixed, hands flat on the bar, his heart beating loud in his chest now, his throat feeling tight and constricted, wide as a drinking straw.

Suddenly another song began, broke Panky's illusion of silence. The throbbing red and green lights of the stereo brought new life and energy to the room, sounds that pushed aside the foreboding atmosphere, but brought with them a distinct message of their own. First came the rhythmic tapping of a snare drum, tight and military, a heavy bass line followed and developed the sound, wobbled and plodded from the speakers,

finally an electric guitar screeched and cried and
jangled with feedback, a jagged sound like broken
glass. The drums and bass brought the sounds together,
created some strange and violent kind of harmony. The
Clash filled the coffee shop with dark ominous music;
Paul Simonon snarled the words over a steady hypnotic
beat, and once again the 'Guns of Brixton' rang out.

The Karamazov's glanced from Panky to the
window and back again, saw Sid and D.K. staring,
heard the ominous music.
Panky started to sweat, just waiting for something to
happen, his heartbeat was tight and louder now,
pulsating in his throat, his mouth dry like cotton wool,
trembling hands too and tunnel vision; seeing only Sid
and D.K.
Waiting for something to happen; breathing harder
now... just waiting...
The Karamazov's looked back and forth from Panky
to the punks, waiting for something to happen.
Knowing that it would, knowing that it had to. And then
it happened.
Sid pulled the handguns from his waistband aimed at
Panky and nodded to his brother. D.K. raised the Uzi in
the bright yellow carrier bag, covered his eyes with his
other hand and fired. The Uzi spluttered bullets through
bright yellow plastic, the window shattered, glass
cascaded around their feet and a hot rapid rain filled the
coffee shop. The noise from the Uzi was shocking,
filled the streets with an echoing bark; a sound you
couldn't hide from, a sound you couldn't ignore. D.K.
looked terrified, way out of his depth and way out of

control, but he kept firing, kept waving the Uzi, doing exactly as his brother had told him.

Panky just stood as before, frozen: trembling hands flat on the bar, wide eyes and a mouth full of cotton wool.

The Karamazov's couldn't believe it! Their eyes were shocked and glaring, heads back and forth like avid tennis fans.

Outside Sid smiled grimly down the barrels of his guns. Aiming at Panky.

Panky's vision zoomed to the gun barrels, zoomed to the blackness of them, to the dread. He slowly looked up into Sid's glazed eyes, eyes crazy with vengeance and bloodlust, wild with cocaine clarity. Panky watching the smallest move, thinking: Yep, they're Judy's boys for sure, just as fuckin' mental, just as fuckin' wired.

D.K. changed the magazine, it was easy like Sid had said, and the Uzi continued to spray bullets into the coffee shop; a corkboard full of photos, pictures and flyers got caught in the hail of bullets, ephemeral fragments spiraling into the cordite air like so much confetti. Screams all around now from inside the coffee shop as customers dashed for cover—Chaos, mayhem, and sounds crashing in waves.

Across the street Boris and Vlad sat silent and impotent; watching D.K. wave his Uzi and spray the place with bullets, tattered remnants of the yellow plastic carrier bag fluttering madly around his hand. They watched as Sid held his guns on Panky, taking aim; heard the sounds across the street, the murderous noise, saw the coffee shop fill with hazy smoke and bullets, terrified bodies running for cover. They saw Panky standing behind the bar, a witness to it all.

Julia stepped cautiously out of the gent's toilet confused by the noise, by the panic all around, a huge gentle giant amazed at the flurry of customers diving for cover, amazed by the smell, the fear, the violence in the air.

Panky watched Julia step across the bar, saw him look around in disbelief, watched him step into Sid's line of fire, innocent and unaware, saw him raise an eyebrow as if to say: "What's the story? What's the fuck's happening?" Everything in slow motion now like Peckinpah pictures. It seemed to Panky like he was having an out of body experience. Floating. Watching it all from above. Weird or what?

Sid pulled the triggers on both guns. Still aiming at Panky.

Julia made another step forward. It was his last step. Ever. The first bullet hit Julia in the neck, stopped his body mid-step; the second ripped through his chest, exploded through his body and he crumpled into heap, folded like a giant rag doll with beautiful hair. Fell silently to the floor.

On the street side of the window D.K. had loaded another magazine, was still firing high into the coffee shop, making all that noise, laughing hysterically like a devil in heaven.

Inside the coffee shop customers screamed and cried, threw themselves around in panic. Julia's body lay in a heap on the floor, he coughed and blood oozed thick from his mouth. With shock and surprise in his eyes he coughed again and died.

'The Guns of Brixton' continued to play…

The brothers Karamazov took cover behind their upturned marble topped table. The bigger brother pulled a large handgun from inside his jacket. He looked surprised, but calm.

Jimmy slid from his seat, pushed his table over and copied the Karamazov's. He looked at Julia's body, tried hard to hold back the tears. Screams filled the room.

Outside D.K. kept firing, waving the Uzi, still peeping through his fingers, still amazed at what he was doing. Sid lifted his handguns again, dizzy with excitement, pumped with adrenalin and coke. He aimed, smiled and thought about Zombies.

Panky stood frozen, still couldn't move, he tried to scream but nothing came out.

Carol ran towards him with arms outstretched, tried to take cover behind the bar.

Sid fired his guns.

Carol's momentum going in one direction and the power of the bullets going in the other seemed to hold her in midair; she almost glided across the room towards the bar, towards Panky, but never quite made it. She never made a sound; just collapsed, dropped dead in a heap in front of Panky.

Tears ran down Panky's face, choked in his throat. He *still* couldn't move.

Outside on the pavement D.K. peeped through his fingers and changed his aim, fired through the remains of the window into some hippy customers hiding behind a wooden table, ripped them to pieces. Then he giggled, fired at the little Scandinavian girl sitting against a luminous green alien crying hysterically, too afraid to move.

He got her too!

The Uzi reloaded, went back to the hippies. Bullets slashed into their bodies again, left them twitching and dying, tattered and groaning. A stray bullet hit another of the aliens against the wall, blew it to a million pieces; fiberglass dust filled the air, luminous and green. An extra terrestrial head broke loose and dropped to the floor, it bounced close to Carol's body, seemed to stare into what was left of her face.

The Karamazov with the bandaged nose stood up, tried to run to the toilet.

But Sid was too good... too quick.

Blood slashed across the luminous green face of an alien like paint flicked from a brush. The Russian dropped in his tracks, half his face gone.

Panky couldn't breathe; couldn't move, still felt like he was watching from above, watching from higher ground.

Jimmy hid behind the table curled up in a ball: a shaking, hysterical fetus.

D.K.'s bullets ripped through the table, Jimmy's body jumped around spasmodically. He was dead with the first bullet.

The remaining Karamazov stood up from behind the table, big and defiant, cool under pressure, experienced. He aimed his gun at D.K., pulled the trigger twice. The sound echoed around the tall streets outside.

The Uzi fell silent as D.K. fell to the floor, a look of total surprise plastered across his face, his chest blown apart, blown open.

The remaining Karamazov smiled.

Sid wasn't the only one who was a good shot. Sid looked down at his brother in disbelief. He gasped and aimed and fired his guns, mad eyes full of vengeance for his little brother, but the big Russian moved just in time, the bullets zipped past his head. Close, but not close enough. Sid under pressure now, near to panic.

The Russian fired back.

The echoes bounced off the buildings outside and filled the night.

Sid stood still, sneering as bullets zipped past him and ricocheted across the street. He smiled and fired again.

The bullets hit their target but low. The remaining Karamazov flew backwards across an overturned table lay with his arms and legs akimbo, gut shot. Smoke, cordite, spiraling confetti and destruction filled the air, and the 'Guns of Brixton' played on. The onslaught had only taken a couple of minutes. It seemed like hours. It seemed like a lifetime. Like fucking eons.

Panky's pounding heart filled his ears, adrenaline pumped through his veins, his head was spinning, tears ran wet down his cheeks, he was deaf and dizzy and he *still* couldn't fucking move.

Outside Sid looked down at his dead brother, guns hanging heavy in his hands, Dr Marten boots crunching glass with his smallest movement. "It wasn't s'pose to be like this mum!" he shouted madly, looking up into the sullen darkness of the night, looking up towards the God he'd never believed in, talking to his mum, hoping that maybe she was up there too. "S'pose to be easy..." he mumbled through his tears, "easy like the Zombies!" Tears rolled down his cheeks, he wiped the snot from his nose on the sleeve of his leather jacket, giggled stupidly through his tears. "He didn't even know what a semi-fuckin'-colon was..." he bellowed to the sky, "He never even kissed a proper girl!"

The gut shot Russian with the swollen Adam's apple groaned and stood up looked at his open wounds and snarled, "Vykovskyi!" With the last remaining power in his huge body he aimed and pulled the trigger.

The sound echoed as Sid's neck took the bullet; his arms flew high, almost gracefully, into the air. He fell onto the pavement, gurgled for a second or two, edged his way towards his brother and died.

The big Russian smiled, slid down the upturned table and slumped onto the floor groaning, holding his gut, blood oozing between his fat fingers.

The coffee shop was suddenly quiet again; just a few dying groans, muttered prayers from the recently converted.

Panky stood perfectly still. He *still* couldn't move.

The coffee shop stood like an acid trip abattoir; splashed, sprayed and splattered. Red and horrific. Dead aliens smoking in pieces, acrid smoldering fiberglass thick in the air, the faint crackle and sizzle of loose electric wires, sparks and dim flickering lights.

Panky heard wailing sirens in the background, sirens getting closer and fast.

Suddenly car doors slammed like tumbling dominoes, Walkie-talkie voices shattered the fragile silence.

Panky grabbed the bottle of Chivas on the bar and took a massive swig, he grabbed his small leather holdall from beneath the bar and jumped feet first into the cellar. He was outta there!

Leary was lurking in the shadows of the cellar, hiding behind a shelf of silver beer barrels, looking scared and bewildered. His look changed to overjoyed when he realised it was Panky and that he was ok, he was still alive. The guys shared a hasty high five and ran through the dimly lit tunnel that led to 'Van Gee's' bar next door. They didn't say a word, didn't need to. It was time to be somewhere else. Anywhere.

They hurtled themselves up the creaking stairs three at a time, side-by-side, panting.

They surfaced behind the bar, stood for just a second grinning at the bar staff, people who knew their faces, people who didn't want to get involved, people who'd heard that they'd done this shit before on occasion, this fast moving, urgent escape routine.

Panky and Leary said nothing, grinned lamely and barged their way through the 'Van Gee's' drinkers, stumbled out into the street, still panting, hearts like frantic techno beats. They saw blue red flashing lights swirling against the tall darkness of the buildings; saw black clad SWAT team members taking position, edging their way towards the coffee shop. They heard harsh Walkie-talkie voices snap commands, saw a faint plume of smoke rise from the coffee shop and twist into the clear night air.

Tall cops held back curious onlookers. Ambulances screeched to the crime scene, more flashing lights, more sirens and anxious voices. Medics jumped out of their wagons before they'd even stopped and ran to the rescue, gathered pointlessly around the two young punks lying dead on the pavement: searching for pulses, kneeling in blood, shaking their heads. Now the shooting had finally stopped a large crowd gathered in the street, morbid inquisitive faces, whispering chatter all around. Talk about gangsters and drug deals gone awry in the air. It wasn't too far from the truth.

Panky spotted a Mercedes taxicab on the other side of the road, watched the two blonde hookers and the Arab guy climb out smiling.

Panky grabbed at Leary's shirtsleeve, dragged him across the street. He opened the cab door, shuffled across the back seat. Leary followed, slammed the door behind him.

"Schipol airport," Leary said and the driver nodded, clicked on the meter, turned on the stereo and they drove slowly through the peering crowds, into the night and towards the airport.

The stereo played 'Shall I stay or shall I go' by The Clash. Ominous and scary.

Panky shook his head in mild disbelief, looked at Leary who was grinning.

"Dude, you know you gotta go, right? Gotta get outta here," said Leary.

Panky nodded, he knew.

The guys sat in silence for a while, listened to the music.

Panky said, "But what about…"

"Hey! Don't worry about me dude… I'm low profile; they don't even know I exist…"

"But s'posing…"

"Forget it man, ok? Go… get the hell out of here. I'll text you if they catch me, ok? I promise you," said Leary with his impish grin.

Panky wasn't sure if he was serious or not. There was every chance that if the Russians did catch up with Leary, they'd kill him for sure, eventually. They'd kill him because he was a friend of Panky's and because they could. That's the way they did business. Panky gazed out of the car window, they were nearly at the airport now; he saw a huge 747 climbing high into the night sky, bright lights and white noise. He looked at Leary and smiled, he was grateful and he knew he'd miss his friend.

He watched the 747 continue to climb and wondered what the hell the Philippines were like.

FORTY-ONE

Chris, Clara and Mai-Ling had hardly moved since Panky started his story. They just sat and listened intently; their faces filled with a mixture of emotions, no one quite sure what to say or whether to speak at all.

Panky grinned at them awkwardly, not sure either. Not sure if he should be ashamed of his story or proud of his escape. Not really sure about anything now, wishing he'd just kept his mouth shut.

His friends lounged back into the comfort of the rattan sofa, breathed small anxious breathes as they thought about the story some more.

Panky sighed heavily; the story and the memories had sobered him up. He reached for a bottle of champagne and drank from it eagerly.

Chris leaned forward, grabbed his glass from the coffee table, swallowed champagne and poured more and filled the girl's glasses too. Clara and Mai-Ling silently followed suit and drank more.

Panky lit a much-needed cigarette, blew the first deep puff towards the balcony doors and sent quick furtive glances to his friends amongst the cushions. The urgency and pace of the story had left the room feeling strangely empty, left the audience silent and uncertain, weary. It *was* quite a story.

Chris, Clara and Mai-Ling sat quiet sipping their drinks.

Panky stared down at his bare feet and smoked his cigarette. The huge green potted plant behind him shimmered with aircon orchestration; once again he threw fleeting glances around the room, hoping they'd pierce the awkward silence, hoping they'd bring him back to where he wanted to be. After a couple of minutes nothing had changed, so he decided he might as well continue.

"Frankly, it was a total fuckin' disaster…" he said looking up and praying for some support, some sympathy or at the least a little eye contact, "My friends were dead, Carol, Julia, Jimmy… all dead! I'd lost about a dozen customers too, all dead… my deal was ruined beyond belief and the chances of making my money was gone for sure. Bish, bash, bosh! Everything just gone!" He paused and smoked some more. "Un-fuckin'-believable… and I still hadn't paid Zoltan any money."

Chris, Clara and Mai-Ling remained silent, sipping, staring at their drinks like connoisseurs, reluctant to comment.

Panky sighed, "So… I made a long distance call to my old mate Chris here and a few hours later I was sitting on board a 747 on my way to the Philippines."

He smiled at his friends and they all smiled back.

Panky almost melted with relief—they smiled! He drank more champagne and sighed again. He wanted to cry but felt it was inappropriate in front of the women, so instead he continued. "Although I didn't know much about the Philippines it seemed like the perfect place to go… probably 'cos it was 10,000 miles away."

Chris, Clara and Mai-Ling smiled a little more—still not giving much away; but at least they'd smiled again.

Panky grinned, starting to feel less like a turd in Jacuzzi.

Clara was the first to speak: "So the punks thought you were using their mother, Judy, to smuggle cocaine into England, like a mule or whatever they call it?"

"Right!" said Panky, "But it wasn't me was it? Judy told me she was going to start smuggling with her new boyfriend… trying to impress me maybe, make me jealous… I don't know, I told her good luck, said I'm not interested, goodbye… thanks for everything."

Panky looked across at Mai-Ling, tried, but couldn't quite read the expression on her face, "So it wasn't my fault, was it?" he said, "Not *really*… I lost my friends, my customers, all my money from the deal and I probably lost my job too."

Chris snorted with laughter, nearly choked on his champagne.

"Basically, I lost everything and I *still* owed the fucking Russians" Panky smiled weakly, "Excuse my language, the rest as they say is geography."

"History!" said Clara.

"History, geography… whatever… at least I'm somewhere safe now," said Panky and he smiled again hoping his friends would smile back.

FORTY-TWO

Boris and Vlad loved the Philippines, lapping up the luxury of the Shangri La hotel. Their fifteenth floor suite was first class with a panoramic view across the noisy sprawl of Manila, modern elegance every step of the way, so different from the best that Moscow could even hope to offer. There were polished granite floors with plush Persian rugs, colourful local artworks depicting fighting cocks and folksy peasant scenes, hand carved quality furnishings, huge green plants in colourful Chinese pots, subtle wall lights on subtle walls and the expanse of pleated curtain contrasted perfectly with the crimson silken bedclothes. Third world opulence at its best, thought Boris, and all paid for by Zoltan.

It was early morning now; *loud* cartoon noises poured from the speakers of the huge plasma TV and filled the suite, the sound was harsh and deafening, Tom and Jerry *still* kicking the fuck out of each other, still battling it out after decades of domestic violence. Toddler entertainment.

The vast and muscular Vlad laid naked, hairy and scarred amongst the rumpled silken sheets of his king sized bed. Guest Relations Officer number 12 lay one side of him, her friend, Guest Relations Officer number 13, lay on the other, both girls disheveled in their slumber, snoring sweetly like only young girls can. They had considered slipping the big guys a *mickey* and robbing them, but decided against it, considered it a little too risky. The girls had good reason to sleep soundly; like the room, the girls had *certainly* seen some action during the night, Vlad had certainly got value for Zoltan's money. The room said it all, half eaten meals sat on trays, discarded coke cans scattered all around, candy bar, condom and Viagra wrappers lurked in the unlikeliest of places. Vlad had had a great night.

Vlad yawned, stretched, glanced at the clock and turned the volume down on the TV with the remote control. Next to his naked bulk the sleeping girls looked tiny, Vlad glanced at them almost lovingly, smiled almost sweetly as he remembered the night before.

On the way back to the hotel Boris had flicked through a tourist guidebook, discovered there was an authentic Russian restaurant in the Ortigas district, just a few minutes limo ride from where they were staying. So without hesitation off they went.

Boris was delighted and Vlad was amazed.

Boris read from the guidebook as they headed towards the restaurant. "Truly authentic Russian cuisine is now available in Manila, the first in The Philippines." To the henchmen it was a culinary coup—it didn't matter to them that the proprietors were Koreans financed by Japanese capital with all the hard work done by Filipinos on minimum wage. The food was Russian and authentic, so authentic they served stuff you rarely saw in Moscow. The waiters provided real service too; didn't just take your order and vanish off the face of the earth; so different to Moscow. The guys were more than impressed.

With eyes as big as their appetites and smiles like bears with honey they ordered: caviar, potatoes, raw herring, celery, potatoes, stuffed olives, plump red radishes, minced red cabbage, potatoes and pickled mushrooms; all washed down with strong Czech beer and frozen vodka. Perfect.

The girls were not impressed with the menu, said they wanted Big Macs and French fries, settled for coca cola and the promise of a visit to McDonalds later.

The restaurant was called 'The Perestroika'. The décor was Russian kitsch at its finest: a huge stuffed bear stood in the corner and watched the festivities with beady glass eyes, Soviet medals and badges sat proud in display cases, Soviet flags hung everywhere, red the predominant colour. Posters of Lenin and Trotsky adorned the walls; faded photographs of Red Square and the Kremlin added a little period authenticity. (The posters of Lenin and Trotsky were printed in Taiwan; the Soviet flags were made in China.)

Boris, Vlad and the girls sat at a huge round table in flickering candlelight surrounded by Filipino waiters dressed as Cossacks, happy and eager to serve. Quaint Old Russian folk songs played quietly in the background. Boris loved the place.

"This place… or should I say this menu, it takes me back, many, many years… remind me of a restaurant in Moscow… 'The Glazur'," said Boris, almost teary eyed.

Vlad was gazing around now, checking out the décor, but listening.

"The Glazur was run by a co-operative, successfully too," said Boris with some authority, "One of the first in Soviet Union, backed by a major Belgian brewery."

Vlad was chewing bread from the basket, listening intently, still gazing around. The girls sat bored and chewing gum, longing for McDonalds, confused by the music and the conversation.

Boris grinned and continued, "The place, was an overnight success... overnight, really... when Zoltan heard about it, he wanted a piece of the action... is natural, no?" Boris smiled when he thought of his brother, "But they refused to pay us! These stupid foreigners, these Belgians! Tell us they have insurance already... Ha! What don't they understand?"

Vlad listened and nodded, reaching for more bread, smiling at the girls with their tiny bored faces.

"So Zoltan gave orders, I firebomb the place a few nights later, was very easy job," Boris said with a smile, "Far as I know 'The Glazur' is a burned out ruin still."

Vlad smiled, not at Boris's words, but at the pleasure Boris took in expressing himself.

"You know what Vladimir? I know we were hungry, but sometimes... just *sometimes*, I miss the good old days," said Boris with a small nostalgic smile.

They had a fantastic meal, paid, over tipped and promised the Korean manager they'd be back again; the manager found it hard to understand them, just smiled a lot and nodded, ignored the looks from the waiters as he put the tip in his pocket.

Vlad gazed sleepily around the hotel suite, smiled at the sheer comfort and modernity of it all; he looked again at the sleeping girls, grinned with some inner satisfaction. It had certainly been a night to remember, memorable in so many ways, to him the girls were a bonus, sweet and sticky icing on the cake. Vlad hoped he'd never see Russia or be hungry again; apart from the blistering heat and the humidity, Manila reminded Vlad of Moscow: the slow pace, snarling traffic, the lack of opportunity for the average man and of course the huge divide between the wealthy elite and the starving majority. Vlad loved it; so different from the wishy-washy guilt ridden liberalism of the Netherlands.

Boris' growling voice boomed from across the other side of the suite, jolted Vlad from his early morning reverie, brought him back to reality. "You know Vladimir, I love just this third world... all this luxury."

Vlad sat up in bed and stretched some more, flexed his massive biceps, turned his huge neck in small circles, listened to the strange gristly sounds it made and smiled again.

"And later, we must buy guns... then we find our friend... our little comrade," Boris said from the comfort of his bedroom and then he chuckled deeply like the big old Muscovite that he was. To Vlad Boris' voice sounded warm and content, had a strange syrupy edge, a certain DJ sleaziness to it that he hadn't heard before.

Boris lay propped up in bed on a sea of pillows, silk sheets partially covering his muscular enormity and his thick gray body hair. GRO number 68 laid one side of him fast asleep and his/her friend GRO number 69 slept on the other side. Boris was wearing a huge cheesy smile; his face like his body was smeared and smothered with lipstick, scratches and tiny bite marks.

Boris turned his head and smiled at each of the geezer birds next to him, 'Strictly for the weirdoes' the fat Australian bar manager had said and of course he was absolutely right.

FORTY-THREE

Panky sat at a table by Chris' swimming pool, wearing Chris' shorts again, smoking one of the cigarettes he'd bought with Chris' money, enjoying the morning sunlight, watching the glimmering water, realising he owed Chris so much.

He was sipping a cold beer, trying to lose his hangover; it wasn't working but he didn't care, he had too much on his mind. The previous night's storytelling had left him feeling a little anxious, all those crazy memories flooding back, all that bad stuff coming back to the surface again. It wasn't easy to handle. Not only that, but the first thing he noticed when he woke up was his mobile phone sitting on the nightstand next to his bed—his only worldly possession. He was pleased to see it—at first he was anyway. Someone –probably Mai-Ling –was kind enough to charge the phone and leave it next to the bed for him; he hadn't looked at it for days—hadn't needed to. Who's likely to call?

With sleepy eyes he lay in bed and gazed blankly at the phone, saw two words: Message received. Who the hell was *that* from?

Barely awake he read the message. It was from Leary Katz and Panky knew what was coming. Even before he read it, he wanted to die, wanted to perish, to be no more, wanted to tumble into the bowels of Hell and burn slowly forever. He just knew that Leary was dead and despite what Panky had said the night before—proclaiming his innocence, he knew that it was *his* fault: Carol, Julia, Jimmy, his dozen or so customers, the retro punks, even the Karamazov brothers, they were all dead because of him and now Leary Katz was dead too.

He pressed 'read message' and his mind swirled madly with emotion. Nice start to the day! He read: *Hasta la vista baby!* He winced at the words, tears welled in his eyes and his throat tightened, Leary was dead for sure. Breathing deeply, holding back a flood of emotion and the certainty of hysterical weeping, Panky sat in the sun, nursed his beer, smoked his cigarette and pushed the thoughts of the recent past to the back of his mind.

He sat watching Chris and Clara's children playing noisily in the depths and the fragrance of the colourful garden; breathed in the cool morning air, enjoyed the freshness, the vitality of it. He sipped his beer, listened to the manic squawking of jungle birds high in the trees, smelled the sweet coffee blossom mixed with the spicy smoke of the gardener's bonfire and watched the waves of thin blue smoke as they danced in the dappled sunlight. Nice.

It was still early, but already about thirty five degrees; weather wise another beautiful day lay ahead. Panky breathed deeply, maybe a dozen times, tried to clear his mind. He finished the beer and the cigarette, breathed deeply some more. It seemed to help. Despite the merciless heat and his troubled thoughts, he suddenly felt quite calm; he felt relaxed now, strangely and suddenly at peace. It was a rare moment.

He smiled and turned his head, focused on the glimmering clear blueness of the pool and then *bosh*! His mood changed completely. He suddenly felt overcome, stifled, engulfed by a heavy wave of sadness, quickly and unexpectedly deflated like a tired old balloon. The feeling brought a touch of dizziness, a smattering of nausea; a chill crept along his spine, made him shiver slightly: goose bumps, chicken skin. Gazing around at nothing he sighed heavily. Wishing he had more beer he looked around the garden some more. Mixed emotions for breakfast or what? He sat bewildered, felt drained like his beer in the growing heat of the morning.

A pretty young waitress walked softly towards his table, brought him the beer he'd requested earlier—keep 'em coming sweetheart, he'd said—he sat searching for solace in the suds, lit another cigarette. He looked up and saw Mai-Ling climbing from the pool smiling at him; he hadn't noticed her floating quietly up there in the deep end, he was too mixed up with his thoughts, too confused and emotional. As always she looked amazing, so young and nubile, her tanned body glistening wet in the sunlight.

She padded towards his table dripping, dark and sultry; her bright eyes sparkled, her soft warm smile was full of secrets and promises. Panky watched her get closer, remembered again the time he got tasered.

She walked up to him, looked down into his face and smiled. Silent, she pulled his head gently towards her and carefully examined his stitches—an efficient young nurse with a sexy look of concern in her eyes.

Panky watched the children playing in the distance as Mai-Ling moved behind him and completed her inspection. His deep stuttering sigh released a hundred mixed emotions, but with Mai-Ling's touch the morning sun suddenly felt good, suddenly felt warm again. Panky's nurse moved back to face him and as she looked into his eyes again he suddenly felt calm, clear minded about what he had to do. He wasn't exactly happy about the situation, but he realised now that he had no choice.

"I'm leaving soon," he said quietly, just the hint of an awkward smile, "Thanks for all your help and everything... "

Mai-Ling was clearly shocked, she took a step back tried hard not to make it obvious, she said, "What?" and then added, "But why?"

Panky found it hard to look at her. His eyes went back and forth between her and the shrieking, galloping children as he spoke. "Why am I leaving? Well... I know Clara still hates me, ok? Even though she pretends not to, and I can't handle that, I really can't handle it..."

Mai-Ling was about to speak, but didn't get the chance.

Panky continued: "And I really can't resist telling stories about the past, especially after a few drinks—he laughed—and I really can't resist a few drinks, you know that, right?" He smiled at his humour and paused, seemed to search for the words, "Chris just doesn't need that... does he? Especially on a daily basis... and there's so many stories, believe me... so many," he smiled again, looked into Mai-Ling's dark eyes.

Mai-Ling said, "But Panky, Clara doesn't hate you, really, she's my best friend, she's..."

Panky held up his hands, stopped her again: "Besides… I can't just live here indefinitely, can I? It wouldn't be fair, I'm not one for free loading, it's not my style Mai-Ling… I hate freeloaders… and anyway, I don't want to spoil things for Chris… or Clara… they seem so happy, so normal. I've done enough damage in the world recently, haven't I? You heard the story."

Mai-Ling ignored his question and said, "You're just being paranoid Panky, Clara's ok, really… she knows you've had a bad week."

Panky nearly laughed out loud, it really *had* been a bad week. In fact the last decade hadn't been exactly wonderful, the life in Amsterdam was ok until you stopped and thought about it.

Mai-Ling stretched out her arms and pulled him towards her and kissed him firmly on the mouth.

Panky was surprised, but soon got into it, eventually they separated, breathless and smiling. "What's a nice girl like you doing in a face like this?" he said with a grin.

Mai-Ling closed her eyes and kissed him again, held him tight against her. Panky groaned, swept away by her innocence, by her youthful enthusiasm. Mai-Ling pushed herself away gently, "I knew you'd come," she said.

Panky looked and sounded surprised. "I didn't… I just groaned…"

"No, I mean I knew you'd come *here*… eventually, I just knew it."

Panky looked puzzled, confused as she continued, "Ever since I started working here I knew we'd meet… I didn't know when, but I knew we would, I just knew it." She smiled into his confusion, "Every day I'd see that photograph of you and Chris... when you were kids, punks... you know the one, from the newspaper and I knew that one day we'd meet... I knew one day we'd be together, it's a destiny thing."

Panky's growing smile hid his confusion, Mai-Ling's words were full of promise, sounded romantic even, but the more he thought about them the more weird they became. Women's intuition is one thing, but this was bordering the spooky. Maybe it was some religious thing, some kind of voodoo? "You serious?" he whispered eyes darting left and right. He'd always considered his long term destiny to be alone and self reliant.

"No..." she said and she laughed out loud, "Of course I'm not serious silly, I'm making fun of you, it's my turn or did you forget what you said about your grandmother, poor grandma on her deathbed?"

Panky laughed now, remembered what he'd said the day Mai-Ling shaved his head, it seemed like months ago rather than days.

Mai-Ling smiled, "But why not stay a little longer, take it easy for a while? Sober up a bit more?"

Panky grabbed his beer from the table, gulped it down. "No, I've tried sober, it's overrated believe me."

"So, you don't you like it here? Is that it? You're bored already, huh?"

"No, of course not, I love it... really... I told you I love it on the beach... remember? But I'd better go, really," he said, "Don't want to cause any more problems, if you know what I mean?" Panky sighed, finished his beer and said, "I guess all this wholesome family stuff just isn't my scene."

Mai-Ling held her stare, "So what exactly *is* your scene Panky?" she asked.

Panky grinned at her, "I'm not too sure if I really know any more," he said, chuckling quietly at his own dilemma, "I'm not too sure about anything just lately."

FORTY-FOUR

Boris and Vlad's white Mercedes cruised quietly away from Manila, away from the hustle and bustle and the endless noise of the city. They were headed south towards Tagaytay; the traffic was light for a change. The bleating horns, the rattling engines of the jeepneys and the torturous heat of the sun were outside and the Russians were thankful; inside the car it was cool, comfortable and quiet.

Vlad was at the wheel looking tired; Boris sat beside him still grinning slightly. They were both wearing new Hawaiian suits, Vlad in tropical green today with white sampaguita blossoms, Boris in pale yellow with pale green blossoms.

Neither of them was keen to leave the city, they'd had such fun there, but now they had work to do. Now they had the information they needed it was time to get the job done. Time to get Zoltan's little problem resolved.

Huge colourful billboards flicked by and filled the windows of the car from every direction, turned them into gigantic fleeting screens, TV visions on wheels: Levis, McDonalds, Kentucky Fried, Pizza Hut, Palmolive, Ford and Colgate said farewell from the city. God bless America. God bless consumerism. God bless the American dream.

Vlad looked into the rear view, watched the city disappear into the shimmering hazy distance. For a while the suburbs flicked by, still congested and noisy, people everywhere, but it wasn't as severe as central Manila. Finally came open countryside; fields, trees, farmers, bamboo huts, provincial tranquility all around. Boris and Vlad hated it. They hated places that were quiet, where every day was the same, where people lived simple lives, they didn't care too much for clean and green, couldn't see the appeal. They sat silent as endless verdant scenery zipped by left and right, both guys yearning, thirsting almost for the sleazy sophistication of the city. They were keen to get the job done quickly and head back to the luxury of the hotel, keen to eat more authentic Russian food and go bar hopping again.

Boris pulled two old hand guns from the bag on his lap, held them up for his partner to see.

Vlad glanced at the two revolvers, blue and black, looking cold to the touch, old and oiled and lethal.

"Souvenirs of the Philippines," said Boris admiring the guns, curious about their history, wondering how many people's lives they'd ruined or ended, how much damage they'd done. "You know… it's easier to buy two guns here than it is to buy a pair of size twelve shoes!" exclaimed Boris with a chuckle.

Vlad said nothing at first, kept his eyes on the road. He glanced quickly at the weapons as the road straightened out. "Who'd you buy those from Boris? Davy Crockett? They're older than I am!" he said, "I hope they work."

Boris hadn't thought of this, his eyes quickly said as much, he hadn't considered that someone might sell guns that didn't actually work, even in a third world country. And who the hell was this Davy Crockett?

Boris grunted quietly, sneered a little and pressed a button on the dashboard. The window at his side slid down, opened with a quiet electric hum. "Slow down, slow down, slow down," he said quickly and Vlad slowed the car a little.

Boris cocked the guns in unison; the sound was strange like breaking bones.

He pointed the barrels out the window. In his sights he saw a huge carabao; the animal standing motionless chewing grass, its thick gray skin was covered with drying mud, it flicked the flies away from its rear with its tail. An easy target.

"Slower, slower," said Boris. Vlad slowed the limo to a gentle crawl.

Maybe Vlad was first to see the two young children skipping happily along the road hand in hand, he wasn't sure. He glanced at Boris, saw something register in his beady eyes, saw his mean little smile grow bigger and knew instantly that Boris had seen the children too. Boris looked down the barrels, through the sights at the massive beast of burden. He moved the guns just slightly; saw the children clearly in his sights. His mean little smile grew bigger, his piggy eyes got smaller. Two easy targets.

Vlad saw what was happening, his stomach tied suddenly in knots, his heartbeat raced and sweat formed lightly on his brow. He remembered his promise to Zoltan, considered Boris' problem, his *'moments of weakness'*. Vlad just knew that Zoltan would hold him responsible for whatever happened; he suddenly felt impotent and breathless, unable to say a word if words were what was called for. He looked across the limo at

Boris and felt it was all too late anyway; the situation was ongoing, unfolding before his eyes.

Boris stared at the happy faces of the children.

The car crawled closer towards them.

Boris saw their big white smiles, could hear their childish banter now, giggling as they skipped along hand in hand.

Vlad held the steering wheel white knuckle tight, the car continued slowly towards the skipping youngsters. Vlad was unsure of what he was witnessing now, almost scared of what was going to happen, seeing the guns, seeing Boris' weird smile. His mind flooded with visions of the past, remembered vividly all the heinous crimes that Boris had carried out before—with so much poise and delight—the carnage that Vlad had witnessed back in Amsterdam. Anything was possible now and Vlad knew it.

Boris could hear the children now and clearly, had them in his sights. An easy shot, two easy shots!

As Boris squeezed the triggers Vlad's heart pounded in his ears, adrenalin pumped hard through his veins, he could hardly breathe, his mouth drier than chalk dust in the desert.

The children suddenly stopped in their tracks, happy smiles turned to looks of horror.

The handguns barked decibels of death from the limo window. *Bang! Bang*! Loud and merciless barking!

Four young eyes grew wide with fear and realisation, two young mouths gaped open feeling the pain before it happened and the roar of the guns filled the limo.

Vlad felt dizzy, unbalanced by the deafening sound.

Boris' perspiration and the smell of cordite filled the air.

The brains of the carabao sprayed dark and high against the cloudless sky. Vlad thought of spaghetti sauce and meatballs, couldn't deny that from such a distance they were pretty good shots.

The children watched in awe as the bovine beast collapsed, splashed into the mud, died without a sound.

"Ok," said Boris putting the guns back into the bag, closing the car window with a quiet buzz, "We're in business Vladimir, they work! Let's go do this thing!"

"You shot a cow Boris!" said Vlad, relieved and almost surprised it was only a cow, as he hit the gas and the car pulled away with a screech of tires, as they zoomed away past the shocked and horrified children. "You shot... a fucking cow..." Vlad's head was back and forth from the road to Boris' face in rapid succession as he spoke, "You *shot* a cow! This... I cannot believe," he said.

"Is not a cow Vladimir, is a carabao... ok?" said Boris.

FORTY-FIVE

Panky sat by the pool in the sunshine sipping his third early morning beer, smoking another cigarette. Mai-Ling had been gone a while but her words; her tearful farewell whispers were still ringing softly in his ears. He really didn't want to leave her, not like this, but he'd convinced himself that he had no choice.

Chris strolled out of the house wearing his faded khaki beach shorts and a solemn face. He sat next to Panky without saying a word, they stared at the glimmering pool, listened to the dry palm fronds fluttering gently in the warm breeze, the sound like small birds taking flight. They sat there for a while, silent.

"Mai-Ling says you're leaving," said Chris finally, his eyes fixed on the sparkling surface of the pool.

Panky sipped his beer and nodded—he didn't want to speak. He didn't want to get too emotional so early in the day. There was plenty of time for emotional stuff, but not right now, so again the guys sat in silence for a while just watching the children hacking around the garden, all whoops and screams and cries of laughter. Panky noticing for the first time that Chris' son looked exactly like him, the spitting image of Chris in every way, it made Panky smile and wish perhaps that *his* life was a little different, but he said nothing.

"You're really not a problema mate," said Chris, "Clara understands, really she does…"

Panky looked at his oldest friend and sighed quietly; he loved the familiarity of his features, the lines of his face, the sincerity in his voice, but he knew he'd got to go. It didn't matter *what* Chris said, Panky just had to get away and soon. "I'm glad she understands," he said looking at Chris and smiling slightly, "But I just need to get away... need a bit of time alone, you know... get myself sorted, a few days to get my head together."

Chris beamed. "Do you think a few days'll be enough?"

They sat in the simmering heat by the Hockney pool and smiled and chuckled together quietly like the old mates they were. Panky finished his beer and they fell silent again listening to the roosters going cock-a-doodle crazy in the background. Dawn was hours ago, but to the roosters it didn't seem to matter.

Chris wanted to give his old mate some advice from the heart, wanted to help him find a little direction, but he didn't want to preach to him, didn't want to appear too obvious. Panky wasn't into people preaching to him, never had been—not even preachers. He looked over at his mate and finally broke the silence, "You know what Panky? It seems to me that men of our age should have... err... how can I put it? There's... well, there's certain things we should've come to terms with in life by now... d'you know what I mean?"

Panky sat in the sun and looked blankly at Chris. He was clearly not on the same page and Chris wondered if maybe he was being a bit too vague; decided he was, took a different approach. "What I'm trying to say is... we might not like it, right? but as more... as more mature men, there's certain things we should have by now," Chris smiled feeling that he was making a little headway, "D'you know what I'm saying geezer?"

Panky cracked a grin, "What, like hemorrhoids or something?

"No, no, no, not hemorrhoids Panky… I'm talking about something completely different, something important, something…"

"Oh I get it! You mean false teeth; we should get false teeth, right? Keep that confident smile and everything? Fresh breath… of course, yeah… that *is* important."

"No, Panky you're really not with me are you? Not even fuckin' close…" Chris sighed heavily, "There's stuff a geezer should gain more of, get more of as he gets older, d'you know what I'm saying? I mean *really* important stuff," said Chris wondering if Panky was having a little dig about his newly capped teeth, wondered maybe if he was just a tad jealous.

"Oh right… now I'm with you," said Panky, "You mean hairs right?" Chris rolled his eyes, wanted to continue but Panky beat him to it. "You're talking about hairs, right?" Panky thinking that Chris was taking the piss about his shaved head.

Chris wasn't sure if Panky was having a laugh, whether *he* was taking the piss or not, he said, "No Panky, no… what I'm actually talking about… is not hairs ok? What I'm talking about is wisdom, ok? We should get a little wisdom as we get older."

"Oooooooh, now I'm with you, wisdom… right." Panky drew heavily on his cigarette, "A rare commodity wisdom… well yeah, guess it goes without saying really…" Panky wasn't sure what Chris was getting at so he stubbed out his cigarette and swigged the last of his beer.

Chris was pretty sure by now that Panky had no idea what he was trying to get at, decided to try another different approach, but later. They sat silent again for a while.

One of the girls brought Panky another cold beer, which he held against the sweat on his forehead and smiled. Chris shared the smile and once again broke the silence, he felt he had to say *something,* but didn't want to sound boring like someone's dad, didn't really want to lecture his old mate.

"Look we're not teenagers any more Panky... you know that dontcha? We're middle-fuckin'-aged mate and there's no getting away from it..." he said, "Like it or not!"

Panky nodded, solemn now like a gambler with empty pockets and a full house.

"Have a word with yourself Panky," said Chris getting a little louder now, "Sort yourself out geezer! Its time to kick back mate... it's time to get in touch with reality!"

Panky said, "Reality?" He'd heard of it, wasn't sure what it really was, considered it all a bit subjective.

Chris said, "Yeah, reality Panky, look ahead a little... slow down geezer, leave all the mad stuff behind... start taking it easy... I hate the phrase 'settle down' but ... you know... another ten years or so we'll be looking at sixty and that's old Panky, that's really old, right? Maybe it's time to cut limbo?"

Panky stared at the swimming pool taking it all in, realizing that of course Chris was right, thinking about being sixty, thinking of playing bingo, doing basket weaving, losing bowel control and going completely gaga. He looked away from the pool, stared Chris in the eyes, swigged his beer and grinned, said, "Easy for you to say... you're the man with everything aren't you? 'Mr. Rags to Riches' himself," said Panky shielding the sun from his eyes, holding back his emotions, praying that his voice wouldn't fail him when he needed it most, "See... things are different for me Chris, I can't just cut limbo as you called it, the mad stuff's all I've got."

FORTY-SIX

Vlad and Boris' limo cruised silently towards Tagaytay village. They were nearly there, nearly on target.

Boris sat with the guns on his lap, ready for action.

Trees zipped by left and right, a green blur.

Boris could smell the oil on the guns, could feel the coolness of the blue black metal, the roughness of the grips felt good against the flesh of his palms, the weight of the guns gave him a certain confidence and a slight erection. He could hardly wait to see the look on Panky's face.

It was obvious to Vlad that Boris was getting excited, but when he spoke his voice sounded controlled and strangely casual, he said, "Of course Vladimir if our plan doesn't work out we can always buy some gasoline, is so cheap here."

Vlad took his eyes of the road and glanced at Boris in mild disbelief.

"In fact we can buy *lots* of gasoline..." Boris smiled at Vlad's expression. "And then we can flush him out," Boris chuckled at his words, thought of Panky as something stuck in a toilet somewhere, "Flush him out, capture him, torture him, get the money... simple no? Give *him* a little heat for a change."

Vlad kept his eyes on the road and said nothing. He was still upset about the cow, the carabao; thought it was reckless and unnecessary. As far as he was concerned killing people was never a problem, they usually deserved it and anyway it was their job, but killing defenseless animals and scaring innocent children seemed so pointless.

"To me... this mission is very easy," said Boris fondling the old guns.

Vlad kept his eyes on the road thinking: Yeah, is very easy because you're a fucking psycho.

As the Russians got closer to their destination, Ding-Dong's bright yellow Datsun pulled into Chris' driveway. A cloud of shimmering heat and dust suddenly appeared: a battered, beaten old car with a strange mirage like persona stood waiting and the sound of rattling pistons echoed around the grounds shattering the morning tranquility. Ding-Dong was hanging out the window, overjoyed at being called by his new friend; his face all smiles and enthusiasm; his feet pumping on the pedals raring to go. The cars exhaust coughed and spluttered black smoke, oil dripped silently onto the flagstone driveway.

Panky stood up and smiled, moved around the table and threw his arm around Chris' shoulder saying, "Here's my old mate Ding-Dong the dog eater with my lovely limo."

Chris looked a little shocked but said nothing. He had visions of Ding-Dong and Panky pushing the old banger along the motorway somewhere, steam pouring out of the engine, but said nothing.

Panky picked up his small bag from under the table and strolled towards the car, Chris followed close behind. "I'd better go now, I s'pose," said Panky,

"Before I change my mind or start crying or something."

Chris could see the small beginnings of tears in Panky's eyes and felt a lump in his throat he found hard to ignore. He was really going to miss Panky, that much was sure.

Panky struggled with the door of the Datsun and eventually opened it. He climbed into the back seat and opened the window as far as it would go. Ding-Dong was revving the engine and grinning, proud of Panky's loyalty, amazed by Chris' mansion.

Panky stuck his head out the window and said, "Say goodbye to Clara and the kids for me… and give Mai-Ling a big hug and a sloppy kiss, she's amazing, really… way too good for the likes of me!"

Chris stood with his hands in his pockets, the sun bright in his eyes; he nodded and felt sad.

Panky shouted, "Thanks geezer… you know I love ya! And you know I owe one don't you? At least one!"

Chris watched the Datsun vanish noisily into a cloud of swirling dust. "Nice limo!" he shouted as he wiped the tears from his eyes, but he wasn't sure if Panky heard him.

Ding-Dong sat at the wheel of the spluttering Datsun as it rumbled along the highway. He was happy to be working for Mr. Panky again, very happy, hadn't forgotten that Mr. Panky was Breeteesh either. He was trying his best to whistle a medley of Lennon and McCartney tunes, wanted his customer to feel relaxed and at home. Decided not to mention Panky's new hairstyle or the stitches in his head, but thought he looked younger, cleaner too.

As they headed north towards Manila they didn't notice the white Mercedes limo heading south towards Chris' house. They didn't see Boris in the passenger's seat grinning, holding a couple of old handguns. They didn't see Vlad looking pissed off in the drivers' seat either.

Panky sat in the back of the Datsun with a spring up his arse, but all he felt was empty and alone, uncertain now about everything: especially his hasty departure. He felt paranoid and his stomach felt as heavy as a sack of rice. He'd wanted to explain so much to Chris, but never got the chance, wanted to ask so many questions too, but the time never seemed right. How had Chris made so much money?

"You ok boss?" said Ding-Dong, tired eyes in the rear view mirror.

"Yeah, I guess," said Panky staring out the window watching the trees zip by, fields of rice and pineapples going on forever, "Got a lot on my mind Ding-Dong... that's all." And of course, he had. He'd wanted to say things to Mai-Ling too, a lot of things, but he didn't want to lead her on, he didn't want to give her any false allusions; it wouldn't be fair, she was a nice girl—he didn't want to break her heart. "Besides," he said to himself as the car struggled along and he stared blankly out the window, "My track record with women isn't *that good* just lately is it? All my women seem to end up dead!" (He didn't even know about Soozie and probably never would!) So leaving everyone to their happy peaceful lives seemed the only way to go; seemed the only way to preserve the sanctity of it and keep it all in tact.

Panky sat in the back of the car staring blankly out of the window, bouncing along the highway, sweating, tired and confused, thinking: Chris is so lucky; he's got the stuff that dreams are made of. That's how it seemed to Panky.

"So where to boss?" asked Ding-Dong over the noise of the engine.

"Just drive Ding-Dong," said Panky, "I'm not sure... just drive..."

"Maybe you're looking for nice girl huh?" asked Ding-Dong, his rheumy old eyes full of mischief.

"No... I'm not looking for a *nice* girl," shouted Panky as he lit a cigarette and wondered why he was leaving so much behind him, leaving so much unresolved. "I'm looking for a bad one Ding-Dong... a very bad one... in fact... even better... I'm looking for a couple of very bad ones."

Ding-Dong's dark eyes filled the rear view and he laughed. He liked Mr. Panky; liked his sense of humour, his sense of adventure.

"I want to get very drunk," said Panky realising he'd left his vitamin B tablets behind, "Completely, totally, can't remember my name shitfaced... and I want sleaze." The way he said it sounded like sleeeeeaze...

Ding-Dong's face was alight with anticipation.

Panky continued, but more quietly, more thoughtful now, "All that domestic shit was doing my head in Ding-Dong. It's nice if you can handle it, it's a fuckin' nightmare if you can't!" His voice got suddenly louder, "You know sleaze Ding-Dong?"

"Oh yes sir, I know sleaze!"

"That's good, that's what I need right now and lots of it!"

"No problema Mr. Panky… you want sleaze I take you right there… direck… I take you city of angels; I take you Angeles City. Plenty of sleaze there sir! Is a berry sleazy place," said Ding-Dong licking the saliva from his lips, wiping his brow with his forearm.

And off they went towards the sleaze.

Boris and Vlad's limo cruised the quiet tree lined streets of Tagaytay; they'd finally made it and were looking for the house where Panky was supposedly staying.

"It was not a '*moment of weakness*'," said Boris, "I was checking the guns… that's what I have to do, you ask me if they work, remember? So I check for you… was not a '*moment of weakness*',"

"Checking… the guns?" said Vlad as the car crawled through the quiet village, past rows of big imposing houses set back from the road, "You shot a fucking cow for no reason!" Vlad didn't want to upset Boris, but felt he had to say something.

"A carabao," said Boris, "Not a cow! And I have the reason, testing the guns like you asked, ok ?"

They continued through the village looking for the house in silence, hoping they'd find it soon and get this shit over with, get back to Manila, the food, the clubs and the bars.

"Don't you think it's gonna get eaten anyway?" said Boris with a grin, "Eventually…"

Vlad said nothing, stayed deadpan and driving, eyes on the road.

"Maybe you think it's a pet carabao, huh?"

Vlad didn't react, didn't even blink.

"Maybe you think it sleeps on the bed at night?" Boris laughed at his own bizarre imagery.

Vlad huffed like a huge muscular Russian girl.

"Hey Vladimir relax, I'm just speeding up the food chain."

Vlad huffed again and tried not to smile.

After a few minutes Vlad saw a sign that said 'Sunset Village, Tagaytay', slowed the limo to a crawl. He then saw Chris' Range Rover in the driveway, the vanity plate reading CHR15 and he stopped the car.

Vlad: "This is it!"

Boris: "This is what?"

Vlad: "It! Where Panky's staying… is here."

Boris: "Huh?"

Vlad: "The old cab driver, Ding-Dong or something, said Panky got picked up by a new Ranger Rover right? Chauffeur driven, remember?"

Boris: "Uh huh and?"

Vlad: "And the girls from the bar, the G.R.O.'s, numbers 12 and 13 said he had an address in the wallet they stole… 'Sunset Village, Tagaytay… remember?"

Boris: "Uh huh and?"

Vlad: "And this is it! 'Sunset Village'… the sign, over there… see it?"

Boris looked over at the sign and nodded, but Vlad wasn't sure if he fully understood.

Vlad: "The cab driver, the old guy said Panky's friends name was Chris, I remember… the number plate on the Ranger Rover is CHR15… what does that tell you?"

Boris: "Ah, I see… so CHR15, that means Chris right?"

Vlad nodded and sighed, rolled his eyes, mumbled under his breath, "You don't have to be Sherlock fucking Holmes to work that one out do you Boris?"

Boris looked puzzled, luckily he hadn't heard Vlad's comment; he sat and stroked his guns lovingly.

Vlad said, "Let's go have a drink, come back when it's dark, ok?"

Boris nodded yes, he was hot and thirsty, so Vlad turned the car full circle with a small screech of rubber and said, "I saw a nice little bar just up the street here, we can get a cold beer and I'll explain who Sherlock Holmes is, ok?"

Boris nodded.

"Is a bar called Bongs," said Vlad, "funny name huh?"

Boris stroked his guns some more and nodded, it was a funny name. "You know Vladimir? All this dust, this heat, this tropical stuff... I could kill for an ice cold beer."

Vlad kept his eyes on the road, thinking: Of course you could Boris... you're a fucking psycho.

FORTY-SEVEN

When Ding-Dong's Datsun eventually pulled into the City of Angels Panky woke up and peered out of the dusty rear window, saw it was nighttime. He saw rows of flashing neon lights, heard a cacophony of 'night club' music beating in the warm evening air. He'd been asleep for more than six hours; his body ached nearly as much as his head, inside the car was as hot as a pizza oven, but stuffier.

Ding-Dong decided to cruise the busy streets for a while letting his customer take in the sights; get to fully appreciate the place, the full variety of sleaze. Panky listened as Ding-Dong spouted his tour guide spiel, filled Panky in on the place, told him a little history about Angeles City.

"When the Americans were here boss, on Clarke base, at Subic Bay, fighting Vietnam War," said Ding-Dong, "This city berry, berry busy, many, many soldiers, sailors too and many, many girls here... girls make big money, big big money."

Panky watched the noisy colourful bars zip by as they cruised along, the choices seemed endless. Since the Mount Pinatubo volcanic eruption—one of the biggest in history— and the Filipino governments change of policy, the American soldiers and sailors had mostly all gone; only the ones with nothing to go back to had remained. Regardless of local history, to Panky the place seemed perfect.

As they drove along through the potholes and puddles, he couldn't help but notice that nearly every bar had young girls perched outside beckoning in the tourists with big eyes and alluring smiles; coercing gullible and willing guys into the darkness with promises of hidden pleasures and willing flesh. "Come inside, sir," the girls said sweetly, the younger ones probably unaware of the heavy ambiguity of their words and naturally for most men it was an offer they couldn't refuse, in they went without a moment's hesitation.

As the Datsun cruised along noisily Panky couldn't help but noticed the small army of fat old ex-pats wandering up and down the dusty strip; some with small young girls in tow, others alone but obviously on the look out for some female company. The forty or fifty year's difference in the couple's ages seemed of no apparent consequence. Panky watching them, thinking: How else are girls like that going to get by? No education, no money, no prospects, a family back in the province needing money all the time. No welfare state in this part of the world, no benefit system here in the Third World! Panky guessed that to them it probably seemed a small price to pay: three meals a day and roof over your head—however leaky—the occasional presents when the geezer got his pension cheque, a few nights on the town if and when he had the energy, trips to McDonalds when the new toys came out; in many ways the girls were probably loving life.

Ding-Dong looked up at his customer in the rear view.

"It's pretty weird seeing an eighteen year old nubile strolling arm in arm with a three hundred pound coffin dodger," Panky said looking around and still amazed, "Funny thing is… the girls don't seem to mind… some of the guys have got limbs and things missing."

Ding-Dong turned and looked at Panky, he was going to explain that some of the girls were younger than eighteen, it was simply a survival thing, most of the girls had families and/or kids to feed, but he didn't want to state the obvious, didn't want to get into the tragic politics of it all.

Panky sighed heavily as he looked around some more; found it all quite hard to believe. The strangest thing was, most of the girls looked genuinely happy, happier than many a wife or girlfriend he'd ever seen in England and on reflection he decided that maybe the situation wasn't that bad at all. The girls actually looked pleased with their crumbly companions, seemed oblivious of the heavy paunches, the withered liver spotted flesh, the time beaten demeanours, the curlicue varicose veins; the girls seemed oblivious to it all.

As the mismatched couples strolled along the busy streets the girls held on tight and stared with grateful, almost loving eyes at their wizened paramours; the guys might be old and toothless and way, way, way past their prime, but to the girls they were some small token of success. The old geezers might be as ugly than the H B of Notre D. and grumpy and preoccupied with the prospect of death, but as far as the girls were concerned they'd actually hit the big time. Meal ticket city or what? thought Panky as he peered out the window sweat running from his brow. "Luckiest fuckin' coffin dodgers in the world!" he said.

Ding-Dong smiled and nodded, not exactly sure what a coffin dodger was.

The old Datsun Cherry pulled up outside a bar called 'Pussy Galore' and Ding-Dong's smile filled the rear view.

Panky looked around before he climbed out of the taxi. The first thing he noticed was a pert young girl sitting on a stool outside the bar. She was smiling at him; big eyes and a slender finger beckoned him inside. He smiled and nodded, then slowly turned his head to look across the street, checking things out now, no reason to hurry. He saw a small colourful group of transvestites or transsexuals in clip clopping high heels sashaying slowly down the dark neon street; he wasn't sure which kind of trannies they were and didn't really care, he was just looking. The street was like cabaret.

Ding-Dong turned his head quickly, saw his passenger looking at the mutton dressed up as lamb and said, "You be very careful here boss, ok?"

Panky grinned into the rear view, grateful for Ding-Dong's concern, pleased to have someone local watching his back. He looked out again, couldn't help but snigger at the 'geezer birds', tight hugged butts in tiny miniskirts, fishnet stocking legs, and the highest of heels—way too sexy to be real women. Panky sniggered some more, watched them amble down the dusty street arm in arm, glittery and giggling and obvious. He saw a couple of them looking back and grinning at him, waving now, enthralled no doubt with his rakish good looks and his Colin Farrell similarity.

Panky's eyes met Ding-Dong's in the rear view, they shared a knowing little smile; almost giggled at the absurdity of it all.

One of the giggly 'geezer-birds' escaped from the slow moving gaggle and skipped on tiptoe back towards Ding-Dong's Datsun: heels like machine guns, limp wrists, Lycra and lashes, a small cloud of dust low in the wake of her heels. Wearing more make-up than Elizabeth Taylor at an Avon party she stared through the dusty car window and gasped at the manly vision before her. It must've been love at first sight, she gasped again like a well seasoned thespian, her slender red nailed fingers went to her mouth in avid appreciation, her fingers quivered like small broken wings and black spider eyelashes fluttered in unison. She made strange breathless whimpering noises like she was going to cry.

Panky couldn't help but smile, and then he laughed.

She ran wildly back to her silicon buddies practically squawking; hands waving theatrically in the air, shrieks of desire and delight gushing from her mad painted mouth as she told her giggly gang that she'd finally found true love. She'd found her papa!

Ding-Dong sat up front smiling.

Panky looked across the other side of the street still checking things out, saw a bevy of bar girls competing for the passing men's attention; the younger ones catcalling and blowing imaginary dicks held tightly in their grasp, the older more experienced ones brushing invisible lint from their cleavage with great concentration, bending and stooping and hinting at what's on offer.

Panky watching it all silently, thinking: Heaven! He got out of the car and strolled around to the front, stooped down to talk to Ding-Dong through the open window. "Looks like you brought me to the right place Double Dee!"

Ding-Dong beamed happily, pleased with his new nickname.

"You wait for me here, ok?"

Double Dee nodded, no problema.

"If I'm not back in a week… send out a search party, ok?"

"Yes sir, Mr. Panky sir," said Ding-Dong easing back into the seat, preparing for a good long sleep.

Panky took a deep breath, ignored the warm smell of piss rising up from the open sewer in the street, turned towards the beckoning nubile and walked towards 'Pussy Galore', he stepped closer to the girl sitting outside and smiled.

"Come inside sir," she said.

Panky gave her no marks for originality, but watched as she licked her lips; saw just the pink hint of a snakelike tongue. Nice. Her Bambi eyes sparkled like small beacons and she smiled just like the Mamasan had taught her.

Panky gave her full marks for presentation.

The girl leaned back from her stool and pulled open the heavy wooden door behind her; Panky slid through a blaze of red velvet curtains, pushed aside the heavy plush symbolism with sweaty hands and stepped inside the bar. The place was busy and buzzing, the lights were mostly dim except for those on the stage. The music was loud, but its beat was warm and erotic: The Stranglers sang 'Golden Brown' and the hundred or so semi clad girls on the stage swayed gently to the rhythm. Nice.

Panky smiled at the girl behind the bar. "Two cold beers and a double Jack Daniels on the rocks please." He really needed a drink now, he was thirsty too, the journey had been long and tiring, his throat felt two or three sizes too small.

Once served Panky found a table not too far from the stage, sat down and lit a cigarette; eager eyes fixed on the girls. The seemingly endless rows of dancers were in various stages of undress, a veritable potpourri of lingerie, erotica and movement. Panky drank with enthusiasm; the cold beer was invigorating and refreshing, quickly swept away the warm dust of the journey, in contrast the Jack Daniels burned gently in his throat, crept down to warm the cockles of his heart. *Aaahhhh...*

The drinks had given him a nice little buzz, the fact that he hadn't eaten for God knows how long probably had something to do with it, but he wasn't worried. He watched the blur of flesh and frills and fantasy gyrate around the stage; big white willing smiles in ultra violet light, soft brown undulating flesh, young... *Phew!*

Panky sat quiet, just staring, lost in thought now, but feeling revived with the necessary liquids; he was thinking again: "It's funny that Chris talked about settling down, 'cos it's something I've been thinking about for ages... for years." He sighed, knocked back a shot, called the waitress for more; thinking: "Of course I know in ten years I'll be heading for sixty, scary... and of course I know that being sixty is old, it's undeniably old, seriously fuckin' old... and of course... that's if I even make it that far... maybe it really is time to cut limbo?" He sipped the rest of his beer and stared at the stage again, watched the willing and wiggling girls with their eyes lost in the mirrors, minds lost in music, he watched them: swaying, gyrating, stretching, posing and beckoning. So many enticing young girls making promises that most of them would never keep;

"OK," he said to himself as he lit another cigarette. "Cut limbo it is, but where do I fuckin' start?" He gazed around the bar, "So where and when does this 'renaissance' begin? Not here surely?" he said looking around some more, nearly laughing to himself at the word 'renaissance'.

Panky stared and drank and smoked, thinking: Maybe I just need a good woman? Not just a great shag this time… but a *good* woman. He wasn't really sure what he needed. His eyes searched the room: saw girls in every direction, all types, every different shape and size imaginable, he took it all as he listened to The Stranglers, the music took him back a while, again and he liked that, was it really just a coincidence? all the old punk songs?

A young girl walked slowly towards him; she was pert and sexy and she knew it, her smile was red and exciting, her mouth looked as tasty as sin itself. She put her soft brown hands on Panky's bare shoulders, looked into his eyes with a smoldering distant glare. "Hello handsome," she said.

Panky sipped his drink said, "Hi." Thinking: Ok, forget the *good* women idea, looks like I'll have to settle for a great shag again. Up close the girl looked young, but not too young.

"Americano huh?" she asked caressing his shoulder. "You alone handsome?"

Panky smiled, his interest was perhaps a little less now.

"Americano?" he said.

As her cool hand slipped inside the leg of his borrowed shorts his opinion immediately changed. "My name's Girlie," she purred, slender fingers well inside his shorts now, rubbing his inner thigh gently, making the hairs on his arms among other things stand to attention.

"You looking for a nice girl, huh?" she asked.

Panky sipped his drink, wiped the liquid from his chin, thinking: This girl's looking better by the second—sensible name, not too imaginative but easy to remember.

"Wanna have a good time with me tonight honey, huh? You like? I'm berry good!" she said eye lashes flicking like humming bird wings.

For probably the first time in his entire life he didn't want to have a good time with a good girl and grinning he said as much. "Funny you should ask," he said with a just small laugh, "but no, I'm not looking for a nice girl..."

Her sweet face turned to sulky; she huffed a little, put her hands on her small hips.

"I'm looking for a *ba...aaaad* girl," said Panky and he stretched the small bad word long like thin elastic and smiled as the girl withdrew her hand from his shorts and let it writhe on his lap, fingers like skinny brown snakes, fingernails like sharp red teeth. *Phew!*

"I'm looking for... a *ba...aaaad* girl," he stretched the word again liking the way it sounded, having fun now, he continued, " *And* her friend... *And* a *really* good time."

"Hey no problema," said the G.R.O. as her face changed to thoughtful and feline; her voice suddenly different—ten years older, suddenly so full of experience. "I can do bad girl," she said and Panky believed her.

He was feeling hot now, so he drained another beer, glanced at the girls on the stage and smiled, saw a couple of them waving, vying for his attention.

"Hey big boy... look at me not them," said Girlie, hands all over her prospect like goose bumps, "I can do bad real good ok? An' you so berry handsome... my fren she come too ok? we hab party... you know what I mean?"

Panky knew exactly what she meant, he looked casually at his watch and smiled at Girlie, thinking: Now that was pretty quick.

Way down south in Tagaytay the 'nightlife' was a little more lively than usual, outside Bong's bar the gray shingle car park was full to capacity, packed with jeepneys and tricycles. The strange, incongruous white Mercedes parked gleaming among the beaten up jeepneys and the rattling tricycles, looked like some futuristic beast: polished, poised and ready to pounce. Despite the crowd's curiosity no one went near it.

The outside of the old bamboo bar was alive with a queue of vibrant partygoers, excited and noisy, jostling for position, colourful hanging lights swung to and fro in the soft breeze above them.

Inside the place was lit up like Christmas day, buzzing like New Year's Eve, like 11.58 pm and counting; smoke, laughter, music and a mass of excited voices billowed from the open bamboo windows, drifted slowly through the warm night air, promising so much to the restless queue outside. Above it all, way up on the roof, a large Welsh flag fluttered in the breeze. The rumours were true; this wasn't just another disco or a sixties revival, Crispy Junior was doing another tribute to his hero… Tom Jones.

The bamboo hut was already jammed with people of all ages, shoulder-to-shoulder, back-to-back in faint flickering candlelight, drinking, laughing, smoking and having fun, small groups of kids running in all directions. Spirits were running high, cheap warm beer – and a lot of foam – was flowing freely and the noise like the smoke was overwhelming. Bong's small scabby pink skinned dog lay curled up in the corner in his usual position, one furtive rheumy eye barely open, but fixed on the bustling crowd; a quick flash of sharp little teeth appeared and a small throaty growl was heard every time someone got too close to him.

When Crispy finally hit the tiny stage the crowd went berserk, as he started the opening bars of 'Delilah' the furor became mind numbing. To the locals Crispy was a God, a man unequaled, a local legend in the world of entertainment. Tonight he was looking good, looking fit too. He didn't look a day over ninety. He sang with arms outstretched in his usual flamboyant manner, gyrating his skinny hips, moving with practiced style and precision, he even added a little 'moon walking' to his performance, courtesy of Michael J. (the children's favourite) Crispy was a pro; he had the crowd in the palm his hand. He strutted, grooved and sweated profusely in his body fit Union Jack t-shirt, his shiny black flares as always were soiled and stretched at the knee; his aviator shades hid the fleshy redness of his tired eyes and as he reached the final chorus his brown old wrinkly hands shook like bats in the night.

The crowd went ballistic. They loved it. Like the beer and the foam, they drank it up.

The dizzying noise of applause and whistles and calls for more bounced around the smoky little bar. Crispy stood panting on the stage; he grabbed the mike stand dramatically and stared at the worshipping crowd. His face was bright and shiny with his sweat, spotlight on Crispy as he spoke. "And now..." he said panting but clearly happy, "We hab a berry special request from our two Canadian frens... our distinguished guests... Sir Boris and Sir Vladimir... came all the way from New Brunswick, Canada just to be here tonight."

The spotlight left Crispy and wandered the boisterous crowd, searched the sea of excited faces and found its target, the 'Canadians'. The spotlight stopped and lit up their faces, it dazzled them. Boris and Vlad smiled awkwardly at the attention and nodded their heads gratefully, feeling a little like celebrities; they lifted their glasses in a toast to the crowd and drank some more. They were sitting at a long bamboo table and Bong sat between them grinning, looking smaller than ever. Drinks, bottles, food, smoke and smiles filled the table. The Russian assassins were looking a little drunk now, big flushed faces, glazed eyes and slightly silly grins.

Boris looked among the drinks, dishes and debris on the table, searched and finally focused on the bony remains of a large grilled fish sitting cold on a cheap plastic platter. He pulled an eye from its charred blackened head and crunched it with enthusiasm, sucked down the juices from inside the eye. Yummy!

He was pretty drunk now; fortunately it was a good drunk, a funny, amusing drunk, nothing heinous or malevolent. He was saving that for later.

Vlad sat the other side of Bong, his bulging arm around Honeygirl's hefty shoulder; he was holding her close and could smell the pungent kitchen aromas lingering in her hair. Honeygirl had powdered over her zits and the result was ok-ish, she was looking a tad coy and swooning still, she'd been swooning ever since she first sat next to the handsome foreigner with the big muscles. After a few drinks Vlad explained to her that he liked buxom women very much, that he liked voluptuous; naturally Honeygirl took it as a compliment, fluttered her eyelashes as she casually nibbled on a fresh loaf of bread.

Honeygirl sat staring into Vlad's turquoise eyes, ignoring their bloodshot sheen, savoring that sacred moment of real potential love, a sacred moment she never thought she'd find. Vlad thought she seemed a little desperate, but said nothing.

Poor Bong had drunk so much he couldn't speak, even breathing was an effort, his grin was fixed and his head was spinning, apart from that he felt fine.

Crispy's macho sons, the melon chopping machete boys, were in the car park now on their knees, puking up, begging for God's mercy and speaking in tongues. They'd only had a few beers, but they couldn't handle it, they were done and they were dusted. They'd promised not to splash puke on the Mercedes, promised faithfully to keep away from it.

The night was a great result. Absolutely everyone was having a good time. Crispy's concert—as expected—was an undeniable success.

Spotlight back on Crispy now as he held the mike and continued; "Theez special request from our Canadian frens is an old favorite of ours... from the Beatles." The crowd went mental, cheering, shouting, screams of joy all around, unbridled jubilation... it was clear the Beatles still meant a lot to them. It took them back in time—like music often does—took them back to the days of President Marcos and martial law, to a time when things were good and under control, when problems weren't allowed, when problems like undesirable people just disappeared.

Crispy put the mike back on the stand, threw his skinny brown arms into the air and bellowed, "It's... 'Back in the U.S.S.R.'!!!!"

The crowd jumped cheering to their feet; the place went crazy ape's shit.

Vlad and Boris shared an amused drunken smile—Boris wondering if they'd heard of Herman's Hermits? The killers sighed heavily in unison and clinked their glasses; they had to admit they were having a great time. Filipino hospitality was everything people had said it was, but now, sadly, it was time to get to work.

While Crispy was strutting his stuff to the Beatles in Tagaytay, the 'Pussy Galore' bar in Angeles City got busier and busier.

Panky sat close to the stage, drank steadily as he watched the entertainment. A tall, heavy set guy came up and sat a couple of stools from him, ordered a beer and lit a cigarette. Panky couldn't really see the guy too well; he was in the shadows, sitting almost draped among the folds of the velvet curtains, he looked a big guy and somehow military. Panky ignored him until he spoke.

"British right?" the big guy said and thrust out a large hairy hand.

Panky wondered how the guy knew, shook the hand, admired its steely grip, said, "Yeah, I'm glad someone can tell." He paused and lit another cigarette, looked up and said, "My name's Panky d'you want a beer mate?"

The big guy smiled, white-capped teeth bright in the shadows. "Sure I wanna beer man; I always wanna beer... that's just one of my problems."

The two guys chuckled together like old drinking buddies and Panky ordered more.

"I'm Dick O'Sullivan, U.S. marine corps," the big guy said, slowly sliding off his bar stool in the shadows. Once on his feet the big guy stood deadpan and straight, stamped his feet, then saluted dramatically. Patriotic or what?

Panky nearly laughed, wasn't sure if the guy was serious or taking the piss, couldn't see him too good there in the shadows, guessed his age at late fifties, maybe sixty looking at his craggy profile, noticing now the gray in his salt and pepper sideburns, in his straggly handle bar moustache. The big stranger wore denim and plaid, looked like the Marlboro man, and sounded like him too, husky, and proud and American.

Panky looked down expecting cowboy boots and smiled when he saw them, looked up as the big guy continued. "I'm retired now buddy, of course," the cowboy said, "But I'm still a marine and I'm still an American and proud." The cowboy climbed back onto his stool, sucked on his bottle of beer and scanned the bar with a lecherous eye.

Panky smiled at his new friend, liked him immediately, still wasn't sure if he was a fanatical patriot or just fucking around. It was hard to tell.

"They call me Dicko, son," the cowboy bellowed holding up his bottle; he'd finished the beer in two long gulps and ordered more. "Don't bother with that broad you spoke to earlier man," he said, a hint of authority in his gravely voice, "She's all show and no go, believe me... the guys here call her 'Tomorrow'... 'Cos she never comes, and her friend's as ugly as...'"

Panky waited for the punch line, swigging at his beer, grinning, nodding with anticipation.

"Ugly as... err... as err..." The cowboy was searching hard for the words... not finding much.

"Ugly as a bull dog lickin' piss of a thistle?" offered Panky.

The American sat conjuring up the gruesome image for maybe five seconds, then slapped his hands flat on the bar and whooped with crazy laughter, as he slapped his denim thighs, tears rolled down his ruddy cheeks, he coughed, choked and spluttered on his laughter.

Panky grinned. He didn't think it was *that* funny, but he said nothing.

"Ugly as a bulldog lickin' piss off a thistle!" he bellowed, "Exactly!" and he laughed some more sounding slightly insane, "You must have seen her already buddy," he said wiping foam off his hairy face with the back of his hand.

The night continued and the guys drank their way to oblivion; girls came and went in the shadows. Dicko's gropes inspired screams and occasional soft groans of pleasure from the girls; they all seemed to know him, called him Papa Dicko. He was a veteran by any distinction and he sure knew how to have fun.

Girlie approached Panky, her fat friend close behind her. Dicko was absolutely right: A bulldog and one with a bad pedigree, skin like yesterday's pizza, designer flab *and* cellulite.

"Sorry I take so long handsome," said Girlie, her hands like snakes again all over Panky, instant like noodles.

Panky turned and winked at Dicko before he spoke, "Girlie, right?"

The girl known as 'Tomorrow' smiled.

"That was six hours ago!" Panky said, as he glanced at the clock on the wall. "So where you been babe?"

"See him, dere?" she said, pointing to a fat Nazi looking guy, pale bullyboy features, tattoos, and a skinhead pate. "He my boyfren, he German, he berry rich too."

Ok thought Panky, he certainly looks German, not too sure about berry rich or boyfren.

"He pay bar fine, take me an' my fren… he hab *real* good time…" she said licking her lips, trying to look coy and sound sexy but not pulling it off, "You like? Huh?"

"What… follow the Furheur?" said Panky with another wink to his new drinking buddy, "I don't think so sweetheart, not my style…"

Dicko chuckled in the shadows, waved at the barmaid, ordered more drinks.

Girlie grabbed her bulldog friend and stormed off in a huff, stuck out her tongue as she vanished into the crowd.

Dicko slouched across the bar, smoke trailing up from his nostrils as he smoked; his cigarette glowed, lit up his craggy face and he laughed like the crazy, happy drunk that he was.

Boris and Vlad sat in their limo savouring the aircon; they were drunk but pumped with adrenaline. They were ready for some action, ready for some violence, well, almost ready.

The big Mercedes was parked under some trees, dappled by moonlight, the branches of the trees shivered slightly in the night air. They weren't too far from Chris' house now; they could see the moonlit rooftops above the tall perimeter wall.

Boris took the revolvers from the bag on his lap, passed one to Vlad and grinned.

"Are you *sure* these guns are ok?" asked Vlad.

"I shot the carabao, you don't remember that?" said Boris like it was some major Olympic achievement.

"Boris…. believe me, it's something I'll never forget, ok? Not as long as I live!" said Vlad, "But d'you really think they'll have carabao's guarding a big house like this?"

Boris gave it his best 'fuck you' smile and climbed out of the car, shut the door behind him.

Vlad climbed out, shut the door quietly and followed Boris across the grass through the shadows of the trees. Cicadas and crickets filled the night air with weird electric noise and frogs went '*Grr…iick*' in the grass.

The huge drunk Russians crept quietly along the old perimeter wall, antique revolvers held tightly in their hands, poised, ready to shoot anything that moved. They looked comical and ungainly as they tip toed along, the green and yellow fabric of their suits with the delicate white blossoms shone bright in the light of the moon, looked mad like a camouflage parody. They looked surreal almost, two huge Muscovites in tight Hawaiian outfits, dark woolen socks and leather sandals, scuttling along in the moonlight, heads turning left and right, ready for practically anything. The guys kept running unsure of what to expect. Panting and breathless they stopped and faced each other. Boris was bent double, hands on his knees, anxious for air, he looked up at Vlad: "Ok, let's get over this wall..."

"No... not here," said Vlad staring at the old revolver in his hand.

"Not here? Why not?"

"I'm not sure, but is not the best place... I've got this feeling... I..."

Boris interrupted saying: "Hey Vlad, remember what Zoltan said ok? Feelings are for the social workers... right?" and he began to scale the wall, his feet scuffing for purchase, trying hard to find a foothold. "C'mon rookie," he said reaching the top, "We got work to do..."

Vlad looked up as Boris toppled awkwardly over the wall and fell backwards, saw his sandals vanish into the night. He heard him give a stifled yelp and then land with a decisive thud on the other side. Vlad couldn't help but snigger and then, still sniggering, he too scaled the wall and jumped over landing firmly on his feet.

The two big Russians stood breathless in the garden looking around. Vlad sniggering slightly between gulps of air, Boris panting and sneering as he rubbed his bruises.

The grotto with its trickling water was directly behind them, candles flickered in the breeze, the Virgin Mary stood serenely with open arms. Silence now apart from the trickling water and the big panting Russians. They stood quiet with their guns poised ready, eager armed assassins still looking around in the darkness.

Boris had an infrared dot wavering slightly between his eyes, but was oblivious to its presence; he had no idea what was happening. Vlad had one too, but was also totally unaware; he was far too busy looking at Boris, looking at the infrared dot wavering slightly between his gray bushy eyebrows. "I hate to tell you this Boris… but err… you got like a red dot between your eyes."

Boris stared ahead into the dark, raised his hand, and ran his sausage fingers across his forehead. "What… you mean like a pimple?"

Vlad remained calm, "No, I think this is a little more significant than a pimple Boris…"

The Russians stood motionless in the moonlight, the Virgin Mary still smiling behind them with outstretched arms, softly trickling water the only sound now. The red dots between their eyes were wavering, but just slightly. Waiting.

Suddenly powerful halogen spotlights came alive.

Boris and Vlad stood frozen like headlight rabbits, dazzled and vulnerable, bathed in brightness; big faces squinting and confused, wide eyed, suddenly sober.

"Ok drop the revolvers," said a Filipino voice.

The sound of two old Colt forty fives on concrete echoed around the grounds in perfect unison. Boris felt the coldness of a gun barrel against his temple. He didn't move.

Vlad also felt the coldness of a gun barrel on his temple too. He didn't move either.

The Morales brothers, the cops, turned their heads, looked squinting towards the spotlights, saw Boy come slowly into vision, saw him walking silently towards them, then saw the uniformed guards holding their Armalites with the infrared devices.

"I think you guys have made a serious mistake," said Boy, "A *very* serious mistake." Boy's face was inches from Boris' now; staring into Boris' small eyes.

Boris towered above Boy and snorted breath through his nostrils; it was a small but slightly arrogant sound. Boy said nothing, just pulled his arm back and punched his considerable weight into Boris' throat: the punch was hard and clean and accurate. Boris fell choking and purple faced, clutching at his windpipe, gasping. As he fell to the ground Boy punched him hard in the temple, finished him off.

Vlad stood trembling now, shocked, he gazed at his partner's fallen body. Shit! No one took Boris out with just two punches. No one!

"You want some too my fren?" asked Boy and the Morales brothers and the guards all laughed.

Vlad stood silent and still, both guns on him now; one poised ready on each sweat-covered temple.

Boy stood close to Vlad, smelled the beer and fish on his laboured breath, noticed the 'fit to burst' seams on his yellow Hawaiian suit, saw his dark socks pulled up high above his leather sandals. Boy thinking: Hmm stylish. Again Boy said nothing, just punched Vlad *hard* on the nose. *Whack!*

Blood spilt on the concrete before Vlad's body hit the ground, but he wasn't far behind. His face landed and bounced in his own little red puddle.

Boy looked at the cops and the guards and smiled, everyone agreed there was little doubt: Boy was *definitely* the best driver/bodyguard Sir Chris had ever had.

Panky and Dicko sat perched on their bar stools, drinkers limbs damp on the bar among the bottles and glasses. Dicko's face was actually *on* the bar, his profile on a soggy mat, his smile was twisted and his face lit up with every puff of the cigarette clamped tightly between his teeth. The music blaring from the speakers was Devo, another blast from the past. The girls danced robotically on the stage, having fun with this 'different' sound. Devo, like Panky, not getting any satisfaction despite the surroundings.

Thirty or forty girls left the stage and thirty or forty more marched through the bar and took their place.

Panky looked around and smoked his cigarette. Oh no! He couldn't believe it! He shook his head and looked again. There they were!

Sid and D.K. stared across the bar at him, waving and mocking him, laughing together. They were bloodied and gory still, their flesh ripped and tattered like their clothes, but their wounds had gotten darker, decay was setting in. They looked pale and gaunt now, like dead people.

Panky swallowed beer, shook his head and puffed out his breath slowly; he turned his eyes towards the stage where thankfully everything seemed normal. At first anyway.

Suddenly every female face on the stage began to morph and change shape; every face slowly became someone else. Every female face was suddenly Mai-Ling! Mai-Ling smiling happily at Panky, giving him that very special look of hers.

Panky slammed his beer onto the bar, held his head in his hands, pogo heart pounding in his chest.

"You ok buddy?" said Dicko concern in his voice and on his lips.

Panky peeped through his fingers at the stage; everything seemed normal again. *Phew*!

"Yeah Dicko, I'm fine… not too bad anyway."

Dicko grinned in the shadows, ordered more beer.

Panky wanted to take his mind off things, "So what brings you here then Dicko? What's your story?"

Dicko slammed another beer in front of Panky and grunted. "Where else in this Goddamn world can a sixty year old geezer like me go out on a Saturday night and get drunk—and I mean real drunk man, —and then go home with two sixteen year old girls… and *still* have change out of fifty dollars?"

Panky grinned, thinking: Fair enough and why wouldn't you? It's gotta beat bingo and basket weaving.

"So who are all these other old guys just sitting around?" asked Panky, feeling a little better, younger almost, but sweating profusely, still shaking slightly.

Dicko lifted his head up from the bar a little. "Same as me Panky, vets from Viet-nam man, this is where we came for a little R 'n' R… six months chasing Charlie through the jungle and we needed it… you know what I'm saying son?"

Panky had a vague idea, so he nodded before he drank.

"It's kinda hard to go home you know? After all *that* shit and some of us had nothin' to go back to man, we sure weren't the same young boys that left the US of A." Dicko's voice had softened and saddened, his face was awash with memories. Bad ones.

A girl approached Panky from behind; she startled him, made him jump as she slid her cool hands over his eyes. The hands felt soft and female so he let them stay. "Hi handsome," the girl whispered into Panky's ear.

Panky grimaced at her lack of originality, but smiled as she rubbed her breasts against his back. He could smell her perfume, he liked the sweetness of it and liked the softness of her breasts too. The girl continued whispering, "My name Josephine… you like boom boom big boy?"

Dicko was slumped across the bar smoking and grinning.

Josephine removed her hands, swiveled the bar stool around so that Panky was facing her. She was looking good.

"Hey, I'd love to, really," said Panky, "I would… I'd love to, but not tonight Josephine."

Dicko hooted with laughter in the shadows.

Josephine was determined; she opened her blouse and revealed her exquisite breasts. Both were beauties and with small brown nipples. Semi erect. "You no like these honey?" she whispered.

Panky stared down at the soft brownness of her cleavage and gasped, full marks again for presentation. He looked up and into her eyes. Oh my God! She'd fucking morphed! She looked exactly like Mai-Ling! Hallucinations or what? Panky was panicked and panting, covered his eyes with the palms of his hands and groaned.

Dicko wasn't too sure what was happening, he just chuckled in the darkness.

"Go away," Panky said to Josephine, "Just go away…" As she strolled away Josephine turned back, her face was her own again, not a trace of Mai-Ling. Panky saw it and sighed with relief.

"You okay Panky?" said Dicko as he slid off his stool and moved through the shadows over toward his new drinking buddy, "Is there sumthin' wrong here son?"

Panky grabbed a shot of Tequila from the bar and downed it.

"No… nothing wrong, I'm ok," he said, "Got a lot on my mind… tryin' to put a few things behind me… if you know what I mean?"

"Women problems son?" asked Dicko in a fatherly voice.

"No… not women problems Dicko, not this time, well not really," Panky chuckled at his words, stared down at his feet again as he spoke, "Probably just too many drugs… that's all… and alcohol and way too much violence." Panky looked up and for the first time saw Dicko's face full on and out of the shadows. It was more than a shock, much more. Panky couldn't help but gasp slightly when he realised that Dicko had only half a face.

He looked down at his shoes and prayed that Dicko hadn't heard the small sound of shock, but guessed by his expression that he had.

When Panky looked up again, he saw that his drinking buddy was Harvey Dent ugly and had skin like warm corned beef. He couldn't help but gasp again, he just couldn't help it. Dicko looked saddened, but not shocked by the response, he stared into Panky's face; saw guilt and shame all over it.

Panky was breathing hard, thinking: So what the fuck's going on now? Is this Dicko guy for real or what?

Dicko had a face with pieces missing, a face without a face somehow and lots of scars, small wonder he hid in the shadows and didn't want to go home. His right profile was 100% warm corned beef; he had wounds that looked as though they never healed, wounds that were old and putrid. Panky sat shocked, found it hard to look, almost impossible, he wanted to sob and cry for his newfound friend, but knew that he couldn't do that. Knew it wouldn't help either one of them.

Dicko stood there with his hands on his hips grinning; after thirty years of deformity he was used to such reactions.

Panky stood there wondering what to say, thinking: What the fuck can I say?

Dicko laughed out loud, swallowed some beer, slammed the empty bottle on the counter and yelled out for more. He turned back towards Panky, grinned some more as he lit another cigarette; this situation was typical, nothing new and he was used to it, it meant nothing to him. Not really, not after thirty years. Dicko spoke as though nothing had happened. "You were saying son? 'Probably just too many drugs… that's all… and way too much violence, am I right?"

Panky nodded yes, looked up at his buddy.

Dicko climbed back onto his bar stool, belched loudly, wiped the boozy dribble off his face, scratched madly at the scabs on his chin with his dirty fingernails and rolled his red eyes. "You know Panky... if there's one thing I learned in Viet-nam... that's too many drugs and too much violence really *can* affect a man's mind and I mean *really* affect a man's mind! You know what I'm sayin' here son?" Dicko smiled and chuckled, laid his face in the dampness of the bar, smoked his cigarette. "You drop a little acid, you smoke a little weed, go running through the jungle shooting Charlie and his family, you gonna end up not knowing which way is up son, you can take that from me. You lose the sense of right and wrong, you know what I'm saying here son?" Despite the macho talk there was sadness in Dicko's eyes. "I tried to stop those sons of bitches in My Lai son, I really did." Dicko finished his beer, grabbed another from the bar. "Twisted on psychedelics like Viking warriors they were Panky, berserk was the word of the day son, waving the Stars and Stripes, whooping like Goddamned Geronimo... killed the children, the babies, the livestock too, killed everything alive. I tried to stop 'em, but they held me down and kicked half my face off—Dicko pointed to his face as though there might be some doubt—I tried to stop 'em son, really I did."

Panky was speechless, what can you say?

"Got me a real good pension though," said Dicko with a gasp and a laugh and a slap of his thigh.

Panky wasn't sure if he was joking or serious, could see now that Dicko was a total fuckin' loon, but still liked him: the guy really knew how to drink and he was certainly entertaining, but not quite entertaining enough for Panky to stick around.

Panky slid off his seat, finished his beer and started towards the door, he turned to say goodbye to Dicko, but Dicko was chuckling in the shadows, girls all around him, kissing and groping and having some fun.

"I'll see you around Dicko," shouted Panky as he wandered off sadly, hating the consequences of war and the people that controlled it.

Dicko's big hand waved in the air. He knew he'd never see Panky again and he really didn't care too much.

Panky pushed through the crowded bar, headed towards the door. Oh no! He saw Sid and D.K. sitting there again, surrounded by girls, laughing at his hasty departure, giving him the finger, calling him a wanker. Panky was out of there and fast.

Gasping just slightly, he stopped at the entrance door, casually brushed the ash and beer off his rumpled clothes, breathed the fresh but warm night air, saw stars high up above him and savoured a touch of reality. Nice. He obviously needed more vitamin B and he needed it fast.

The girl on the stool at the entrance smiled and said, "Thank you sir, come again." Panky grinned and sniffed at his armpits, they smelled of vinegar and neglect, but he didn't care, there wasn't much he could do anyway. He heard a song, faint and in the distance, a familiar song: 'I want to be straight' by Ian Dury and the Blockheads, another classic. The words were clear and to Panky more than a little ominous: Being straight seemed like a good choice for once.

"Great song," said Panky to no one in particular as he walked towards Ding-Dong's car, "Great, great song."

Ding-Dong awoke as Panky tapped gently on the window. Sounding anxious and desperate Panky said, "Ding-Dong I... I need vitamin B complex... I need a lot of it, I won't be a minute, and then we go, ok?"

"Ok sir, no problema," said Double Dee yawning, wiping sleep from his eyes like cobwebs.

Panky spun on his heels, stumbled towards the pharmacy next to the bar. As he staggered through the door he saw two young sales assistants slumped across the counter sleeping, snoring quietly. He looked at the clock on the wall: ok, it *was* getting late. One of the young girls managed to open an eye, she peered at her disheveled customer, saw him wipe his nose on the back of his hand and casually sniff once again at both his armpits.

Panky hung onto the counter by his fingertips, tried to control his swaying. He was stinking of booze and cigarettes, had dribble on his unshaven chin; a stranger might've been fooled into thinking he was a little crazy; he certainly looked it. "Hi," he said to the girl with the one open eye.

Panky thought she looked weird lying with her head on the counter like that, peering at him with one sleepy eye. He wondered if she knew Dicko, but decided to say nothing. He was finding it hard to talk.

"Hi Joe," said the girl sitting up, proving she had a complete face; "You want Viagra?"

"Viagra? No," said Panky and he smiled and added, "Not right now."

"Condoms, then, huh?"

"No, not condoms."

"Oh... ok, you must want penicillin then, huh?"

Panky was swaying and seeing double much better than he was communicating with the sleepy girl—much, much better. "No not penicillin either," he slurred quickly, "I'm having these hallucin…"

The girl looked suddenly lost and bewildered, she didn't catch a word, she was wide-eyed and open mouthed, he was speaking much too fast, slurring far too heavily. Her friend across the store woke up, peered sleepily at Panky; saw the mess he was in.

"It's the hallucina…" he mumbled and slurred, "I need vitamin B complex, ok? And I need a lot of it… it's the alco.. hol."

Both girls looked confused, shared a puzzled look across the store, a raised eyebrow now on either side. They understood the word alco.. hol that was easy; they could smell it, but what was it he actually wanted?

"Look, its simple right, I need vitamin B complex, ok?" he slurred the words again, but even quicker. It didn't help.

The girls clearly didn't understand a word and Panky was getting annoyed now.

"This is a pharmacy right?" he bellowed looking around in case he'd made a silly mistake. Both girls nodded that it was; they looked scared now, wide-awake.

"I want vit-a-min B com-plex… you got that? You un-der-stand?"

Both girls nodded, but without much conviction.

"So give me some vit-a-min B com-plex and give it to me NOW! Purleeeeze!"

The girls still looked confused; one of them mouthed 'Bitamin V comflex' to the other. The bravest girl spoke, "You mean you need bitamin V comflex sir?"

Panky's eyes grew wide; he grinned, dribbled slightly, swayed and then snorted a little air from his nostrils. "Yeah... that's right, that's what I need," he said fumbling for some pesos, "Bitamin V comflex and hurry up... please."

The girl handed over a bottle of pills and took Panky's pesos, her friend got closer and they stood side by side and stared at the weird and clearly desperate foreigner.

Shaking a handful of pills from the bottle and stuffing them into his mouth with wholesale delight, Panky blundered drunkenly from the store and headed out towards Ding Dong's old car.

Ding-Dong slid up in the driver's seat and started the engine, he looked over at Panky and wondered how he'd got in such a state: the dribble, the disheveled clothes, the manic look, the chewed up pills stuck on his face, around his mouth. Panky opened the Datsun door, slumped into the back seat and sighed with relief. He turned and looked out of the back window of the car, wanted a final sleazy peek at the city of angels. Oh no!

The love struck transsexual—the 'geezer bird' that stared at Panky through the car window eight or nine hours ago and found true love—was clip clopping up the street in her heels, waving her delicate painted hands in the air and screaming.

"Papa, papa I lub you, I lub you... don't leeb me, don't leeb me!"

"Let's get the hell outta here Double Dee," said Panky through a fresh mouthful of pills, "And let's make it fast..."

The old Datsun Cherry pulled away as sharply as it could; Double Dee's eyes filled the rear view. He said, "I guess you no like, huh?"

Panky looked up, "I guess not," he said and huddled down into the seat, felt that comforting old spring in his arse again.

"Where we go now boss?" asked Double Dee swerving to miss the transsexual.

"Take me back to Tagaytay, Double Dee, back to Sir Chris'… I got some major apologising to do."

Panky was sweating already; he looked at the small hand held battery operated fan on the dashboard. "And pass the aircon Double Dee, it's fuckin' boiling in the back here…"

The speakers in Chris' basement were big and powerful: 'No more Heroes' by The Stranglers was *booming* out, filling the dingy room; making the glass in the tiny high window vibrate, flicker like the wings of a panicking moth.

Boris and Vlad were stripped to their Calvin Klein underpants and tied to chairs with wire, strong gray duct tape stuck across their mouths.

The room was stiflingly hot; the huge Russians were dripping with sweat, they were beaten, bruised and bleeding, looking scared.

The music was *so loud*—the same song playing over and over and over again. To Boris and Vlad the situation seemed surreal, dreamlike, their blank expressions said as much. Neither of them was too sure what had actually happened, they both remembered climbing the wall—Boris remembered falling—and they remembered seeing the Virgin Mary. The rest was a blank.

They sat in their chairs the heat of the spotlights bright in their eyes, wondering what was coming next, not expecting too much fun, not expecting a lot of laughs. Earlier their captors had tried a little interrogation, but the Muscovites said nothing; maintained they were tourists, from Canada they said, from New Brunswick, said they were lost, scared of getting kidnapped, hence the guns. They sat like that for hours or at least that's how it seemed—The Stranglers playing over and over and *so loud*.

Finally the basement door opened and the Morales brothers, the cops, strolled in smiling and switched on the strip lights. One of them wearing a big yellow Hawaiian suit with white sampaguita blossoms, his brother wearing the same but in green, the suits needed a little adjustment, they were way, way too big, but the cops didn't seem too bothered. Boy followed behind them smoking a cigarette, grinning; they hadn't got very far with their earlier interrogation so he'd decided to take a different route. A more traditional route. Torture.

The Hawaiian suited cops carried a strange assortment of kitchen equipment, tools from the garage; their smiles became cruel like their eyes as they entered the room.

Boy stamped his cigarette out on the floor, turned off the music and said, "Don't worry guys I'll turn it back on when we're finished, ok?" The cops laughed.

Boris and Vlad's eyes followed Boy's every move.

The cops put the equipment down on the table at the side of the room; brown faces full of menace, black eyes shining with anticipation.

Boy saw Boris and Vlad staring at the kitchen equipment, at the tools. "Their standard torture stuff is at the police station," he said to the Russians and he smiled, "So they're gonna have to improvise a little," he held up a liquidizer and grinned.

Boy started pacing up and down in front of the failed assassins, building a little tension, spreading a little fear, "The Morales brothers are police... you understand that?"

The big Russians nodded in unison. They understood.

"They're extremely good at making people talk... police training here very good, very thorough."

Boris and Vlad looked terrified.

Ecto, the cop in the big green Hawaiian suit, padded over to Boris and *riiiiipppped* the duct tape off his mouth.

"*Yeow!*" screamed Boris, tears running down his face for the first time in thirty years.

Peo strolled over, grinning he bent down and looked Boris in the eyes; sweat dripped off his brown face and landed on Boris' big pink knees. Peo said, "Ok I'll ask you again my fren... where you prom?"

"Puck you," said Boris, remembering the Leary Katz execution and feeling a certain irony.

Peo gazed around the room shaking his head from side to side, tutting quietly; this was not good, not what he expected at all. These big guys were no push over; they were going to have to go a little harder. He pulled back his fist and punched Boris hard in the mouth.

Boris grunted. It was quite a punch. Instant blood.

"So, I ask again ok? Where... you... prom big guy?" Peo looked down at his aching knuckles, shook his hand slightly and winced.

"I tol' you..." said Boris through swollen, bleeding lips, "We're tourists, Canadian tourists... prom New Brunswick, look at the passports again, you'll see..."

Boy stepped forward with their two passports in his hand. "Boris Morozov and Vladimir Brodsky, the Canadians? said Boy, "I don't think so, I think these names... they are not very Canadian, ok? ... And something else, you don't sound too Canadian either, not to my ears anyway, ok?"

"We're from New Brunswick," said Boris, spitting blood.

Vlad sat sweating wishing he could speak, wishing he could breathe a little easier.

Ecto walked towards Boris, smiled, pulled back his fist and smashed Boris hard in the mouth. "I theenk you should tell us the troot," said Ecto, smiling at his brother, shaking his hand and checking his knuckles.

"Puck you too... vykovskyi," said Boris and spat a mouthful of blood and mucus into Ecto's face— considering the circumstances it was a pretty good shot. Ecto stepped back, wiped the mess onto the baggy sleeve of his new Hawaiian suit and wondered what 'vykovskyi' meant.

Peo grabbed a Jalapeno pepper from the table, bit off the end, spat it on floor and moved over towards Boris.

Vlad looked scared, turned his head slightly, saw Boris all blood and sweat now, looking terrified.

Peo rammed the Jalapeno pepper into Boris' left eye, rubbed it around a little.

"*Aaaaaahhhh*!" screamed Boris. His face went from bruised tourist pink to tortured person purple in seconds. "Vykovskyi! Vykovskyi!" he bellowed wiggling in his seat like an eel out of water.

Vlad sat completely still.

"You theenk that hurt? Huh? You pat puck!" said Peo getting mad and also wondering now what 'vykovskyi' meant. As always, the more excited Peo became the worse his P and F confusion became, V's and B's were just the same, Ecto and Boy had the same problem, it was a Filipino thing.

Ecto and Boy were chuckling quietly.

Peo whispered into Boris's ear, "Wait 'til we go further down my fren... you unnerstan?"

Boy clapped his hands together, "Ok let's go drink some Margaritas, it's hot and I'm thirsty," he said with a wicked grin, turning the stereo back on *loud*, smiling at the familiar punk sound of the Stranglers. "We come back later, when we're refreshed," said Boy to his prisoners, "And maybe a little drunk, huh?" He looked at the Morales brothers, winked and said, "We drink and then maybe we kill these 'Canadian terrorists', burn their fat bodies in the jungle, no problema? Ok, let's go guys, it's Margarita time." The cops looked delighted at the prospect of Margaritas and a bit of body burning; it was becoming quite a night, they were actually having some fun with these big stupid tourists, and despite the loose fit, they loved their new outfits. Ecto picked up the liquidizer as they left the room laughing; he turned off the main lights and left the two beaten Muscovites in the hot glow of the spotlights, tied tight to the chairs with the Stranglers *loud* in their ears.

Vlad winced at the sound of the Stranglers, *so fucking loud*, looked at the state of Boris' face and winced again. Boris' eye was red and swollen, puckered like a sick poodle's asshole, awash with stinging tears; his mouth was swollen and split. Vlad's eyes were sympathetic; it was the best he could do.

"So, they're making Margaritas," said Boris through his busted lips, "I was beginning to get a little worried."

Panky sat in the back of Double Dee's Datsun, the aircon held tightly in his hand and a spring up his arse—for some reason the spring was more comforting than the aircon. At least he felt safe again.

He'd made the decision to return to Chris' and tolerate the domestic scene, maybe it wasn't *that* bad after all. Panky suddenly felt good about the future, he'd come to terms with it, decided to get his act together while he still could. He couldn't wait to see Mai-Ling, tell he was sorry and explain how he felt.

The old car hammered and coughed its way up the highway toward Chris' house. Double Dee's eyes filled the rear view. "I forgot to tell you sir; I speak with your frenz? Did they find you in the end?"

Panky looked up, puzzled, "My friends?"

"Yeah the big guys, the Canadians, you meet them?"

Panky looked puzzled: Canadians?

"Boris and Vladimir I think? Your good frenz.... right? They want a check you're in Tagaytay still; they want to surprise you they say."

Panky's mouth fell open as intense hyperventilation kicked in. He was thinking: Oh fucking no! Not Boris and Vlad, not after all this… purleeeeze!

Double Dee nodded happily; unaware of the problem, pleased he hadn't spoiled the big surprise.

"OK, step on it Double Dee, fast as you can…"

Double Dee nodded and slammed his foot on the accelerator, but nothing much happened, a little black smoke spluttered from the exhaust, but that was about all.

Vlad and Boris sat tied to the chairs still, sweating in the spotlights, listening to the Stranglers still, *so fucking loud*. The air was thick and damp, heavy with heat; the music was omnipresent. They sat and they sat and they sat, just listening and sweating. Boris did a little bleeding too.

During the 'lifetime' that the Russians were left unattended they realised that they were being watched; there was probably at least one camera on them at all times. There was also a time when both the spotlights and the Stranglers on the stereo were suddenly switched off.

"Disorientation is very old trick," Boris said, through his busted lips.

So for a while they sat in total darkness sweating quietly, Vlad almost missing the music, but unable to say anything with the duct tape still across his mouth. Suddenly the spotlights came back on.

The disorientation didn't bother them so much; it was the waiting that really got to them. The waiting was bad, the dread and anticipation worse than any pain they could receive. Boris and Vlad sat in the hot spotlights without music for a while. Waiting.

While they sat quiet Boris showed his rookie partner a little compassion, but not much, he said, "You ok rookie?"

Vlad nodded yes and that was it.

Boris couldn't find anything else to say, words were not his forte, but after an hour or two he looked at Vlad, a hint of inspiration in one eye, a road map of red veins in the other.

"That Crispy Junior was pretty good, huh?"

Vlad didn't even nod.

Finally the door *burst* open. Their captors strolled back in, looking drunk and boisterous.

Boris looked up thinking: Not a good situation.

Boy turned the stereo down, but not off—he liked the Stranglers. He paced up and down in front of the Russians, scowling and sighing, making up his mind about something.

Boris saw the cops, Peo and Ecto playing with the kitchen equipment and the tools, like kids with Lego, imaginations running wild, making agonized noises and laughing as they played. Peo held up a pair of pliers, a look of delight smeared across brown his face, he said, "These Canadians have the bad teeth, no? We can play dentist? Is fun to play dentist, remember?"

Vlad suddenly remembered Leary Katz in the warehouse, glanced at Boris thinking: This is *really* not good. Is Karma?

Boy ripped a piece of duct tape from the roll they'd used earlier, wound it round Boris's head a couple of times and covered his mouth, tightly. Boy looked across at the cops smirked and snorted a little air from his nostrils—a stifled laugh—he moved casually over to the table and picked up a solid wooden rolling pin.

Playing dentist was fun, he remembered it well—how could he ever forget? But he had a better idea, a much better idea.

"Teeth we can do later Peo, I promise, ok? We can even borrow the drill again, play 'Marathon Man' like before, you can be Olivier and Boris here can be Hoffman, ok?"

Peo cracked a smile and nodded, put back the pliers, tried to hide his disappointment.

Boy looked at the rolling pin like it was a rare Egyptian artifact, eyes sparkling, full of wonder, he said, "You know how much just a little tiny knock on the shin can hurt you? Huh? You know? *So* much pain just a little knock, yeah?"

Boris was sweating more than ever, he glanced over at Vlad; Vlad was sweating more than ever too. The Russians knew nothing of 'Marathon Man'—Boris hated running, he knew that—but they knew about shins and they knew about their tenderness. This was not good at all.

"This pain it makes you wanna die it hurt so much, right?" said Boy.

The cops sniggered over there by the table. They knew what was coming.

Boy stooped slightly and swung the heavy rolling pin hard like a baseball bat, smashed Vlad's shin as hard as he could.

"*Aaaaaaahhhhhh*," screamed Vlad from behind his duct tape, bright blue eyes almost jumping out of their sockets like a cartoon character.

Boy swung again, harder, smashed the tender bone on the other shin.

"*Aaaaaaahhhhh*," screamed Vlad with big red cartoon eyes. The sound so sickening Boris wanted to puke on his underwear.

Boy *riiiiipppped* the duct tape from Vlad's mouth; heard him gag and gasp for air, heard him groan and gasp some more, watched his red eyes roll as he gagged.

Boris saw Boy looking down at *his* fat pink shins now, sizing them up. Oh no! Boris was next! Boris mumbled and screamed behind his duct tape, he wanted to speak, he wanted to do something before it was too late… he was rocking back and forth in his chair making those strange muffled noises that only terrified, gagged people can make.

Boy *riiiiipppped* the duct tape from Boris's mouth; heard him inhale, breath like a drowning geriatric. "Ok, ok… we're…" Boris gasped, tried hard to speak before the rolling pin swung again, "We're…" It wasn't easy. "We're…"

The basement door swung open, in walked Chris with a big grin and Panky close behind him.

Peo and Ecto, the cops, gave Panky the thumbs up, big smiles of recognition like long lost friends. Boy nodded and grinned at Panky, held open his hands; spread his arms, proud of their captives and the treatment they were getting.

Boris hawked loudly and gobbed on the floor near Panky's feet, he shouted, "We're looking for that vykovskyi just walked in," and then he stared and sneered at Panky, it was all he could do.

"You keep saying vykovskyi! What is this vykovskyi?" barked Boy up close, into Boris's red face.

"It means wanker,' said Panky with a little smirk and an internationally recognisable hand gesture.

Boy stood back a little, shrugged like he had no choice, swung the rolling pin as hard as he could and smashed Boris' left shin to pieces. The sound was gut wrenching, Panky nearly puked, almost felt sorry Boris. Almost.

Vlad kept his eyes closed as Boris' scream filled the room. Ecto laughed a little as he wound more tape around Boris' mouth and muffled his pain and his panting.

Chris just grinned, he'd been in the Philippines a while now, he'd seen it all before, knew it was a mistake to fuck with the wrong people here.

Chris and Panky stood looking at the Russians, wondering what the hell to do next. It wasn't an easy decision, sure they could burn the bodies that would be easy, but would it keep Zoltan off Panky's back?

They decided it probably wouldn't and looked for a different angle.

"Which one's Zoltan's brother?" asked Chris.

"The fat one with the pink puckered eye and the wobbly legs," said Panky.

Boy and the Morales laughed as they poured more Margaritas passed one to Panky and Chris.

"Boy gave me their mobile phones when they first arrived," said Chris sipping his drink, licking casually at the salted rim, "I found a number under Z in the directory." All eyes on Chris now. "It's an Amsterdam number too; good chance its Zoltan, hey? Unless of course it's Zorro, but I don't think he lives in Amsterdam any more, heard he couldn't handle the nightlife."

Panky laughed a little and then agreed. It probably was Zoltan.

Vlad looked at Boris.

The Morales brothers and Boy smoked cigarettes and mixed more Margaritas.

"Let's have a little conference call shall we?" said Chris and he walked across the room, picked up a telephone, punched it onto speakerphone and dialed the number. All eyes on the telephone as the dial tone droned out of the speaker, finally someone picked up.

"Hello, Boris? Vladimir? Hello?"

It was Zoltan.

Panky looked at Chris and smiled.

Boy and the Morales brothers looked at Chris and smiled.

Boris and Vlad looked at each other. Worried.

Panky stooped a little towards the speaker grinning, "We got your boys here Zoltan."

Heavy breathing oozed from the speaker and finally, "Pay your debts Panky and I'll leave you alone ok? Is not so difficult."

"Listen Zoltan, I had most of it," Panky said, "… another couple of days you could've had it all… but you had to put on the pressure didn't you?"

Zoltan continued, "Hey, you were late, remember, I had no choice… I'm sure *you* understand *that*, this is just business Panky."

Panky said, "Look, what happened in the coffeeshop, wasn't my fault… right? I'm sure *you* understand *that*?" Panky took a Margarita from Boy, sipped it noisily, looked over at Boris and Vlad and toasted their health.

They were sweating pretty good now, probably thirsty too.

"Why'd you kill Leary Katz Zoltan? he had nothing to do with this." Panky wasn't 100% sure that Zoltan had killed him, but he'd got Leary's text, knew that the Russians had got to him one way or another. It was the way Zoltan worked; Leary'd be considered a lose end, loose ends need tying up, end of story.

"Who told you this?" asked Zoltan wondering if Boris or Vlad had been stupid enough to mention it.

"It doesn't matter who mentioned it, why'd you do it?"

"Hey look I'm sorry ok? Stupid American insulted me... I got mad." Zoltan paused, he was thinking, "I guess it was just a *'moment of weakness'*."

Boris wanted to scream, but realised he couldn't and mumbling just wasn't the same. So his eyes screamed instead, his fat face reddened to beetroot, even his ears screamed and that's not easy.

Vlad watched Boris' face, laughed uncontrollably behind his duct tape, silently, shoulders up and down like honeymoon bedsprings.

Eventually Zoltan's voice filled the speaker again; by his tone Leary's death was of little importance, "Tell me Panky about the money, what d'you mean... you *had* most of it?

"What I say, I *had* most of it," said Panky.

"Ok look... maybe most of it will do, ok? I'm getting sick of all this bullshit; it's costing me money." The speaker went quiet, Zoltan was thinking. "So where is my money now? You saying it's not with you? Is that what you're saying?" Zoltan was getting a little anxious now, sounding frustrated, bordering desperate.

"It's probably still on my houseboat Zoltan," said Panky with a smile, "Probably still under my bed."

Boris glanced at Vlad and started to whimper.

"*On the fucking houseboat*!" bellowed Zoltan, "*On the fucking houseboat*! The speaker went quiet, but they could hear Zoltan's seething breath, "Boris, you stupid vykovskyi! This I cannot believe!"

Everyone except Boris laughed at the word 'vykovskyi', Vlad chuckled quietly behind his duct tape.

Zoltan continued, "You stupid, psychotic sonofabitch, I'll kill you... I will kill you!"

Vlad glanced at Boris.

Chris smiled at Panky. This was fun.

"Zoltan," shouted Panky strolling around looking at the Russians, enjoying their obvious discomfort, "Before you have a coronary, tell me... was it you told those two punks, those crazy kids that it was me supplying their mother with cocaine?"

"And why would I do this?" asked Zoltan, "Maybe you should ask Vlad, this Judy the mother, she was *his* girlfriend not mine."

Panky nodded, now he understood everything, he looked at Vlad, watched him blushing behind his duct tape.

Zoltan continued, "What I want to know is what fucking lunatic sold guns to those crazy kids? Huh? We don't have enough customers for guns?"

Vlad gulped audibly and Boris sweated some more. Things weren't going too well for them—it really wasn't their day.

"So, what do we do now Zoltan? Shall we kill these idiots for you, save you the hassle?"

The speaker went quiet again.

Finally Zoltan said, "Yes, ok, kill them! Do it now… but make it slow!"

The Morales brothers and Boy looked delighted, knocked back their drinks and poured some more.

Boris looked at Vlad in total disbelief. His own brother for God's sake!

"Wait," said Zoltan, "wait, leave it on speaker phone… this I must hear."

The Morales brothers ambled across the room and each picked up a clear plastic bag, smiling they slipped them casually over the Russian's heads and pulled the pull strings as tight as they'd go. Boris and Vlad struggled and squirmed for their life like puppies in a sack near the river. Faces instantly purple and eyes bulging fit to pop. As their breathing filled the bags with sweaty condensation, their faces began to fade; the plastic moved in and out like labouring lungs.

"No wait… wait," bellowed Zoltan.

Chris held up his hand and the cops released the bags, gagging and choking noises, panting filled the room.

"I'll kill them myself… is better for me that way," said Zoltan, "Maybe I can be total bastard… send them back to Moscow!" Through the panting, sweat, blood and misery Boris and Vlad looked more gutted than ever. Not Moscow!

Chris and Panky shared a smile, but the cops looked disappointed.

"I see you in Amsterdam again Panky I will shoot you dead, you know me huh? You know this is no idle threat, ok?"

Panky stooped towards the speaker and said, "Ok, you got a deal."

"Send my boys back today, in one piece... otherwise I hunt you down, kill you with my bare hands, this you understand too?"

"Sure." Panky paused, "It didn't have to be this way Zoltan, we'd always worked well together you and me, if only you'd waited... we..."

"What's done is done... I never see your face again Panky! I mean that." *Click...* Zoltan hung up.

All eyes on Panky now. "Sorry guys," Panky said to the cops, "hate to spoil your fun, but no death today...it's deportation time."

The cops looked disappointed.

"Can we at least keep the suits?" asked Peo.

Boris and Vlad looked both relieved and worried. Surely they didn't expect them to fly back to Amsterdam in their boxer shorts?

FORTY- EIGHT

Three weeks later, Panky and Chris sat by Chris' pool getting some sun and relaxing. They sat in silence watching the children hacking around the garden, all whoops and screams and crazy cries of laughter, still noisy in the morning. Panky noticing once more that Chris' son looked exactly like him, the spitting image of Chris in every way, the little daughter beautiful like Clara: amazing or what? It made Panky smile; maybe having some kids wasn't such a bad idea? He figured he's about the right age—late forties, ideal time to settle down.

The guys sipped their orange juice, waved to their women in the pool.

Clara and Mai-Ling were looking happy and relaxed too. They waved back. Clara floated on her back in the warm blue water, she said, "So d'you think he'll stay?"

Mai-Ling sat on the side of the pool, feet splashing gently in the water, "Hard to tell," she said, "Probably."

Clara stood and smiled, "Told you my plan would work didn't I?"

Mai-Ling grinned, "Uh-huh."

Clara waded across the pool and stood looking up at Mai-Ling, "Like I said if you seem too eager, too keen with these foreigners, they take advantage of you; they walk all over you… I told you that didn't I? Especially good looking ones, remember?"

"You did, yeah."

Clara smiled happy with the way things had turned out, "If you'd told him about your real feelings… *pfft*… first he'd think you were completely crazy, second he'd run a mile."

Mai-Ling said, "I remembered what you said, but I told him anyway…"

"You did what?" asked Clara, eyebrows in her hairline.

"I told him… I said I saw his photo every day… the one when Chris and him were kids, punks, I said I knew we'd spend time together… said I had a feeling about it… told him it was a destiny thing."

Clara was a little shocked, "How come he didn't run?"

Mai-Ling said, "I told him I was joking."

Mai-Ling and Clara looked over at the guys and waved again. They both knew that having Chris and Panky together could only be a good thing, Chris loved having him around and Panky not only loved being with him but needed to finally settle down and take life a little easier, to finally cut limbo as Chris called it. Mai-Ling and Clara's plan had worked out well.

Chris and Panky waved back.

Chris looked over at Panky and said, "So the vitamin B complex worked ok then?"

"Like a dream," said Panky, "Never felt better in my life, everything's hunky-fucking-dory geezer… copasetic as they say."

Panky was looking much healthier, his hair had grown back a little, he'd put some weight on, he was almost tanned, his eyes were bright and clear and best of all he looked happy. Very.

Mai-Ling climbed glistening from the pool, big smiles and that luscious physique, waving at the guys again.

Panky smiling like a Cheshire cat with a bucket of cream, mice on the side.

"And there's another good reason to stay," said Chris looking at Mai-Ling.

Panky smiled, "You think she likes me?"

Chris chuckled, "Let's say I think you're in with a pretty good chance, she thinks you look a bit like Colin Farrell... not sure if that's a good thing?"

The guys sat quiet for a while, grinning at how well things had turned out, hoping that Clara and Mai-Ling would be ok about everything.

"So how'd you make all this money then? What's the story geezer?"

Chris grinned, "Thought you'd never ask... it was *a miracle* Panky, really, a fuckin' miracle."

Panky smiled, "So that's why you've gone all religious on me is it? Because of *a miracle*?"

Chris grinned, sipped his O.J. noisily.

Panky said, "Knowing you mate, as I do... I thought you'd been up to something naughty, really... that's what I thought."

"Of course I've been up to something naughty Panky," said Chris with a beaming smile, How the hell could a guy like me earn this much money otherwise?"

"But you just said it was *a miracle*?"

"Oh it was mate... it was a miracle I didn't get caught!"

The guys laughed in the sunlight.

"I'll tell you all about it one day Panky I promise, but not right now, it's a long story, really long,"

"Sordid?" asked Panky.

"Course it's sordid, what d'ya take me for?"

They sat quiet for a while enjoying the heat and the tranquility. The roosters were going mental as always, but the 'partners in grime' ignored the noise. They were used to it.

Chris sighed heavily, "So, you staying then or what?" He really wanted to know.

Panky shrugged and smirked.

"Ain't a lot of nightlife here mate," said Chris, "If you stay you'll miss all the mad stuff won't you?"

"No, I won't miss it... I'm sure of that," said Panky, "The novelty wears off after twenty-five years or so..."

They laughed together like the old mates they were.

Chris said, "Shame you left all that money on the houseboat geezer, big, big shame."

"Didn't leave it on the houseboat, did I?"

"You didn't?" Chris with a huge smile and a throaty gasp of surprise.

"Course not, I'm not stupid Chris! I left it at the airport... I know some very good hiding places at Schipol airport... you oughta know that!"

THE END

The songs

"Holidays in the Sun", The Sex Pistols, Virgin, circa 1977

"Hot in the City", Billy Idol, Chrysalis, circa 1982

"The Passenger", Iggy Pop, RCA, circ 1977

"Watching the Detectives", Elvis Costello, Stiff, circa 1977

"Peaches", The Stranglers, United Artists, circa 1977

"The Guns of Brixton", The Clash, CBS, circa 1979

"Public Image", Public Image Ltd., Virgin, circa 1978

"At Home He's a Tourist", Gang of Four, EMI, circa 1979

"Memories", Public Image Ltd., Virgin, circa 1979

"Damaged Goods", Gang of Four, EMI, circa 1979

"Guns on the roof", The Clash, CBS, circa 1978

"Sex and Drugs and Rock and Roll", Ian Dury and the
  Blockheads, Stiff, circa 1977

"Warning Sign", Talking Heads, Sire, circa 1978

"Judy is Punk", The Ramones, Sire, circa 1976

"Should I Stay or Should I go" The Clash, Epic, circa 1982

"Golden Brown", The Stranglers, Liberty, circa 1982

"Satisfaction (I can't get no)" Devo, Warner Brothers, circa 1978

"I Want to Be Straight", Ian Dury, Stiff, circa 1980

"No more Heroes", The Stranglers, United Artists, circa 1977

2829281R00227

Printed in Great Britain
by Amazon.co.uk, Ltd.,
Marston Gate.